Dreams of
Steam

Dreams of Steam

Anthology engineered by
Kimberly Richardson

Dreams of Steam

Cover design by Darrell Osborn

Published by
Kerlak Enterprises, Inc.
Kerlak Publishing
Memphis, TN
www.kerlakpublishing.com

ISBN 13: 978-0-9823745-5-9
Library of Congress Control Number: 2010931586
First Printing: 2010

Special thanks to everyone at Kerlak Publishing for all of the encouragement and assistance.

This book is printed on acid free paper.

Printed in the United States of America

Dedications:

To my family and dear friends, as always.

To all Steampunkers - Glory to the Power of Steam!

To Kerlak Publishing - Thank you for letting me wear the Editor's Bowler for this anthology.

To Sophie Jewett, Oscar Wilde, Charles Dickens, George Washington Carver, Leo Tolstoy, Sir Arthur Conan Doyle, Edgar Rice Burroughs, Wilkie Collins, George Elliot, Thomas Alva Edison, Nikola Tesla, Edgar Allan Poe, Bram Stoker, Henry David Thoreau, Emile Zola, Robert Louis Stevenson, James McNeill Whistler, Emily Dickinson, HG Wells, Mark Twain, and many others who lived during such an exciting time. This is for you.

Editor's Note

My lords and ladies, I am pleased to present to you *Dreams of Steam*, Kerlak Publishing's Steampunk anthology. In this tome, you will find stories of adventure and daring rescues, dashing men and innovative women, inventions of progress, and leaps into the unknown future. I am grateful to have been a part of this project and I hope you will enjoy the end results of said project. For all of you, however, who may be asking, "Just what exactly IS Steampunk?" I will answer you with this: Steampunk reflects a time in history when the world was a different place while the people living in that world had certain standards while asking the eternal question "What If?" With that in mind, Steampunk, then, is what you make of it, no matter your background or interest. *Dreams of Steam* is Kerlak's and my own way of showing appreciation for that exciting and groundbreaking period of history.

So, without further ado, I bring to you - *Dreams of Steam*.

Thank you all and God Speed!

Lady Agnes Viridian, Adventuress and Maker of a Good Cup of Tea
(Kimberly Richardson - Editor, Kerlak Publishing)

Copyright Acknowledgements

Contents

Flight of the Dragon

Rachel Pixie

Smoke from the factories, from the houses, from the airships and the steamers, from all kinds of technology, covered any densely-populated area with almost constant night. Amelia hated the clinging darkness and the sooty air of the big city, and she hated the way the Mississippi sludge crawled along the banks.

But that wasn't why she was waiting impatiently at the docks. She had lived in Memphis her whole life; it wasn't the desire to escape that brought her to obtain passage on a seedy transport out…it was pure business. She fanned herself, hoping the oppressive heat would let up soon, so that the even more oppressive smell might fade.

An urchin in a low cap bumped into her.

Amelia wasn't a fool. She felt the lift, and caught the boy. "I'd rather like my wallet back, thanks," she said, mouth hard.

The urchin grinned toothily. "Waitin' for 'ee cap'n, idn'tcha?" he asked, nearly unintelligible through some sort of quasi-British brogue.

She frowned. "Captain Dyson Mays of the Drakkina. He was meant to meet me here."

"Oh aye, aye. 'ee sent me on to bring ye in. Follow me, lady." He didn't offer to take her luggage. Amelia muttered unhappily and dragged it behind her, glad of the small wheels at the other end.

She lingered a little, watching him work his way through the crowd – and work the wallets and purses away from their owners.

Something about his hat nagged at her. It settled oddly on his head. It was a moment before she realized why that must be.

"You're an elf!" she gasped, when the urchin had danced back to hurry her along.

He laughed. "Well, yer more an' less observant than I thought." He didn't say anything else until they reached the Drakkina's mooring. "Up ye get!"

She looked. The airship was grounded for the moment, but its massive hull made for a long ascent regardless. It was still small, by airship standards: forty feet of brass and wood, with slimmer engines than most aviators bothered with. The thick canvas sails were furled for docking.

"How am I supposed to get up?" she asked.

"There's 'ee ladder there, or we can lift ye with yer trunk," the urchin pointed. The luggage lift was a metal slab wrapped with ropes and a large pulley-crane gathered the rope for easier hauling. It had no seat or rails. She shuddered.

"I'll climb, thanks," Amelia said, though she didn't sound thankful at all.

The urchin giggled, climbing up ahead of her with the agility of a monkey.

A surly looking dwarf was paying the urchin a handful of coins when Amelia hauled herself over the rail of the airship. "Thanks for nothing," she mumbled to herself, used to males of all species offering a hand to a lady – not that she usually considered herself a "lady."

"Ygrin doesn't lift a finger 'less 'e's paid to. 'e's Merkak dwarf...only kind worth hirin' for airships. All the rest get sick if'n they're further off the ground'n they can jump theyselves."

Ygrin bared his sharp teeth. He was no rosy-cheeked mining dwarf. "Most of 'em can't jump more'n three inches 'less ye stab 'em jus' righ', anyhow," he hissed.

Bloodthirsty, Amelia thought to herself. Merkaks are assassins and mercenaries. What kind of ship have I signed onto? She knew perfectly well that the Drakkina did not strictly perform the legal cargo pick-up and carry that its manifesto claimed. She had anticipated a weapon-savvy crew; anticipated and desired. The skies were no safer than the seas or anywhere else from piracy and robberies.

She needed secrecy. She needed independence. She needed the crew to leave her alone, not ask questions, and not tell anyone she existed. She needed to speak to the captain.

"When can I speak to Mays?" she asked the dwarf.

He looked at her like she was mad. Then he glanced back at the urchin, as though seeing him for the first time.

"Up to yer old tricks, Dyson?" he sneered derisively.

"Hardly worthy of being called 'tricks,'" Dyson grinned, throwing off the cap and removing his shabby overcoat with a flourishing bow.

"Captain Dyson Mays, at your service. What is it you wished to discuss, milady?" He had replaced the gutter talk with a courtly, even more out-of-place posh accent.

She probably should have expected it. She'd known the captain was not well thought of because of his race. Not having heard what it was, she'd rather foolishly hoped he would be black – or part black – like her. His skin was leathery brown from years of outdoor work, his hair short and roughly cut, but he was very clearly not African.

"In private," she said, through gritted teeth.

"Naturally, whatever the lady wants," the captain beamed, offering her his arm. She took it on reflex, walking with him to his cabin. "Please, have a seat," he gestured to the desk chair. He lounged on his bed as he waited for her to speak.

They spent an hour going over her living arrangements on the airship (private quarters, with a lock), the destinations the Drakkina would be mooring at (five or six cities between Memphis and New York City), for what purposes (supply, fuel, cargo transfer), and Amelia's intentions for her stay. At first she had been coy, as she had been when she searched for transport. But the captain asked her point-blank, with the threat of leaving her behind if he was deceived.

She licked her lips. "There's a company in New York City. They work with technology and magic, and my source tells me they're looking for a way to control people's minds – make them slaves. They tested their work first with paralyzed limbs, and for certain conditions, they can give people control over lost limbs, or even artificial ones, if certain connections are made." She licked her lips again, nervous and anticipatory. "That purpose is noble. The other is alarming and foul. I plan to ensure the latter is never seen to fruition."

"Bold words from a little lady. Why do you need me?" Mays asked, fingers drumming on his knee.

She held out her hands. "Airships are no place for a woman, as I'm often told. The crews are rougher, they smell, the smoke gets everywhere. But more importantly… they move faster. I don't want to allow this company the chance to get their product to market: a day could make all the difference."

"You have some sort of alibi in place, I assume?" Mays raised a thin eyebrow.

"Of course I've an alibi. My father is ill. As far as anyone knows, I left in a hurry for Georgia. A neighbor is seeing to my cats and plants."

"And is your father aware of this plan?"

"I haven't spoken to my father in ten years, and no one in Memphis knows my real name. Also, he lives in Alabama. But there's a quiet old man in Georgia who knew me quite well for a while, and he's willing to pretend for my sake, if anyone comes asking."

Mays leaned back. "That sounds well enough. Would you like to see your quarters now?"

"Yes, thank you," Amelia nodded her head.

The cabin was small, a thin bed crammed in one corner with her trunk at the foot and less than a yard of space between trunk and wall. A little vanity was squeezed into the other corner with a child-size stool. If she'd had any real choice in the matter, Amelia would have insisted on more space. As it was, she was fairly sure only she and the captain had private rooms. The crew most likely shared quarters.

"This was Ygrin's room, so don't mind him if he's a bit tetchy with you. Honestly, he's tetchy with everyone," Mays grinned.

Amelia frowned at him. There was something she was forgetting. She opened her purse, and her eyes widened. "I just had it…"

The grin got wider. The captain held up a simple, sturdy wooden flute. "Looking for this?" he asked teasingly.

"But it was – you really are quick with your hands," she said, grudgingly admiring his skill. She was sure he hadn't had her purse more than a moment or two, when he'd done the lift at the docks.

"I've had practice. Wasn't always a 'respectable' merchant, after all," he laughed. "You did quite well. No trouble acquiring it, I trust?"

She shrugged. "The museum didn't seem to care too much about a plain old flute."

Mays smile faded into a fond, sad shadow. "Three hundred years old, in fact. And it was beautifully carved once…but years of wear rubbed it nearly smooth again."

"Does it still play?"

He put it to his mouth and blew a few clean notes, then a simple tune.

"Aye…still plays," Mays said unnecessarily. "Petra was always better at it than I was, though."

"Petra the Pirate?" Amelia asked, stunned. "But she was human, and she sailed in the 1400s, as first mate to Captain Addison Mayleaf…"

"You know a great deal about pirates, milady. But it's as I said earlier: you're both more and less intelligent than I expected. What's my name?" he teased.

"Dyson Mays… Dyson… Addison Mayleaf," she shook her head. "You aren't even trying, are you?"

"But still, people are fooled," Dyson shrugged, grinning. "At any rate, I'm glad to have Petra's old flute back."

"Is it true, then – that she was your wife?" Amelia asked hesitantly, realizing she was prying but wanting an answer too much to keep silent.

"After a fashion. No church or lawman would marry a pirate to a former monk… even if the monk turned out to be a girl. Perhaps especially so. Even more if the pirate was an elf; in the Middle Ages, it was we who were slaves, little girl. Africa was a vast unknown. So we were married once under false names, with me pretending to be a human man. And I married us on my ship, once. But we were already common-law married by then, broom jumping and all."

Dyson played another little ditty on the flute. Amelia recognized it as a gospel song she'd heard in a black church when she was younger, and couldn't pass for white as easily.

She sang along. Music had always been a part of her life; these days, it was a part of her cover. The affluent performer Amelia Rose was a fixture of the Memphis nightlife, performing in gentlemen's clubs and bars other women were categorically banned from entering. It had given her a somewhat scandalous reputation and invitations into the homes of many wealthy men.

If little things went missing, they weren't about to tell their wives who they had let in.

The little cabin had been getting darker as they spoke. Dyson glanced at the porthole. "The crew should be aboard by now. Dinner will be soon. I'll fetch you for it. I've jobs that need doing." He bowed a little and left the little room.

Amelia lit a gas lamp to journal by. She was occupied for less than half an hour before someone came knocking. Amelia tucked the little diary in her bodice and opened the door.

Dinner was nearly unpalatable, and the airship lurched into flight halfway through, ruining what little appetite she had.

"How well have you planned this heist of yours?" he asked her, all business.

"It's my business," she frowned, affronted.

"I'm afraid it isn't. Your 'source' is the first mate that Ygrin replaced, Jellicoe McCreddan. Didn't you think it a bit convenient we were in the area when you happened to need transport to the place we were going?"

"I plan the heist, I make it happen, I pay you, and then we go our separate ways," she said firmly.

"Or you plan the heist, you get caught, and I don't get paid."

"You don't get paid return fare if there's no one to return," Amelia scowled. "I paid for my passage to New York already."

"Why were we transporting an unescorted woman? She didn't have any letters of intent to anyone in New York City. She's got no relatives there, no job references, no reason for going – wealth enough for a maid but no maid coming along, and all manner of other inconsistencies. What did we think we were doing? It's not proper. And it's only a short jump from 'not proper' to 'not legal.' And then they start searching my hulls and I certainly have things I don't want them finding. So forgive me if I want to be as sure as possible that you don't get caught, Miss Farrier."

Her lips tightened. "How do you know that name?"

"I know a lot about you, Amelia Rose. I don't let just anyone onto my ship. I certainly don't tell just anyone when there's a heist that needs be done. I have to make sure I can trust them – to do what I expect them to. Tell me what you've got planned, and I'll see if I can't make your plans more flawless." He spread a long roll of paper onto the table he had bolted to the floor.

He had a blueprint to the company laboratory.

"No harm in some advice," Amelia murmured. She outlined her plan.

He had several good ideas. She worked them in, refining the plan for three hours, feeling like she was giving a voice recital to an exacting teacher.

He leaned back. "You're ready. It'll take us a week to get to New York. Memorize the plan," he handed over his notes on their discussion, "and try not to get cornered by any of the crew."

Her eyebrows shot up. Amelia realized belatedly this would be the second time she left the captain's quarters in one day. She had been in his company since arriving. The crew had seen her with him, seen him finish her dinner… "You want them to think I'm your woman, don't you?" she asked, the pieces fitting together suddenly.

Dyson chuckled. "Less and more intelligent," he repeated. "I've been dropping hints all day. Go to bed, lassie. Look a bit rumpled if you like."

She bit her lip. "I'm not sure I approve of this plan."

"It keeps you safer. If they tease you more than your tender soul can bear, let me know…I'll reinforce their belief by beating the tar out of them," Dyson said dismissively.

She stalked off in a huff, locking her cabin door behind her. The crew were chuckling amongst themselves and singing lewd songs. She could hear them through the door. Screaming her frustration into her pillow, Amelia struggled to fall asleep.

*****

"Amy – can I call you Amy? – Amy, time to get up," a wickedly perky Captain Mays murmured in her ear.

She nearly leapt out of bed in shock. "That door was locked!" she gasped.

"Aye. And I unlocked it," Mays grinned, dangling a key in front of her face, snatching it back when she reached out. "See, I don't hold with having a part of my ship that I can't get into easy-peasy. Don't worry, little missy, I've had enough of human female parts to last me a lifetime." He laughed. "I suppose, together, they have been a few human lifetimes." He tossed the key in the air, caught it, and tossed it again. The ease of motion marked it as something of a habit.

"Aren't elf women the same… essentially?" Amelia blushed, trying to deflect his attention.

"Elf women don't much hold with an old ragamuffin like me, anyhow. But! Enough chitchat, I came to fetch you for breakfast, and fetch I shall."

"Breakfast? What time is it?"

Mays glanced at the grimy, rusted porthole. "Sometime in the region of 4:30 of the morning, I suspect."

"Ye gods, it's not yet dawn! You have breakfast at this uncivilized hour?" Amelia cried out.

Another seal's bark of a laugh, but no real answer.

"Will I be getting this delightful wake-up call every morning, or is this a special occasion?" Amelia sneered.

"I could leave you be, I suppose. But where's the fun in that?" He ruffled her hair, always a wiry mess, but especially awful in the mornings.

She glared at him until he shut the door behind himself on his way out, and then flopped back down on the bed. Her two bites of dinner hadn't sated her at the time, and she was even hungrier now. Seeing as she was already awake...

With a sigh, she began to dress.

Breakfast looked like dinner revisited, this time with a side of stale biscuits. She finished two biscuits and nearly half the stew by dipping the hard bread into the bowl.

"Getting used to the fare already, I see," Dyson said mock-proudly.

She ignored him.

Most of the week passed like that – bad food and worse company. The brief stops at ports were solely for resupplying, and Dyson effectively discouraged her from stepping off the ship without using a single word. He let her look at the city with a spyglass instead. Considering they always made port in the cargo ship docks, which were nearly always the absolute worst part of town, Amelia had no desire to disembark. The crew she mostly avoided.

*****

New York City was a different matter entirely. Dyson had forced the crew to clean the ship as they made the last leg of their journey, until the hull was gleaming brass and the decks were polished wood. For the next day or so, the Drakkina – or Lindwurm, as the hull now claimed, for the sake of discretion – was pretending to be what she was originally designed for: a pleasure yacht registered to a wealthy Louisiana socialite, Lavinia Stanhope...sometimes known as Amelia Rose, or even Rosa Farrier.

Captain "Jehane S. Platt" moored at the marina, paying five times the docking cost he would have at the cargo bay. The Lindwurm was a pretty little sparrow roosting with peacocks. He contented himself with the fact that sparrows could fly, and did so quite quickly. Peacocks were notoriously earth-bound.

"Enjoy your stay in the City," the marina dock-master smiled at Captain Platt.

"Thank you," Mays said curtly. "My employer wishes to put in motion plans to surprise a family friend in a few months. Can you ensure the ship's name is...misplaced for a year or so?" he asked artfully.

The marina man smiled wider. "I am of course more than willing to oblige our honored customers...but such a service is somewhat hazardous for me, is it not?"

Mays offered up a small stack of bills, mentally adding it to Amelia's return airfare.

Amelia wore her "thieving clothes" under the dress she had brought for the one fancy dinner of the trip. Mays would be attending with her, and had obtained a discreet carriage for them both. He drove them to the restaurant in silence.

The meal was much better than usual, but still sat awkwardly in Amelia's stomach. She had, up until this point, robbed very few large companies. She hated to think of it as nerves, but it must have been. Mays drove the carriage toward the laboratory while she undressed in the back seat. Dark grey clothes and soft-soled boots, paired with a head-wrap to disguise her face and hair…she could have been any age, race, or gender, Mays noticed with satisfaction.

She picked the lock on a side door and slipped in.

Fifty paces north, she thought, counting off mentally as she strolled down the dark hallway. One hand trailed along the wall to ensure she didn't miss the turn for thirty paces east, and then twelve paces south, sixty-five paces east, ten paces south…here we are. This door was also locked. The windowless, empty corridors were black as pitch. She felt for her lock-picks and opened it by feel and sound. Constantly burning forges left the room filled with a soft orange glow. She minced her way through the lab tables, collecting a stack of documents and a bag of experimental equipment.

She had to trust Mays' informant was correct, that all the information about this project was limited to this lab, and that none of the engineers and scientists working on it had brought anything home. But in light of how close-mouthed companies were about trade secrets, Amelia found she did trust that assertion.

She retraced her steps out of the lab and slid into the carriage, knocking twice. The carriage started to move. A lamp flickered to life and she saw a strange man in the back, with Mays tied up and unconscious on the floor. Amelia gasped, before the man covered her mouth with a cloth. The lamp seemed to separate into three little lights, which swirled in nauseating circles as the world tilted forward. She blacked out.

*****

She woke up in a cramped, wooden room, tied to a chair. A man with more fingers than teeth grinned at her.

"Up, are we?" he asked, far too cheerfully. "Now then, youse just explain what it is you was doin' in Boss Carmichael's alley, an' mebbe we'll be letting you go with youse hands still attached."

Amelia paled. "I'm sure I have no idea what you're talking about," she said.

"Mebbe not. So I'll explain in little words. You had youse hopper parked in Boss Carmichael's alley. That alley means a lot to him. Me an' Zedock, we keep it clear for him night an' day. We knock out the little elf-thing once you leave and wait for you to get back. We knock you out. Why was youse parked there?"

"We had… business with the laboratory."

"Medicorp men go home at 8 p.m., every day. No one around for business. No one around but the little elfthing and the little patchy girl."

Amelia couldn't help herself – she glared. Most mixed children were a soft blend of their parents' skin tones. She had patches of white, patches of pale pink, and patches of chocolate brown. She rarely tolerated people speaking of it, especially if they were being uncomplimentary.

"I – " she struggled for a good enough lie. "My uncle works there. I was fetching something for him. He left it at work."

"Youse fetched lots of things, patchy girl. Whole bag of shinies an' another bag of papers. Youse uncle is forgetful." He didn't believe her. She wouldn't believe an excuse that flimsy either.

She fought against the ropes uselessly, trying to think. "H-he was just fired…he wanted me to steal it back, okay? But he didn't dare go himself or they'd know who to track."

"Ah…so youse uncle doesn't care for you much, then."

"A-apparently not," Amelia gave a strained smile.

"Good little girls shouldn't make friends with elfthings. Theyse tricky."

"W-well I needed someone tricky, didn't I?" she tried.

The poorly toothed man considered this. "S'pose you did," he agreed grudgingly. "What was youse stealin'?"

"My uncle's work. It's not fair for the company to use it if they aren't paying him for it."

"Boss Carmichael can use it," the man said slowly. "Boss Carmichael even pay your uncle. Pay him with your life."

"Please don't hurt me," Amelia said, trying to force herself to cry. Maybe a few tears would persuade him.

He mulled the plea over. "Boss Carmichael decides. Youse in Boss Carmichael's alley. Boss Carmichael knows what to do with you." He dragged her, chair and all, into a different room. Captain Mays looked quite battered. A man in a work shirt with the sleeves rolled up had just finished punching the elf in the gut. The man glanced up.

"Murdstone," the man said, voice low, "you were supposed to leave the girl in the other room. She doesn't need to see this. It's not right for a lady."

"But Zedock, she said they was stealin' something to make a company off of. Boss Carmichael should be the one who decides what to do with 'em. So he can get a company."

Zedock sighed the sigh of a man tested to the end of his patience. "Murdstone. Carmichael has plenty of companies. He doesn't need whatever silly contraption these people think they have."

"But – "

"Murdstone. Take the girl back in the other room so I can finish interrogating her man. Servant. Elf-thing," he fumbled for the correct noun and gave up.

Mays' head lolled limply. Blood was dripping from his mouth. He managed to lift his dull brown eyes a bit. "Carmichael…" he said, coughing red. "Solomon Carmichael?"

Zedock kicked Mays into the wall. "'ow do you know that name!?" he yelled.

"Tell Solomon that Adi wants a word." Mays fell unconscious. No, Amelia thought, her eyes narrowed.

He fell asleep. The very nerve, she thought, was not to be believed.

Zedock looked at the elf in confusion, and then shrugged. "Fine. Leave 'em in here." He dragged Murdstone out by the arm. Amelia concentrated on escaping the ropes, not that it did her much good.

*****

An angry-looking white-haired old man stormed into the room, nudging Mays with his foot. "Why didn't you tell me you'd be in my part of town, you… Zounds, you look uglier'n homemade sin. My boys worked you over pretty well, didn't they?"

Dyson chuckled, sitting up gingerly. "That they did, Sol. Wanna help out your old cap'n?"

Solomon cut the ropes off them both.

"What brings you this far up North, cap'?" Solomon asked as he bandaged Dyson's worst injuries.

"A heist. You tell him, little missy," he nodded to Amelia, who then spilled everything she knew about Medicorp and the technology that could help thousands or enslave millions.

Solomon nodded in all the right places and rubbed the feeling back into her hands. "You got everything you needed?"

She nodded.

"Well, I wish't you'd told me something ahead of time, Adi. I've had those dumb boys watching that alley so they don't get in my way. But now they expect some sort of ransom, at the very least. And they'll probably want a reward."

"Tell 'em the truth…they beat the tar out of an old friend and they get a warning, not a reward," Mays shrugged.

Solomon didn't move.

Mays sighed. "Five percent profits."

Solomon frowned a little.

"Ten, then, but no more than that," Mays said insistently.

"Aren't you glad to see an old friend at all?" Solomon shook his head.

Dyson paused for a long moment. "Thirty. Don't expect any more, Sol. I have a crew to feed."

"From what I recall, you spend more money on guns than on food. Not everyone can live off stale bread and stew that's based from the stock of last night's stew…your cooky has been remaking the same stew at least as long as I was aboard."

Mays scowled. "Thirty-five, then."

"Of returns, not profits," Solomon said firmly.

"You'll beggar me!"

"I doubt that. You're a stingy old seadog. You live cheaply on a boat you built yourself, and pay your crew a pittance."

"Thirty-five percent of returns," Mays held out a hand. Solomon shook it. "Now would you get us out of here?"

"My pleasure," Solomon grinned. Their carriage was a little scraped up from Murdstone's wild driving. Dyson probably wouldn't be getting his security deposit back.

Dyson drove the carriage back to the marina and Amelia locked herself in her quarters, hugging the lumpy pillow and trying not to see Dyson's bludgeoned face whenever she closed her eyes. She had never been so glad to be on the Drakkina, even if its hull still said Lindwurm. This whole trip had turned into far more of an adventure than she had really wanted.

All Amelia wanted now was to return to her quiet, simple life of honest work... with a bit of thievery now and again to keep things exciting. She wanted to return to the city where no one called her "Patchy" without some gentleman challenging the insulter to a duel.

The captain barged into her room without even the courtesy of a knock. She hadn't heard him unlocking the door.

"That went rather well," he said brightly. His face was a bruised purple.

"With all due respect, I'm inclined to disagree," Amelia said shortly.

Dyson blinked at her in surprise. "What? We got the loot, Medicorp has no idea, the police are likewise unaware, and we walked away under our own power! I'd count that as a win."

"You're a bloody mess and you owe Carmichael 35 percent of something...I'm still not entirely sure what."

The captain waved that off dismissively. "He's not entirely sure what...which means it'll be 35 percent of your return fare. So long as I've a five percent cut in your business profits off the tech you stole, seeing as I was the one beaten for it and the one who got you out of hot water."

Amelia frowned, but five percent was a small cut, and she did feel rather as though she owed Dyson her life. She shook hands on the deal.

"You really are quite a good thief," Dyson complimented with a smile.

She was momentarily flummoxed as to a response. Compliments should be returned with compliments, screamed years of etiquette training, even compliments that dubious.

"...Thank you," she said slowly. "You're, um, an excellent marksman. Elf," she corrected herself with a flinch.

"Marks-elf," Dyson chuckled. "That's a new one. When have you even seen me shoot?"

"I, er, didn't precisely see you. But you were mentioned in a lady's magazine I subscribe to."

"Oh? What magazine?"

She licked her lips, wishing she hadn't brought it up. "Reasons to Risk Hell. Most of it's rather a joke – recipes for guilty-pleasures foods, or foods that Christians aren't strictly allowed to eat, but everyone does… like shellfish. But sometimes they discuss men or masculine humanoids, and, well," she broke off, blushing.

Dyson was grinning. She very much wished she hadn't mentioned it.

"So… how long have you been reading 'those' sort of magazines?" Dyson teased.

"OUT!" she yelled.

He laughed and paused in the doorway. "By the way, my dear – I don't know if that was the interview when I mentioned Friends of the Dragon. Rest assured, you are one."

She didn't move for a long moment, and was still searching her memory long after he had left. The Drakkina, she knew, meant dragon in some ancient language or another. But this sounded like a special sort of title.

There seemed to be some niggling remembrance of protection and long memories of the elves.

She groaned, but was a little flattered, actually. What little she remembered said she could expect protection and heroic rescues if Dyson Mays ever heard she was in trouble. She wondered how, in hardly a week of knowing him, she could have managed to impress him that much, especially considering how onerous she had been to him most of the time.

Then she remembered how abrasive Ygrin was, and how his insults made Dyson laugh.

Maybe the elf was just crazy.

It was an uneventful – verging on boring – trip to her departure point in Georgia. She spent most of the time on the deck, watching mountains and forests crawl by far below. Amelia's alibi was as good an excuse as any to visit Nicodemus Hornege, one of her very old friends, and she was impatient to try his peach cobbler again.

She could see him on the Marietta docks. She waved, and went to help Dyson load her trunk on the lift.

"It was lovely working with a real professional," Dyson smiled. He pecked her cheek, slapped the luggage lift – Ygrin began to lower it – and vanished back into his cabin. Her eyes narrowed. She checked her purse. She was missing a few coins, but more importantly, there was a piece of paper she knew she hadn't put in there.

Amy – you never did answer if I could call you Amy –

Amy,

There's a law firm in Indianapolis that's been swindling poor blacks out of their homes, and a church has put up a reward for proof...

Let me know if you're interested.

-Captain Mays

With a little growl of frustration, she was finally the one to barge into his quarters.

It looked like Georgia – and Memphis – would have to wait.

Dead Man's Hand

Jared Millet

August 25, 1888

To Whom It May Concern,

I, Daniel Cotton, of Capek & Lang Automatonics, do hereby attest that I am of sound mind in offering this deposition. To any authorities reading this document, I sincerely apologize for the mess I have dropped into your lap. As some details of my account may otherwise seem incredible, I hope the means by which I have chosen to convey my story will lend it plausibility.

The automated humaniform simulacrum, or "dogsbody," in which I have recorded this message is a Capek & Lang Model Nine, manufactured in Prague and assembled at our company's workshop on Magazine St. in New Orleans. Obviously, since you are reading this, you followed the instructions I scratched on its housing and provided it with pen and ink. You will note that the Model Nine's ambulatory system allows a degree of articulation in the fingers, arms and legs to rival that of a living man. If everything has gone according to plan, then you found this dogsbody on the grounds of Knockwood Plantation, the property of my client, Mr. Jean-Baptiste Perrilloux.

I have never met Mr. Perrilloux in person, though he once did considerable business with my predecessor in the hope that our machines could be made to work his plantation in place of human labor. Alas, the application of clockwork automata in such an unpredictable terrain as a cane field is an ambition that remains unrealized.

Nevertheless, Mr. Perrilloux maintained a number of mechanical servants in his household and on occasion would wire us an order for replacement parts or the latest model, which we would ship upriver to his estate. I did not visit Knockwood in person until the evening of

Monday, July 2, in response to a telegram requesting the aid of a technician.

Since the request was nonspecific, I came with a full maintenance kit and enough spare parts to construct an entire dogsbody from scratch should the need arise. However, I underestimated the effects of recent rains on the roads in this part of the state, and as a result the weight of my equipment was too much for the wagon I hired to transport me from the boat landing.

When my driver at last deposited me at the plantation, I was covered in mud from the many ruts in which we had become mired. I dreaded the thought of greeting my client in such a condition, but the hour was nearing sunset. With no other accommodation available, I saw no other choice.

Hat in hand, I left my luggage by the road and walked the mercifully dry path to the house itself. It was unnaturally quiet, and from what I could tell no lamps had been lit inside. Though giant oaks shaded the estate, light still bled from the fields beyond. The sugar cane, not yet tall as a man, looked wild and untended even to my untrained eye.

The Perrilloux mansion sat four feet off the ground on stout cypress piers. I could still see marks where the spring floods had washed under the building. A porch adorned the front of the house with a matching balcony above. Columns supported the overhanging roof, and though there were many windows the interior was black as pitch. Fearing that my client had vacated the premises and left me in the lurch, I nevertheless mounted the steps and knocked on the door.

There was no reply.

Nor was there any traffic on the road that might take me, bedraggled as I was, to better lodgings. Once I had satisfied myself that no one was home, I retrieved my luggage and prepared for a miserable night out of doors. I did not wish to sleep in the abandoned, insect-ridden servant quarters, nor did I wish to soil the house's porch any more than I already had. I elected to remain on the steps until dawn and then make my way to the nearest village.

It was a moonless evening. Nights are quiet in the country, once one becomes accustomed to the ambient symphony of crickets and katydids. Wait long enough and every sound becomes magnified tenfold. After sunset I heard a dog yelping in the distance. Later I heard a steamboat paddling up the Mississippi. I considered running to the levee and waving them ashore, but they wouldn't have seen me in the darkness. I heard laughter and a band playing, and I felt somewhat lonely until the riverboat passed.

Later, though I thought it my imagination at the time, I heard a woman singing. Her voice was faint but angelic. The melody was that of a Negro spiritual, but I couldn't place the tune.

I must have slept, because eventually I woke. It was not yet dawn. The last quarter moon had risen and the estate was bathed in that cold blue radiance that can make even the most rational man believe in ghosts.

But it was a noise that woke me.

It came again: a footstep and the creak of a board. Then a rattling whir. Then another step. And another, each with a telltale rattle.

There was a dogsbody moving in the house. Its footfalls grew louder as it descended the staircase inside. When it reached the bottom it trod toward the door.

I held my breath, feeling exposed in the light of the moon. It was foolish, I know. Automatons can no more see than they can hear, and no more understand their actions than a clock knows the time. Therefore I cannot explain the chill that gripped me as those deliberate, mechanical footfalls approached the door and stopped.

Was it a scarecrow? I had myself encoded such behaviors into clients' dogsbodies to frighten away prowlers and the like. But why had it come forth now? Had I, in my sleep, triggered some tripwire that activated the mechanical sentinel? It occurred to me that an automaton tasked to protect a residence so far from the city might be designed to employ a deadlier response than mere intimidation. Carefully, I backed down the stairs.

After a moment its footfalls resumed as it retraced its steps. Once it was gone, I sat in the grass while my pulse subsided.

It was then that I noticed another sound, so faint that the earlier susurrus of nightly insects had drowned it out. I recognized it immediately and circled the building to find its source.

The cable was hard to see in the darkness, hidden as it was by oak branches. Snaking through the trees and approaching the house from the rear, it hung from a pole and slipped like a thief into an overhanging eave. In the stillness of the night, the cable hummed with power.

*****

Dawn came. With my belongings stowed out of sight, I walked down the road in what I hoped was the direction of civilization. I had not gone far when I was hailed by a well-dressed young Creole on horseback who informed me that if I meant to head into town, I was going the wrong way.

I introduced myself and explained my business. He told me his name was Marcus Despre and that he had ridden to Knockwood that morning to find me. He was employed by Mr. Perrilloux, and the telegram that should have informed him of my arrival had been delayed by a downed cable. He offered to take me to his family's house where I might refresh myself, and I gladly accepted.

Though small, my rescuer's home seemed like an oasis. I greeted Mr. Despre's wife and young children, changed into less sodden attire, and ate a breakfast of fresh cornbread while Marcus explained why I had been summoned.

"Mr. Perrilloux's been overseas on business since last December. I keep a watch on the house and look out for any carpetbaggers that might have an eye on the property, you know. The place pretty much takes care of itself. With the dogsbodies, I mean. If there's ever a problem they can't handle, that engine in the attic just wires Mr. P. and lets him know."

I almost choked. "An engine?" I asked. "A difference engine? In the attic?"

Marcus nodded. "He set it up when he had the house electrified." With that, he passed me a slip of paper from the local telegraph office.

LIVERPOOL, ENGLAND, JUNE 30, 1888
MARCUS DESPRE, SOTILE, LOUISIANA

HOUSE REPORTS MODEL 8 FAILURE NORTH HALLWAY SECOND FLOOR STOP MEET TECHNICIAN FROM CAPEK LANG JULY SECOND STOP ASSIST AS NEEDED STOP SMML

JB PERRILLOUX

I queried as to the meaning of the last four letters.

"Send Miri My Love," Marcus answered. "That's his daughter, Miss Mirielle, still lives there. I'm bringin' her dinner when we go back."

I was shocked, to say the least. "Do you mean someone's living in that house and they let me spend the night on the steps?"

"If you'll pardon my saying so, Mr. Cotton sir, I wouldn't have let you into my house, looking the way you did. But Miss Miri's kind of funny. She's always been shy. Now she hardly ever comes down from her room. We bring her something to eat every day, but I hardly ever see her. What we bring, those dogsbodies take up to her and that's that."

"Do you suppose there's something wrong with her?" I asked.

"Can't speak to that," said Marcus, then he continued with a sly grin. "If you'll pardon my saying so, being touched in the head is a luxury only white folk can afford."

*****

We returned to Knockwood later that morning. Marcus unlocked the door and a pair of Model Eights greeted us. According to my records, Mr. Perrilloux owned three Eights and an assortment of Sixes and Sevens. The two Eights in the foyer had been painted in the attire of household servants. They wore black coats, white wigs, and their faces were blank. Painted faces are unnerving to some, so we leave that detail to our customers' preference.

Marcus pressed two buttons on a panel next to the door. One was labeled with his name, the other with the word "guest." Other buttons bore the names of Mr. Perrilloux, his daughter, and gentlemen whom I presumed were business associates.

"Do this when you come in or out," said Marcus, "to let the dogsbodies know who you are."

"You must be joking."

"No, sir. When Mr. Perrilloux comes back, I'll tell him to make a button just for you."

I shook my head. Dogsbodies can't know anything; they simply move through series of preset actions enscripted by a technician or, if he is mechanically inclined, the owner. Then I remembered the computing engine in the attic and began to work through the possibilities.

Marcus went to the dogsbody on the left and pressed one of the buttons on its chest. This, of course, is the usual method for triggering a preset behavior. The dogsbody lifted its arms and Marcus handed it a covered basket that smelled of roasted vegetables. He pressed another button and it proceeded to walk up the stairs with its burden.

"Miss Miri?" Marcus called. "I'm here with the man from the dogsbody company. He's gonna fix the one broke down in the hall up there. Is there anything else I can get you?"

There was silence, then a voice like an angel's. "No, Mr. Despre. I'm quite all right. Please tell your wife that the mushroom sauce she sent yesterday was heavenly."

"I will, ma'am. Thank you. We'll have some ham to bring you tomorrow."

There was no answer. Marcus shrugged. "Just head up and make a right. I got to check a few things around the property. Holler if you need anything."

I thanked him and took the stairs to the second floor. The other Model Eight followed, mimicking my footsteps. I felt the same disquiet that I had the night before, though not as strongly. I imagined pressure plates under the floor that signaled my movements to the difference engine. But how was it telling the dogsbody what to do?

At the head of the staircase, a hall stretched left and right. Light poured through windows at either end. The hall was decorated with pastoral paintings and wallpaper that may have once been green, but was now a sickly yellow. Electric lights hung from the ceiling, but none were lit. I would have expected a carpet runner, but there was none. At the end of the hall to my right, the inoperative dogsbody lay crumpled on the floor exactly like a discarded marionette.

I immediately diagnosed the problem. The automaton's knee had seized and sprung out of place. There were gouges in the floor where the machine had tried to go about its business until its motive power exhausted itself. Older models ran on tightly wound springs, but Sevens and above come with the option (for an additional fee) of a chemical battery. Since I had a hard time imagining the reclusive Mirielle winding up her mechanical retinue every day, I presumed these dogsbodies ran on electricity.

I rolled the machine over and inspected the faulty knee. Dogsbody legs are as problematic as those of humans, since the joints must be flexible as well as load bearing. In this instance I would have to replace the entire spring assembly. I had brought my toolkit, but I would have to return to my luggage for the parts.

My dogsbody chaperone followed as far as the door. When I returned, I slipped around it. The instant I did, three more automatons stepped out of the darkness and surrounded me.

I froze, more from shock than fear. These were Model Sevens, and their age showed in their faded varnish. They wore gray instead of black and were painted in the semblance of Confederate soldiers. One approached from the parlor to the right, one from a darkened room to the left, and the third from an alcove behind the stairs.

I took another step, and the three advanced again. When I retreated, however, they did not respond. "My" dogsbody remained rooted but turned to face me. I stepped back again and all four of them tracked my movement, as if they could see with eyes they didn't have.

Realizing my mistake, I went to the panel by the door and pressed the "guest" button. The soldiers did not retreat, but neither did they hinder me. I hastily returned to my work with only my original automaton for company.

The repair took perhaps an hour. I spread canvas under the injured leg to prevent oil from staining the floorboards. It took much longer to remove the damaged joint than to install the new one. I noted that the damaged knee had gouged the rod that served as the dogsbody's femur. My repair would hold for a while, but it would be susceptible to similar breakdowns. I resolved to recommend to Mr. Perrilloux the purchase of a Model Nine.

I rolled the dogsbody over to inspect my work from a different angle. Doing so, I noticed something that was not a part of our standard design. On the undamaged leg, running upward from the heel like a hamstring, a copper wire led into the service panel on the dogsbody's back. My curiosity aroused, I pulled off its coat so I could open the panel and investigate.

What I found astonished me. Modern dogsbody designs employ grooved wax cylinders to record behavior patterns, replacing the rigid clockwork of earlier models. In this machine, I found neither. There was a memory cylinder, but it was metal. How it should work was beyond my immediate comprehension. I presumed that it did work, for there was nothing else within the dogsbody's frame to supply the machine's motivation.

Whoever designed this, whether another engineer or Mr. Perrilloux himself, was an innovator of the highest caliber. I wondered if he had yet applied for a patent, and I could not help but consider removing the apparatus and doing so myself.

I closed the panel, locked the dogsbody's legs, and hoisted it onto its feet. I straightened its coat and wondered about that mysterious copper wire while doing so. Leaving the dogsbody in place, I knelt and inspected the floor.

There, between the boards, was another wire. Of course! Not only could the house's difference engine monitor its dogsbodies' comings and goings, but it could command them via electrical impulses. Ingenious! Now all I had to do was figure out how that metal cylinder worked and I would be set for life.

I banished the thought from my mind and packed away my tools. When I activated the dogsbody, it did nothing. Its battery must have been drained, and I had yet to see any place where such equipment might be recharged. Marcus would know, but before asking him I followed a hunch and shifted the dogsbody so that its heel connected with the wire in the floor.

The thing jerked to life. I sprang back so as not to injure myself, should it be trapped in the performance of some previous task. I needn't have worried. It backed toward the window at the end of the hall where, no doubt, it would remain at rest until recharged. I smiled at my handiwork, and then frowned at the grease that blackened my hands.

I looked at the other dogsbody standing sentinel in the hall. "I don't suppose you could point me toward a washroom?" It didn't answer, and I would have been appalled if it had. Given the layout of the house, I guessed that the room I wanted was directly across from the stairs, and twice in as many minutes my hunch proved correct. To my relief, the house had running water. I had seen no cistern, but since Mr. Perrilloux spared no expense on technology I suspected that water was supplied by an electric pump. While I scrubbed the grime off my hands, I heard Marcus call for me.

I stepped into the hall to answer and beheld a vision in white. Her hair had an almost golden sheen and her skin was like the petals of an orchid. She seemed even more surprised than I was. I hunted for the proper words to excuse myself, but before I could do so she screamed and ran.

"Miss Perrilloux!" I shouted, and in my impropriety I ran after her. She slammed a door behind her before I had gone two strides, but it was another sound that froze me in my tracks - that of pistols being cocked.

I turned carefully. Both the dogsbodies in the hall, the one that had followed me and the one I'd repaired, pointed their left arms at me. Gun barrels protruded from hidden panels therein.

Marcus poked his head around the first of them. "Mr. Cotton," he said, "pardon my saying so, but you better walk back this way real slow."

*****

A month later, a letter arrived. It was brief, but penned in a practiced, exacting hand.

Dear Mr. Cotton,

Thank you for your commendable service. The house reports that the malfunctioning automaton is now performing satisfactorily. In response to your telegram, I agree that my household would benefit from the addition of a more recent model. Please deliver one to my estate as soon as is convenient. I expect nothing less than the finest your company has to offer, but I prefer its motive core to be tabula rasa. My usual accountant will handle payment.

Sincerely,
Jean-Baptiste Perrilloux

I set aside all other projects and assembled the requested Model Nine as quickly as I could. I was eager to return to Knockwood and hoped for an excuse to examine the difference engine itself. I had checked the recent patent index on file at Tulane University and found nothing registered under the name Perrilloux or any description resembling the metal cylinder I'd seen.

Marcus met me at the Sotile boat landing. Since the Nine's motive cylinder was blank, it couldn't walk on its own. We bore it in a stretcher and laid it in the back of a wagon like an invalid, all the while drawing the attention of a small crowd of Marcus's fellow townsfolk.

It was two o'clock when we arrived at the estate. It had not rained for days, and the moisture in the air seemed to steam up from the ground. We made for the shade as quickly as we could. The doors to the house were open and a pair of dogsbodies waited inside.

"Good afternoon," sang Mirielle's heavenly voice from the bowels of the mansion. "Mr. Despre, Mr. Cotton, if you would be so kind, please lay the new manservant across the threshold."

We did as asked. Once inside, I saw that Mirielle was watching from atop the main staircase. I took off my hat.

"Good afternoon, ma'am. I'm sorry I startled you last time."

She smiled, but it was the smile of a doll. "Not at all. I reacted foolishly. Please come in and have some tea." She gestured to the parlor on my right and I went inside. I wondered if she meant to join me in person, or if she would do so by mechanical proxy.

The room was free of dust, but it felt as if it was rarely used. I sat so that I could watch the dogsbodies at work in the hallway. They knelt over their newly fashioned kinsman, and for all the world it appeared as if they were feeling it like a pair of blind men. Marcus guided their hands until they gained purchase on the new automaton's chassis, then they lifted it in unison and carried it out of sight. Marcus tipped his hat and stepped outside.

It was not long before a Model Seven dressed as a housemaid entered the sitting room with a tea set. It poured two cups, then daintily picked one up and presented it to me in a clockwork ballet that was all the more astonishing since I knew exactly how complicated such a display was to perform. I took the cup and nodded in thanks.

"She is marvelous, isn't she?" said Mirielle from the doorway. "I call her Josephine. Sugar?"

I would have said "no," but I wanted to see how the dogsbody would react. "Yes, please." The lady of the house tapped her toe twice on a floorboard and "Josephine" spun around, picked up a sugar cube, and proffered it for my cup.

"Amazing," I said. "Did your father script all your dogsbodies' actions himself?"

Mirielle walked along the far wall. It wasn't lost on me that she was keeping as far away as she could.

"Not directly," she said. "He built the engine that runs the house, and it controls the automatons from a set of general guidelines."

"I can't wait to meet him," I admitted. "I feel as if I could learn as much in a single conversation as I did during all my years at college. Do you believe he will return soon?"

"I hope he will." She ran her hand along the windowsill and glanced out at the empty estate. "It's not that I'm lonely, and I'm quite well protected."

"As I discovered before."

She gave her first true smile. "Yes, I suppose you did. But I do miss him. He writes to me every week and promises to hurry back, but something always keeps him away."

"I don't mean to impose," I said, picking my words carefully, "but I'm concerned as to what might happen should the difference engine malfunction. Would you permit me to examine it while I'm here, so that I might see it in proper working order?"

There was an accusation in the look she gave me. "I'm not a fool, Mr. Cotton. Father's designs are worth a lot of money. I have enough trouble with rich Yankees trying to steal the house from under me. Why should I trust you not to attempt the same with its treasure?"

She'd caught me, and I felt the need to cover myself. "Miss Perrilloux," I said, "I appreciate your concern, but I'm not an inventor. I'm a technician. It's my business to know how machinery works so that I can put it back together when it falls apart. That's my only concern, and since your estate is dependent on a machine, it would be in your best interest to have a capable pair of hands on retainer should anything go amiss."

She didn't answer at first. I wondered if I had been too bold.

"Very well," she finally said. "I'll allow it, but I shall wire Father immediately that I have done so. That way, if his designs should suddenly appear on the market, he shall know who is to blame."

*****

Mirielle and "Josephine" followed me up the stairs, though at a distance. Two more automatons waited at the top. Both were soldiers. Both were undoubtedly armed.

Mirielle slipped around me (using a dogsbody for cover) and walked down the hall to the left, where she shifted one of the paintings and pressed a button set in the wall. When she did, a panel in the ceiling swung open and a stout ladder unfolded from above.

As I climbed into the attic, I wondered what I was doing. Did I really think that I would be able to fathom the workings of Mr. Perrilloux's engine if I couldn't solve the riddle of his dogsbody modifications? Would I be able to glean enough of its design to even service it, let alone duplicate it as Mirielle feared?

The attic was dark, but a bulb flickered to life when I was halfway up the ladder. I poked my head through the opening and beheld a chamber of gleaming clockwork such as I had never seen. Rows upon rows of brass pistons fired to a cadence as complex as rain on a tin roof. Gears of polished steel churned like watermills in an invisible current. Spiderwebs of copper laced the room, the electric lifeblood of the house coursing through them.

In the nearest corner of the attic was a tidy little office. There was a desk and chair, a typewriter, a cupful of quills, and a stoppered pot of ink. On a shelf above the desk was a row of hand-bound journals. My mouth began to water. Surely these must have included Mr. Perrilloux's notes, his research, and his most secret designs. I took another step upward.

In the other direction I saw a workbench that, because of what lay there, reminded me of an operating table in a surgical theatre. On it, the Model Nine I had delivered not half an hour before lay prone with its back panel open. As I watched, long, many-jointed arms reached from the ceiling and gently removed the wax cylinder at its heart, no doubt to replace it with one of metal.

I was in awe. To the layman all computing machines are as magic, but this was so far beyond the state of modern science that even I, who am familiar with such things, was struck mute.

I leaned forward and placed my hand on a floorboard for support. That must have been the trigger. The arms whirled upward like those of an agitated spider and another piece of equipment dropped from a hidden chamber above.

It was a Gatling gun.

I ducked under the door and leapt off the ladder just as it let loose the first round. Bullets tore through rungs that a moment before had been sheltered by my chest. I twisted my ankle when I landed and rolled forward to escape the weapon's line of fire.

I rolled toward Mirielle. Both her guardians moved forward, raising their arms. The hidden gun barrels sprang from within. In that instant, I realized there would be no warning shot. I had outstayed the house's welcome and it was about to have done with me.

"No!" Mirielle threw herself in front of her protectors and shielded me with her body.

They stayed my execution. I gasped for breath. My mouth was dry. My heart beat so heavily that I barely noticed the stabbing in my ankle.

"Miss Mirielle, I don't think-"

"This is no time for chivalry, Mr. Cotton. It's not a virtue you can afford right now. I'm in no danger here, and as long as we keep close neither are you."

It was true. As their Creator had yet to grant his servants eyes, the house could only "see" us by our weight on the floor. If protecting the lady was its principal directive, it could not risk assaulting me if it might also cause injury to her.

"Let's head for the door," she said. "Step where I step, when I step. That is, if you wish to live to serve your customers another day."

Marching in unison like a pair of dogsbodies ourselves, Mirielle and I walked down the stairs and out to the foyer. I did not let myself limp for fear that it might betray me to the engine. When we reached the door, I worried that the house might open fire should I continue on without Miri.

I needn't have feared. In her father's absence, Mirielle was master. She pressed a sequence of buttons on the panel by the door, then motioned that it was safe to go outside.

"Mr. Cotton," she said, "I'm so terribly sorry for what just happened."

"No need to apologize, ma'am. Your father is understandably protective of his creations. It's my good fortune that he's even more protective of you."

"It's not often that a Southern belle gets to play rescuer to a gentleman in distress. I hope that you are still willing to remain in my service despite this incident."

Sanity told me to never come back. My hunger for another look at her mechanical treasure trove caused me to answer otherwise.

"I am at your beck and call," I said with a bow. She grinned.

"Next time, I promise the house will be better behaved."

*****

The next time I came to Knockwood, it was not by invitation. The Great Storm struck on the 19th of August, disabling every power and telegraph line in New Orleans. While the river poured over the levee, it was all my fellow technicians and I could do to move our merchandise to our workshop's upper floor and pray the hurricane wouldn't bring the building down.

Even before the storm reached its peak, I found myself fretting about Miri, alone in her house by the river and dependent upon machines that surely wouldn't function once the plantation's power went out.

Thanks to luck and the grace of God, our workshop lost only its roof. There was nothing to be done until the floodwaters subsided, so I borrowed certain funds from the company vault and bribed the captain of a surviving steamboat to deposit me near Knockwood on his way to Baton Rouge. The landing at Sotile was completely destroyed, so the captain sent me to shore in a dinghy. Before heading to the plantation, I first sought out Marcus in the hope that he'd already seen to Mirielle's safety.

I was horrified at what I found. The Despres' home had been completely flattened. Its sides had caved in and pieces of roof were scattered everywhere. There was a mound in the rubble that marked the site of Mrs. Despre's cast-iron stove.

The rest of the village was in the same condition. The storm had struck with such ferocity that it left nothing standing save the church, which had been saved by its stone walls. There I found Marcus along with the other survivors. Before I even had a chance to inquire after his family, he shouted, "Mr. Cotton! Thank God you've come!"

"What's the matter? Did something happen to Miss Perrilloux?"

"I don't rightly know. It's that house. I think it's finally gone crazy."

"Crazy?" I asked. "What are you talking about? Do you mean it's still running?"

Marcus nodded. "But the dogsbodies started acting funny right after the last time you were here. After the storm I went down there and those damn things shot at me! 'Scuse my language."

My head was spinning. "What about Miri? Did you see her?"

"Couldn't get close enough. I hope she ain't hurt, but we hadn't brought her anything to eat since Sunday afternoon."

"Is your family all right?" I asked. "Can you come to Knockwood, or do you need to see to them?"

"They're fine. I sent 'em to my uncle's."

"Come on, then. We can't waste any time."

The road to Knockwood was still under water, so we trekked cross-country instead. Marcus's horses, turned loose before the storm, had yet to return, so we made our way on foot. We took a hidden path that had once been used by runaway slaves, and after several hours it brought us to the cane fields behind the Perrilloux estate.

The house had survived, though most of the outlying buildings hadn't. Mr. Perrilloux had learned the lessons of the tempests that struck in the past and planned accordingly. Most of the shingles were gone, but underneath was a roof of solid metal. Siding had been ripped away, revealing the stout cypress framework that held the building in place. All the windows I could see had been shattered or cracked, leaving empty maws full of jagged crystal teeth waiting to tear at anyone who tried to climb through.

As soon as we were near enough, I called out for Miri. There was no answer. We circled the house, Marcus and I shouting her name repeatedly. The front doors had been blown open and a lone dogsbody stood guard. I almost ran inside, but Marcus stopped me.

"Soon as I set foot on the first step," he said, "that fellow started shooting. I don't know how many bullets he's got, but I'm sure he's reloaded since then."

The blind automaton stared grimly ahead. I tried to think of another way in. The windows were higher off the ground than I could reach, but between the two of us Marcus and I could possibly scale the wall.

"We can try," he said. "I can't think of anything better."

"But I don't understand," I said. "How can the house be operating without power?"

"I can tell you that," said Marcus. "Mr. Perrilloux put a couple of big vats in one of the back rooms. Said they were batteries and if the power went out they could run the house for weeks."

I ground my teeth. Foresight is a blessing, but damn the man for thinking so far ahead.

"If only the telegraphs were working," I said, "we could reach him in England. He probably has a failsafe code he can wire into the engine from abroad and shut it down."

Marcus hung his head. "About that, sir..." He suddenly spoke like a truant schoolboy. "There won't be no wiring Mr. Perrilloux."

"What do you mean?" I asked. "Has something happened to him?"

"You might say that." He glanced at one of the upper windows, and it struck me that he was struggling with the act of breaking a confidence. "Mr. Perrilloux ain't in England. He ain't never been." He pointed to a grove south of the house. "He's buried in a clearing yonder. He passed last Christmas Eve."

It all came to me then. I would never have suspected, yet it made perfect sense. A wealthy father dying unexpectedly, his unmarried daughter left to fend for herself. The charade of her father's "trip abroad." Her fear of strangers coming to steal what was hers, and a retinue of mechanical men to cater to her every whim.

Or did they? I remembered how she'd protected me during my earlier visit. Did the house truly answer to her, or was it still following the directives of the hand that had set it in motion? With horror I realized that it was very much the ghost of the late Jean-Baptiste Perrilloux with whom we would have to contend.

Let me be clear that I didn't believe Mr. Perrilloux's spirit was somehow living inside the machine, but I had no doubt that the house's engine was imbued with its Creator's will – which was focused on nothing but the protection of his daughter from every conceivable threat.

I wished I knew more about the layout inside. Even if we broke into the first floor, the stairs would become a shooting gallery. Should we somehow make it to the hall above, there was the Gatling gun in the attic to deal with. Looking at the empty windows around the back of the house, I wondered what other defenses waited behind each.

"Marcus," I said, "was there no servant's entrance?" The house had no doors except for those on the porch.

"At one time, sir," he said, pointing to the mansion's north face. "When Mr. Perrilloux added that wing, it became part of the inside."

An addition to the building - a weak point in the structure? I wondered if the storm might have damaged some of the house's defenses at the join between sections of the building. If so, the master engine might now be partially blind. Could we be so fortunate?

I went to the north wall. The space below was high enough to crouch under, but the sodden ground beneath was a mire. The wooden skirting that protected the home from such intrusion had been sufficiently loosened in the storm for Marcus and I to pull a section away, so I squelched underneath in mud to my ankles to investigate.

The underside of the house was festooned with what appeared to be piano wire. It was so wondrous that for a moment I forgot my purpose. Each step on a board must have made a particular wire sing, sending a vibration through the network that somewhere must have funneled to the engine above. If I could find that nexus and disable it, the house would be rendered blind.

Alas, the forward-thinking Mr. Perrilloux thwarted me by enclosing what I sought behind a shield of iron. I thought about cutting the cables one by one, but the wire-shears in my toolkit weren't up to the task. There were two regions of the crawlspace that were not crossed by wire, but both were likewise protected by metal plates. One was around the pump that fed water into the building. The other guarded what may have been the house's batteries.

I examined the seam between the old part of the house and the northern addition. It was easy enough to find. Most of the wires had survived intact, but a handful had snapped. In that section at least, the house was partially impaired. Would it be enough?

I would certainly find out. I crawled into the open and had Marcus hoist me to the nearest window. He was reluctant, but I insisted. I tore the sleeves from my jacket and wrapped them around my hands so I wouldn't cut myself on the glass. I'm not as athletic as I once was, but I pulled myself over the sill just in time for an armed dogsbody to enter the room.

I crouched and it fired over my head. I rolled and it tracked me along the floor, the sharp report of its gun spurring me ever on. I reached the far wall, then spun on my heels to face it. As long as I kept moving, I might get a chance to knock it off its feet.

The dogsbody stopped tracking me. Its gun pointed at a section of wall some four feet behind where I now stood. Sheer luck must have brought me to one of the floorboards that the house could no longer detect.

I strained to recall the pattern of broken wire I had noted while crawling below. In one area, it had seemed as if every other board was still connected. I couldn't remain against the wall forever, so I gingerly stepped to the next board over.

The dogsbody did not react.

I shifted my weight and moved two boards closer to my opponent. Again, it didn't move. If my luck held for a moment longer, I would have one less automaton to worry about.

I stepped on the third board. The dogsbody swung at my head, its aim uncanny. I ducked and blocked its arm with my own. The gun went off mere inches from my face.

There was heat and noise. Not knowing if I'd been shot, I lunged and wrestled it to the floor. It threw a punch – an automated response, no doubt. If I'd been fighting a man, I would have struck its jaw. Instead, I reached under its breastplate and pushed my hand into the spinning gears of its guts. Twisting metal tore at my flesh, but I screamed through the pain and reached the steel rod that held several important components in place. I yanked it out of joint, and the mechanical man shuddered to its death.

I lay there for a moment across its crumpled body. As my hearing returned, I noticed Marcus shouting outside. I examined the bleeding mass of my hand as if it were someone else's and told Marcus that I was all right.

There were footsteps in the house. The door to the room I was in (a study, by the look of it) was ajar, but there were no other dogsbodies in the passage beyond. If one found me, I wasn't sure what I could do.

The machine I'd crippled was a Model Eight. I recognized it, in fact, as the very machine I had first come to Knockwood to repair. I felt a twinge at seeing my own handiwork gone to waste, but I buried it under my concern for Mirielle.

I stood. The footsteps above were in tune with the others I heard throughout the residence. The dogsbodies on patrol moved in lockstep as they did their rounds.

Could it be that simple? I couldn't go any further undetected, but the house's engine was just a machine: blind, deaf, and dumb. I listened to the rhythm of the automatons' march and walked out of the room in time with their cadence.

The stride of a Model Eight dogsbody is two feet, six inches. My own is slightly shorter, so I made an effort to adjust it. At a bend in the hall, I made a sharp, military turn as dogsbodies are built to perform. My path took me toward the house's foyer and the base of the stairs. A Seven in Confederate gray stood guard at the entrance but paid me no notice.

I had no way of knowing what commands the master engine was sending the Model Eight whom I was impersonating, but I had to hope that the dogsbodies were instructed to return upstairs for maintenance in case of malfunction. I turned the corner, once again in military fashion, and marched upward.

The hall above was patrolled by the new Model Nine. I couldn't pause to consider my options. In order to maintain my ruse, I had to keep moving. The Nine went left, in the direction of Mirielle's chamber, so when I reached the top I turned right and walked to the end of the hall. There I did a precise about-face and stopped moving.

The Nine regarded me in silence. I'm certain the difference engine was confused. The Nine walked toward me. On a whim, I marched in place and matched its steps.

It halted before me, raised its arm, and poked me in the shoulder where, were I an automaton, there would have been a button to return me to my "home" position. I didn't react. I wasn't sure what the house expected to happen.

The Nine resumed its patrol. I followed it in lock-step, praying not to tip my hand. I couldn't help but notice that the attic panel was open and I would soon be in range of the engine's deadliest weapon.

As I neared Miri's room I called to her. This time there was a weak reply. Her door cracked open. When it did, I pushed the Nine off its feet and dove inside. Gunfire rained from above and the boards where I'd been standing exploded into splinters. Lunging through the door, I knocked Mirielle off her feet.

The gunfire stopped, but the Nine rose from the floor. I slammed the door just in time as it fired. Shells punctured the heavy oak, but the door held. Its ammunition spent, the Nine began pounding on it with its fist.

"Mr. Cotton," said Miri, "you came for me."

"Please," I replied, "I would be honored if you'd call me Daniel."

She looked very frail. She wore only a night-dress, and it had obviously been soiled by the debris that had blown through her shattered window during the hurricane. She was shivering, no doubt from exposure to the elements. She had trouble standing, so I helped her to her bed. The Nine continued to pound on the door.

"Why didn't you leave after the storm?" I asked. "Marcus would've been happy to help you."

"The house wouldn't let me," she said. "I tried. I did. I think it's scared. It tries so hard to keep me safe."

"Let me keep you safe. You can't stay here any more, and the house will starve you if it won't let anyone else inside. Your father wouldn't have wanted that."

Fear flashed in her eyes, then she nodded. "It's all I have left of him."

"I know. I'm sorry. But it's time to leave."

The door was starting to rattle under the Nine's pressure. I cleared the broken glass from the window and called down to Marcus. Miri and I quickly fashioned a rope out of linens and dresses, and I made her blanket into a harness with which to lower her to the ground.

The Nine was relentless, and it sounded as if the hinges were about to buckle. As I lowered Mirielle out the window, I pressed my wallet into her hands.

"There's money here for passage down the river. Have Marcus take you to the Sisters of Charity Hospital in the Fauborg St. Marie. It survived the storm and they can care for you there."

"Daniel," she said, "aren't you coming too?"

Just as she spoke, the door burst open. I lowered her to Marcus's waiting arms as quickly as I dared. The dogsbody grabbed at me and the rope slipped out of my hands, trapping me in the house.

That was just as well. My business wasn't done.

I let the dogsbody grab my wrist, then used my weight to pull it off its feet. The Nine's responses were more complex than the Eight's, but since it had spent its store of bullets I could afford to disable it properly. I wrested it over to expose its back, then I used my good hand to open the panel and turn it off.

I took a moment to tend to my injury, binding my hand with some scraps of Miri's clothing. My fingers were already so stiff as to be useless.

Marcus shouted outside. I told him to carry Miri back to Sotile and take the first boat to New Orleans, and that I would catch up later. I prayed I wasn't lying. I still had a gauntlet to run, but since there was no longer any life at stake but my own I could take my time.

As long as it remained active, the difference engine would be a menace to anyone who approached Knockwood unawares. I had to disable it, either directly or by sabotaging the batteries. I didn't know how to do either, but I guessed that the answer lay in the journals I'd glimpsed in the attic. I had an idea as to how to reach them safely, but it would be a gamble.

I stood the Nine on its feet and pressed the reset button on its shoulder. It immediately marched into the hall and, as I'd hoped, waited for the ladder to descend. I went with it, careful to only walk on the boards that had been damaged by the Gatling.

I followed as the Nine ascended. I had to help it past the rung that had been damaged earlier, and I heard dogsbodies elsewhere in the house react as the engine deduced my location once again.

I was betting my life that the engine would not destroy one of its own dogsbodies nor the workspace of its Creator. When the Nine took its last step off the ladder, I scurried around it and into the chair in front of the desk.

The dogsbody faced me. The Gatling gun swiveled to aim at me. Neither took any further action.

I sighed with relief, then set myself to the tasks of disabling the house and planning my escape. I had to do both, or never leave the attic alive.

*****

I have spent many hours poring over Mr. Perrilloux's journals. Here is what I have discovered. The difference engine is indeed the product of Jean-Baptiste Perrilloux's genius. It is the true wealth of Knockwood and it belongs solely to his heir and only kin, Mirielle.

It is possible to instruct the difference engine by entering commands into the typewriter on Mr. Perrilloux's desk, but the codes he devised for doing so are too complex for me to decipher in the amount of time I have left. I will attempt instead to destroy the battery. I do not know for certain that I will succeed.

What I am able to do from my perch is to issue commands to the dogsbodies, which respond to the standard enscripting code that is familiar to me. I have only been successful with the Model Nine. The engine seems to cancel any commands I send to the other automatons in the house.

I have discovered that Mr. Perrilloux devised a way for a dogsbody to mimic his own handwriting so that his daughter could conduct his affairs in his absence. I think back to the "hand-written" letter I received from him, and I can imagine Mirielle dictating it to one of her servants from this very seat via the typewriter I am using now.

This is what I intend. I will send the Nine before me down the steps. I will mimic its movements so that the house will be confused as to which of us is its enemy. When we reach the first floor, the Nine will walk out the front and I will head for the battery room. With luck, the house will mistake the Model Nine for myself long enough for me to disable the source of its power.

I have confidence that I will survive this venture and that all will work out for the best. I know how dogsbodies "think," and I believe that I can outsmart them. Since I must follow after Mirielle immediately upon leaving the house, I have enscripted my tale into this Model Nine's memory for the benefit of those who may come here inquiring after the affairs of this estate.

If everything has gone according to plan, you will find me in New Orleans tending to the needs of Miss Perrilloux. If I have failed, then you will find my remains somewhere in the house, but I urge you not to enter if you detect any movement within. If I live, please accept this document as my statement of the facts in this matter. If I do not, then consider this my final testament, rendered unto you (appropriately enough) in a dead man's hand.

So Sworn this 25th of August,
Daniel Cotton,
Knockwood Plantation,
Sotile, Louisiana

The Bunker

Stephanie Osborn

"What's that you have there, Henry?" the man asked, turning as his apprentice trundled in a large wooden crate on a hand truck.

"Delivery for you, sir," Henry, a tall, lank youth, noted, easing the hand truck to the floor of the room. "This came with it." He proffered a letter.

His master took the letter and opened it, scanning down through it. "Oh. My, my, my. Sooner than I would have thought. I'd forgotten all about this thing. Get a pry bar, lad."

Henry ran for the pry bar on the tool rack and came back. His teacher held out his hand, and Henry placed the bar into it and then watched as his senior eased the lid off the crate. The apprentice helped remove the kapok packing, then stared down at a wonder of brass, metal, and wood. "What is it?" he whispered, awed.

His mentor laughed. "No, you wouldn't know about it," he said. "Sit down by the fire, Henry, and let me tell you a little tale…"

They moved to the fireplace in the far corner of the room. There, a rocking chair sat on one side of the fire, a short three-legged stool on the other side. Henry took the stool as the teacher settled into the rocker. A light tap of the master's toes set the chair in motion, and as he began his story, his voice was in counterpoint to the soft creak of wooden joints.

"Some years back," the man said, "when I was a few years older than you are now, I was a telegrapher. A damn fine one, if I do say so. I was working in the Midwest that summer when an urgent message came in – for me. I was called immediately to… well, it wasn't Washington, D.C. precisely. It was a town nearby in Virginia called White Sulphur Springs, and I was told to approach the front desk of The Grand Central Hotel and speak with the man who would be waiting there. Not only that, but my rail fare would be taken care of by the mere mention of my name."

Henry gaped.

"Exactly," his teacher chuckled. "I daresay my expression was much the same at the time. At any rate, I ran home, gathered my things, and set off, for the message came from a VERY high and reliable source, and brooked no delay.

"It was a long journey, and I can tell you, I was damned tired of the train by the time I reached my destination. I got directions and found my way from the station to the hotel, where I approached the desk clerk and gave him my name. His eyes widened. 'Yes sir,' he said, 'we've been waiting for you. Follow me, please sir.' Sir. To me. A young whippersnapper of... mm, I think I might have been all of nineteen, if memory serves. And you'll never guess what happened next."

"I'm sure I shan't," Henry avowed.

"He led me into a back room and opened... a secret door, Henry! I followed him in, and we went down a set of spiral stairs. Down, and down, and down. At the bottom was a cave, for the hotel was built on the site of a sulphur spring, where people would take the waters. And in that cave was a fair beehive of people. I couldn't begin to tell you everything that was going on there, even if I were permitted, which I am not... as yet. But this much I CAN say: I was brought there to coordinate, collate, send and receive the most urgent of telegraphy messages – for we were being invaded."

"INVADED?! Sir!" Henry exclaimed, eyes wide.

"Yes, Henry, invaded. And not from Europe or Mexico or the like. No, these invaders... were from another planet."

"You're joshing, sir." Henry's face closed in displeasure, thinking his adored mentor was teasing him.

"Upon my life, Henry, I am not! I should not have believed it either, had I not been there. It was no longer a cave, lad, but a bunker. THE Bunker. One of the last bastions of humanity. Oh, they were treacherous creatures, they were. And utterly ruthless. I am not permitted to tell you from whence they came. But their craft were scattered over the planet, and it became necessary for us to unite as one species to defend ourselves if we could. And thus my summons.

"Imagine if you will, creatures as unlike us as it is possible to be; creatures whose technology dwarfed ours as we dwarf the ants. Creatures whose sole purpose was to wipe out all existing life on Earth and replace it with their own. Beings who did not know the meaning of mercy, who were uninterested in dialogue, with whom one could not even plead. That is what we were up against, Henry."

"I was a boy then – how come I didn't hear about it?" Henry protested.

His teacher shook his head. "Ah, Henry," he sighed. "You know how long it takes for news to be transmitted and disseminated from place to place, even with the telegraph. And now we have the trans-Atlantic cable – but we were fortunate that one of the earlier cables was still functional at the time. However, regular civilians thought it was broken, for its transmissions were entirely devoted to our desperate cause. And Henry, few there were who saw these monstrous things who lived to tell the tale. I daresay NO civilian, and precious few soldiers. And those, not for long, as a general rule.

"They themselves were from a planet that…" he caught himself, "well, let us say that our gravitational energies are considerably greater than they were used to. Still and all, that did not stop the… the Things. They created great, powerful conveyances for themselves, with horrible weapons – death beams, poisonous fumes, and the like. And the strength of the conveyances was enough to knock down stone buildings, Henry! It was dreadful."

"Did you see 'em, sir?" Henry breathed, shocked.

"No, Henry, I did not – fortunately for me, for I do not think I would have survived the experience. Nimble of feet I may be, but not THAT nimble."

"Then how d'ya know all that?"

"I told you, son, I was the… I suppose one might call it the communications officer. Every message that came into The Bunker came through my hands, and every one that left, departed by my hand. I was charged with organizing the messages: descriptions of the creatures, descriptions of their space vessels, descriptions of their conveyances, of their weapons, of their movements. Positions of our soldiers, of our allies' soldiers. Troop movements. New arrivals of space vessels. Reports of casualties. Dear God, the casualties. And their descriptions. Charred piles of ash; bloodless carcasses; crumpled, broken bodies; crushed jelly; roasted, dead meat. All… in these hands." He looked down at his calloused, nimble fingers and sighed. The sound was shaky.

"It did not take very long at all before we realized that ordinary infantry and cavalry were utterly useless against them. Not even Maxim guns were effective. Heavy artillery worked, but only once. As soon as one artillery unit managed to take out their…" he thought, came up with, "ground vehicles, the artillery unit itself were simply…" he paused.

"I suppose 'incinerated' is as good a word to use as any. Finding the right words to describe it is hard, Henry. I hope you will forgive me for these frequent pauses as I search for words. We have yet to comprehend their weaponry.

"So all our weapons of warfare were, as one report said, like bows and arrows in their effectiveness. It became patently evident that we should not win the battle for our planet through normal means. They had extraordinary weapons; it behooved US to develop extraordinary weapons to use in counterpoint. And so we began to work.

"Initially we considered some of the more recent designs in artillery: steam powered cannon, Chinese rocket explosives, and the like. But all these had the same problems as regular artillery – they simply did not destroy efficiently and quickly enough, and their crews would have but a single shot before being wiped out, to a man.

"Being a rather imaginative young gentleman, I considered the possibility of devising a way of turning their own weapons against them, after a fashion – that we should build a kind of death ray of our own. Something that would work as far away, if not farther, than theirs, that killed as swiftly and as often, and something that was within our ability and our science. A kind of Maxim gun with rays instead of a projectile, THAT was what we wanted, what we sorely needed. Those of us in The Bunker considered the matter with all the gravity we could muster, and concluded we should develop light beams and sound beams. Given my handiness in developing means to improve my telegraphy system, I added this fiddling-about to my other duties."

"In heaven's name, when did you sleep?"

"Infrequently, my dear boy, infrequently. And you have, I suppose, noted it is a habit I continue to this day. It was not a time for sleep. It was a time for action. It was not," he added, "something I particularly wished to do; the notion of beings from another world fascinates me to this day, and I would much rather have developed a means of communication, of learning. But communication cannot be one-sided, and the Others did not desire to communicate. So, with self-preservation in mind, I turned my thoughts to the production of a weapon, or weapons."

"But... you don't..."

"Not now, lad, I don't, very true. And precisely because of all the death of which I saw and read back then. But at the time..." He shrugged. "It was essential. We HAD to have something! You cannot play chess if all you hold is shy a score of pawns against equally as many queens! And so I turned my attention to the evaluation of light and sound as weapons against the monsters. Fortunately I was not alone, but there were only a handful of us working on the matter.

"Relatively soon we had ascertained that, with our resources so limited, devising a way to make a death ray of a beam of light was not practical. A gas jet produces considerable light, and even more heat, but it is difficult to harness in any such useful fashion, and the fuel dangerously explosive, especially in the vicinity of one of the enemy's death rays. I still believe it possible, though not with gaslight, but we were running out of time. More and more of the damned space vessels were landing, disgorging more and more of their land vehicles. We were like to be overrun."

"So you turned to sound?"

"Yes, Henry, I turned to sound. Everyone knows that a properly trained soprano is capable of shattering fine crystal with her voice. My goal was to find a way to shatter those otherworldly mechanisms. Perhaps even to reduce to jelly the beings inside them."

"Eugh."

"Desperate times, son, desperate times. My task was to develop a way of creating the sound. I had a young friend, Nicky, who was about your age then, I think. He was brilliant and cunning and altogether right for his task."

"Which was?" Henry was leaning forward, elbows on knees, chin in cupped hands, eyes wider than his tutor had ever seen them, completely enthralled by the story his mentor unraveled before him. His teacher suppressed a tolerant smile.

"He was to determine the frequency at which the blasted things resonated," the older man continued. "It was absolutely essential that we know. For, you see, if we chose the wrong frequency, our weapon would do nothing save make a great racket. It might even do more harm to humanity's own structures or creatures."

"And?!"

"I considered the matter for a full two days – two days which could hardly be spared – then sketched a design. Some of the scientists in The Bunker looked it over and pronounced the fundamentals sound. Then I requested a quantity of brass, tin, a bit of iron and steel, copper, good solid oak, a hammer and anvil, crucibles and wax for molds, screws, nails, a metal lathe, and hand tools. And thus, working day and night, I built a prototype weapon. Oh, it was a thing of beauty. How the brass directional cone shone, the wooden housing richly polished! All the connections smooth and even, the movements like clockwork. It was easily portable and easily operated. But it was not large enough; it was only a test machine. To fight the monstrosities from space, it would need to be scaled up."

"And then?"

"And then I waited. Waited for Nicky to send the resonant frequency. It was the one thing that lacked in my design, and I had no way to determine it myself. It was dangerous work Nicky had taken on, possibly even suicide, but he chose to do so. He volunteered."

Henry looked disturbed. "What happened?"

His mentor scowled. "He never sent it. Never even determined it. We – he and I – had it all planned, how he should determine it – how he would lure one of the things into a church by playing a pipe organ. How he would use the frequencies of the pipes and listen for beats as the monster plowed into the building, then slip out the back at the last moment before the church was fully breached. But when the time came, when the final test arrived, the immaturity of the boy he still was overcame the courage of the man he thought he was. He could not do it. He chose to hide instead. You believe a traitor assassinated the President? I know better. He was on his way to The Bunker and safety when the Others caught him. They FED on him, Henry. Sucked his blood dry. With no more thought than we would crack an egg. And it could have been stopped if Nicky had had the courage to follow through on the course he chose. I think I shall never forgive him for that." Henry's mentor sounded harsh and bitter.

"But... but... sir, would you think so ill of me in such a circumstance? I don't know if I..."

"You weren't there, Henry," his mentor snapped. "The lives of millions, of a world, rested upon Nicky's shoulders." He drew a deep breath, calming himself. "He has tried to atone for it since. I have heard he even experiments constantly with resonating frequencies and harmonics. The damned man nearly brought down a building with his infernal experiments! But it is not the same."

"What... what happened? We're still here... there aren't any space monsters..."

"Nature, Henry," his tutor explained. "Nature happened. I never got to build the weapon, and in the end, I never had to. Even as the Indians were unused to the diseases of the white man when the Europeans landed in America, so too were these creatures. Just as the Indians were wiped out by the thousands, so these beings from... another planet, died the death."

"Well... then why aren't there any of them lying around, or on display in museums?"

"Ah. The governments of the world decided that it might be better for things to remain... secret. As I told you at the first, there were few who survived observation. So the dead beings and their mechanisms were gathered up and disposed of, and the locales of their rampages rebuilt – or blamed on pre-existing conflicts. Poor Atlanta..." He broke off. "I do believe the United States government gathered up those on our soil and shipped them via train somewhere out West. Buried them in the desert out there." He pondered a moment. "It's been secret ever since. I left this," he pointed at the object in the crate, "in The Bunker, just in case it was ever needed again. I suppose this new administration decided to clear out what we left in The Bunker, for its own purposes. I did hear, however, that some writer over in England has been tasked by Queen Victoria to write the whole mess up as a story – a fiction. A string of truths laced and knotted together with a considerable quantity of fable, in order to discredit the thing to the general public. I expect it will take him awhile, though. I shouldn't want the task."

"I... don't understand," Henry complained.

His teacher smiled. "It's very simple, Henry. Once the book is published, anyone who mentions beings from another planet, space vessels, death rays, and the like, will seem to be discussing the book. No one will take it seriously, because 'it's just a fantastical story.'"

"Oh."

"Come now, help me get this blasted thing out of the crate and over onto the workbench. Then you need to return to your studies, if you ever want to fulfill your own dreams."

"Yes, sir."

Ever so gently, the two men reached inside the crate and grasped opposite sides of the prototype's base. "On one... two... three... lift," the elder said, and they eased the mechanism out of the crate. Walking sideways, they carried it to the worktable and sat it down, ensuring it was level. Henry's teacher gave it a considering eye. "It should be safe like that. Now get your notebook, and let us sit back down and see what you've done."

Henry fetched his notebook and they sat back down again, Henry on his stool, his tutor in his chair by the fireplace. But neither of them looked at the notebook.

"So that's the prototype," Henry mused, studying its design: a wooden platform surmounted by a hand-crank, a metallic cylindrical generator, and a now-tarnished brass-aiming cone, all linearly aligned. The boy imagined it scaled up to cannon-size and mounted on a wheeled, horse-drawn base; a formidable weapon, indeed. More so, he decided, if the horses – prone to fright in combat – could be eliminated. He wondered how it might be managed. "It is a frightening thing, even so small."

"It is," his teacher replied. "A bit the worse for sitting in a cave, I suppose. It certainly is not the shining wonder my memory makes it. Ah, but sulphur is notorious for tarnishing metals. And the humidity did the wood no favors, either. It needs a bit of maintenance, I fear." He paused, staring in deliberation. "I wonder if the damned thing still works."

He rose from his chair and moved to the machine, insensible to his apprentice's sudden fit of tremors. Lifting off the generator's cover, he moved a small arm onto a tin cylinder and initiated the device. Instantly, his own disembodied voice sounded in the air, issuing from the brass horn on the machine.

Mary had a little lamb,
Its fleece was white as snow.
And everywhere that Mary went,
The lamb was sure to go.

The young Henry Ford looked up at him. "That's amazing. What are you going to do with it, Mr. Edison?"

Thomas Alva Edison shook his head. "I don't know yet, Henry. But I'll think of something. I always do."

Black Rhino

M. Keaton

Sometimes at night, it seems as if the embers in Selous' pipe are the heart of Africa, its pulse a calm wax and wane in the midst of an eternal storm.

While the other men look into the camp's fire, I watch him. Fredrick Selous—the man that killed seventy-eight elephants in three years on foot, survived more trampling and goring than I care to remember, and who is more at peace in the acacia than in bed. The man that has, unknown to most, served on Her Majesty's Other Secret Service for more than twenty years.

Tonight, he is uneasy. The others cannot see it; Corwall is lost in retelling his fight with the Cape buffalo to the men we guide; the native porters have retired to their own fire. I do not consider myself a native any longer. I am part of Selous—his "long black shadow" as Corwall says—like his rifle. I stay at the white man's fire.

He smokes his pipe, sips his tea, and listens to the cackling bark of the hyena in the darkness. He hates the hyena. We all do, but they are like the flies, something to be endured, part of Africa, the good and the bad. He stands and leaves the fire. I take my rifle and follow. No man goes alone into the bush. Ever.

We walk to the crest of a rise. The acacia trees are thin here; grass rises almost to his waist, sharp enough to cut the skin like a knife. Hot wind sighs through it, makes it hiss. Selous stands and smokes, a steady red pulse in the velvet night. His beard swings in the wind; it is more gray than brown now. Africa does not care about its men; it uses them harshly, casts them aside.

He is looking at the stars that dot the sky like scattered diamonds. A low rumble like thunder sounds in the distance, grows to a shrill trumpeting, then falls off with a grunt.

"She'll lose the calf," he says softly. "Damned hyena'll get it." I say nothing; it is bad when an elephant calves at night, an unnatural thing, an evil omen. He draws on his pipe again and the heart of the jungle burns bright. "Have you ever seen the Tswana hunt lion, Ramazan?" he asks me. His voice is like smoke, quiet and tired, but not soft.

"No, bwana." I am a Bushman; we understand the hunt, the honest contest and clean kill. The Tswana are weak, pothunters.

"They tie ostrich feathers to branches, and drive them into the ground in front of them."

I smile. The idea of the Tswana hiding behind feathers amuses me.

He does not see my grin. Selous is still looking at the night, at nothing, at Africa. "The lion attacks the feathers and the hunters jump away. While the lion mauls the decoy, they spear him. Sometimes a strong male will tear through twenty or more of the feathered spikes before he goes down. He might even get hold of one of the hunters if they're too slow. But, in the end, the Tswana win. Like the hyena. Nip, nip, nip, the slow kill." He stops. I wait. I have borne his gun for many years; he will speak when he is ready. "If the Tswana had stood together, they might have stopped Mzilikazi when he marched south. One man almost did."

I know of Mzilikazi, King of the Matabele, the Abaka-Zulu. "One man? Stop the great Black Bull? I cannot see this."

It is Selous who smiles now. "He was no ordinary man. When he was born, his mother took him to Kuruman, left him for the missionaries to raise. The Reverend Moffat sent him back to England to be schooled. He must have done well. He was allowed to study with the machiners."

I snort. "They are toy makers."

"More than toys, Ramazan. You have not seen what they build in England—great steam-powered trains, cabled lifts, machines that let men glide like birds. And weapons, guns of light and electricity, armored golems powered by steams. No, you have not seen." He says the last in a fading voice. He is speaking, I believe, to himself, not to me.

"Whatever his reasons," he continues with renewed energy, "grown to a man, he returned to his people. They called him Tumbo."

The Belly. I laugh, saying, "They fed him well in England."

"Indeed," replies Selous grinning around the stem of his pipe. "But he was knowledgeable and good for his tribe, so they proclaimed him a witchdoctor. For many years, I rather suspect, he spent most of his time lancing boils and extracting blow-fly larva."

"Until the Matabele came."

He nods. "Until the Matabele came. Then he pulled out all the books he brought back with him from England and all the parts and pieces he could scrounge. And he built, as you would say, a toy. A very big toy with the heart of a steam tractor and bones of iron, covered in the skin of a rhino and coated in the sap of the fever acacia. He filled it with water, stoked its fire, and sent the great black beast charging toward the Matabele."

The night air fills with the yipping, barking cackle of hyenas and I see Selous' eyes narrow in anger. "We could ride down and shoot them," I offer.

"Waste of bullets. There are always hyenas, wherever you go." I wait, he smokes. After a bit, he speaks again. "The Matabele attacked Tumbo's black rhino. But every assegais they threw just stuck in the sap, and when they attacked it with knives, it trampled over them."

I grin. I have no love for the Zulu. "Mzilikazi was beaten?"

"The Black Bull did not give up so easy. He ordered his warriors to capture Tumbo and said that if Tumbo didn't stop the beast, he would be bound and thrown in front of it. Tumbo said that was fine, just so long as Mzilikazi didn't throw him into the whistling thorn tree instead."

I flinched. "He threw him in the thorns." It was, truly, a painful threat. Bad enough that the tree has large thorns on its branches, but terrible biting ants live within it as well.

"Had his warriors pitch him right into the thick of it and left him for dead. He got out, of course. Escaping the thorns was just a matter of pain and patience. Even though he was born Tswana, he was raised an Englishman and there's nothing an Englishman cannot overcome with pluck and courage." When he says this last, he is smiling at some humor I do not understand. The smile fades and I wait for more of his story. It does not come. His mind has returned to the dark thoughts of earlier.

"What happened?" I prompt him.

He shrugs. "The Matabele kept killing Tswana until the Boers started beating them to it. You can still find rusted parts of Tumbo's black rhino around his village. Mzilikazi died a few years later. I guess he just ran out of steam."

I am not sure if he means the rhino or Mzilikazi. I am confused. He is talking around something, stalking it like he would an elephant, looking for the best angle to take his shot. "Bwana, I do not understand."

"News from England. There is war coming," he says, his voice full of bitterness. "Worse than anything you or I have ever seen, worse than the Zulu, worse than the Boer. The Germans want to rule the world. They train armies; they build engines of war that make even what the English machiners create look like children's toys. They will engulf the globe in their madness and no household will remain untouched." He is very sad and his voice is filled with sounds like ashes. "There is a great war coming and there is nothing I can do to stop it. They are like the hyenas, always hunting, always hungry."

"You fear for Africa?" I do not understand his concern; there are always wars.

He surprises me by laughing. "Africa is bigger than man. She is like a great pit of tar, sucking up men like Tumbo's rhino sucked up spears. No, once a man has seen Africa, something changes inside him and no other place can ever be home. No," he falls serious again, "I fear what most men fear. Death and I are friends of old, but I fear the long death of feathered branches and hyenas." He takes a deep pull from his pipe, sighs the smoke out in a slow stream. "I do not wish to see the pain and ugliness, the heavy suffering of war again in my lifetime. Perhaps I won't. This war may yet be many years off. You and I may be dead well before." He turns his head and smiles at me. It is a weak smile, but a kind gesture. "Especially if we tangle with another herd of buffalo like we did last week."

"If the war comes, we will go to England? To fight the Germans?"

Before he can answer we hear Corwall yell up the hill. "I say lads, is everything all right? You've been gone a rather long while."

Selous rolls his eyes toward the sky and yells back. "Coming back now. No worries." He puts his arm around my shoulders and speaks near my ear. "If the war comes while we yet live, old friend, I shall say to Her Majesty's recruiter, 'Send us where you will, but please, oh please, don't throw us into that thorn tree that is Africa.'"

We both laugh as we return to the fire.

January 1917, a German sniper at Behobeho killed Captain Frederick Selous. He was sixty-six.

The Ballad of Angelina Calamity
Angelia Sparrow

The tale is told around the campfires and the song is sung in bawdy houses and barrooms of a woman airship pirate, a wicked one-eyed woman, tall as a man and with a worse temper to boot. They say she ranged from Kansas City to San Francisco, from Dakota Territory to Old Mexico before the States' War. No one knows the truth of it these days and no two singers tell the story alike. But here it is as it was told to me.

From out of the sun and down from the moon,
The airship came apace.
And over its hold a strong lady bold
with hunger in her face.
Aye, with hunger in her face.

From fine drawing room to rude pirate ship,
Lady's maid to captain now,
She sails the wide world with her flag unfurled
And wealthy men do bow.
Aye, and wealthy men do bow.

Her Hangman's Strumpet, the ship bore us down.
The ship all black and cruel.
And Angelina on deck she was seen,
Cursing us all for fools.
Aye, cursing us all for fools.

The wild Calamity woman, she ranged
Down from out of the sky

And bore down our ship with goods so rich
The fair people did cry.
Aye, the fair people did cry.

It's broadside and grapple and boarding hook,
And o'er the rail they came.
Without so much as a "by your good leave"
They bore this boy home again.
Aye, they bore this boy home again.

The wild captain came to divide her prize,
The loot and young boy, too.
Her lone eye shone bright, her lips went white.
She knew what she must do.
Aye, she knew what she must do.

"Oh tell me why to stay my hand," she cried
"Or will you join my band?
From dry Deseret to Texas well-met
And take the riches in hand?"
Aye, and take the riches in hand.

High over the hills and desert they flew.
Life passed before his eyes
Until he said with a smile, "I'll fly every mile
And give you all my prize."
Aye, and give you all my prize.

From Frisco bay to old Mexico way
they plundered, stole and flew.
Till the boy said "Aye, as captain I'd try
and be better than you."
Aye, and be better than you.

With knife and corselet, to cutting they went.
The blood flowed deep and red.
Angelina struck, to our boy's bad luck,
And had stabbed him quite dead.
Aye, and had stabbed him quite dead.

The Strumpet sails on through the western sky,
Angelina captain still,
Cured of lovely boys and fine pretty toys
She pirates where she will.
Aye, she pirates where she will.

Endeavour of the Rose:

A Chronicle of Atlantis
Sidney M. Reese

Prologue:
Hello travelers, I want to tell you the story of when I was almost lost forever…

Let's start by getting acquainted with the year. Two things were happening in this year of our Lord 1922 A.D.: the Industrial Revolution was steaming along at a furious rate and those who sought to stave off the advances of science by means of magic were rousting their followers for the culmination of ages. We found ourselves right smack in the middle of it all with a man. This was a man who among other things was flying his blood red airship across the sky towards what was Europe to meet with an old friend. His name was Lucian Bane and he was by no means ordinary.

Chapter 1: The Mad Scientist

"Lucian, Lucian, how goes my Rose?" asked a man hunched over next to a giant Tesla coil as he fiddled with the wires.

"It's my Rose now, Professor," Lucian stated with a grin as he crossed the enormous laboratory. "I earned her at our last match up."

"So you did, so you did. I still say you rigged it somehow and I swear I'll find out how you did it my boy. Losing my airship like that… if I have to use every one of my metallic crows to keep an eye on you for the rest of your life, I will find out how you did it," fumed the old coot.

"Listen, not every one has the skill it takes to play pinochle. And you know my grandmother was the best. Plus you're the one who bet the airship; I just ended up with a better hand. Now, you know I love a good game, but enough of the pleasantries old man. Why did you call me away from a deserved vacation, I'd like to know."

"Well, speaking of your grandmother… did I tell you about the time Ruby and I searched for the lost city of Atlantis and almost found it? If it weren't for those damn automatons-- they were ancient, but moved as if built yesterday. Now that's craftsmanship for ya. I barely escaped with both my legs," replied the Professor as he pulled up his pant leg to show his automated leg.

"Cyrus, come on. What in hell did you find now, the Key to Atlantis?" Lucian scoffed.

"By all rights, Lucian, I think Ruby did," Cyrus said with a look that would have quieted a banshee. "I was with Ruby in Egypt before she passed on last year and I tell ya that woman had more spirit in her than one thousand Fire Mares. I don't think she died the way the doctors said she did though." A tear rolled down the creases in his leathery face as he spoke.

"So, you're trying to tell me that my grandmother was what? Murdered? You know as well as I do that the woman was pushing one hundred years old!" Lucian said almost in a rage.

"Boy how long has it been since you went on an adventure with your granny?" he reflected as he sat watching Lucian's dumbfounded look. "Yeah, that's what I thought! Now you listen and listen well; Ruby gave me something to hide and told me if anything happened to her to wait one year then give it to you. She said for you to 'remember your home' and you'd know what to do with it all. Now it's been a year and it's been driving me crazy! What does it all mean?"

"I have no idea," Lucian said.

"What!? What do you mean you have no idea? I waited a whole year for this; built thousands of machines to avenge her death and now you are telling me you have no idea why?"

"Cyrus! You need to show me what she left first!" spouted Lucian as he ground his teeth in frustration.

"Oh, oh right! That does make sense; you need to see IT first," Cyrus stammered.

"You call this thing an IT?" Lucian queried.

As if in another world and then snapped back into reality, Cyrus replied, "I think Ruby got herself into something she didn't want the world to know about. I called the Book an IT because I swear that thing is alive!"

As they walked through the castle's innards, Lucian noticed the many machinations of a mad scientist with a grudge to settle and he thought to himself, "I would hate to be on the Sid's bad side." In one stone hallway that smelled of elderberries, Lucian saw rows upon rows of what looked like stone men and a cold shiver went up his spine.

Why so many of them and didn't Cyrus say something about automatons? Did he make these to clash with the ones at the cave? Was Cyrus ready to go to war over Ruby's death? He wondered to himself.

But asking seemed like a moot point as they came to a large locked door. The opening looked in the vein of a giant sea whales' mouth portal with great tentacles protruding out of the stone frame. It was a bit monstrous compared to the vault that lay inside of this room.

Queer thought Lucian.

Chapter 2: The Book Is Alive

After acquiring the strange cargo from Prof. Cyrus, Lucian sat at the helm of his airship contemplating the night's strange happenings and the Book he now possessed. Cyrus was right; the Book had a strange aura about it as if it was breathing. When Lucian had first set eyes on it in the giant Edinburgh vault, he shuddered at the thought that this Book was the key to that very cavern that almost destroyed his grandmother and took the leg of her dear friend. But one thing had become clear: "I will find you! You, who did this and I will make you pay!" Lucian bellowed from his perch on the Rose, his long brown hair and captain's coat flowing with the rage of his voice. In dissatisfaction Lucian reached into his coat and lifted a scroll from an inner pocket. He received something else from Cyrus: a map that showed the exact spot his grandmother Ruby and the Professor had apparently stumbled upon and almost lost their lives.

To find Atlantis and close it off . . . why would my grandmother not share this find with the world? Why would she hide it away? He kept thinking to himself.

With the book nestled in the belly of the airship, Lucian's first move was to acquire his crew. They were a motley bunch, but each had their place in the puzzle. He had his monkey wrencher—Spur. This tiny girl was the mutt of the crew. Different ethnicities aside, her intelligence surpassed normal human standards, so the idea of acting like a girl was intolerable to her. She was happy working with grease and gears. Her tiny stature and thin hands made it all the more reasonable for her to work with the machines. She wore ocular devices that made her eyes seem like large orbs and because of the cold depths of the Rose, all her clothes contained feathers for added warmth. She did it all and kept the ship looking beautiful all the time; of course, this meant at first glance most people couldn't tell if she was a boy or girl due to all the grease. She, however, only cared for the grind, and she loved the solitude of the humming machinery in the ship's stomach. She strongly protested the Book being on board. Saying with a sniff, "It feels wrong; my machines don't like it! They tell me it's not natural! And you know they never lie to me!" Oh, if he had just listened to her.

Now we see the first mate who was a monster of a man—Gaunt. Seven feet of muscle and bones, this man was no novice to war. If it is not obvious by the stature of his being, his expertise came in the form of battle. He was a fighter and a brilliant tactician in air, sea and land warfare. For him, glory would be to die taking the head of his enemy with him to the gates of Valhalla. He was a brutish man, yet, when it came to women, he was the gentle giant. In fact he risked arm and leg to defend and protect the precious beauties.

He made known his feelings as he always did in his own way. Looking at Spur, Gaunt spoke with a thick accent, "Ze greasy baby owl is most right. Ze old ones talked of that Book and the end of times. Ve should destroy it and go back to ze beautiful women with grass skirts. Very nice."

As he drained the last of his ale, Spur rebutted, "Who looks like a baby owl?"

They all began to laugh a little… then silence again.

One among them let the fates be her guide—Twilight. The white cloak she wore hid a woman that was clad in all white ribbons looking as though she had just come out of 'curse of the mummy's mum' with only her crystal clear eyes showing for the world to see. She used her charms and potions mixed with a little alchemy to ensure the victory of every mission her crew took to course. Nature was hers to play with like a child. She used it to bend the very fabrics of the human body and soul. She saw the nature of the Book the way it truly was: Evil.

Taking a cue from Gaunt, she stated, "Out of all of you, I know the Book. It is alive and it will be the death of us. If we choose to go, we die; if we don't, we live. The fates cannot be tricked or bargained with; our fate is sealed either way." Maybe she was right.

Lucian listened to them bicker among themselves and finally spoke, "We all have a choice in this mission. If you want out, I'll drop you off and go myself. I don't care; the people who killed my grandmother are looking for this Book and need it to open the cavern to Atlantis. I will use it to bring the lot of them down, with or without you all!"

In the airship's cabin he stood not facing the crew, but glaring into the open entrance leading to the Book's makeshift prison. On the side of the wall Lucian flipped a switch and the table they had all been gathered around opened with a smelting pot rising to the top. Each member of the group looking intently at the cauldron now set before them, all wishing they were still on vacation. With a silent hum, the ship headed towards their new destination.

Chapter 3: The Die Is Cast

Without hesitation, the crew threw each of their identical pendants into the pot. Even if death was to have them, each member owed a debt to the captain that no money could repay. Those pendants were their tie to the captain, but that is another story... for now, understand that their lives were not their own without the captain.

The ship headed to the Province of Thera near the southern part of the Aegean Sea to the western shores of Santorini; this crescent shaped isle was said to neighbor another island that sank into the ocean. The land mass was destroyed by an incredible volcanic eruption around the 17th century B.C. which created the caldera our crew was heading toward now. This sunken island was thought to be the lost city of Atlantis, as the crew headed to one of the many cave houses carved into the myriad parts of the island made up of volcanic rock to prove this theory.

As the shore crept up the bow of the ship, the crew turned to the captain for the next move. Lucian finally spoke, "The map that Cyrus gave me shows an opening to a cavern at the right side of the island. We can make it by using our rudder ship…"

"But that hasn't been tested, checked and tested again. You said I had time to prepare it before you would use it; she's my baby and I won't let you…" Spur started gibbering, her words turning into grating mumbles that only dogs could hear.

"Spur, calm yourself! The ship works fine. I took it out the other day and the only thing that happened was a little sea foam changed the color of it," Lucian jibed at her.

Shocked and appalled, Spur squealed, "You what?! How dare you, Sir! You may be the captain, but you know how I dislike people touching my things! I gave her life, and I should have been the one to have first crack at her on the ocean!"

Laughing uncontrollably Lucian spurted, "I . . . was . . . just . . . kidding . . . Spur! It was . . . one tease I couldn't pass up . . . you're too easy to poke, kid."

"I'm a lady dammit, and don't you forget it!" Spur chided him.

"Zo, when did you become woman? I never zee you with a man, and you're just a baby owl. You grow up; I'll show you how to be woman. Ha!" replied Gaunt, throwing his worthless two cents into the mix.

"Eeeeewww, you are so gross! Baka! Hentai! Pervert! You know I'm saving myself for when I get married," Spur yelled, disgusted.

At last Twilight spoke with a voice so tranquil, "Please, calm yourselves. It was entertaining for a moment. Now it is becoming grotesque."

With everyone settled, they bundled up the Book and hauled into the Rudder. This boat was quite the wonder of technology. Spur had outdone herself by packing in all sorts of gadgets including an addition to the engine: a Mr. Tugwell's Endothermic Propulsion Guidance System or the EPG for short. In layman's terms, this fancy dancy device kept the Rudder on pace with the fastest airship in the sky without the engine exploding. Because of the enormous heat it generates at top speeds of Mach 2, a large amount of the water surrounding the boat is thrust around the engine in a series of tiny cylinders and while the EPG guides and steadies the ship at incredible speeds, it cools it at the same time.

However, there is one reason why everyone in the world does not have one: Mr. Tugwell was notorious for his gaffs and tricks on the common inventor; in this case, he added to his invention a dual personality. So, to actually get anything done, you first have to convince the personality that was dominant at the time that the cause was a good one. Only then would the machine work and you could hit speeds faster than the infamous Nautilus. It seems that our little Spur came upon one of these magnificent, but almost hindering, devices and actually gained both personalities' affections. In the game of love there is always a winner and a loser. Alas, her innocence that blinds all mend will also be her undoing.

Chapter 4: The Cavern

Before they left the airship Twilight did one last reading with her special tarot cards. A Miss Finklestotch, whom it was said to sway not only mechanical beings of every sort, but every living creature, gave these tarot cards to her. All would kowtow to her whim with only a flick of her wrist. In Twilight's life, she had only ever loved two people: Finklestotch was one of these. For now, we are waiting to see the results of this incredible skill that was passed on to our lovely Twilight. At each turn of the card, she read the same every time: The Book and Death. This revelation was kept to herself so as not to create panic.

The side of the caldera was deep, but in one area the sea seemed to part unnaturally and Lucian steered them towards their objective. They followed the map to a cavity at the base of the gradient where the water had subsided as they approached. They neared the entrance of the cave and Spur noticed on either side of the cave that there were pictographs or pictos for short. Excitedly, she started getting her gear ready to disembark and study the carvings that were etched into the volcanic rock. Before she was let off, the EPG's dominant personality at the time started professing its love and fear that she might be hurt if she left the safety confines of the Rudder. It tried, reluctantly, to lock her in the guts of the boat by moaning and complaining of pain, knowing she would come rushing to its side to make the pain stop for her baby. Gaunt smacked the jar that kept the personalities safe in a liquid coolant/ether bath and ushered Spur up to the deck. With a Spur full of tears at the rudeness of Gaunt's action, the crew made their way down the opening of the cave having to literally drag Spur away. She kept hollering in many different languages that if for no other reason she needed to learn the writings linguistic origins if she was to decipher the pictos. As they spelunked deeper into the cavern they noted that after a ways down, there were stairs carved into the stone not made by a human apparatus. With a squeak everyone turned to find Spur crawling up Gaunt's back to get a better look at one pictos in particular. Commenting on the styling of pictographs scrawled about this wall, Spur spoke, "Now see here, I've almost figured this language out and if I don't have a little bit of time to do it right, you will feel my vex! Stop fidgeting Gaunt... Looky here, these creatures depicted on the wall. They are like those things Professor Cyrus told you about Lucian. But see here . . .", crossing from one shoulder to his other, pointing to one pictos in particular that had crystals for eyes that glowed when they got close to it, "...this mannish thing seems to be mechanical and made with magic; hence, the glowing crystally stuff surrounds this one guy here."

"Wait a minute, Spur; you really need to break it down better than that. I love the fact that you're so enthusiastic about these things, but you're losing us," said Lucian.

"Okay, look here, this pictographs show a human shaman-like character infusing this metal hulking-like thing here with what looks like magic, see? Well, that should be impossible, right, Twilight? I mean magic and technology are like water and oil. That's been the way it's been since the beginning, right?" said Spur in a puzzled voice.

Twilight had taken the book from Spur and while examining it stated, "Lucian, if she is interpreting these pictographs correctly, then that means the people of Atlantis found a way to combine magic with machinery. Your grandmother Ruby and Cyrus got this far and were stalemated by these things. They spent the rest of the time looking for the Book. But isn't this Book supposed to open the doorway to Atlantis, not manipulate metal with magic. And if the Book does hold the knowledge to control the creation of something like that, shouldn't it also hold what could prevent harm from such atrocities? Theoretically?" Twilight held the Book out to Lucian.

"Well, whatever this Book is, we have it now. We are going to set up camp over by that corridor. Spur, keep on the pictographs; I want to know everything possible about those things. No, surprises! Gaunt, stay with her, and you two behave!" Chided Lucian.

"Come on my little baby owl; I take care of you and make sure you read the pictures on the vall correct," Gaunt poked her with a large finger.

"What do you take me for, a complete idiot? I'm at least way smarter than you! HAH! One for me; zero for you!" With a lick of the finger and a mark in the air, Spur took her victory a bit short sighted.

"You may be smarter than most 19-years-olds, but you act like a 6-year-old vith a crush. Hah! Now ve are even!" Gaunt guffawed, duplicating the same motion in the air as Spur had.

Chapter 5: The Unfortunate Backtrack

The next morning brought with it an inopportune enlightenment. The pictographs on the wall proved that the goliaths in the carvings on the wall were real and very dangerous. Poor Spur stumbled across a marking shaped like a strange squid-like face that opened a door to a hallway. In that hallway, a sea of glowing eyes stared back at her. Out of the darkness grew an arm that swatted at our baby owl. With a squeal she was thrown over Gaunt's shoulder and he rushed down the cavern back to the camp. Gaunt grabbed her and held her tight with a look of determination and survival imprinted on his face. "I von't loze you yet; let's get back to ze camp!" Gaunt slipped her a smile as he pinched her bottom and made her squeak. Spur, retaliating with fruitless swats to Gaunt's head, stopped flailing about and held on as his speed picked up with the sounds of thunder that followed behind them.

In one moment Lucian heard the thunder, heard Gaunt's voice, "MOVE!" and followed him with the crew in step all in one felt swoop. Laughing at Spur who looked content resting on Gaunt's shoulder, Lucian yelled "What-in-all-that-is-HOLY are we running from and are we out of luck?"

"Not if we keep moving Cap'n!" Spur yelped back to him as they ran. "I messed up…"

"Ze curious monkey on my back, opened ze hallway vith dose tings trying to skveesh her like a bug!" Gaunt poked at an already embarrassed Spur.

"I thought it was a joke, it looked like a joke… Baka nan desu ka? I'm such an idiot!" a sulking Spur responded as she put her face in her hands and began to cry.

As they scurried back to the Rudder and took to the big blue, Lucian looked back in time to see an army of glowing Golems staring back at him and slowly receding to their resting place.

63

At last back on the airship, they breathed a sigh of relief.

"What in the hell were those things? I knew they were drawings and that a shaman guy created them... oh, and I thought the Book was supposed to protect us? What was that, a ruse? I'm gonna kill Cyrus!" Lucian steamed.

"Forgive me for stating the obvious, but we did not stick around long enough to find out if the Book would protect us," Twilight pointed out abruptly.

"Well, shite! I didn't think of that!" Lucian said pondering over their quick retreat. "What did you two find out, other than how to piss off an army of what were those...Golems?"

"Cap'n I really am sor...," Spur tried to sputter out.

"No worries, accidents happen and you shouldn't be upset; we are alive and we can learn from what happened. So, let's learn what happened," Lucian queried.

"Well, (sniff) the markings on the wall showed us the shaman guys creating the Golems-thingies with the Book. (sniff) What they didn't show us was why it was a good thing for us to run (sniff) — there was an object needed to control them other than the Book."

Still composing herself, Spur added, "If my translation of the pictographs is correct and my translations always are; then the object needed is called the Eye of Nagoth."

And a chill filled the room.

Chapter 6: The Eye

"The last known holders of the Eye were the dugpas, ancient black sorcerers that were evil of the darkest sort. You know the ritual sacrifices of the young to elder gods of old; they wanted ultimate power at any cost and did some really sick stuff to attain it. They stole the Eye from the Atlantians in hopes of obtaining the Book and entering Atlantis to gain all the power that laid therein," Spur continued. "As far as the pictos stated; all of the dugpas were wiped out in a great war that sent Atlantis under the water. Boss, there is somethin' else you should know. We aren't the only ones who know this; we found this while searching the area." She pulled a smoking pipe out of her satchel, "I think you know whose this is?"

"Phineas Blockwell! How is he involved, Spur?" growled Lucian.

"I've got more bad news boss..." Spur sputtered, "...that Eye of Nagoth? It's supposed to be the eye of a mythical giant monster from the bottom of the ocean. With the power it contains, Atlantis stayed afloat; almost floating in the air for Christ's sake! When it was stolen, Atlantis sank and the only thing that kept them alive was the Book. So, us havin' the Book means that is the reason why everyone is not livin.'"

"It makes sense doesn't it?" Twilight chimed in finally, "Then, that is the reason Atlantis sunk—the Eye and the Book aren't there anymore. Which means the dugpas had the eye and Mr. Blockwell knew this? Lucian, do you think he has it? Will he sell it or use it for his own gains?"

Lucian stared into the clouds outside the window to the main cabin, not responding to the query. The tension now in the room was so thick that it could be cut with a Rotating Hand-Crank Tendon Saw.

Without moving from his view, Lucian spoke, "We need to find that bastard, Phineas Blockwell! No doubt, by now he has what? . . . A 2-3 day start on us, Spur?"

"Yeah boss! At least . . .," she quipped.

"Then we do what we do best . . . let him get the Eye, take the Eye from him, and carve him up one nice and deep across the belly," stated Lucian.

Chapter 7: Crimeny, What Now?

The crew went back to Professor Sid's lab, angry at the betrayal by one of their own turned wicked.

"So we now know the power of the Eye. What about the Book?" asked Twilight.

"Whatya mean?" asked Spur.

"We all know that thing is evil. If that is the key, does that make the Eye the doorway? I mean, what happens if we put the Book and the Eye in the same room?" she shuddered.

As the ship made its way back into the hanger at the base of Prof. Sid's castle, Lucian thought only of the history he had with Mr. Blockwell; the horrible night, the explosion, the betrayal and the loss of his one true love at the hands of a friend. Lucian's guilt drove him into the bottom of the deepest bottle of rum—until Ruby pulled him out of his funk and slapped the sillywog out of him. Because of her, he lived on; because of her, he saved others like himself. He owed her everything and nothing. Prof. Cyrus also owed Ruby; he never told Lucian why, but he knew he could find his answer somewhere in that huge castle of ingenuity. If Mr. Blockwell had the Eye; then they needed a way to track it, and if the Eye was a power source, then Lucian knew what he needed.

"Cyrus!" Lucian grilled, "Where is the Stumbleon-Bylock? Blockwell has the damn Eye and that thing can gain us the revenge we seek!"

Now what is a Stumbleon-Bylock? This amazing invention is the size of one silver dollar. Inside this device is harnessed the power of the Aethernet. Just tell it to find something or someone, and then pick a direction for each side. Then, this is the easy part: fix a strong cup of tea and toss the SB in it, because everyone knows the only way for the SB to truly work is if you pitch it in the Grey and it stands up on its side letting you know the tea has steeped to perfection. Once it stands on its side, you then pull it out, flip it and the SB will land on the side it wants you to follow. You may just end up in the place you need to be, and so far it has a 1/1 accuracy rate. Lucian and his crew faired pretty well with it.

"My boy, it's in the back and how about a 'Hi? Glad to see you, you old coot!' Is that too much to ask..." Cyrus trailed off when he saw the look on Lucian's face.

"Blikes, sorry, it's right over there. I'll put the kettle on," Cyrus said apologetically.

"Sorry, Cyrus. It's just that now we were too late to get the Eye, and now we know how to find him and crush him. We can finally avenge Bryony and Ruby's deaths," Lucian said through his gritted teeth.

That was the first time he spoke her name since the day she was taken from him in an explosion thought to be caused by Mr. Blockwell's bad judgment on the timer of an experimental bomb set to kill Lucian. I would love to tell you more right now, but why ruin the fun ending. It's teatime...

Tea Time

Oh my, look at the time... my Earl Grey has steeped long enough, a little cream and— Voila!— greatness. Sorry, ladies and gents, I'll have to tell you about when I was almost lost next time. Cheers and away.

Chapter 8: One-Dimensional SB

Alright followers, thank you for stopping for tea. Now let us return to the meat of the story. By now you would think the SB would have been flipped and the course set to find Blockwell. Unfortunately, a problem occurred; they didn't foresee the SB would have a flavor change. Who would have thought the SB had a bit of an expensive taste. When it wouldn't stand up on its side, Cyrus was a bit perturbed. It was then hooked up to the Aether-cage so it could tell Cyrus why it didn't want to work, and it immediately started professing its love for Ceylon tea from the Orient. Apparently, it had heard a conversation between the Queen (God Save the Queen) and an aristocrat that had just returned from the Orient. They conversed about how only a few hundred pounds of Silver Tips were harvested a year, making them rare and expensive. After realizing the shallowness of the SB, the crew skittered to find the rare white tea and steep it nice and long.

Absolutely inconceivable, the SB is at an angle and it's only giving our crew a half reading of where Mr. Blockwell has hidden himself. It looks as though the conversation between the Queen (God Save the Queen) and the aristocrat was a flodge, made up by the vile Phineas Blockwell! The white tea turned out to be tainted, which in turn put the SB on its rocker. Due to this catastrophe, the SB ended up O.D.ing on the horrible concoction!

"I'm gonna kill him, oh, Odin help me, I'm gonna break him, I'm gonna skin him!" fumed Lucian. "First, we need help!"

"Aw hell, you're not thinking of HIM, are ya? The man is a madcap, and reckless to boot! All he does is drink and then flies off the handle! Why would we possibly bring him with us... I just think that's not a very responsible thing to do, boss! Plus, he is a creepy otaku! Baka nan desu ka? That is not very smart, boss, I'm just sayin'..." again Spur's voice got higher and out of the world of intelligible.

"Oh, iz zee little woman afraid of ze drunk man?" teased Gaunt.

"You two cut it out! We need information and as crazy as he is, the Mad Gasser of Mattoon is our only lead right now." Lucian quipped.

"Well, wouldn't you know it, looks like the crew is going to be headed to an old favorite pub."

"It's time for us to see an old friend ..." Lucian smiled maniacally.

Chapter 9: The Mad Gasser of Matoon

In the town of Mattoon, Illinois the Mad Gasser reined with a noxious hand. The Mad Gasser, you see, had a penchant for jumping in front of open windows of unsuspecting females and gassing them. Well, what most thought he did it for was just plain vulgar. The truth was and is still, he loved practical jokes; his favorites being to draw a moustache, beards, dirty words, and other unpleasant things on their sleeping faces or place the girls' hands in warm water. But think about it, who would take you seriously about such a confrontation if you had "POPPYCOCK" written on your forehead. So the parents or the guardians of the girls would tell tall tales of dastardly deeds to the officials of the town and frighten the children into locking their windows at night. In reality the Mad Gasser was neither Otaku nor a pervert, he was just an older brother who never had a little sister to harass and thought girls who went "Eeek!" or "Eeeew!" were just plain fun to traumatize. After so long in Mattoon, he opted to take his fun elsewhere to devastate the female populace of the world and not just in his hometown. This grown man hiding behind a full array of hoses and tanks with bags of tricks at his side now hunched over in a tavern in the underbelly of Europe's lower class of mongrels. At first glance most people would have thought a giant sea monster had crawled out of the ocean to have a pint, what with his huge black eyes that hid his real ones from the billows he used on the innocent. But our crew knew exactly what was under that air breathing apparatus, a man who had seen the world and heard all the news through listening to others tell the tales of new and old. If nothing else this man knew it all, but you had to ask the right questions or risk going in circles. Lucian and the crew slipped past the dancers who remained unfettered even at the sight of Gaunt who by the standards of the men in the room was the perfect man, Lucian aside of course. As they hovered next to the man that looked like a squid turned upside down, he slowly looked up from his mug of ale and gave an insidious smile at them.

"So, you have finally come for this…" Gasser removed his hand from under the table and tossed what he held at Lucian.

Lucian caught it with little effort, and then held it open for the rest of the crew to see. It was one of the first pendants made and it had seen its fare share of days. The wily old man sat up straight and looked directly at Spur.

"Oh, my, it seems my favorite little girl has finally grown up. Hah!" Gasser sniped.

"Don't even think about it you old perv! I won't deal with any of your jokes on this job! You are not funny and another thing is you and Gaunt need to be refined! Why can't you both just be normal! Why do you have to act like children when you get around each other!" complained Spur.

"Spur!" Lucian declared, "You shouldn't talk to your elders like that even if his sense of humor is in the gutter with Gaunt's."

"Argh, don't go and smudge my name with his! I'm not a pervert like he is! Heh! But Shorty should be used to it by now if anything. I give her enough hell!" proclaimed Gaunt.

"Please, can we all just get on with it?" asked Gasser. "I'm getting too old for this nonsense!"

In one flash, all of the crewmembers pulled their guns and aimed them at the pseudo Gasser!

"Where is the real Mad Gasser?" Lucian asked with a stern voice that would have gained the attention of Poseidon himself.

"Well now, did I give myself away that easily, darn and I had wanted to at least get back on the ship and gut a few o'ya for da masta!" his speech becoming more dreg as his form started to take its true self. His body contorted and started to swell as if about to explode, while the occupants of the hostelry noticed without a blinking eye what was about to transpire and fled.

Lucian asked again, "Where is Mad Gasser, Fiend! Oh! I see…"

With a crunch, the thing flung the table aside and stood before Lucian. It was a formidable beast with arms swinging from all parts of its grotesque and bloated body. What wallowed before the crew was neither man nor fishy thing; no, it was something more abominable.

"A Nergil? Here?!" Twilight let out a gasp as a hooked tentacle lashed for her neck.

She dodged its razor tip by moments. As its wretched talon made a full turn, Lucian literally disarmed it. With a flash of silver, he sliced the arm clean in two. The Nergil pulled back, obviously in shock and pain at the proverbial slap to the face by what was left of its arm.

"Now is time to fight! I want to hear it scream some more!" yelled Gaunt as he reached his entire forearm into a pouch on his right leg.

What he pulled out could only be described as a bracer that had a trigger handle in the front for the hand to grip and two parallel pistons with a solid rode connecting them. At the tip were three probes that looked like knucks. To say the least, it was one hell of a knuckle-duster. In the time it took for Gaunt to reach in his pouch and out again, he was a foot from the Nergil, arm reared back and the trigger held firmly down. His blow struck the beast between what could have easily been mistaken as a pair of eyes. His finger depressed the trigger setting off the function of this amazing weapon. Electricity surged thru the gauntlet to the tip of the three knuckles and as his fist crunched bones and scales, the duster tip sent a shock straight to its nervous system. The bulbous creature sloshed to the floor in a heap of mess. All of its undigested excrements released in one foul movement.

"Kor! Why didja haf to go an do dat?! We coulda gibben it a good whacken an been done wif it!" Spur yelled as she covered her nose with both hands.

"Right! A bit much, I know, I know... but when else do I get to use the HOG*."

"Preferably in a more open area with the wind gusting through our noses. I mean good god man! That smell could burn the nose hairs off a dead nun!" Lucian remarked.

"Put that damn thing away and help me cut this damn thing open, it already stinks so it won't matter if we do it here."

"Why prêt ells, are we about to open that thing up, cap'n?" whimpered Spur.

"How does a Nergil take the form of its victim? Answer: It devours them whole and then can manipulate its body into the form and even the memories of the victim; kinda like a flat worm, but not. If my guess is right..." With a slice from his vorpal blade from stomach to sternum, Lucian shoved his arm into the innards of this odious monstrosity.

As his arm galorpingly squished its way back out, another hand was seen held firmly in Lucians. A bit more effort and he pulled the old man from the creature. The old man sprawled on the bar floor.

"...Twilight... he isn't breathing! I think that shock from the HOG* stopped his heart. I need a resuscitating spell now or we lose him."

"I don't know any of those spells!" Twilight regretted.

Spur then chimed in, "What? Lem'me at 'em!"

She rushed to the Gasser's side and presented a small cylinder from out of one of her pockets. Placing the small rod above his heart she yelled out, "CLEAR!" and thrust it down. A spark went shimmering throughout the Gasser's body. They all waited in anticipation, and then slowly, the Mad Gasser's hand moved. It moved up to Spur and suddenly grabbed a handful of her buttocks.

Aghast, Spur said, "Hentai otaku! Get your stinky grimy sick pervert hands off a me you dirty sneaky shite! I save your worthless life and this is what I get? A Christmas goose early?!? I wish I'd never saved you!"

"Oh, now how is that acting like that to your father's brother?" Mad Gasser said in a groggy voice. "And I didn't know it was you, I swear it!"

"You are only my uncle thru marriage. Your brother married my mum and that is that, you sick dirty man!" Spur sputtered almost in tears.

"Right, whatever. I wouldn't mind not showering all the time, but this is a bit unsanitary; take me ta the inn, would ya?" stammered Mad Gasser. "By the way, Spur, what was that little gadget you used to start me heart again?"

"Oh, that's my D.P.Z. It stands for Dirty Pervert Zapper. I keep it handy cause as you can see, a blossoming young woman such as myself needs to protect herself from dirty sickos like you! Truth be known, I was trying to make sure you stayed down, but unfortunately it had the reverse effect."

"Where is this blossomed woman, little greasy..." Gaunt beleaguered.

And ZAP! THUD! He hit the floor unconscious, with Spur walking past him with a triumphant smirk on her face as she slid the D.P.Z. back into its holster. They lifted him from the floor and slowly made their way back to the lodgings after first burning the remains of the Nergil.

"Idiot," Twilight muttered. "That is what you get for messing with her."

Chapter 10: The Real Mad Gasser of Matoon

The Mad Gasser walked from the men's bath; he looked at the room where the Book was kept and a shudder went up his spine. Spur came tumbling up from below with hands flailing as usual.

"What in the blazes happened to you? You old fogey!" Spur sputtered.

"Well, there I was looking completely dapper;" started the Mad Gasser like he was just waiting for his cue, "...then this young lady asks to buy me a drink and then WAMMO! I gets swallowed up like a whale downs some krill. I tell you what? If I wasn't a lady killer this wouldn't a happened."

"Bwahahahaaaa! You?! A lady-killer?! Stop it, you're killing me!? Your wrinkly butt couldn't get a woman to save your life! Even your voice is harsh on the ears!" Spur guffawed.

With a bitter stare, the Mad Gasser went to the rear of the ship and looked out the main portal. The man that stood in front of our crew may have been old, but as he watched the clouds pass by, his eyes showed a youth no one could understand.

"I saw what that thing was planning for whoever sent it when I was up in its guts. A fight is comin and we are in the middle and that damn Book is the main reason. Cap'n, if'n I can speak freely we need to be rid of it and run for the hills," Mad Gasser stated.

"Why is that, old man?" Spur sparked.

"Well, that Nergil was just the beginin: ya'll have heard of the Old Ones right? Heard of Yog'Sothoth, Nyarolthep and Cthulhu? Well, they are all there in that Book. The Atlanteans knew what they were doin by destroying themselves and leaving the secret of the Book right where it should've stayed till your poor grammy, God rest her soul, found the damn Book and here it is for all of us to... WAIT! My lord, have you idiots' read IT yet? NO!? What do ya mean, NO?!" Mad Gasser fumed.

"Ve are stuperstitious bout Book," Gaunt hesitated to say.

"Well, you should be. There is blacker magik in that Book than all the magic in the world. That is why your old partner Blockwell wants it; not just to get the Eye... but to unlock the very secrets of the universe," Mad Gasser said eerily while doing that thing where you try to make what you are saying more scary by fluttering your fingers at the recipient of the story.

With a scoff Lucian said, "If Blockwell wanted this Book and he knew we had it why didn't he tail us to the island and steal the Book while we were in the caverns being chased by little miss 'I'm-gonna-touch-everything's plunder?"

"Kor! I said I was sorry!" whimpered Spur.

"Hmm. I only got three words to say about that. I DON'T KNOW." Mad Gasser stated.

"Actually, that would be four words, but now we are just talkin' semantics cause 'don't' is a contraction." Spur said all smarmy-like.

"Are you really trying to wax intellectually with Gaunt? No offense Gaunt." Lucian queried.

"None taken!" Gaunt grunted.

"Ha! That's ma gurl!" said Mad Gasser. "Always going for the dumb ones. Hah!"

Chapter 11: The End is Nigh

So while the other crew members slept, Twilight read and read and read…

It consumed her night and day until three days later she came up for air.

Around the center of the airship she gathered the crew and told them what had transpired.

"The Book offers so much, I heard its whispers and promises to me. It offered the world and more powerful spells than any could imagine. I nearly lost my soul to it had it not been for Spur's two pet brains in the bottom of the ship. They pulled me back into this world by their sheer combined will. I owe them my life."

"So what did the Book say? Is there anything in it that we can use to stop It and the Eye?" asked Lucian.

"I'm sorry, Lucian, I was unable to obtain any information other than a few memories that are so fragmented I cannot place them in order or understandings. I failed…" Twilight said noticeably upset, tears of fear welling in her eyes.

"Nonsense gurl, you got lucky and you're alive without a scratch. I had to cut a finger off to get my soul back to reality. So, don't go thinking you failed; you gained more than my sorry butt did. That Book should have outright eaten my soul, but you have a magik soul about you that it needs to fulfill this doomsday scenario. You now have in your head more information than any of us could ever dream and you have your soul intact and unfettered. Praise be to the Mother!" understandingly said by Mad Gasser.

"I need to get some air!" Twilight said while she made her way to the deck with the crew following her.

"Where do we go from here? We could just keep the Book and keep flying. I mean for all we know, if we just do that until after the specific time then we should be in da clear. Right, boss?" asked Spur,

"We have to fight and we will. Don't ask to run again. Are we copasetic?" Lucian grilled. "Twilight... Twilight, what can we do and where should we go?"

"I don't know, but a name keeps running through my head... Azgoth. I'm sure it's a place; I just don't know where," Twilight said holding her head.

Everyone was quiet until Spur started up again about at least keeping the airship moving and not staying in one place when she bent forward as if in pain or throwing up.

Then with invisible arms around her waist she was pulled over the mast and through some clouds. In shock and disbelief the crew watched her as she disappeared, parting the cloud and revealing another airship and a man standing on the stern holding a round orb in his hand aimed at Spur.

"Blockwell! It's Blockwell! Get the ship airborne, dammit! Gasser downstairs! Gaunt on the guns! For Pete's Sake, someone give me a heading! Twilight..."

"I'm on it sir!" Twilight yelled rushing to the steering.

As everyone was in motion, a loud static charge screeched and then a voice came...

"Well, well, looky what I caught? She's gotten as big as a marlin!" Blockwell gagged. "'Bout time she grew up! It's just in time for the big finale! I do hope you don't mind me taking the last of the unicorn hunters. Do you, Lucian? I mean, you don't even know what to do with her, let alone where? Gawd, always the one-step behind wonder!

I figure this will be a like a gift to me for blowing up the love of our lives... Yes? No? Nah, I think you owe me a lot more than just the world's loneliest nerd girl. She is only the main ingredient for this god smack I plan to lay on this world! Not even close to being compensation for what you took from me! That's enough gloating for now. When next we meet I will be a GOD! And I'll wear your head as a fob! Mwahahaha!"

"DAMN YOU BLOCKWELL!" yelled Lucian.

"Nope, too bad, can't hear you! The Eye lets you do some amazing things, doesn't it? The only thing is it only allows you to do only one thing at a time. So, I can talk to you, but I can't hear a stupid thing you say out of your stupid mouth, STUPID! Cheerio!" Blockwell said as he made his exit.

As Lucian and the crew stood there in a stupor the Mad Gasser of Mattoon stood up and said his piece.

"I think it's time we paid Mr. Big a visit!"

"Who is Mr. Big?" Lucian asked.

"Haven't you guys figured it out yet? It's the one man who hasn't been in the story since the beginning!" stated Gasser.

"But wait! If it IS Professor Cyrus, why did he give us the Book and send us on that wild goose chase to find Atlantis? If he is the bad guy, he needs the Book and the Eye to make this work. What does Spur have to do with it?" Lucian asked.

"He gave It to you to keep the Book out of Blockwell's hands until he could finalize the deal to get the Eye. He needs Spur to make a deal with Yogsothoth and bring back the Old Ones. She is the last unicorn hunter after all," said Gasser.

"How and why do you know all this, cause of your bond with that Nergil?" asked Twilight.

"I thought that was obvious..." Mad Gasser said as he pulled a very large gun out of his side pouch and aimed it at the crew, "...I'm helping him. Now if you don't mind we need to get back to Cyrus' castle. Twilight will let you know I told you to read the Book because I knew it would drain you and confuse your focus on reality. Seeing how concerned you are for the rest of the crew, let me add; you don't have to worry about Gaunt. He is taken care of and safe or at least safe until the world ends in a fiery hell. Hah! Now enough fidgeting, Blockwell wants you to meet and watch him become a God. Let's hop to it then, shall we?"

"What's in it for you?" Lucian asked.

"I'm going to live for ever, when you get to my age you start reflecting and want more time. With this..." pulling the Book out of his backpack, "...I will be immortal."

"You won't live that long, I swear it!" Lucian said gritting his teeth.

Chapter 12: Final Resolve

The airship docked at the castle as the darkness rolled in across the sky. Lucian cursed himself for not noticing the same styling of his ship compared to Blockwell's. It was there staring at him that Cyrus was behind this. They came to the main chamber where Lucian noticed the huge door and saw that the room had somehow become larger almost pulsating. In the middle, lay Spur unconscious in some kind of ceremonial robe, Cyrus hovered over her, when the ceiling opened up and the moon turning the color of black sackcloth could be seen.

"It is about time... no words from you Lucian, you of all people should know why I did this. Rose wanted this, but her resolve failed and I had to press on without her. I want this; do know how long they have waited for me? Eons? Millennia? Tonight we let them loose on the world and they will give us power and immortality for our faith! Let us begin."

Cyrus took the Book from Mad Gasser and looked to Blockwell for the Eye...

"This doesn't happen without the Eye, Blockwell. Let's have it."

Reluctantly, the Eye was handed over. The Eye was held in Cyrus' left hand while the right was free to move the pages of the Book. Cyrus spoke aloud the words that would damn them all in an unknown language.

The ground in front of them gave way, cracks in the stone masonry opened to a massive slimy thing that spilled forth towards the altar as the gatekeeper made its way to Spur. As Lucian and Twilight could only watch, a tendril wrapped around Spur and started to pull her to its gigantic tooth filled maw... then with a monstrous cry and as quickly as it had encompassed her, it threw her to the floor with the creature's tentacle writhing in pain as if acid had been thrown on it. The gatekeeper moved to Cyrus who was frantically flipping the pages to find some remedy to his now very real f.u.b.a.r.-ed situation. The tentacle snatched him up and pulled him in two and with a loud crunch devoured him. When the gatekeepers' appetite was satiated, it dissolved back from where it came and left the room deathly quiet.

"What? What happened?! You did this, didn't you, Lucian! I will get you for this! I will make you pay. I could have brought her back with the power! I could have!" yelled Blockwell as he made his escape.

What did happen? Lucian thought to himself as he thumbed his teeth at Blockwell, *yeah yeah, whatever…Shithead!*

As he made his way to Spur he saw that the Mad Gasser of Mattoon had fled as well. When he made it to Spur, he noticed there wasn't even a scratch on her.

They made their way back to the ship and found Gaunt on the stern untied, yet out like a stump. Spur started to wake up and noticed Gaunt.

"Gaunt? Gaunt wake up, please wake up, mon chere! Please, for me, wake up baby!" She cried out with no notice of the shocked looks on Lucian and the crew's faces. With a smack to the head, Lucian woke Gaunt out of his snore.

"Hahaha! She's not a VIRGIN! You son of a bitch! When did you two have time, or hell, I don't even care! This is amazing!" Lucian laughed.

There was a note pinned to his chest.

Dear Lucian,

Well, I know what you may think of me now and that is deserved; but I'm the one that pushed these two kids together. For that I took the Eye and aim to have a whole heap of fun. You can keep that infernal Book. I say destroy it if I was you. If you think we should settle this, if you think we are enemies, then I will be waiting for you. I hope we aren't at the end, boy. It was never about the immortality and power. I had to put myself inside to save the world and I hope you will understand that one day.

The Mad Gasser

"What do ya know? The old perve was actually trying to be a saint. Till next time then." Lucian smiled.

Now, what to do with this Book? Well, if he said burn the Book, then…

Lucian headed to the furnace when Twilight grabbed his arm. She held her hand out in wanting and Lucian slowly gave up and handed it to her. She turned and moved to her quarters with an evil grin slowly moving up her face. The possession of Twilight is another story for another time. For now, all is well and the world is safe for the crew of the Rose since they have the Book. Sleep tight and don't let the creepy slimy things bite!

End Log

And with that let me just say this trip was amazing, I almost got crushed by a stone monster, then I was threatened to be burned alive. If I had one more life threatening thing befall me today I think I may just destroy this whole planet and have a nap. Oh I never did introduce myself, did I? But I'm sure you being the smart little human you are figured that out... my name is the Book of the Dead or Necronomicon. I know-not that exciting and kind of cliché as of late. So what, it is what I have to work with. Oh, and now I have a crew to boot! I know I said that all of them were going to die, but I'm a Book! You are listening to a Book and with all rights I can say whatever I want. Since I'm not lost forever, I will accompany this fine vessel with a very eclectic crew of sideshow freaks. You shouldn't worry, I will be back and we will have more adventures. The crew will want to go back to Atlantis now that they know its location and they will need the Eye. They have a lot to do and I will be there the whole way tempting them and promising them for there are many ways to bring back the Old Ones and many ways to skin our cats. Until then, cheers with a warm cup. I will be waiting...

Blood and Brass:

The Poem of Sylvia Weathersby
Kimberly Richardson

There was once was a woman named Sylvia Weathersby
Who lived to the ripe old age of 103.
She lived alone with no spouse or mate
Spending time building machines or engaging in debate.

She was born in the year 1824
Just before the Steam Glass War
When Conductors built constructs immense and tall,
Squat and little, or strong and small.

When Sylvia was young, her father and mother dear
Taught her the science of constructs and gears.
The child was delighted with metal and brass
And also learned daily of the War of Steam and Glass.

As she grew up, her mind expanded beyond expectations
Giving way to hopes and dreams as well as frustrations.
For Sylvia asked many questions, to know the world in whole,
Studying the designs of machines that were fueled with coal.

At 17, she designed her first construct named Tim
It was taller than her, metal sleek and slim.
Walking around her studio, making loud whistles and pops
Tim was fueled, while she made sure it would not stop.

When she turned 24 in 1848
Sylvia built construct Number 38.
Each one more dazzling than the one before
People wondered, "Would she ever get bored?"

Her constructs were used mainly for good
While Sylvia created as many as she could.
She supported the war, to drive the evil out-
Those who hated the Conductors, their minds full of doubt.

"Why must we live according to their rules and laws
When they can live without any flaws?"
These were the folks who were evil and full of hate
Thinking that progress could most assuredly wait.

But people like Sylvia wanted more in life
Than buying tea and cakes and complaining of strife.
She dreamed of a day when man and machine would
Work together as they truly should.

So she walked and pondered and thought of a way
To make her dream come to life some day.
Every morning, she walked along the streets
Passing by florists and butchers with fresh meats.

She would walk from day till twilight
Watching the street boys light up the gas lights.
And, every night she would go home
Back to her own unfinished work, back to being alone.

No thought came into her mind that would bring peace
Ending the entire war, suffering to be released.
She wanted to do her part for the Great Cause
To prove that the war was greatly flawed.

One night, around a quarter to three
Sylvia lay in her mechanical bed, rocking with misery.
Her thoughts kept her up late into the night
But none of them would work, none of them had the bite!

For years and years, the war raged on through the land
While more and more people began to take a stand
Against the brutal fights and the blood spilled on the ground
From dead bodies that fell without a sound.

The skies turned black with soot and ash
Caused from the cannons that BOOMed with flash.
Mechanical soldiers, of brass and steel
Fought the humans with bloodthirsty zeal.

Then, suddenly, in the year 1893
Around the time for afternoon tea
The war was over, much to everyone's surprise
Causing many a person to stupidly rub their eyes.

A truce was made between the warring sides
No one was the victor, no one secured the prize.
People could finally go home after so many years
To families who missed them, their eyes full of tears.

Sylvia watched women reunite with their broken men
Knowing that they would never fight again.
There was much praise and fanfare
People screamed and laughed without any cares.

Within a year, everyone was back to their lives
Women with their husbands, men with their wives.
Conductors continued to build for the good of all
Remembering what happened before, thereby saving them all.

Yet the horrors of the war continued to remain
For blood still ran freshly along the plains.
No machine could remove the blood from the ground
While those who died were placed in a burning mound.

Fires consumed massive graves night and day
Sending putrid smoke along the way.
People would look up to the smog ridden skies
Wondering why there was a war to secure humanity's prize.

The Age of Steam still rolled on with dreams and progress
Giving people what they wanted with less stress
And soon the skies did turn back to what they knew
Fluffy clouds among a sea of clear blue.

Sylvia Weathersby lived till she was 103
Still working on gears and learning alchemy.
When she died many mourned her death
Thinking of the exact time when she took her last breath.

Many learned from her teachings and her published works
For they were worthwhile and not full of quirks.
Man and machine must support each other, it was said
This was an idea that would never become dead.

"The war taught me much", she would say
"And I am glad it is better this way.
Conductors are here for all, no matter what you think
Assisting with growth of food or better water to drink."

And now my tale has ended, the lesson learned well
For I, as a Conductor, will not go to Hell.
I work my magick to help those in need
Still remembering the war, when many were in need.

Five Copper Bowls
Dale Carothers

I felt my anger rising and accidentally snapped the paintbrush in my hand. I searched through my cluttered brush box for another one.

"What is the delay, Mr. Donderman?" Madame Atherton asked.

I took a calming breath, smoothed my waistcoat and bowed. "Sorry, Madame. This will take but a moment."

It took all of my artistic skills, which were considerable, to make her youngest daughter, Renee, beautiful. She had a fat face and hair like a bush in dire need of pruning. I'd managed to make her voluptuous with a head of seductive curls.

"We've a gala to attend, Mr. Donderman. Expediency is essential." Madame was fat too, but tried to hide it with a tight corset, which contributed to her mood.

Tonight, amongst the amber gaslights in the glass dome atop the Center Tower, dapper gentlemen would twirl their highborn ladies about the dance floor and dine on exquisite food. I'd crashed five Center Tower galas. After those, galas in the South Tower, where I lived, seemed trivial and shoddy.

A lock of my long black hair fell out of the ribbon tied at the back of my neck. I put my brush in my teeth, causing Madame Atherton to cluck her tongue in irritation, and gathered my hair and wound the ribbon around it, pulling the ribbon tight. Then I pushed the anger down deep; but not so deep that I couldn't find it when I needed it.

I laid the last brushstroke, adding a glint to Renee's eye. "Finished."

Madame Atherton's stiff petticoats rustled as she rose from her brocaded chair, making sure not to step on the drop cloth I used to protect her fine carpets. She stuck a pince-nez on the bridge of her nose, looked at the painting and sniffed, "Adequate."

My upper lip twitched and I bowed to hide my rage. "Thank you, Madame."

Renee examined the painting. She almost smiled. I'd made her more beautiful than she could've dreamed. But then she remembered her station. "I guess it will have to do."

"You honor me," I said. It was easy enough to excuse her words; she was a spoiled Center Tower girl. If she'd only smiled I wouldn't have gone into the Waste Around, trolling for another victim.

I gathered my things and left, forgetting to clean the drying paint from my hands, and made it to the steam-driven glass elevator before the doors closed. I looked through the glass at the city. The five towers of The Elegant City were arrayed like the pips on a gaming die, similar to those that you might find in a gambling house in the Waste Around. The Center Tower was one hundred feet higher than the others; each of them standing at the cardinal points of the compass.

I shared the elevator with the conductor and a black-suited butler holding hands with his daughter. She was a pretty young girl, much like the version of Renee Atherton that I'd just finished painting, with flowing curls and a perfect little neck kept warm by a woolen scarf.

When the elevator let us out in the Garden, they followed the path toward the servants' entrance in the Border Hedge. I sprinted to South Tower elevator. Drake, the conductor, was there in his blue livery and brass buttons.

"Take these up for me would you," I said to Drake, handing him my paints and brush box. "I don't want to keep the lady waiting."

"Not a problem sir," Drake said with a wink. "Be back late I suppose?"

I smiled, showing too much teeth, like a manic dog. To avoid killing him, I ran toward the Border Hedge.

When I got to the other side of the tower I spotted the butler and his daughter walking along the path lit by gaslights. I followed them through the servants' entrance into the Waste Around; where all of the servants who worked in The Elegant City lived.

They turned right down Hedgerow Street, walking past a line of crude of shops and pubs. A lamplighter lit the oil lamps along the street, shedding a faint yellow light on the worn cobbles. I tried to blend into the crowd, but my attire made it impossible, and I was given a wide berth.

The butler stopped and handed his daughter some money. "Can you run to the butcher's shop for me? Your mother is waiting for me to bring Drew's medicine home."

"Will he get better soon poppa?"

"Don't worry darling. I won't let anything happen to either of you." The butler saw me, recognized my station and bowed. I turned away and brought my hand up to scratch my ear. Had he seen my face? If so, did it matter? Men from The Elegant City often went slumming for Waste Around whores. Let him think what he wanted.

"Be quick at the butcher's and hurry home," the butler said, walking away.

I couldn't imagine letting my daughter, though I'd never want one, walk alone here. It was shabby and dangerous by anyone's standards.

The girl walked up to me and said, "Why did my father bow to you?"

"Because I live in the Center Tower." The lie didn't matter. Who was she going to tell?

Her face turned red and she curtsied. "Sorry sir. I didn't know." But then she got her nerve back. "What are you doing here then?"

I laughed. She needed to learn her station in life. "I've a mind to have steak for dinner. And I know the butcher well. If I go around back, he'll give me the best cut of meat in the store." I didn't want to give her the time to question why I wasn't just going into the store, so I distracted her. "You're a pretty little girl. I'll wager that he gives you the same deal."

I stuck out my elbow and she took it.

"What a lovely scarf," I said.

"My mother made it."

We walked together into the dark alley between the rough stone wall of the butcher's shop and the sagging warehouse next door.

My rage grew. I needed release. "I'm sorry," I said, stopping and looking down at her. "But, I lied. I think your mother makes the ugliest scarves I've ever seen."

Before she could reply I grabbed the ends of the scarf and pulled it tight around her neck. Her mouth opened and her eyes bulged. Then her face went still. I'd frozen Renee Atherton's face on the canvas and frozen this little girl's face in death. She was my twenty-seventh victim. Her death didn't matter. She had nothing to live for.

*****

My door burst open a few hours after sunrise. Constables charged into my bedchamber, pulled me out of bed and hauled me into my parlor. They threw me to the floor at the feet of a man from the Inspector's Bureau. He wore a brown checked suit and had a red mustache. One of his jacket pockets bulged, giving his belly a lopsided look.

"What is the meaning of this?" I pulled my nightshirt down to my knees, trying to maintain my dignity.

"Let's see his hands," the inspector said.

Two constables peeled my clenched hands away from my chest and stretched them out in front of me.

"They still got paint on them sir," a constable said.

The inspector pulled a bundle wrapped in white butcher's paper, out of his pocket. He opened the paper and pulled out a woolen scarf.

I kept my composure.

The inspector compared the flecks of paint on the scarf to the paint on my hands. "Thomas Donderman. You stand accused of the murder of Veda Cuttle, daughter to Malcolm Cuttle, the favored personal servant of Lord Randall Wim."

I nearly collapsed. Lord Wim owned the entire top level of The Center Tower. His family had founded The Elegant City.

They coerced me to confess to the other twenty-six murders with drugs and sleep deprivation. My trial was quick, and when the tribunal judged me guilty the crowd cheered.

I was stripped to my undergarments and driven down the path to the servants' entrance of the Border Hedge. A crowd waited for me on the other side.

Lord Randall Wim himself made the proclamation. "You are no longer a noble of The Elegant City. We cast you out."

A pair of constables shoved me through the servant's entrance in the Border Hedge. I imagined the leaves closing behind me.

The crowd parted and then encircled me, waiting. I turned, watching them, trying to figure out who was going to attack me first.

Someone screamed, "Murderer!"

A rock smashed into my ear and I swayed. The second rock sent me to my knees. The crowd's howling rose up around me like a homicidal chorus. They beat me until my body went numb. At least I wouldn't feel pain when I died.

One voice cut through the din. "Burn him!"

Kerosene sloshed over my back. Someone had come prepared.
I gagged against the smell of my burning flesh.

*****

I awoke screaming, my body felt like it'd been ripped apart and then stitched back together. I writhed, drowning in a wash of acerbic chemicals in the center of an enormous vibrating copper bowl. I sloshed towards the edge, heaved my head up over the rim and vomited into the darkness below.

A masked and be-goggled giant loomed above me. He made a grab for me with a set of tongs. I tried to dodge the instrument but lacked the strength. The giant pinned me to the bottom of the bowl with a long-handled spoon, nearly drowning me, and then gripped me under my armpits with the tongs. He supported my buttocks with the spoon, turned to dip me into a basin of warm water, and then set me gently on a folded towel.

I stood unsteadily on the towel and hid my privates with my hands. "What's going on?"

"Dry yourself please," the giant said. "I have been waiting ages to talk to you."

"Why? Who are you?"

He returned to the apparatus in the middle of the room and turned the handle of a screw-press, releasing the pressure on the crystals in the glass cylinder below. The five copper bowls stopped vibrating. The bowls were set atop what looked like a stubby candelabra, each bowl sat in a place normally occupied by a candle. Tubes and wires ran from the base of each bowl, down to the glass cylinder.

The giant took off his goggles and his mask and set them on the table. He ran his hands through his dirty blonde hair and then scratched his bulbous nose. "Thomas Donderman, painter and murderer, my name is Lymon Marbry and I have admired your work for a long time."

I gaped at him. I couldn't get my mind around what was happening.

Lymon set his elbows on the table and his chin in his hands, "I followed them when they drove you out into the Waste Around. News of your murders traveled fast. Their plan was to beat you to death and drag you through the streets, but I stopped them."

"Thank you for trying to help me."

"I was the one who told them to burn you."

I had no idea what to say. First he'd been my savior and then he'd become an accomplice in my destruction. I sat on the towel and cried. I bunched my hands into tight fists and covered my eyes. Tears dappled my whitened knuckles.

"They weren't about to refuse orders from a gentleman of the Elegant City," Lymon said.

I wanted to kill him, but my size and situation made it impossible.

"I needed them to burn you for my experiment to work. When it was all over I collected a handful of your ashes in this," Lymon said, pulling a small silver urn out of his pocket. "And brought you back here. Congratulations! You are my first success. I've made so many mistakes." He gestured at a glass jar. Pickled obscurities of anatomy floated within.

Lymon put his goggles back on and appraised me. "Turn around."

I complied, embarrassed by my bare buttocks. The situation was so strange I didn't know what else to do.

"You are a triumph of modern alchemy!" Lymon clapped his hands like a child at a puppet show.

*****

The only light came from beneath the door. It didn't matter, I'd been here for months, and I could've described the room's contents in the dark. It had the damp chill of an underground chamber and its walls were made of stone. Lymon owned an apartment on the bottom level and half of the basement of the South Tower. My own apartment was several floors above. Wooden shelves and tables, stacked with the glassware required for alchemical experimentation, lined the walls.

I walked across my birdcage and grabbed the water dish that hung from the wires, unhooking it and setting it on the floor. I gripped the loose bar, braced my feet on either side of it and pulled. The bar screeched as it traced a scratch on the floor of the cage.

Footsteps echoed in the stairwell and the shadows of Lymon's feet appeared at the base of the door. I shoved the bar back into place, gritting my teeth at the noise it made, and hoping that Lymon hadn't heard it. I managed to fumble the water dish back into place.

On the other side of the door Lymon dropped his keys. "Damn!" he said, kicking the door. He came in with a scowl on his face and tossed his bowler and topcoat into the corner. "Arrogant bastards! When I make a decision I expect it to stick." Lymon coughed so hard it bent him over. "I should've quit. Let's see those Center Tower pricks find qualified gardeners without me." He pulled out a match, struck it, turned a valve, and then lit the gaslights near the door. "I need some eledite flakes Thomas! Time for you to get to work!"

I had no idea what the eledite was for, but I knew that Lymon needed lots of it. He stored it in a glass vial that he kept in his jacket pocket.

I pulled some doll's gloves out of my pocket. Before putting them on, I examined my hands. They used to be so delicate, so precise. I'd been capable of painting the individual hairs on a person's head with a fine brush, but every time Lymon came home angry I went to work on the eledite, earning thick yellow calluses.

Lymon took my cage down from the shelf above and slammed it on the counter below. I managed to stay on my feet, but the shock of the impact ran up my shins. Lymon opened my cage and set a chunk of eledite on the table near a mortar and pestle. He gave me a tiny hammer and chisel, and a thimble for the eledite.

Lymon propped a little ladder against the mortar. "Hurry now, I can't wait for you all night."

I dug the metallic eledite flakes out of the rock, filling my thimble, hauling them up the ladder and dumping them in, over and over.

After a few hours, Lymon examined the amount of eledite in the mortar. "I guess that's enough. Why does it always take you so long? There are little girls in Mercer that work faster than you."

Lymon had come from Mercer years ago. He and the members of the Society for the Advancement of Alchemical Research ran a sweatshop filled with little girls. It took delicate hands to chisel the thin veins of eledite from the stone. Lymon was still a member of the Society, but only through correspondence.

I rested my aching back against the side of the mortar.

"I have some new ashes," Lymon said, smiling and pulling the silver urn from his pocket. "Soon we'll have company." Lymon's moods always changed for the better after watching me work.

"It will be nice to have some new companions," Lymon said. "Not that you aren't enough for me, Thomas. Over the past few months your tales of murder have kept me entertained. You'll always be my best friend, but I worry that you get lonely when I'm at work."

"I do get lonely," I said. "But the time we spend together makes up for it."

"You flatter me. We both know that you are the celebrity." Lymon set the urn on the table, walked across the room and turned the handle atop the screw press, squeezing the crystals within. The crystals cracked and emitted a purple glow. The wires stiffened and conducted power to the bowls. The edges of the bowls blurred and hummed.

Lymon stepped back to my cage. He looked side to side theatrically to make sure nobody else was listening, and then leaned in to whisper, "I've been working on a solution to your predicament. You'll be so happy. I can't wait to tell you about it."

Lymon set the silver urn on the cart and hung my cage on a chain dangling above the bowls. The cage swung back and forth so I gripped the wire bars, waiting for it to stop. I felt like I was in an airship, bouncing in the turbulence, looking down on the land of giants.

Lymon pulled on his mask, goggles and gloves. "I'm going to try something new tonight. When I collected your ashes I knew what I was getting." Flickering gaslight flames were reflected in the lenses of his goggles. "You were the only person burned that day on that spot. It was an ideal situation. I had enough time to get a big scoop of you before anybody knew what I was doing. And I was able to get a clean sample. You're lucky that you didn't fall on an insect when that man knocked you down. Otherwise you might have a few extra legs, or antennae." Lymon mimed antennae against his forehead with his tongs and his long spoon.

"What's new about tonight?" I asked.

Lymon pushed a cart over to the bowls; bottles, jars, tools and decanters danced atop the cart as he rolled it across the rough floor. "I slipped into a crematorium in the Waste Around today and stole some ashes out of the oven. They'd burned at least seven people that day. I barely got out of there before the night watchman came." Lymon reached into the clutter on the cart and pulled out the silver urn. "I have no idea who is in here. I'm looking forward to the surprise."

Lymon checked the vibration of the bowls and adjusted the plunger pressure on the crystals. The purple light darkened and then a low thrumming shook my teeth in their sockets.

"Looks like we're ready to begin." Lymon ran a finger around the center bowl and made it sing.

Lymon selected a jar from the cart and dumped its contents into the center bowl. The blue liquid rippled and bubbled. He dipped his spoon into a bowl of yellow powder and tipped it into the liquid. Vapors rose.

"How did you learn how to bring people back?" I asked. "And why am I so small?"

Lymon mixed more chemicals into the bowl. "It would take a long time to explain how I got to this point, and I don't think that you'd understand, but I'll give you the idea.

"I've been experimenting with the reanimation of the dead for some time, but I have only ever been able to bring life to ashes reconstituted within these chemicals." Lymon said, pointing at the cart. "A fleeting portion of your life essence was still bound to what remained of your physical body after it was burned. I was able to insert it into a doll-sized version of your body using the energy from the crystals. The harmonic vibration of the copper bowls bound that essence to your new body. You're small because I don't have the money for the equipment to do this on a larger scale. Also, I've never been able to bind more than a tiny amount of essence to a body, so a larger body, at this time, would do you no good.

"Though now, I think I've worked out a possible solution. I can reduce you to pure essence again by bathing you in this." Lymon held up a glass bottle of orange liquid. "You've lived in an approximation of your body long enough for your essence to bind itself to the physical world again. Once I dissolve you, I can capture the gasses that will, essentially, be you, and introduce them into another man's brain by way of the nasal passage. He'd have to be on death's door for it to work and it would be hard for you to take over if he had too tight a hold on his body.

"Sorry that you won't be you, old friend. But we could hardly live together and continue your murderous work if you came back in your original body. Don't worry Thomas. I'll find a suitable replacement for your old one. But, I have to say, that it's been so much fun having you here. I'd followed the rumors surrounding the Waste Around murders obsessively, and after I found out that it was you who'd done the deed, I was happy to collect you. I knew you'd understand me. "

I slumped down to the floor of my cage. I'd dreamed my whole life of being a celebrated painter, but in the end, murder made me famous.

Lymon flinched. "Damn! Listen to me carrying on. Look how dark the solution is getting." Lymon put the bottle of orange liquid back on the cart and picked up the silver urn. He dumped the ashes into the center bowl and then pulled his tool tray to him. "Let's have some company, shall we?"

Pale shapes formed in the roiling blue liquid. Lymon separated them with his tongs. A tiny leg, an arm and a torso with breasts formed.

"It looks like we have at least one woman," Lymon sucked up some liquid with a glass pipette and squirted it into the upper left bowl. He transferred the torso to it and searched for her head. "Here she is." Lymon picked it up by its chestnut hair and showed it to me. "She's quite a beauty. Don't you think?"

Lymon spread the body parts around the center bowl to keep them from touching. He adjusted the plunger on the crystals. The vibrating hum lowered in intensity. "Better slow it down, too much happening at once." His voice cracked and he coughed. I couldn't tell if it was from strain or excitement.

Lymon assembled the woman. Her eyes stayed closed, but blue froth burbled from her lips. When Lymon attached her arm it twitched, making her breasts bounce. I felt a guilty stirring in my crotch. He checked the bits still growing in the center bowl and moved a shoulder away from a foot. "Let me know if any of them get close to touching. I don't want them to bind."

He returned his attention to the woman. He found her legs and her other arm and then squirted blue liquid into the lower left bowl and moved her unattached limbs into it. He held her down with his spoon and plucked her arm from the lower left bowl. Lymon leaned in close, adjusted his goggles and spent several seconds lining up her arm before he applied it to her shoulder.

A torso floated into an arm and they fused together, but I didn't feel the need to tell Lymon.

Lymon flipped her over onto her stomach and then grabbed one of her legs. It seemed misshapen, until I realized that one of her buttocks hung from it, the other buttock jutted from her torso. Lymon aligned the buttocks and held the leg in place until it began to twitch. "Did you ever have a woman so fine?"

"Never." I didn't agree, but I saw no reason to argue.

Lymon finished assembling the woman, forgetting the other parts melting together in the center bowl. With each passing moment more pieces boiled to the surface. A cluster of arms and legs formed. A head had fused at the center. One of the eyes opened. And then the creature coughed, exposing broken teeth.

"What was that?" Lymon looked into the bowl and saw the cluster. "You were looking at her weren't you? Stop it. She's mine."

Lymon took up a ladle, sloshed some liquid into the upper right bowl, scooped up the creature and dumped it in. "There's no telling how many people I could have made tonight. They were all going to be perfect. Now look what you've done!" He separated the bits in the center bowl. "Keep an eye on it or I'll chop you up and toss you into the mix." He took the woman to the counter and rinsed her in a warm bath.

"There's a hand that's about to touch a knee!" I said.

"Just a moment!"

"Hurry!" I was worried that he'd punish me for his own incompetence.

"Let me get her into the cage."

Lymon closed her cage and rushed back to the bowls. He separated the hand and the knee. Lymon smacked the ladle against the cage. It rang and it swayed. "I give the orders."

I fell to the floor of the cage, my ears ringing.

The woman coughed and then sobbed. Lymon shot me a glance, testing to see if I watched the bowls or the woman. Luckily I had resisted the urge to look.

Lymon assembled a man below me. He started with the head and then put him together piece by piece; the neck, the ribcage and the small of the back. Nothing matched. The little man convulsed and tried to crawl away, but Lymon pinned him between his tongs.

"This isn't working," Lymon said. "I'll wager that the parts I need are on that thing." He gestured at the creature in the upper right bowl. He put his hand to his chin and thought for moment. "I wonder if it would work?" Lymon trimmed a limb from the creature with a scalpel and attempted to stick it to the man's shoulder. It wouldn't take. "Damn, damn, damn!"

The creature wailed. I covered my ears.

Lymon worked well into the night, but to no avail. By the time he'd finished the man was dead. All he had left was the woman, the thing, and me.

Lymon unhooked my cage from the chain and set it up on the shelf. The woman's cage remained below on the table. Lymon doused the creature in a bath of warm water and dropped it into an open-topped cage. It flailed at the bars but wasn't able to lift itself.

"Well Thomas, because of your ineptitude you're officially father to this beast, maybe you'd like to spend some time with him." Lymon set its cage next to mine.

It stopped trying to climb. The creature rolled to the edge of its cage and groped for me between our bars. I backed against the far edge of my own cage. It strained at me until a growth on its shoulder popped between the bars, trapping its arm. It yelped and yanked with all its might, trying to free its limb. It gritted its teeth and spittle flecked its two chins. Sweat broke out on its lumpy forehead. The growth pulsed and turned red. A tiny rivulet of blood streamed from partially healed scab. I figured that it was the stump left over after Lymon sliced one of its arms off during the bonding in the copper bowls.

"He just wants to be near you." Lymon had removed his goggles and mask. He sat on a stool, watching us and giggling. "He seems very excited. Do you want to share accommodations with him?"

What made it male in Lymon's eyes? Had he seen a part of its anatomy that I hadn't?

"I just noticed that he has eight limbs, like an octopus," Lymon said.

I counted five arms, one near each shoulder, two coming from different angles out of its back, and one in the middle of its chest. It had three legs. The creature planted one of its feet on a bar and pulled. The shoulder popped through the gap and the creature tumbled and came up cradling the growth. It cried and glared at me.

"He doesn't like you very much," Lymon said.

"I didn't do anything."

"No you didn't. He was trapped and you just sat there. Some father you are."

"He would've pulled my skin off."

"I think that we should name him Octopus."

"What about her?" I pointed to the cage on the table.

"That is none of your concern! She's mine."

Lymon checked her cage. She lay there, asleep. I wondered if she'd live through the night.

Lymon wrapped her in a swatch of red velvet. He stroked her face with a fingertip and then went to the door. "The experiment failed because of you. This was supposed to be perfect. You're lucky that I like you so much." Lymon slammed the door, as he left. He'd forgotten to extinguish the gaslights.

*****

Octopus sobbed in his cage. I pitied him because I felt responsible. Had I just paid attention, he wouldn't exist. I squeezed my eyes shut as hard as I could and wrapped my dirty blanket around my ears, but I could still hear his crying.

Octopus stopped weeping, tumbled to the side of his cage and looked down at the table.

A voice rose from below. It was the voice of the woman. Her song soothed Octopus.

The sparkling stars
Won't ever be bright as your smile
When you wake up in my bed
The next morning

Octopus relaxed as she sang. His breathing slowed until he fell asleep. I wanted to call out, to thank her, but I didn't want to wake the unfortunate creature.

I was confused. Lymon had said that he'd gotten the ashes in the Waste Around and her song was one that daring young women sang to the boys while dancing in the domes atop the towers. I'd heard it more than once myself. I couldn't imagine a tower girl being burned in a Waste Around crematorium. Her family must've fallen from favor.

The next morning Lymon clomped about in his rooms above, getting ready for work. Dust from the cracks in the floorboards sprinkled on my head. I checked Octopus. He was still asleep.

I crawled to the edge of my cage and peeked down at her. She didn't have any clothes yet, but she was wrapped in the scrap of red velvet that Lymon had used to dry her. Her pale foot poked out from under her makeshift blanket and she rolled over.

Something yanked at my sleeve. I jumped back, but Octopus had a hold of me. His thick yellow fingernails scratched my forearm. Suddenly, I was singing.

We'll clean your floors
We'll tend your flowers
But we'd just as soon
Tear down your towers

Octopus let me go and grimaced. My voice was nothing compared to hers. It cracked like that of a pubescent boy. I'd heard the song late one night in a Waste Around pub, while looking for a place to hide from the authorities just after I'd killed a little girl.

The woman laughed at me.

"That wasn't funny," I said.

"Your voice is awful." She stood wrapped in her blanket, her face framed between the bars of her cage. Curly chestnut hair fell past her naked shoulders. Her nose was a little too long, and her eyebrows were heavy and mannish. Her charms lay solely in her voice.

"He wants to kill me," I said.

"There were times when I wanted to kill my father too."

"You heard that? I thought you were asleep."

"I was pretending."

"Anyway, I'm too pretty to be his father," I said, smiling. "What's your name?"

"Myra. And yours?"

"Thomas."

Octopus shifted his gaze back and forth. When our eyes met he gave me a crooked nod. Did he want me to sing again?

"What tower did you live in?" I said. "Before your family…"

"Before my family what?"

"Lymon said-"

"Who?"

"The man who holds us prisoner. He told me that he'd found your ashes in the Waste Around, but you must've lived in the towers at one point. That is, before your family fell out of favor."

Her face went blank.

"I'm sorry," I said. "I was just curious."

"I'm from the Waste Around." She looked at me defiantly. "What made you think I was from the towers?"

"How do you know that song?"

"I used to serve wine at tower parties. I heard the song and liked the tune."

Servants had always been nearly invisible to me and Myra wouldn't have earned a second glance.

Octopus pummeled the floor of his cage and wailed.

I retreated, startled by the clamor. "Shut up, you monster!"

"That isn't any way to talk to our baby," Myra said loudly over the din.

Octopus stopped, he pointed at Myra with two of his arms and nodded.

"Our baby?" I said.

"Lymon called you his father, and there must be part of me somewhere inside him, which makes me his mommy."

Something was wrong with this woman; the melding had addled her brains. "We'll I've seen his teeth. Unless you've got callused nipples, I'd advise against nursing."

She pulled the blanket tighter around her chest and turned away.

"What makes what you said funny, and what I said not?" I asked.

"There's no reason to be cruel."

"And you calling me the father of that monster isn't cruel?"

"This is the worst thing that will ever happen to me. Why can't you be kind?" Myra slid to her floor and sobbed. Octopus did the same.

I'm sorry!" I said, trying to scream louder than Octopus cried. "Please forgive me. You're right. All we have is each other. You, me, and our baby."

Myra rose and wiped her tears away with a corner of her blanket and said, "Thank you."

Myra sang until Octopus fell asleep and then we talked. I learned about her life and she learned about mine. I left out the murders. I'd just gotten her to like me again. I didn't want my only friend to become my enemy.

Later that afternoon, when we heard Lymon's footsteps in the stairwell, Myra said, "I never woke up, we never talked." She flopped to the floor and covered her face with her blanket.

Lymon opened the door.

The sound woke Octopus, who immediately howled and waved at Myra, demanding that she sing another song.

"What's with all the racket?" Lymon asked. "Shut him up!"

I sang my Waste Around song again, but Octopus didn't like it. He rolled to my cage and kicked at it and then rolled back and pointed at Myra again. He bobbed in place and pointed again.

"What's been going on down here, Thomas?" Lymon asked. He strode toward me. "Did she wake up? Did you talk to her? I told you that she wasn't any of your business. I made her for me." Lymon banged on the table near Myra's cage.

Octopus growled and clawed at him between the bars. Myra stuck her head out from under her blankets, but Lymon didn't see her. He was too focused on Octopus and I.

"You've both grown too attached to my girl," Lymon said. "How did you know to sing when Octopus got upset? Why did he stop you and point at her? She must've been awake at some point. Tell me what you talked about. Was it about me?" Lymon leaned in towards my cage and laughed. "You aren't planning on running off together are you? Did you tell her about the little girls?"

I looked at Myra and saw the question in her gaze.

"Please don't," I said. We'd only known each other for a day, but we were stuck here, at this size. It bound us together.

"Please don't what?" Lymon said. "Please don't tell her that you are... Wait a moment. Let's do this face to face. I want you to see her reaction when you tell her."

Lymon took a deep wooden tray from under the table and then opened my cage and groped for me. I tried to get away, but he caught me. Lymon set me in the tray; the sides were made of rough wood and stood as high as my shoulder.

Octopus howled and spat while Lymon fished for Myra.

"Get away from me," Myra screamed.

I ran to the side of the tray. Myra's cage rattled as his hand chased her about. She had managed to keep herself wrapped in the blanket.

I hoisted myself up on the side of the tray, "Myra!"

Lymon turned and flicked me back into the tray. I skidded halfway across it. My lip was bloody and I'd lost a few teeth. I tried to stand but I was too dizzy.

Lymon dropped Myra into the tray. I ran to her but Lymon brushed me back and then he plucked Octopus out of his cage.

"I want some answers or I'll set him loose in the tray with you. Damn! It bit me." Lymon dropped Octopus to the bottom of the tray and then pinned him with his palm. "Let's hear some of that singing Myra."

Myra stood speechless.

"Now!" Lymon raised his hand and held it in place. Octopus struggled to get up, but Lymon slapped him to the bottom of the tray again.

Octopus grunted and then attacked Lymon's hand with renewed ferocity.

Myra sang. Her voice stirred my mind. I imagined that her red scrap of cloth blanket was a crimson ball gown for a moment and saw her curls piled high atop her head in the latest fashion. Halfway into the song she turned and sang to me.

"Stop that!" Lymon screamed. "I knew something was going on between you two."

Myra quit singing and came to me. I wrapped my arms around her. Though I didn't find her attractive, when I had her in my arms, her smell enchanted me. Her curly brown hair was soft against my chin.

"He's a murderer you know," Lymon said. "Tell her about the little girls."

Myra stiffened and pulled her head back to look at me. Her mannish eyebrows rose. Tears came to my eyes. I couldn't tell her. Myra let go and stepped back. "What is he talking about?"

"I..." My lips froze. I could still smell her.

"Say it," Lymon said smiling. "Tell her that you are Thomas Donderman, strangler of twenty-seven girls from the Waste Around."

Myra's eyes widened with shock, her hands went to her mouth, "My niece Katerina."

"It wasn't me," I said. It was almost true. I hadn't been the same man since I'd been resurrected. There was enough of me missing for me to assume that my murderous rage hadn't made it into the mix.

"Liar!" Lymon said. "You've told me the details of every murder. I have a memento upstairs that you might recognize."

I couldn't imagine what it might be.

"You're the liar," Myra said to Lymon. She turned to me. "He's making you say this somehow isn't he? Please say you didn't kill Katerina. You were my only comfort."

I stayed silent.

"I can't believe this," Lymon said, pressing Octopus viciously against the bottom of the tray. Octopus flailed and tried to bite Lymon's fingers. "He killed your niece. Look into his eyes and see his guilt."

Myra looked at me for a moment and then seemed to have a revelation. She pointed at Lymon. "You know the details of the murders because you committed them. A man was burned alive by an angry mob for your crimes, you bastard!"

I hadn't told Myra about the little silver urn and how Lymon had resurrected us. She didn't know that I was the burned man. I hadn't even told her that I was a painter. She might've made the connection.

"How dare you accuse me, you ignorant bitch!" Lymon lifted a fist and smashed Myra under it. He opened the fist and shook the gore from his hand, before looking at me. "Look what you've made me do!"

Lymon raised his fist and brought it down. Instead of smashing Octopus, his wrist banged into the side of the tray, flipping it up and flinging Octopus onto his face. Myra and I rolled into the side of the tray. When it slammed back down onto the table, we rolled back toward the center.

I crawled to Myra's side. One of her eyes was still open and her mouth opened again and again like a fish dying on the seashore. "You shouldn't have said that, Myra. I'm sorry about what happened."

Her mouth had stopped moving. She was dead and I'd been too weak to confess.

Lymon screamed and I turned to see Octopus forcing himself into Lymon's mouth. Lymon fell to the floor choking.

I laid Myra down gently and then covered her ruined face with the blanket.

I hoisted myself over the lip of the tray and saw Lymon twitching on the floor, clawing at his throat, with blood on his teeth. A tiny arm was stuck in the spittle on his cheek. Soon, he'd be dead. I knew instantly what I had to do.

I sprinted down the length of the table, thankful that they ran along the walls and were joined at the corners. I dodged past jars, tubes, and vials, and found the bottle of orange liquid that Lymon had told me about. I dragged it back around to the tray.

Lymon was still and his eyes were closed. He lay on his back with his mouth open. He was close enough to the table to pad my fall. I didn't know if Lymon had ever tested the orange chemical before or how he knew it would work. But, I did know that I didn't want to be this size forever. I also knew that I didn't have time to think about it. Lymon had said that the other person needed to be on death's door for this to work.

I hauled the bottle to the edge and made sure that it would fall on Lymon and not the stone floor. I pushed it over. The bottle rolled off of Lymon's chest and shattered on the floor. At first I was angry, but then I realized that the bottle was open. Would I have had another way of opening it at my size?

I lined up with Lymon's fat stomach and jumped. I turned in the air so that I would land on my back. I bounced and stopped myself by grabbing a wrinkle in Lymon's shirt before I hit the floor. I didn't want to land in the orange liquid just yet.

I climbed up Lymon's abdomen and across his chest. I needed to get Octopus out of Lymon's throat. It would do me no good to take over Lymon's body only to choke to death the instant after it happened. I made my way to Lymon's mouth and looked inside. Octopus was lodged at the base of Lymon's tongue and he'd been chewed. I grasped Octopus's arm and pulled, but he didn't budge.

I didn't have the strength to move him. I planted my feet against Lymon's teeth and pulled again. I strained until my shoulders threatened to pop out of their sockets. I let go and cried. If I were my normal size I'd have the strength to do it.

An idea came to me in a flash. I stripped off my clothes, knotted them together, tied my sleeve to Octopus's arm and trailed the makeshift rope out of Lymon's mouth.

I slid to the floor and rushed over to the broken bottle. The orange liquid had pooled in a depression in the stone floor. I pulled the glass out of the pool and plunged in, coating my entire body

I floated into an upright position. I could see the floor through my translucent orange hands. They left shimmering trails when I moved them. I was momentarily hypnotized. Then I began to disintegrate.

I swam through the air toward Lymon's nose chanting these words. "Pull it out of your mouth when you wake up."

I sat up choking and clawing at my throat. My eyes bulged. I knew that I was going to die, until I heard a little voice in my head.

"Pull it out of your mouth when you wake up."

There was a thick string stuck to my lip. I grabbed it and yanked. A meaty, bloody mass flew out of my mouth and hit the floor. I coughed up phlegm and blood and a tiny foot.

I crawled across the room and then upstairs and into Lymon's bed.

*****

In the weeks it took me to sell Lymon's things I'd learned what the eledite flakes were for and about Lymon's addiction. The morning after I'd collapsed in his bed, I'd found his set-up on his nightstand. There was a bottle of cheap brandy next to a little metal cup; and a spoon with the remnants of eledite flakes on it. I'd sniffed the cup and recognized the scents of liquor and eledite. I couldn't imagine drinking such a concoction. But as the day wore on, I'd thought about the little cup more and more. By dusk, I'd mixed a cup and swallowed it. I'd coughed so hard that my ribs ached. I'd remembered him coughing, but had never made the connection. Soon after my eyelids drooped and my skin had grown tingly, and once I'd had that first dose, Lymon's addiction had a hold on me.

I'd made plenty of money selling Lymon's apartment and basement work room to the Waste Around family that was at the top of the waiting list. I'd sold all of Lymon's alchemical equipment and burned all of his research journals and any evidence of his experiments. The apparatus of the five copper bowls was the hardest to dispose of, but a good hammer and a pry bar can do wonders if you have the inclination.

On the day I'd planned to leave, I picked up Veda Cuttle's scarf. I had no idea how he got it, but I'd found it in Lymon's wardrobe. I ran my fingers along the rough gray weave. Flecks of white, green and brown paint were caught up in the tassels. I packed it in my suitcase to remind myself of what I'd done and set my luggage near the door, patting my pockets to make sure that I had my steamship ticket, my financial papers and my identification.

I checked myself in the oval mirror above the washbasin stand. I smoothed the lapels of the dark green woolen jacket that I'd found. There were matching pants and a bowler with a hatband of an even darker green. I waxed the points of my new mustache and beard with a gloved hand; the hair served to sharpen Lymon's doughy face. I oiled my hair back and admired my overlarge ears before donning the bowler.

I still felt uncomfortable in his skin. I could still feel Lymon shambling around in my head when I was tired. He was a major player in all of my dreams.

I grabbed my luggage, shined my pale ivory spats on the backs of my trouser legs, and headed through the Garden. I hired a coach to take me to the docks and boarded my ship to Mercer.

*****

I chased the girl into the alley. It wasn't hard to catch up with her; she had such stubby little legs. I tackled her and we rolled into the garbage. She hollered and pummeled me with tiny useless fists.

"Calm down and stop your screaming," I said in the gentlest voice I could muster. I coughed blue phlegm onto the dirty cobbles of the alley. The chase had left me out of breath and wheezing.

"You just want to take me back," she said. "I can't do that work no more."

"You don't have to work." I kept her cornered in the alley. "I have a new place for you."

Her eyes darted, looking for an escape route. "You're lying! Let me go! I said I can't work any more. My fingers are all bloody." Her fingernails were cracked and broken and her hands were covered in scabs.

"I'll take care of you."

"No!" Her face showed a suspicion of adults that brought tears to my eyes. "Why are you crying?" she asked.

Another coughing fit shook my body. I raised a handkerchief to my mouth.

Greta came into the alley and put her hand on my shoulder. "He cried when he came for me too, Letty."

"Greta," she cried, recognizing her friend and running into her arms.

I let Greta do the work, soothing the child, telling her that I was a nice man and that everything would be all right. "I'll wait in the carriage."

Greta was the first child I'd found after I'd shut the sweatshop down. I'd come to Mercer to find Lymon's old cronies at the Society for the Advancement of Alchemical Research, and when I'd gotten there all I found were a few broken down old men running a workshop full of orphan slaves. The Society had been behind on their mortgage, and the bank men were ready to give them the boot, so I'd bought the building, insured it, kicked them out and burned the place down. With the insurance money, and the money left over in my accounts, I'd purchased a country estate outside of Mercer.

Of course, I'd taken all of the Society's eledite before kicking them out. I needed it to feed my addiction and to soothe my murderous rage. It'd come back a few weeks after I'd started the orphanage. And now every time I felt the rage, I drugged myself into a stupor.

Greta kept Letty comfortable on the other seat of the carriage. I smiled at her but she turned away. The gentle rocking of the carriage eventually lulled her to sleep.

When the carriage neared our grounds I signaled Greta to wake her. Letty rubbed her eyes and gazed at her new home, a sprawling ivy-covered stone house with a high-peaked roof and a porch that ran along the front side. Children ran playing in the yard. Marten, one of the older boys, gave lessons under the weeping willow.

"You're safe now," I said, hoping that it was true.

While Greta took Letty off to meet the other children, I went to see Betina, the matron I'd hired to help me look after the children. She was of middle age, unmarried, and childless. She favored colorless dresses that belied her cheery disposition.

"Good day, Mr. Marbry," she said.

I'd taken Lymon's face; why not take his name as well? "And to you Betina. Could you come with me to my office?"

"Have I done something wrong?"

"No, quite the opposite. Please, just come with me."

Betina followed me to my office.

"Have a seat." I said, and pulled some papers out of my breast pocket. I started coughing. I pulled out my handkerchief and covered my mouth, before pulling out a little bottle of brandy mixed with eledite. I'd been drinking so much of the concoction lately that I was almost out of eledite.

"That handkerchief is filthy," Betina said, pulling out a clean one. "Take this and leave that dirty thing in the laundry."

"Thank you," I said, taking the handkerchief.

"You alright, sir?"

"I'm fine." I straightened in my chair and flattened the sheaf of papers on the blotter. "I've had my accountant draw up some papers. In the event of my death; all of my money, my land, and this house will pass to you. If you'll just sign here." I held the papers and a pen out to her.

Betina's eyes went wide. "Your death, sir? You mean your illness has gotten worse?"

"I'm afraid so."

She sobbed. "But you've been so good to me."

"I need you to return the favor by taking care of the children. Will you do it?"

"Nothing would suit me better." Betina took the pen and signed her name.

*****

Only a week later, I lay in bed, sweating, my breath wheezing in and out of my body. Blood dribbled down my chin, staining my nightshirt. The eledite had eaten away at my insides. I'd been drinking five cups a day for the last few months. I had to. The rage was growing and it was the only way that I could kill myself and silence my rage.

Children lined the walls and Greta held my clammy hand in hers. Betina stood behind Greta's chair wringing her hands.

I wanted to tell them what they meant to me. What they'd done to change my life. The joy they'd brought. But I only had one word left. So I spoke it.

"Sorry."

"What for?" Greta asked.

I didn't have the strength to explain. And even if I did, would I have the courage to tell them? No, that wouldn't be right. If I told them that I was a monster their new home would become tainted. So I just lay there, surrounded by children. I'd sent so many of them to their deaths. Now they waited for mine.

The End

For the Love of Steam

Missa Dixon

Life changed for us after Daddy left. Mama worked tirelessly, day and night, in her workshop. We never went for walks anymore and although I loved Mrs. Baxter, our housekeeper, she never gave treats like mama did. Now-a-days Mama would wake before dawn, wash, pulled on her petticoats and dress as she ran down the stairs to her shop, picking up the welding goggles she had left hanging on the end of the banister the night before. I would get a soft pat on the head as her skirt brushed by me in the doorway. Off she would go, lost in her dark world. I would take my place on the well-worn rug she lovingly placed under her workbench. Many hours would pass and then well after the light was gone from the windows Mama would drag herself up the stairs pulling off her goggles leaving them on the banister, for another day's toil was now done; a scene to be replayed before the light in the windows returned.

One day, the great steam bell interrupted our daily routine. Mama had replaced the normal door knocker like all the other houses had with a much higher-power noise maker, one so loud she would hear it ring on Mrs. Baxter's day off. Like I wasn't a good enough door bell - I would bark at the milk man, who came every day. Of course I could hear a stranger coming up the stoop and tell her about it. But I don't think she understands my dog barking. Once again, the steam roared through the house. I leaped out off my warm rug and rushed to the door barking all the while.

"Damn it!" Mama cursed, "Mrs. Baxter, please get the door!" She yelled.

Walking up behind me Mama said, "Is it her day off Charlie? I didn't think it was Thursday already."

The great bell rung again. "Coming!" Mama yelled at the door.

Grabbing the handle firmly, Mama flung opened the large, heavy door that thudded as came to an abrupt stop against the adjacent wall. "May I help you?" She angrily challenged the man standing in front of her. She had not even removed her goggles, much less her welding apron. To any stranger Mama probably looked frightful, but I loved her with all my heart and I was not going to let anyone hurt her. I was a good guard dog and I also looked sternly at the man standing on my veranda.

In contrast, the man now standing on the oversized front porch was dress in long, dark pants and a matching shorter frock coat that had become the popular style for upper-class dandies. A light colored shirt and dark bow tie finished his clothing. His dark, worn, leather topcoat was laid over his left arm with his rain stained top hat held in his left hand. He had obviously just dashed through the downpour from the waiting carriage, now parked on the street in front of our house. A puff of steam jettisoned out the back just as he began to speak.

"I'm looking for Miss Stephanie Tapp of 92 Cotton Street." He said in a light, cheery, yet somehow put-off voice.

"I am she. How can I help you?" Mama answered flatly.

"I'm Drake Maloney from the Philadelphia Science Conservatory." He held up a rolled up addition of Scientific American magazine, showing to Mama. "And we've heard of you and your work."

"Anyone can pick up a science journal and any educated man can read it. So once again I ask, how can I help you?" Mama said roughly as she pulled her goggles down off her piercing green eyes. They matched her dress even down to the small golden stripes running down her skirt. Her petticoats were stained gray from years in workshops, but the apron she wore showed off the warm, silky brown of her long hair nicely. She didn't like to go shopping for anything. She preferred to scrounge up useful items and bring them back to life. Now Mrs. Baxter, the housekeeper, did everything to keep the house running, but she drew the line at Mama's personal shopping. The newest thing Mama had on was her welding apron; it was the last thing Daddy had bought for her before he had gone away. Most women would have been horrified at such a gift, but I think Mama liked it better than the ring he had given her when we all went up in the air-ship for the Halloween Ball, now three cold seasons ago. Mama said we became a family that night and that Daddy was now my Daddy and she was still my Mommy, and we would live together forever. Funny how things changed for us.

The man's voice jostled me from my daydream. I had to make sure Mama was safe from this stranger. I stared him down and growled in a low voice just so he would remember that I was there ready to strike if he came closer to us.

"You've heard the World's Fair is coming to America, Philadelphia to be exact. The whole globe is going celebrate one hundred years of freedom in our great land." He said with a slight southern accent. Curious how a man from the south talked about great things happening in a thriving northern city, just ten years after The War Against Northern Aggression. I could tell Mama was intrigued. Plus he had a steam coach. Mama had never seen one before - at least not one so big.

"Yes Mr. Maloney the Centennial International Exhibition will open in your fair city in just over a year – July 4th, 1876 I believe. What has that got to do with me and my work?" My mother repeated a bit warmer than before. I could tell she wanted to know more about what this man had to offer. Maybe even a ride in his carriage.

A wide smile came across the man's face, "You are working on little steam, Miss Tapp. Creating the world's smallest steam engines has excited the curiosity of the selection committee and we would like you to show off your work on the world's biggest stage."

"It is Dr. Tapp, and it's called Micro Steam Mr. Maloney." Mama corrected him. "And I have no interest in being gawked as a freak by strangers who will have no appreciation for the glory of technology." A confused look came over the man's face as Mama slammed the big door on the man with a huff. She turned to find Mrs. Baxter standing behind her having just returned from her errands.

Mrs. Baxter had been Mama's housekeeper since before I came to live with Mama just as the rebels from both sides of the war began their assault on the west – three years after the Great War. Mama found me in the rubble of a warehouse that had been bombed during the last battle on the Mississippi River. She had been looking for scrap metal to continue her work. But instead she found a small white puppy with brown spots. I guess she felt sorry for me and took me home. Mrs. Baxter was there when we walked in, and she appeared to have everything in hand.

I remember Mama explaining to her what had happened. "I was in the bombed cotton warehouse on Front Street, looking through the bits and pieces for anything useful. I found a dead dog under one of the collapsed walls. Kind of unsettling if you ask me, then I heard a noise.

Thinking it might be something useful, gears, steel rods, just anything, I moved some bricks and out toppled this ball of fur."

"I see, my lady." Always very proper was Mrs. Baxter.

"I couldn't leave him there. Plus this place could use some livening up." Mama continued with a happy giggle she no longer had.

Mrs. Baxter, looking very put out if memory serves, "He's going to make a mess. But your father left you the house and you may do as you will with it, but I will not be his caretaker."

"What shall I yell at the dog when he misbehaves?" Mrs. Baxter asked flatly.

Mama looked puzzled at her for a moment. "Oh yes a name!" Mama thought and thought, as Mrs. Baxter put down a warm bowl of soup she had just finished. I remember it was the best thing I ever ate.

"Who was that Englishman who won the Coplay Medal several years ago?" Mama pondered. "You know the survival of the fittest gentleman."

"I most certainly do not." Mrs. Baxter chimed back as she refilled the small bowl on the floor with another ladle of broth.

"Charles. Yes Charles Darwin. We'll call him Charlie." Mama said happily.

I digress into the past, but Mrs. Baxter's voice brought me back to the here and now. "Bad things happen. Your precious Ben died; however, for you, life has gone on. Your father left you with the knowledge and the skills to build yourself up again and carry on disfigured as you think you are." Mrs. Baxter pointed at my mama's left leg - the one that went away with Daddy and she replaced with a brass one. "And even though you hide all day in the dark of your workroom, the sun rose, just as it will rise again tomorrow morning. Charles Darwin Dog Tapp needs to be walked by his mistress." She has always referred to me by my full name. "You need to talk to real people, not the life size dolls you work on every day. You made yourself walk again. Now show the world that they can walk again as well." She turned in a whirl of her black dress, back toward the kitchen. I almost followed her. She always brought me something back from the butcher and the warm memories of happier times called to me, but Mama needed me now. I stayed at her heels just in case a warm dog kiss was needed to salve old wounds.

With a heavy look, a tear dropped from Mama's eye. Then she inhaled more deeply that I had ever seen her do. She grabbed the door and slowly it began to move. "Mr. Maloney!" Mama's voice called out the now open door. "Tell your people I will be there. But I have some conditions."

"Ask for just about anything and I can deliver it you, Miss…" He stopped himself, "Sorry Dr. Tapp."

"I will require medium-sized booth in the Main Exhibition Building at the World's Fair. Also, we will need four-star room and board for myself, Mrs. Baxter, Charles, and our guest." Mama instructed.

"Done." Mr. Maloney answered, revealing more of his Southern ways.

"Don't be so hasty. I'm not done yet, sir. You will pay for all money expenses including travel expenses for us all. A weekly stipend for Mrs. Baxter and our guest in the amount of $5.00 starting now till the fair is over." her voice trailed off.

"That is all very reasonable." He replied with a hint of excitement in his voice. "Anything else?"

"Yes. Our guest. I need a wounded man, a veteran from the war, one that lost one or both legs and is young enough, strong enough, and willing to walk again. Can you find me such a man?" Mama finished.

"Oh yes Dr. Tapp. I know the perfect man. He will be here, where I stand, in one month." Mr. Maloney then dashed down the stairs into the rain and swung open his taxi's door. "You are going to be famous, Dr. Tapp. You just wait and see."

"We shall see." Mama quietly replied as she closed the door.

She wandered into the kitchen with me at her heels, "Mrs. Baxter would you make up the spare room? We will be having a guest."

"Of course, my lady." She said with that proper smile.

For the first time in since Daddy left, Mama pulled off her goggles and ascended the stairs before the light left the sky. I did not follow. I knew she was going to sleep and cry and she would not want me with her in the dark cloud of grief.

*****

In the morning Mama rose after dawn. She began to refit the house with the steam lifts and other devices that she had used after Daddy had gone. Piping that Mama had taken down after she could walk again was relayed. The chairs that connected to the banisters that lifted Mama to her bedroom and from the front stoop were reconnected and tested. She hired a dustman, Mr. Gage, to help her doing the lifting and cleaning up the outside of the house. She wanted everything to look good for the new tenet.

I could tell Mama's heart was still sad, but it seemed there was light in her eyes once again. Mrs. Baxter even said so to Mrs. Trudy Worthington, the next-door housekeeper, when she took me for my walk. "Thank the stars, Trudy. Dr. Tapp appears to have finally turned a corner. She ate a full meal yesterday. And she asked the dustman to clear the back patio of over-growth." She said. "For these last few years, since Ben was killed, I didn't think she was going to come back, even after she built that leg of hers."

Mama had asked Mrs. Baxter to tidy up the house, in hopes of making it more presentable to their guest. Mrs. Baxter hired a girl to help clean the three years of gloom out of the house. Everything that was not nailed down was washed, scrubbed, pressed, polished, shined, remade, re-hung, mended, or thrown out. New white wash was put on the walls, and new paper was hung in all the public formal areas. Of course Mama worked in her workshop, but she spent time "outing the old and ining the new." At least that was what she kept saying. I was even taken to the groomer and bathed and clipped to within an inch of my life. The month had been a true whirlwind. However, the house looked amazing – like somebody lived here – not a dark mausoleum ready for the not-yet-dead. On the last day, Mama even gave me a new collar and leash. We went walking down the street to the park just to try it out. We had not done that in three cold seasons. Life was looking up for my little family.

*****

In the hubbub of the past month I had almost forgotten our guest. As promised, one month later the great bell rung again. Mama rushed passed everyone to open it. She was expecting a grizzled, broken, old man, supporting himself on makeshift crutches and wooden legs. However, the universe had a different idea. A young street urchin stood on her porch.

"Dr. Tapp?" he said in a very southern accent.

"Yes, I'm Dr. Tapp." Mama answered coarsely. She didn't like the street trash. Schools were what these children needed. Let knowledge set them free from their earthly bonds. I growled at the kid, just to make sure he knew Mama meant business and this was no place to play.

He backed up, turned around and ran down the stairs saying, "This is the place Mister. I want my two cents now. And you didn't say nothing about a dog."

Mama eyes followed the child down her steps to the street and what appeared to be the same carriage that had brought Mr. Maloney. It now opened up like a great steam organ and a man appeared sitting in a wheeled chair. The chair was not that different from the one she had made for herself after Ben had been killed and she had lost her leg.

The carriage lowered and the man rolled himself off the lift and on the walk in front of the stairs with great ease. The man covered by a duster-style coat and a large hat, tossed two shinny coins to the boy. "Thanks kid! Now get on - Dr. Tapp doesn't appear to like kids."

He looked around, surveying the area, then asked gently, "May I use your lift?" His voice was southern, but refined and educated.

"Oh yes. I re-erected it for your use." Mama paused. "I'm surprised you know what it is." A smile could be heard in her voice and she could not hide the surprised look on her face by the fact this gentleman knew what her lift was.

"I've seen your designs before - clever to say the least." He commented.

The veteran pulled himself into the waiting chair, reached under the seat, and started the lift. Mama's jaw dropped as the steam rose from the metal banisters and the chair began to rise. With his great arm, he picked up his wheeled chair to use at the top of the stoop. I could see it in her eyes. Who is this? And how does he know how to use my lift? I barked once to bring her back. We were going to be face to face with this man in a minute and Mama needed to be on her toes.

The gentleman placed his chair down on the porch with one graceful motion. Then as if he had done this a thousand times before he transferred himself from the lift to his old chair. A massive light colored hat had been obscuring his features; however, now that he had arrived on stoop, the man removed it and introduced himself. "Dr. Tapp, my name is Vincent Malone. I am your experiment for the next year."

Mama and Mrs. Baxter, who had now joined us on the porch, were speechless. The war had been over for almost ten years – depending on how you asked. And the War in the West had been quiet for almost two years. However, this man was young – no more than mid-thirties - Mama's age. How could he have fought in the war yet kept his vigor? I know Mama was expecting an old, broken man. I had heard her say many times to Mr. Gage, "My biggest challenge will not the making of the devices, but convicting the geezer to use them and get his broken soul to live again."

Mrs. Baxter had also been dubious about an old veteran coming to stay. "He'd better keep his hands to himself." She would explain. "I will put him in his place if he tries anything. I've got knives, and I know how to use them." Mrs. Baxter might have been old, but she was a spry lady when it came to her person.

Mrs. Trudy Worthington would smile back, "If he's that much of a ruffian send him to me. Let him chase me around in that wheeled contraption."

It appeared no one had to worry. Mr. Malone was strong, willing, a true gentleman, and very handsome to boot. Long dark wavy brown hair with just the first hints of gray covered his head. Bright, clear, shinning green eyes twinkled over a well-groomed beard. His slightly western style clothing looked like it was made for him exact. The coat he wore covered his massive arms without straining. His shirt buttoned perfectly over his expansive chest. Even his pants ended in neat hems right above what would have been his knees.

"Not what you were expecting, I see." He broke the silence.

"I apologize, Sir; I meant no disrespect by staring, of course. I know for a fact that the pressure of all those eyes can be infuriating. However, I," she stuttered, "I mean we, were expecting a much different kind of man." My mother answered.

A warm smile came over Mr. Malone's face. "I think my brother did good getting us together. And what needs to get done first?"

"Your brother, sir?" Mama asked with a puzzled look on her face.

"My brother, Drake, he's the one that came to you a month ago and asked for your help." He answered in a matter a fact way.

"I see." Mama mumbled.

"I still need your Micro-Steam, and so do lots of other people Dr. Tapp so let's get started. Introductions and then where do I bunk down?"

Mama held her ground for a minute, and then as if something had lifted, she started the introductions. "Oh yes, well I'm Dr. Stephanie Tapp. Please call me Dr. Tapp and this is Mrs. Baxter my housekeeper." Mr. Malone nodded in recognition.

"Here is your payment Mrs. Baxter." He handed her a dark brown leather envelope. "My brother told me that we had agreed to five dollars a week. This is that payment in full money for my room and board. That should cover it. I put some extra just in case because I eat a lot." He said with a bright laughing smile.

Mama and Mrs. Baxter were so stunned by his gesture that I had been left out of the introductions. I had to bark to remind her to tell him about me.

"Oh yes, this is Charles Darwin. You can call him Charlie. He's our center in this house." She explained to this new human.

He put his hand down for me to smell. I obliged him. I could tell he had been around all kinds of animals and that he understood basic hygiene. Also, he might have no had legs, but that had not stopped him from working with his hands or firing guns.

The rest of the day was spent showing our guest around and loading his things into his quarters. He could already use Mama's helping machines, so the time teaching him how to get around was saved. Mr. Malone explained that he and his brother had seen her ideas in print. Tinkering with those plans the brothers had made their childhood home more accessible. Vincent also let it be known that he had made some improvements on Mama's designs so that he could be lifted onto a horse without scaring the beast to death. I could tell Mama was warming up to this veteran. She was too fascinated by his conversation and at dinner she forgot to give me my part of her steak under the table as she always did.

"Yes Dr. Tapp, I have done everything to make my world fit this body I was left with. However, walking again would bring me to the best part of my life. When I got my copy of that rag last year and saw your steam limb, I just had to get a hold of you." He stated brightly. "What happened that you lost your leg?"

Mama's heart fell. I could see it like a shroud that had been wrapped around her lifted for a short time, but now, with this innocent question, it closed up around her again. I put my paw on top of hers and looked up into her shaking green eyes. I wanted her to feel my love. However, Mama finally answered, "The War. The War in the West took the whole of my life." Then she rose from the dinner table and trudged up the stairs – leaving behind her momentary retreat from the pain of her loss.

Mrs. Baxter placed her hand on Mr. Malone's hand. "She will give you new legs. And I hope to all the Gods above you give her a new heart."

"What happened?" Mr. Malone asked.

"Very simple, actually. Do you remember a few years ago when the rebels reformed and stared attacking outpost up and down the river?" Mrs. Baxter asked.

"Oh yes." Mr. Malone answered. "I couldn't get my livestock to market and I couldn't get supplies in for over a year because of all the trouble."

"Well," Mrs. Baxter continued as she pulled a bit of Yorkshire pudding off the hunk and gave half of it to me. "Dr. Tapp and her beloved Benjamin Watt had met after at a symposium held at the new Arboretum. They were both attending a talk about steam or some such. They were like two peas in a pod; both so into the newest technology. I've never seen two people so in love in all my life. Their – light – was infectious."

"However," Mrs. Baxter continued, "the war flared up again along this Big Old River. And it was not long before Ben, who was an engineer on the river, was pressed into service keeping the river open for traffic. It didn't matter to them – Ben and the Mrs., they gleefully pressed forward with their weeding plans."

"One night late Ben had brought home new welding vests for Stephanie and himself to celebrate her first publication. They were to be married at the next full moon. Ben joked about wearing their new matching vest as part of their wedding attire. Then a knock at the door - a young man had been sent to collect Ben. Someone had destroyed part of a levee that kept the river back. Men who could build with metal were needed. So Ben had to go or part of the Low City would be flooded by morning. Stephanie went with him to help. She had just finished her welding course. There were only a few people who could weld in those days. The River Master was happy for her help."

"They worked all night holding the water back. Charlie and I made a huge breakfast for their return." She patted me on the head and gave me the other half of the pudding. "But they never did."

"What happened to them?" Mr. Malone asked.

"As the sun rose there was another attack. I was told it was the biggest explosion since the war. Ben was killed instantly and Miss Stephanie…" She paused as if a bayonet had stabbed her own heart. "Had lost her left leg. It was blown off as she was trying to weld the last piece of metal in place."

"I finally found her two days later in the hospital. She was still unconscious, but the doctors taken her leg off, repaired the wound, and stabilized her blood loss. They were hopeful she would live, but they knew she would never walk again." Mrs. Baxter continued.

"I moved into the hospital - caring for her day and night. Charlie became the hospital mascot - running each and every floor, visiting with everyone just to cheer them up. I still take him there every week to help out the sick and injured. After three months, they let me take her home. She had not spoken to anyone. The doctors were afraid that she needed to go to a sanitarium for further treatment. I knew I needed to get her home for her to heal."

"As soon as we got to the steps, she flew into action. She had built a wheeled chair in less than a day, and a steam one in about a fortnight. The house had lifts throughout a month after that and she strapped on her first leg in less half a year. So much for what doctors know!" Mrs. Baxter sneered.

"She could walk, but her spirit was as cold as a January morning. Work, write, and cry; that's all she has done lo these many years. Her flame has burned far and wide, but nothing has warmed her since that night so long ago." Now finished with her story, Mrs. Baxter wiped away a tear.

"I didn't know she had lost a leg. I just saw the brilliance of her work and hoped she could help me live just a little better in a world not made for men who have fallen from the grace of perfections." Vincent countered.

"I will see myself to bed. Thanks for letting me know what I'm in for." He rolled away and the great steam lift could be heard churning him up the stairs.

Mrs. Baxter cleaned the table, set up the starter for the bread and went to bed soon after. I went to my Mama's room and slept outside her door just in case she needed me to lick away the tears.

*****

As usual Mama was up, washed, dressed and at her post before the sun rose. Our guest was waiting for her with that wide, bright smile and welding clothes of his own. I could tell Mama was put off and intrigued at the same time. They went straight to work. With the extra money now in the house, Mrs. Baxter had made a fine breakfast, so everyone could get started off on the right foot. I was the only one to partake of her labors. She complained bitterly about our lack of respect for her work and trouble. She even went so far as to threaten to not make lunch or dinner. However, there were sandwiches on the table at the noon hour and braised pork chops in gravy for dinner.

All day Mama and Mr. Malone worked on his legs. Measuring, weighing, planning, arguing it was like a never ending science talk and a high stakes poker game all wrapped up into one. Mama would say something Malone would counter – round and round they went. By the end of the day they ate in different rooms and yelled back and forth to each other about not wanting to talk because the other one had no intelligence. I was happy for the start of the process. I got twice the dinner; one from Mama and one from Mr. Malone. Yummy.

As the weeks worn on, progress seemed to be slow. More arguing, more planning, more ideas to improve Mama's overall design ruled each day. The one thing Mrs. Baxter noticed was that the personal-ness of their first attacks at each other was gone. They were more playful, even throwing her corn muffins at each other one night.

"They made a mess of my dining room last night!" Mrs. Baxter explained to Mrs. Worthington while they were out on a walk. "I have not seen such juvenile behavior since I was in Sunday school."

Mrs. Worthington smiled widely revealing her missing teeth, "Well the lovers' moon might just rise over the Tapp house again. About time don't you think?"

Mrs. Baxter's voice cracked as she answered, "Oh yes! Oh yes my dear. We can hope."

*****

Mr. Malone had been with us for over half a year. Mrs. Baxter had put heavy restriction on how much they could feed me. It appeared I was getting too fat to walk the park with her in the mornings at her normal pace. I couldn't help the fact that I was cute and they loved to feed me. However, Mama and Mr. Malone had stated taking me out in the evening after dinner to scavenge for materials. They didn't do any real scavenging, but it was how they got to know one another and settled the day's differences so no one went to bed mad.

"So, Mrs. Baxter spilled the beans about me. Well fair is fair. How did you lose your legs?" Mama asked one day as we rounded the park.

Mr. Malone smiled, "I was wondering when you were going to ask."

"I was just waiting till we had the time." Mama responded warmly.

She found a bench and sat down. I hopped up next to her and put my paws in her lap. Spring had come, but the evenings were still chilled and I liked my paws warm. Mr. Malone guided the great steam chair next to us, so close he could hold Mama's hand, if things got to scary for her.

"We live of the west side of this great river." He pointed at the mighty Mississippi flowing down below the bluffs. "My family owns a huge ranch not a day's ride west from here. When the war broke out, my father felt it was not our business to get involved. He kept me and my bother home to run the ranch and protect our interest from both sides."

Although Mama never approved of war in the first place, finding me in that building had helped turn her mind against the idea of war as a way to settle conflicts. With her head against the idea, her heart was turned with the death of Daddy. So she approved of Vincent's father's neutral stance as the lunacy raged around them. "Your father was a brave man in those days." She added.

"Both sides did bad things west of the river. Neither one made friends. For many of us Westies, neutrality was the only way to keep your land and your life." He added.

"After Lee signed to Grant, the war in the west took off. In the winter of sixty-six, troops came to the ranch and asked for ten head of cattle to feed themselves over the winter holiday. My father told them to see me – I was the quartermaster in those days - and pay for them. They could have their pick, but only after they paid. They hunted me down in my bunk house and told me to give them ten head. I didn't know what they were talking about, but I told them it would cost them 100 gold dollars if they wanted to cattle. I guess they didn't like my answer because one of the soldiers hit me from behind with the butt of his gun. I fought back of course. Killed two of them, but I just couldn't get them all. One of them clocked me in the back of the head. They took my keys to the steer pin and started shooting the cattle."

"My Dad had an idea something might happen. He mobilized the men we had on hand at the ranch. The solders must have been with a platoon that had artillery, because before my Father's men could take up their post, cannon fire rang out on the ranch. I was coming around after being pistol whipped, when the bunk house exploded around me. All I remember is being thrown to the ground. I woke up in the main house will doctors all around me. My brother and the rest of the ranch hands had finally driven the solders off, but my Dad had been killed in the fight and I had lost both of my legs."

"You must have been upset when you woke up. I know I was so angry and hurt I just couldn't move." Mama said.

"I was pissed that my Father had been killed for ten cattle, but I never gave up. I never let my sadness or hurt take me. My brother was much more the city man than me and he heard about this new steam technology and the wonders it might do. I started working with these great new engines. I made some really helpful improvements to others inventions. I even helped make sheep and cattle herding easier with a steam powered cart. I used one of Rumford's ideas and improved the oven in the house. And I even found you and the idea that I could get new steam legs to walk on so that no one would be the wiser." He reached out to touch Mama's hand that had been petting me. "I just didn't know the person who had invented the idea of Micro-Steam was such a beautiful, smart, talented woman."

Mama blushed and looked away towards the river with an embarrassed smile on her face. I could feel the warmth rising in her body. Mr. Malone raised his hand from Mama's to her face. Genteelly he moved her head so they were starring into each other's eyes. He leaned close to her and she leaned into him almost smushing me in between. Their lips met in a warm, wet exhale. I took the opportunity to lick two faces at once.

"Charlie!" Mama exclaimed. "What are you doing?"

While Mama was distracted, Vincent scooped both of us up with his superhuman arms and placed us on his lap. He encircled Mama, making sure I was outside his arms, and kissed her deeply. Mama melted into his embrace.

"No woman has ever stolen my heart, Dr. Stephanie Tapp." Vincent removed a gold clockwork heart from a chain around his neck. "Here it is. All for you." He said softly.

Mama lit up like one of her torches. She took the charm and slid it into her bustle near her heart. She re-adjusted herself on Vincent's lap, kissing him again, and saying, "Home sir, we have legs to build."

I hopped off her lap and ran behind the steam chair as they raced home. I wondered if he was going to be my new Daddy. Mama had not said anything yet, but she sure acted like it.

*****

The next morning, boxes of all kinds arrive on the front stoop. Most said Tiffany &Co. The rest were just the normal plate brass by the smell of them. Mama and Vincent loaded the boxes into the workshop and didn't leave for four days. The heavy sound of metal work could be heard day and night. Welding of tiny pipes, gears, jewelers' chains took over from the talking and arguing that ruled the first days of their working relationship. Heated discussions could still be heard from time to time emanating from the workshop, but from the most part – work, work, work.

Mrs. Baxter took food at regular intervals and sometimes I heard her scream, "Don't sleep on the tables. It's unseemly. What will the neighbors think? At least pretend to go to bed once a day."

When the light was waning from the windows on the fourth day, Vincent, looking like he had not bathed in a week, with welding soot all over his face and shirt, walked from the workshop with two new legs under him. Mrs. Baxter just about dropped the dinner tray she was carrying into the workshop. Mama came up behind him, and she looked even worse that he did. Her long brown hair was now almost black, and her once green dress was now a dull gray from welding ash. But her face glowed. Pride. Happiness. Relief. Joy. And maybe even a hint of love showed all over her person.

"I can't believe it, Sir. You are standing in this entry way. Tall and strong as any man alive." Mrs. Baxter uttered.

"Yes distinguished lady. I stand. But I would not be the man I am without having lost my legs. I would not have found my love." Vincent turned to Mama, and kneeling down took her hand and said, "Will you marry me, Dr. Tapp."

Mama was aghast. She was a woman true, but she was missing her left leg and how could any man want her - even one that was missing both of his legs. She was damaged goods.

Seeing her mind churning, Vincent clutched her lovingly and exclaimed as if to the world, "I want you even with one leg. Will you have me with none?"

"Yes!" She said through tears coming up in her eyes. "Yes! YES!" Mama continued as Vincent picked her up and whirled her around.

When he put Mama her down, she picked me up and said, "Charlie you have a new Daddy. Aren't you happy?"

Like I didn't know that was coming. I licked her face and wagged my tail as much as I could without my feet on the ground. I could tell Mama was overjoyed; Mrs. Baxter was in tears leaning against the wall giving thanks to everything she could for the positive turn of events; my new Daddy was smiling like I had never seen a man smile before.

From out of nowhere, drinks appeared, and everyone did a shot and threw the small glasses into the fire. Then off to bed, for there was much to do when the sun rose and only half a year to the expo in the far off place called Philadelphia.

*****

Mama and my new Daddy did not waste any time. They were married at the downtown court house the next week. I had to wait outside with the rings tied to my new collar because they had changed the laws. "No Dogs Allowed While Court is in Session" was what the sign said, and getting married was the court being in session. They came out of the court house and right down to the river boat for a month-long honeymoon. I don't think I'd ever seen Mama so happy. During this time Daddy completely mastered his legs; taking them off, putting them on, and filling them with pure water and tiny stones that kept the steam going. And he made love to Mama making her scream for joy on a nightly basis. Their days were filled with talk and walks on the decks taking in all the sights of the mighty Mississippi River.

When the two of them returned they started building the exhibit they would take to the World's Fair. Micro-Steam was going to be all the rage. Once again the house hummed with excitement. But this time no cloud of sad darkness rested over the large Victorian style home, in the middle of Cotton Street. It had been replaced by plumes of steam, the sounds of industry, and always the smell of roasting beef. After all, Daddy was a cattle man from right across the river. Fresh meat was delivered weekly to the house and I couldn't have been happier.

*****

Spring was now waning into summer as a new set of three new steam wagons pulled up to the house. Mr. Gage, who had been working on the exterior of the house repairing and painting, almost fell off his ladder because of surprise. The opening of the World's Fair was only ten weeks away and all submissions must be checked in and operating by June 4th.

"They're amazing Vincent! Where did you get them? How did you get them built? Will they make it all the way to Philadelphia?" Mama asked emphatically.

"I've been having them built at the ranch. I figure we can get to Philly in half the time using steam, even over some of those bad roads crossing the Smoky Mountains." Daddy replied wearing this trademark wide smile framed by his long dark hair and beard. "These are some of the hands that will be helping us load everything and carrying it for us."

One of the men stepped forward, his face obscured by his wide brimmed brown hat. As he looked up, Stephanie recognized him as Drake Maloney the young man that had brought her this new life. "Dr. Tapp," he removed his hat and lowered his eyes in respect. "I can't thank you enough for bring my brother back. It would be my pleasure to take your equipment to show the world a whole life can be lived no matter if the body is whole or not. Everything is paid for and ready to go."

"Well, well, Mr. Maloney or is it Malone like your brother?" Mama asked playfully.

"I say Maloney, Vincent says Malone. Doesn't much matter we're blood just the same and I'm proud to call you my sister." He approached Mama and kissed her hand. I gave him a growl to make sure he knew I was there and watching him. Then he pulled a bone from his pocket and gave it to me.

"Here you go little fellow. I brought a bone for you this time."

How could I disapprove of him now? A big, cooked, marrow-filled bone just for me. This was my favorite treat.

The men started to load each wagon with equipment from Mama's workshop. The day wore on it seems as if the whole house was emptied into these wagons. One wagon was for personal effects. We would be gone for almost two seasons so much of our clothing and personal items must go. The second wagon was for the set up of the booth it's self. Backdrops, demonstrations, parts, engravings, tables, and everything else a booth could need. The last wagon was for us to travel in.

As the light left the sky, the first two wagons were loaded and ready to go. They would start off in the morning. We would follow in a week in the third wagon. Everything went as planned till it was our day to leave.

On the morning we were to leave, the great steam bell rung again. I barked my disapproval of someone interrupting our happy family, but Mama went to the door. As she opened it, a very young man yelled, "The liberty will never die. Death to steam!" He threw a brass ball into the entry way and ran back down the stairs. I ran after him growling and barking him away. When I was satisfied he was gone, I turned for home. At that moment, Daddy ran passed me tossing the bright, shiny orb towards the young man. Reaching his long gun, Daddy shot at the orb setting off a huge explosion.

"That will show those rebels!" He shouted down to me. "It's the love of steam!"

Returning to the home, Mama looked worried. "Thank God you're safe." She said hugging Daddy. "I don't know what is wrong with them."

"Some rebels don't like technology. They find it scary to their world. The faster we get out of here the better and safer."

"Mrs. Baxter is the house ready?"

"Yes Sir. Mrs. Worthington has the house till we return. And Mr. Gage will be staying here to make sure no one does anything to our home."

"Good!" Daddy said assuredly. "Darling, are you ready to be the belle of the technology ball?"

"I'm ready to show the world the smallest engines and what they can do!"

"Then ladies let us go to our wagon and off to Philadelphia." Daddy announced. Mama grabbed me up and off we went in the big caravan of steam carts.

*****

The trip was very nice and much more comfortable that a normal wagon. We saw no rebels or had any attacks, but people stared at us everywhere we went. At each stop to rest or refuel, or eat, or relieve ourselves, people would come out of nowhere just to see our cart and ask questions. Most had never even heard of steam technology much less seen it.

As we pulled into Philly, the wagons we had sent ahead had already arrived. The men had almost everything set up. Mama was so happy to see her work being displayed in a positive way that she had a hard time holding back the tears. Daddy held her and kissed her on the head. "I told you I would make you famous."

"Thank you." Mama whispered back.

The expo was a great success. I got treats almost every day. Mama and Daddy built legs for four different people. Everybody knew the name Dr. Tapp and her miracle limbs.

Mama had kept her promise. Daddy had kept his. And the world now had a way to move about just a little bit easier.

In the Mountain Skies

Stephen Zimmer

The slow creaking of the water wheel, the sharp scents of pine drifting along the breezes, and smoke wafting from a cook-fire made Solomon wish that he were in Schaeffersburg for reasons other than the one that had brought him there. An audible sigh escaped him, as he thought of the arduous task lying before him, which seemed so alien amidst such tranquil, restive environs.

The soft pitter of paws alighting upon wood brought his eyes around to where Harvey had jumped up onto the chair to his right. The stocky brown and white cat never ceased to bring a grin to his face, an increasing necessity after all of the travails that Solomon had witnessed over the past few years ever since giving his oath to the Order of the Numinous.

"Yes, yes, Harvey," he greeted the cat, who was staring expectantly at him. "A fresh mountain trout meal is in order for you, young lad. And for me, for that matter … and all of it is thanks to our wonderful host, of course, and don't you forget that."

*****

The cat emitted a spirited meow, and then jumped into Solomon's lap. Gripping the little fellow under the forelegs, Solomon hoisted the cat up over his right shoulder, and began to gently stroke the cat's back as Harvey settled his head down, resting his chin upon Solomon's shoulder.

It had been a long, taxing journey, one that had begun on the east coast, within sight of sandy beaches and crashing ocean waves. They had gained passage on a dirigible that had brought them most of the way, to the cusp of the great Cloud Mountain range, before setting down. A short jaunt on a steam-ship down the Eagle River followed. It brought them to the river valley where they had hiked on foot the last few miles into the mountain pass that lead to Schaeffersburg.

The stroll through the thickly wooded terrain was taken with caution, fully cognizant of the reason why Solomon had been summoned to the little mountain town. As Harvey padded alongside him on the beaten path, streaked with grooves from wagon wheels and pocked marked with hoof prints, his eyes had incessantly turned skyward, as if expecting to gain a glimpse of the winged terror that had brought such sorrow and fear to the mountain town.

The sound of heavier footsteps across wood planks drew Solomon's attention back to the present, and he glanced up to see that Malcolm Jameson was approaching with a couple of plates in hand. Gently, Solomon lifted Harvey up off of his shoulder, and set the cat down upon the ground.

"A full meal is long overdue, yes?" Malcolm inquired amiably. "I overheard the last bit of your discussion with Harvey."

"But not because of any delay on your part, my friend," Solomon replied with a grin. "You have been very kind to us, and are always far too generous to malcontents such as us."

"I figured that your assistant could use a prodigious meal too," Malcolm commented, with a nod towards the cat, who was eyeing the plates with great interest.

"Probably, even more so than me. I consider fish dinners to be his form of payment anyway, as he doesn't have much use for money."

Malcolm laughed, and set one plate down in front of Solomon. He then leaned over and set the second one down on the timber planks of the flooring. He glanced over towards Solomon. "Don't worry. I did a little extra preparation for Harvey."

The cat could eat just fine when food was cut up in smaller chunks, but he still had his limitations. The cat had been missing most of his teeth when Solomon's sister had taken him in as a stray, along with an assortment of other signs that the feline had been subjected to a heavy dose of the world's cruelties.

Seeing the burly little fellow burying his face happily into the dish of trout, it was hard for Solomon to imagine the frightened, battered cat that his sister had taken days just to coax out from under an armoire in her house in Bodington. The cat possessed an incredible wellspring of spirit, though, and was now a faithful traveling companion to Solomon on his far-flung journeys.

Solomon closed his eyes, as he took in a fork-full of the fresh mountain trout, prepared with butter and herbs in the way that only

Malcolm's wife Agnes was capable of. The succulent flavors swirled in his mouth, bringing great pleasure to Solomon after having been subjected to tavern food for several days in a row. Malcolm left for a few moments, and returned with two glasses of beer, before sitting down at the table with Solomon.

He raised an eyebrow at Solomon. "I assume Harvey does not drink beer."

"No, he has not exhibited a taste for it, at least yet. And my compliments to your wife, Malcolm," Solomon remarked, after swallowing another scrumptious bite. "This tastes just heavenly."

Apparently, Harvey thought so too, as the cat had still not come up for air from his own plate.

Malcolm chuckled. "Ahhh… how the rigors of the road can make a simple meal most delectable."

"No, I assure you, this is simply succulent, on any occasion," Solomon replied, giving Malcolm a wink.

"Well, I must thank you for your compliments, and I will convey your sentiments to my wife, which she will certainly appreciate," Malcolm said.

"I appreciate this very much, as I really needed some sustenance, for my little sojourn into town," Solomon declared.

"So you do plan on going into town today?"

"I don't want to waste even a minute, not with what your town has had to endure over the recent months," Solomon replied, his countenance growing more solemn. "And you think that one of the tribal people might be able to meet with me tonight?"

Malcolm nodded. "Yes, as they have not forgotten their own time of horror, when the shadow of something very similar had fallen across their people. I received your cable, and took the liberty of arranging a meeting with one of them at dusk."

"I will return at dusk promptly, then, and we will see what we can do to bring this trial to an end as soon as possible," Solomon stated, a glint of iron reflecting in his gaze. He dug his fork back into the trout on his plate, and continued his meal, his thoughts already working through the plans that he had settled on.

*****

The stroll down from Malcolm's house into town was pleasant enough, as the sky was clear, and the crisp, fresh breezes were not so cold or gusty as to be discomfiting. There was a little more spring to

Harvey's step after the ample meal, and Solomon watched the cat bound a few paces ahead, as they walked toward the main street that passed through the center of town.

Schaeffersburg was a quaint mountain town, and a very picturesque sight when viewed from the heights of the surrounding slopes. A modest number of dwellings were clustered in the vicinity of the main street, which was flanked by the edifices serving the needs of the community, whether in matters of entertainment, commerce, craft, or law.

Solomon set his iron-tipped walking cane in place, and tipped his hat, as a pair of younger ladies walked by. Both of the women returned his gesture with nods and polite greetings, as they ferried baskets filled with various goods along with them.

"Stick close to me now, Harvey," Solomon said in a low voice, as he heard the approaching clatter of a coach. He looked up and saw the black wagon drawing near, which was being pulled by a stout pair of draft horses.

Seeing their blond manes, he recognized the equine pair as Belgic, a breed he particularly liked due to their friendly demeanors and robust capabilities. Whenever he settled down from his journeys on behalf of the Order of the Numinous, if he survived them somehow, he was determined to secure a couple such horses one day, and specifically active working ones, and give them a luxurious tenure within a spacious pasture.

Harvey dutifully kept close to Solomon, as he edged to the right side of the street. After the coach passed, he continued onward, towards the center of the town. Other than being accompanied by a cat, Solomon did not attract anything more than casual attention. Dressed in a vest and jacket, and topped with a brimmed velvet hat that had been fashioned with a low, rounded crown, Solomon was well attired, but his garb was far from ostentatious.

They had to pause once, as Harvey stopped suddenly to scratch at his right ear, twitching it several times before starting forward again. It was a sight that had occurred several times over the course of the past few weeks, and each time it greatly bothered Solomon, who felt that the cat had already endured far too much in life. He hoped that the apparent irritation was not the onset of another tribulation, but he feared otherwise. The cat recoiled whenever Solomon tried to lightly touch the area, which boded ill.

Slowly, Solomon withdrew the precious spectacles that he harbored in the upper vest pocket over his left breast. The tinted look of the lenses came from the thin, crimson film that dwelled within the midst of the carefully, and meticulously, crafted glass. Solomon was always a little ginger when handling the ornate spectacles, as they were his most valuable possession, and perhaps one of the most valuable possessions in the entire collection of devices and artifacts controlled by the Order of the Numinous.

He slipped them on, and steeled himself, as he always did when donning the spectacles. There were two very good reasons for doing so. The first was because looking through the spectacles brought pain to the viewer from the first instant, as the field of vision that came through them was anything but natural. The second was because he had to always discipline himself, especially within a crowd, not to react to the macabre sights that the spectacles sometimes revealed. The last thing that he ever wanted to do was draw attention to himself, especially from those who had purposefully veiled themselves to the sight of humankind.

Cast in a blood-red hue, the pacific atmosphere of the mountain town evaporated when viewed through the spectacles. There was more to be seen now among the surroundings, as Solomon's gaze was attracted to wisps and tendrils of movement, as dark, shapeless forms drifted around both people and buildings.

Several of the caliginous shapes seemed to be attending to a tall, elegantly dressed man, who was in deep conversation with several other individuals in front of the local bank. That was of little surprise to Solomon, as it was something that he had witnessed many times before. The dark entities seemed to coagulate around the powerful and the wealthy, though not on all occasions, as Solomon was always careful to remind himself. Blanket judgments were never fruitful, and certainly not in a world consisting of individuals.

The little wraiths shunned the small church that was within view, which was encouraging to Solomon, as it was not always the case within a given town or city. When the wraiths could infest church grounds, it usually meant that the corruption by the darker astral realms was widespread, and ran very deep.

Solomon finally removed the spectacles, after just a few minutes, sapped of energy and bestowed with a grand headache; one that he knew would take quite some time to subside. He took several deep breaths, knowing that the walk back to Malcolm's house would be physically demanding after enduring the deleterious effects of the unique spectacles.

He was not ready to take the walk back just yet. His next stop was a visit to the mayor of the town, who he found in a two-story building located at the town's center. After seeing to Solomon's hat and cane, the mayor's assistant ushered him in immediately, to where the city's civil leader sat, ensconced within a high-backed, padded leather chair.

"Hello, Solomon, it is always a pleasure to see you," the mayor greeted warmly as he entered the spacious office. His eyes then lowered to where Harvey padded in close to Solomon's right leg.

"Hello, Mayor Jackson, it is good to see you again…and this time I have my good and loyal assistant Harvey with me, who accompanies me in my work for the Order these days," Solomon replied. Though it had been a couple of years, it felt as if it were only a day since Solomon had last seen the mayor of Schaeffersburg.

The mayor was a gregarious, heavyset man, with a thick, brown beard, and a deep, resonant voice. His eyes sparkled with intelligence, and his demeanor was infectious and congenial. Solomon liked the man a lot, as he was not the usual breed of politician. Erudite and considerate, the mayor possessed qualities not often encountered within the corridors of governmental power.

He had always supported the work of the Order of the Numinous, and it had been both him and Malcolm who had worked to summon Solomon.

The mayor gestured towards another high-backed chair, set before his wide oaken desk. He smiled warmly at Solomon. "I am afraid I may not have a suitable chair for your assistant."

"Harvey tends to adapt pretty well to most situations," Solomon replied, chuckling, as he took the proffered seat. Harvey rested on his haunches by Solomon's high leather boots, his tail flicking back and forth, and ears rotating about as he took in the office space from a feline perspective.

At first, the two men exchanged some pleasantries and small talk regarding Solomon's trip, and the affinity that he held for the town. Yet it was not long before the discussion turned towards the pressing matter at hand.

"I am gratified that you have come to help us in this hour," the mayor stated, his expression growing solemn. "We have endured far too much sorrow lately."

"When was the last incident?" Solomon asked, gently.

"Almost four weeks ago, right after Malcolm and I sent for you," the Mayor replied somberly. His voice grew heavier, and his eyes were downcast. "That was the ninth child taken from our community. And there seems to be nothing we can do. Nothing at all. No matter how many lookouts we post, or where they are, it always seems that they are out of position when the monster comes."

"Do you have any idea at all where this monster comes from?"

"Somewhere high and deep in the mountains. It flies far too fast for any of us to gain a bearing on it," the mayor said. He loosed a long breath. "Believe me, we have tried."

"And how often does the creature strike?" Solomon queried.

"Almost once a month," the mayor answered.

"Is there anything that you can think of which could possibly have started this?"

"No, we are confounded by what is happening to us. There is no reason that anyone can think of for this terrible misfortune," the mayor said, a hint of exasperation within his voice. "This is why we have sent for you. It is something much more suited for one from the Order."

"Something of the unseen world, you think?"

The mayor nodded, with a grim expression on his face. "It is no natural creature ... of that much I am certain. It is demonic, as in every case a strange spell seems to fall upon the house, from where a child is taken."

"If it is demonic, and of the unseen world, I will do everything in my power to find the cause. And if I find the cause, I will move to eliminate it as fast as I can, if it is within my power," Solomon assured the mayor. "That much I can promise you, but I must learn more of this depraved creature before I can find a way to defeat it."

"And that is all that we can ask of you, Solomon. I know that without you, we would be quite helpless right now," the mayor said, with no shame in his voice at the admission.

Solomon gazed back at the man, seeing the sadness and frustration in his eyes. He had seen such a look several times before, from men and women at wits end who were dealing with things that went beyond the boundaries of science and the material world. Solomon was very glad that the Mayor had sent for him, as he strongly suspected that this was indeed such an instance.

*****

A short time later, Solomon walked back into the street, taking a couple of moments to check the timepiece sequestered in his other vest pocket. It was approaching four o'clock in the afternoon, and the shadows would soon be lengthening as evening approached. Solomon knew that he could not stay in town very much longer, as it was important to get back for the meeting with the tribal representative that he had asked Malcolm to assist with.

The main street district was still bustling with activity, and Solomon watched as a few men walked into the front of the tavern. A stout mug of ale would have been a very welcome pursuit on any other occasion, but Solomon knew that he had to keep all of his wits about him under the circumstances.

A group of ladies had just emerged from the front of a storefront across the street, when Harvey went stock-still. His ears perked up and oriented fixedly towards the cluster of women.

Harvey mewled up at Solomon, catching his attention, before sauntering over towards the well-dressed ladies. Solomon watched the cat with interest, knowing that there was something very intentional to the feline's behavior.

The group of women took note of the cat, a few of them even leaning over to pet Harvey, as he wound his way around the bases of their long dresses. Solomon continued to quietly watch from where he stood, wondering what the cat's purpose was, as Harvey meandered through the group of women once again.

Harvey cast a furtive glance back in Solomon's direction, holding the stare just long enough to convey meaning to the sustained look. Solomon's brow furrowed slightly, as the cat began another pass through the women.

As Harvey made his way through the women for a third time, Solomon noted that the cat's attention purposefully excluded a tall, auburn-haired woman in their midst. There did not seem to be anything unusual about her appearance. From her interactions with the others, it seemed as if she had no greater or lesser stature amongst the others, but Harvey had pointedly avoided her all three times.

On a hunch, Solomon pulled out the unique spectacles once more, even though his head was already throbbing with the effects of the brief viewing that he had recently undergone. He slipped the spectacles on, and almost made the mistake of allowing an audible gasp to escape.

Fortunately, he was far enough away that he drew no attention from the one that had caused it.

The woman that Harvey had avoided was no longer the attractive, auburn-haired beauty that Solomon had seen only a moment before. Instead, she had the appearance of a decaying corpse, covered in stretched, sunken, leathery skin, with eyes that were glazed and covered in a white film. The ghastly figure was interacting casually with the other women, who had not changed in their appearance, casting the entire scene under a macabre light.

The cat glanced over at Solomon, and now that Solomon had the spectacles on, Harvey trotted away from the ladies and headed back over towards him. Solomon removed the spectacles without breaking his expression, and placed them back in his upper vest pocket. He squeezed his eyes shut, and pinched the bridge of his nose, as he tried to fight off the piercing effects from the spectacles. He felt even more dizzy and tired, even though he had only put the spectacles back on for a few scant moments.

"That was some very good work, Harvey," he said to the cat, when Harvey had reached him. The cat rubbed up against his legs, before pausing again to scratch at his right ear.

Solomon stood in place for a few more minutes, letting the pounding in his head begin to subside before moving onward. He relied on his walking cane a little more heavily on the way back to Malcolm's, drained as he was from the period of enhanced viewing.

He mulled over the woman whose guise had been pierced by the spectacles as he walked, knowing that she was either non-human, or was human and had given herself fully over to the lower realms. He had little doubt that her presence in the town was no coincidence in regards to the misfortunes that had befallen the townspeople. Solomon just needed a few more pieces of information to understand just how.

*****

"Solomon, this is Deer Runner of the People of the Cloud Mountains. He has graciously come to speak with you about the plight of the people in Schaeffersburg," Malcolm said, introducing the tall man standing at his right side.

Attired in buckskin garments with long tresses of raven-black hair, Deer Runner eyed Solomon with an intense scrutiny. The keen, appraising look did not leave his dark, piercing eyes, even when he nodded in acknowledgement of Malcolm's introduction.

"It is a pleasure to meet you, Deer Runner, and I hope that you can help me gain some wisdom in regards to this adversary," Solomon said. He took no offense to the somber expression on the other man's face. Solomon was an unknown, and likely a very mysterious, commodity to Deer Runner; especially related to the fact that Deer Runner knew that he had been called to Schaeffersburg specifically to deal with the matter of the flying, child-stealing monster.

"Solomon, I can only tell you something of the lore of my own people. They have faced an adversary like this in the past," Deer Runner stated. "It involved a child stealer that came from the skies…which we called the Ulagu."

Harvey traipsed up towards Deer Runner at that moment, rubbing his head against the man's buckskin leggings when he had drawn near. Even from a few paces away, Solomon could hear the low purr resonating from the cat. The reaction told Solomon that Harvey sensed a very good spirit within Deer Runner, and the cat's assessments of people had never proved to be wrong. The hint of a smile touched Deer Runner's mouth, as he leaned over and scratched the cat lightly on the back of the head.

Harvey's head jerked when Deer Runner's fingers graced the back of his ear, but the cat turned his head and pressed against Deer Runner's hand, as if to convey that the spot was an irritation. Deer Runner was careful to avoid the area as he continued to pet Harvey.

"The Ulagu, you say?" queried Solomon, trying to recall the legends and myths in the area that he was aware of.

"Yes, the Ulagu. The tale is a painful one to remember, but it is necessary to never forget such things," Deer Runner said.

The tribesman proceeded to tell Solomon an incredible tale, involving a giant, insect-like creature that had stolen many children in a previous generation of Deer Runner's people. The description mirrored that given to Solomon by the mayor, and he listened very closely to the tale.

Though persistence and guile, the tribe had ferreted out the creature's lair, which consisted of a great cave that was also occupied by many small versions of the winged monstrosity. Fire and smoke had been used to overcome the monstrous predator and its tinier cohorts, and since then such a vile thing had not plagued the mountains, until the present time.

Harvey then paused, and sat back on his haunches, lifting up his right back paw and scratching vigorously at one ear. A look of concern crossed Solomon's face as he observed the cat's actions, an expression that was derived both from the tale, and from the bothersome irritation manifesting again in the cat.

When he looked back to Deer Runner, he saw that the tribesman was quietly regarding him.

"Does your little one have an affliction?" he asked Solomon. "It seemed so when I was greeting him."

"Something distresses him in the right ear, and it is gaining frequency," Solomon replied.

"I can take you to a Sacred Spring of my people, and it may be that the waters can help your friend," Deer Runner stated.

"A Sacred Spring?"

"A touch of the Creator is in the water of this spring," Deer Runner replied. "It has long benefited my people, and I see no reason why it would not benefit another creature of the Sky Father. I can take you there at dawn, before you begin your day's work."

"I would appreciate that, very much so," Solomon replied appreciatively, piqued by the information. Though he was not about to get his hopes up, neither was he going to dismiss possibilities. He had experienced quite enough of the inexplicable to know that it was foolish to shut his mind off fully to such potentialities.

The early morning jaunt would be undertaken for Harvey's benefit, but perhaps it would lead to something else that might be of help, if the waters truly contained special properties.

*****

The damp, cool air within the pre-dawn was invigorating to Solomon's spirits, as he made his way with Deer Runner along the mountain trails to where a small mountain spring tumbled down a short drop to collect in a rocky pool.

"This is the Sacred Spring," Deer Runner commented, as Solomon walked slowly towards the water's edge. "Bring the cat over to me."

Solomon leaned over, and scooped up Harvey, carrying the cat over to where Deer Runner was standing. The tribesman squatted down, and cupped some water in one hand, as Solomon secured the cat more tightly in his embrace.

Deer Runner slowly poured the water out of his hand and onto the cat's head, right over the ear that had been agitating Harvey as of late.

Solomon braced for the cat to react to the touch of water, but strangely, Harvey remained entirely calm. Even more incredibly, Harvey began to purr as the waters tricked down the fur of his neck.

"Not the usual reaction of a cat to water," Solomon commented.

"He senses its nature," Deer Runner said. "Go ahead, see if it helps him."

Solomon took a deep breath, and moved to scratch the cat behind the right ear, steeling himself for the expected, reflexive reaction. To his continued surprise, the cat purred contentedly as he scratched the feline all about the ear that had been giving him so much trouble in recent weeks.

Amazed, Solomon set the cat down upon the ground, and looked up to Deer Runner, who now had a smile spread on his face.

"Thank you, Deer Runner. What a gift you have given me, as there was nothing that I could do to spare that little fellow the discomfort that was afflicting him," Solomon said.

"Thank the Sky Father, for it was His gift; I merely made you aware of it," Deer Runner replied.

Solomon smiled. "Then thank you for making me aware of it, Deer Runner."

"I am happy to be of any help that I can to a man who willingly comes to face the task that you have come for," Deer Runner said, and Solomon could sense the genuine respect within the tribesman's words.

The two men fell silent, and enjoyed the peaceful atmosphere, with whispering breezes and the soft patter of spring water, touching down into the pool from where it flowed over the edge of a higher rock. As Solomon watched Harvey bound around the area, an idea came to him. If the water really did have some sort of sacred, mystical qualities, and it certainly appeared to have that, then perhaps it was something that would be of use in his current endeavor.

He looked towards Deer Runner. "May I take some of this water with me for my purposes, to aid with my effort to contest the thing that plagues this town?"

"The town needs healing, and that is what this spring has been given to us for," Deer Runner replied. "Anything that you do to defend the town and its people would bring healing to this area, so it would be of no disrespect to take water from the spring to help you."

*****

It took a couple of painstaking days, but Solomon finally witnessed the ordeal that the town had been subjected to in recent years.

He had periodically slipped the spectacles on, and had taken note that a number of wraiths were converging upon one of the outlying houses in particular. He knew that something was amiss, and that he had more than a little inkling as to the nature of what was about to happen.

He concentrated his attention upon the house, and placed it under a tighter surveillance when night fell. The wraiths were gathering there in greater number as time passed, and Solomon felt more certain that the town's continuing nightmare was about to fall in force upon the house.

Solomon had tested his idea regarding the water on the first night after the sojourn to the Sacred Spring. After having first put on the spectacles, he had moved over closer to where a few of the drifting, wraith-like forms were loitering about the town's tavern. Taking out the small bottle of water that he had collected from the Sacred Spring, he poured some of the water onto his right hand, and then flicked his fingers in the direction of the nearest wraiths. As if scorched by fire, the wraiths had darted away abruptly, as the droplets of water scattered and fell in amongst them.

The water did indeed have a special property, which had bolstered Solomon greatly as he had taken up a watch on the house where the wraiths were congregating.

During the night that he saw the sky menace for the first time, he had taken note that no wraiths could be seen anywhere in town other than the house. He had not seen any of them drifting in for almost an hour, and suspected that whatever was going to happen was imminent. With the spectacles returned to his pocket, and the bottle gripped in his left hand, Solomon grasped the end of his cane and girded his resolve.

Without further delay, he started towards the house, walking with a quickening stride. As he narrowed the distance to the house, he saw a young girl, of maybe six or seven years of age, stroll out of the house, and down into the open yard in front of the porch. Barefoot, and clad in nothing more than a long nightgown, the child stepped slowly across the grass, as if caught within a dream.

Solomon reached the open yard with the little girl, just as he heard the flapping of wings coming from the night skies above. Limned by moonlight, the huge creature's form was outlined starkly against the sky, as it swept towards the yard and the young child. The child did not react to the approach of the monster, caught as the little girl was within the strange trance that had fallen over her.

The flying creature reminded Solomon of a great insect, though this was no creature that could count its origins within the world in which he dwelled. As it drew closer, Solomon began to come to a full appreciation of its size. Nearly the equal of the house that the child had emerged from, the creature was simply enormous.

At first, a spike of fear drove into Solomon as he gazed upon the winged giant, but he swiftly gathered himself. He breathed deeply and set off at a run towards the child. The sprawling shadow of the creature fell over both the child and himself as he reached the yard. He switched the glass vessel with the spring water over to his right hand, and let the cane fall to the grass. Rearing back, he hurled the glass bottle with all of his strength towards the massive, diabolical creature.

At such a close range, his aim did not have to be exceptional, and the glass bottle shattered into bits as it impacted against the shiny chitin of the creature's outer body. Water and glass shards sprayed outward, spattering the creature in numerous places with the liquid taken from the Sacred Spring.

The night was rent apart by the creature's hellish, piercing shriek. It recoiled with tremendous speed, flapping its wings furiously as it gained altitude, and hastened away from the open yard. Solomon felt a tremendous relief at the response, though his heart was still pounding furiously from within his chest. Throwing the vial was the only chance that he had had against the hulking creature, as if the water had done nothing to it, it would have made very short work of him, and would have taken the little girl.

"Magdeline! ... Oh Magdeline," cried out a female voice, as an adult woman sped out of the house, and raced across the yard, garbed in a long nightgown. Tears were already flowing down the woman's face as the moonlight fell upon her.

The child rubbed at her eyes, and Solomon could sense that the youth was yet groggy from whatever spell had come over her. The woman swept the child up into her arms, as tears ran profusely down her cheeks. Her eyes were bright with fear, as she looked over towards Solomon.

"What ...was that?" she asked, her voice shaking.

"The thing that has been tormenting this town," Solomon said.

"How did ... you drive it away?" she managed to ask, between sobs.

"I believe I found one weakness in it," Solomon said. "And I have a new idea..."

"Thank you, sir ... thank you," the woman stammered, her voice choking up. "May God bless you a hundred fold, sir."

Solomon nodded, feeling awkward as he always did whenever hearing such emotional gratitude. He replied to her gently, "If God just remembers me when all is said and done, then that is all I ask."

*****

When Solomon returned back to Malcolm's, the next step in his efforts had unfolded before him. After a short nap, which was entirely inadequate to address the fatigue in him, he had called for Malcolm and asked that a number of craftsmen be gathered together.

Being of The Order of the Numinous, Solomon had access to some considerable funding, and Solomon made sure that Malcolm conveyed the fact that all of those who participated would be very well compensated for their efforts.

It took several days for the construction of the device that Solomon had conceived of, involving a couple of Malcolm's artisan friends and several assistants, who labored assiduously from dawn till dusk, and a few hours in between, to finish it. Their expertise proved bountiful, as they took in Solomon's idea and made adjustments and improvements to the design. The small team had to cobble together a lot of material, and Solomon could only hope that the winged creature would stay away from the town just long enough to allow his concept to be completed.

Gaining the help of several hardy men from the town, Solomon also collected several barrels of water from the sacred spring, and had them brought back to where the construct was being fashioned. Gradually, a prodigious amount of the special water was collected, as Solomon awaited the completion of the implement that he had envisioned after the night that he had intervened against the winged horror.

*****

The populace of Schaeffersburg woke up to a great mist on the morning following the completion of the design, though it did not come from the moisture of the pre-dawn, or from any mountain lakes or streams. Heated and pumped out of the huge bronze vessel that had been so industriously crafted, and carried through a system of narrow metal tubing to several points at the town's perimeter, the steam was created and distributed with a very intended purpose.

Using a complex system of valves, massive amounts of steam were loosed in a progression that worked its way around the town. The air currents assisted, mostly favorably, in spreading the freed mist all over the town.

Monitoring the situation as much as he could possibly endure through the spectacles, Solomon's heart was lifted rapidly, as he saw the dark wraiths quickly abandoning the town. The black tendrils darted away from the billowing mist, as the town was cleansed of their loathsome presence.

Solomon waited patiently, expecting more than just the wraiths to react, as the mist engulfed the town. He had a theory regarding what had been happening in the town, and his speculation was about to be proven.

A short time later, a shrill cry pierced the air as the mist flowed throughout the center of the town.

The cry had come from the stately house where the woman that Harvey had singled out dwelled, which came as no surprise to Solomon. It was exactly as he had expected. She was the ultimate cause of the town's misery, and her identity was very clear; a sorceress of the dark arts that had taken up residence in Schaeffersburg. The children were sacrifices meant to empower her, whether in prolonging her life, or perhaps giving her arts greater strength. In either case, Solomon was bringing her wickedness to an end, right then and there in the morning light.

The cry came again, and movement above attracted Solomon's attention. He did not need the spectacles to witness what then transpired. A monstrous winged form dove down from the skies, lifting up a moment later, bearing a human form in its clutches. Solomon's heart quailed for a brief moment, until he recognized that the figure was an adult, in a woman's attire.

At once, he knew who the winged monster had come to retrieve.

Before Solomon turned around, he felt a tap upon his shoulder. Turning, he came face to face with Deer Hunter, which was an unexpected sight.

"It would seem you have found the cause," Deer Hunter stated.

Solomon nodded. "And it has been uprooted."

"But you must find a way to finish off the thing that the witch summoned," Deer Hunter said.

Solomon peered into the distance, where the fast flying creature's form was already minuscule. He sighed, "That is a task beyond our capabilities at the moment."

The corners of Deer Hunter's mouth turned up in a grin. "It would have been, but the People of the Cloud Mountains have spread all throughout the trails and overlooks.... Even now, sharp-eyed lookouts are watching the flight of that monster. It has been drawn out under the sun, and cannot use the night to veil itself. When it descends from the sky, we will have a good idea where its lair can be found."

A fresh hope welled up within Solomon, as he looked at Deer Hunter in humbled astonishment.

"Did you think we would not do our part to help you overcome this monster?" Deer Hunter asked him.

*****

The fire was stoked and soon blazed strongly, heating the contents of the bronze vessel that had been carefully lugged for quite a distance. A small collection of pipes that had been used in the town had been fitted together.

Before long, pressure built and expanded, as steam generated from the Sacred Spring's water built in force. When he judged everything ready, Solomon opened the valve, which belched forth a prodigious degree of stream into the gaping mouth of the cave.

The reaction from within the shadowy maw of the cave was swift and explosive.

The winged giant finally emerged from the depths of the cave, spreading its wings and clearly readying for flight. A thick hail of arrows greeted its presence before it could lift off, the feathered shafts riddling the immense form. The cracks of many guns from the townspeople joined in the whoosh of the arrows, as barrels emptied lead towards the beast. Arrowheads and bullets alike had been dipped in the sacred water, and the natural armor of the creature availed it nothing. The creature stabbed outwards with spiky appendages, and snapped several pincers shut, but the tribal archers were too far to reach.

Fragments sprayed off the creature as bullets tore into it, and shafts from arrows were buried all over its body. Riddled with oozing wounds, it emitted a pitiful cry, and stumbled about, sorely disabled from the first volley. The archers and riflemen did not wait for a second, hurrying to prepare their weapons again.

After another great volley, the giant slumped onto the ground, and did not move.

Before anyone knew what was happening, a figure was born upward on leathery wings away from the cave mouth, from behind the inert body of the monstrosity. The new figure flew high into the skies above the mountain slope.

Solomon had only a glimpse of the entity, but it was long enough that he recognized the traces of a human visage in the feral countenance that glared hatefully back at him. Gnashing its spiky teeth, the smaller creature fled through the skies, abandoning the huge winged beast that had long done its bidding.

As Solomon watched the winged entity flying away, he heard Harvey mewling incessantly. Following the sounds of the cat, he jogged over to where Harvey had managed to pin a creature almost half his size to the ground. It was a small version of the winged monster that had been plaguing the town.

"Have you caught me a gift there, Harvey? I believe that a mouse would be a little more manageable," Solomon remarked, appraising the cat's quarry. The cat kept up its yowling, clearly agitated. "Hold on there a second more, let me do this right, Harvey."

Taking up his cane, Solomon poured some sacred spring water from a bottle onto the iron end.

"I'll take care of it from here, Harvey," Solomon said to the cat. "Let it free."

The cat meowed once more, and jumped backwards, releasing the hold on the winged creature. Before it could move away or lift off the ground, Solomon smashed it with his water-coated cane tip. He brought his cane up and down with force a few more times, for good measure. He eyed the pulped body of the creature in the aftermath, and was well satisfied that it would not be growing into a new threat for the mountain town.

"Kind of like squashing a bug, Harvey," Solomon commented to the cat, who was staring at the pulverized remains of the creature.

Deer Runner was standing next to Solomon by then. "We will be sure to do a very careful search of that cave."

"That would be highly advised," Solomon replied, nodding. He looked to where the steam continued to pump into the cave mouth. "But let the misted sacred water do its work before you risk anyone in that cave."

*****

"Are you sure that you can't stay for a day or two?" Malcolm asked.

"I'm sure," Solomon said, grinning. "I have a very uncouth lady to pursue now. She won't show her face in Schaeffersburg anytime soon, not now that her true nature has been unveiled. But she'll seek to practice her arts elsewhere, and I intend to make that very problematic for her."

As if he understood Solomon, Harvey stretched lengthwise, and then rose up to his paws, arching his back for a few moments. The cat sauntered over to Solomon's side, and looked up at him.

"And you espied her first, so I know you understand why we need to go," Solomon remarked to the cat.

The burly cat loosed a robust meow, drawing a hearty chuckle from Malcolm.

"I think he does indeed understand," Malcolm remarked, shaking his head, as Solomon tipped his cap, stepped down from his friend's porch, and started forward with the cat at his side. He slung the strap of his travel bag over his left shoulder. "But don't be a stranger for too long."

Solomon paused, and glanced back at his friend. "I love this little mountain town, Malcolm. You know that! I'll try to be back this way before too much time passes. Keep a barrel of beer handy, and give my regards to the good mayor. God willing we'll see each other soon enough!"

Giving a last wave, Solomon strolled with Harvey on down the trail.

Harry Was One of Us

Sara M. Harvey

"Jo, it's your turn to check the traps." Sam called out from the helm.

The Saint Dismus, a refurbished Army airship, hovered in a fog bank that blanketed the eastern shore of Lake Michigan outside of Chicago. The War Between the States had raged on for eight gruesome years, leaving the country shell-shocked and economically broken. In the aftermath of that all-consuming war, wealth and power accumulated in areas of trade- New York, San Francisco, Miami, Chicago- and the canny pirate knew where to tap that source. For the crew of the Saint Dismus, their favorite hunting ground was the lucrative fur and minerals trade out of Canada that crossed the Great Lakes.

"If it's seagulls again, I am throwing them back. I still have heartburn from the last time we tried to eat one of those oily suckers. If we want pigeon, we really ought to pull inland a little more." Jo kicked off her shoes and sidled out the narrow maintenance hatch.

"Well, Cora don't like the idea of being to close to the city and the captain is backing her up on this one."

"Mick always takes her side," Jo huffed and climbed out into the heavy mist. "Everyone always takes her side."

She swayed a moment, feeling the earth perilously far below, before inching towards the radio receiver and the grid work that held the traps. The wind blew irregularly, making it difficult to concentrate on her task. But one-by-one, she ratcheted up each of the pigeon pots. Three still had their bait intact, two were empty and picked clean, one held a shrieking seagull, and the last held a single fat pigeon.

"One. Great." Jo released the seagull that cried violently at her before hopping off the narrow deck and wheeling away. At least the pigeon was a good size, looking more like a small chicken. Even more surprising was that it stayed still and docile as she drew it from the cage and remained calm in her hands.

"I've got the catch of the day," Jo announced, producing the bird from inside her coat as she shut the hatch door behind her. It sat in her open palms, beak tucked down against its broad chest.

Sam stared at the bird, amazed. "That's the damn biggest pigeon I have ever seen!"

Cora peeked out of the galley. "Wow! That is a fat squab, but I am glad I've got potatoes to pad out the meal. That there bird's not enough to feed us all."

"I'll put more bait out in a bit, still have three traps out though, maybe we'll get lucky."

"You threw the seagulls back again, didn't you?"

Jo didn't answer; she only thrust the pigeon towards her. "Start here and I'll see what else I can scare up."

Cora grabbed the pigeon by the legs and the bird let itself be hung upside down. "And you bring us a stupid bird, to boot." She rolled her eyes. "Hey, what's this?" She plucked a cylinder from the pigeon's ankle.

Jo took the metal container and examined it. "Looks official." She unscrewed the lid and out slid a tiny metal chip.

"Anything else in there?" Sam peered over her shoulder.

"Doesn't look like it. Wonder what it could be?"

"Let's pop it in the reader and find out!"

"Now, now. I think we might want to put it back on the bird and send it back to whoever will surely be looking for it soon," Cora said, already heading towards the hatch.

"Hell no! And give away our dinner?" Sam shook his head. "We'll read the chip, and if it's important, we'll take it to whoever ourselves. Probably get us a nice reward while we're at it, too!"

Sam unlatched the brassbound cover of the central control array. It flipped up with a small squeal revealing a panel of instruments and a small view screen embedded into the cover's interior. He slid the little chip into a larger adapter and plugged that into a slot in the panel.

The system whirred for a long moment before the screen jittered to life. At first there was nothing, but gibberish and symbols, but it soon cleared into text, but no less intelligible.

Sam scratched at the stubble on his cheek. "Hmm, this is official. Gonna take me a bit to translate, call Mick up here to take the helm while I work on this."

"You sure you want to wake the captain up from his nap?"

He turned to Jo, his usually merry brown eyes strangely grave. "This is Federal code."

Jo blanched. "I'll get him right away."

*****

They had settled in to eat a tense dinner by the time Sam had deciphered the message. Although the supper was a masterwork of potatoes and pigeon served with a reduction of black lager, no one's mind was on the meal, at least not the eating of it. They were all pondering where this plump and tasty bird had come from and what message was it carrying.

"It's about Harry."

The table fell silent.

"Harry?" Cora's fork clattered to her enamelware plate. "Harry?"

"Our Harry?" Jo shook her head, comprehending the words, but not understanding them. "Why ever would they send an encrypted code on a pigeon about Harry?"

Sam sighed and slumped into one of two vacant chairs. He glanced at the other. "Because…. Because Harry's dead."

Mick shook his head. "Are you sure it's our Harry? I mean, why would they send that classified?"

"I know it's our Harry, but they don't. They have no idea who he is, save that he is a federal scout. The missive was a rendezvous request; to dispose of the body."

"And you know it's him because…?" Cora's voice nearly drowned in her tears.

Sam nodded. "They describe the body in detail. Down to his dreadlocks, the starburst scar on his ribs, his Saint Dismus tattoo on his back, and…." He trailed off, avoiding Cora's desperate gaze, but still speaking to her. "And the locket he wore with your picture in it."

She gasped and jumped up from the table, sending cups and plates tumbling to the floor. "Harry!"

"Did they say how long he'd been…you know…gone?" Even Mick had a difficult time admitting the truth of the matter.

"A while. Seems that he might have died sometime in the late autumn and the snow and ice up there preserved him pretty well. Some government scouts found him last week when the spring thaw started. There wasn't much of him left that wasn't covered by his clothes, and those were barely holding together. Seems Harry had it rough in the corps."

"I told him not to go!" Cora wailed and cried into her apron. "He never listened to me!"

Harry had been a great scout and spy, an integral member of the crew. He wanted the Saint Dismus to go legit, scout for the government, but the rest of the crew had voted him down. He'd left in the middle of the night at the next port without telling anyone, only leaving a note for Cora. That brought the crew to only four and shifts had been tight ever since. They never looked to bring on a new member, instead, they held Harry's place for him for when he came back.

"Well, we have to go and get him," Jo said.

The others nodded. "Of course we do," Mick said, decisively. "Harry was one of us and he always will be."

"I don't know if I could bear it. I don't know if I could stand to see him...like that."

Jo ignored Cora, "We're going to have to plan this carefully. Sam, I assume you have their position?"

"I do. But, we'll have to move quickly. They mentioned that they sent the note by direct current mail as well, but that will take a day or two to arrive and be downloaded, if they get it at all. D-C-mail is notoriously unpredictable."

"Hence the pigeon." Mick nodded towards the bird's picked-over carcass.

"That would explain why it was so plump and juicy," Jo agreed. "T'was a government bird."

*****

The USS Eagle sat at her moorings not too far north of Chicago, in Milwaukee. Harry's body had been found due east of the city in the remote woodlands between it and Madison. He had been searching for a spring-fed lake, said to be a prized hunting ground and spiritual center for the natives. No one knew if he had ever found it. He lay across a deer track with his head, or what remained of it, pointing vaguely south, as if looking for the Saint Dismus as it made smuggling runs across Lake Michigan.

Jo read the dispatch time and time again, wondering if they had taken that run up to Kenosha, if things might have been different. Maybe they would have robbed the Eagle or whatever ship Harry had been assigned. Maybe they would have spotted him, intercepted his signal, somehow found him in that Wisconsin wilderness.

"You keep thinking in circles like that and you're gonna wear ruts in your brain." Sam leaned into the doorway of the crews' quarters. Cora had the helm and Mick was bottom side, fighting with the navigation system.

"We've been this close the whole time. I mean we dropped him off in Cleveland, how'd we know he'd end up back this side of the lake? And just a few short hours away?"

"I think Cora knew. I think he might have contacted her. She's been so hesitant to get anywhere near Chicago or Milwaukee, even Kenosha, since the end of summer. The feds could have been onto us and if Harry knew that, he'd try and warn us off."

"Harry would do that for us, I know he would. But why contact Cora? Why not me? Or you?"

Sam grinned his lopsided smile and shook his head. "Cora always gets her way, you said it yourself. I don't think Mick would have heard it from me or from you. But Cora.... Especially after Harry left us, leaving Cora alone and heartbroken and ready for him to step into that empty place in her heart. Mick listens to Cora."

"I just wonder if this was a good thing or not under present circumstances. We might have Harry back if he hadn't."

"Well, we'll have Harry back now, won't we?"

Jo sighed. "Only in a manner of speaking."

Mick shouted from below. "Got it! North-Northwest, Cora. Easy does it, I'll be right up!"

"This is it," Jo said, resignation in her tone.

Sam put his arm around her shoulders. "Come on, let's do him proud. Let's go take Harry home."

As they came onto the bridge, Mick was ascending them into the cloud cover. He cut the engines, leaving only the stabilizing propellers turning. It would be enough to maneuver them slowly towards the Eagle without alerting them to their presence.

Through the periscope, Jo could just make out the airship. It was a huge, lumbering thing, but appeared to have much better engines than they did.

"We've got agility on them, but not speed or power."

"We won't have far to go, we just need to get to the island," Mack answered.

Jo glanced back over her shoulder. "Back to Beaver? Are you nuts?"

"They have an airfield. And the Mormons have gone now. Just a bunch of Irish fisherman these days."

"We have been saving that Midleton whiskey for a reason. I'll bet it'll smooth over relations when we land," Sam observed.

Mick nodded. "And Harry was born there. It's as good a place as any to bury him."

Cora remained silent, steering blind through the swath of stratus clouds.

Jo grit her teeth. "It's a risk, Mick. The last time we were there it didn't end so well, if you'll recall."

"Listen, no one got arrested and no one got hurt. And that was years ago. Besides, what other choice do we have? We could try for Mackinac, but I hear the feds have all sorts of summer homes there now. Beaver's the only autonomous island left on the western lakes."

"There's Canada," Sam suggested.

"Not enough fuel for Canada, we'd at least need to stop at Beaver to refuel." Cora's voice sounded flat, distant. "Besides, we can't take Harry to Canada. We can't bury him there. It's bad enough that the feds want him buried in one of their cemeteries. Mick's right, the best place to take him is Beaver. He always spoke lovingly of it, at least his childhood memories, before things went bad between the feds and the Mormons."

"Are we certain the Mormons have left?"

"No," Mick said, "but they'll treat us better than the feds."

"Better is relative."

"Better than federal prison. Or did you somehow get the bounty off your head and didn't tell the rest of us."

"No," Jo admitted, glumly, "I'm still wanted, same as y'all. Just…. You're right. No other recourse."

"We're coming up on the Eagle. Get ready, you three." It had worked out well with Cora not wanting to participate. She had readily agreed to stay with the Saint Dismus.

Jo followed her two crewmates into the teacup, the bowl-shaped extension below the main cabin. It housed what small arsenal they carried and the emergency escape kits: six silk parachutes. She watched Mick and Sam strip to the waist and strap on their lead-lined vests, designed to stop bullets. The Saint Dismus tattoo stood out starkly against their backs, as she knew her own did, and Cora's as well. A thick black cross with manacles hanging over the crossbar symbolized the thief crucified with Jesus. They weren't a religious lot, but the man had remained honorable to the last, proving a friend to the falsely accused messiah until death. As thieves devoted to friendship and honor themselves, the crew had unanimously agreed on both the name of the ship and the design of her logo. To that end, at some point Harry had brought aboard a set of real manacles and hung them above the helm as a sort of lucky charm for the ship. It was an image they each wore, etched indelibly into the flesh between their shoulder blades so no matter what extremity they might lose they could still be identified by it. They had been able to identify Harry this way. It was cold comfort to know how well their idea worked.

Cora brought the Saint Dismus in only a few yards above the Eagle. The federal floater dwarfed them, a long, solid shadow below. They strapped the parachute packs on over the vests and carefully lowered the rope ladder. Mick went ahead, vanishing through the cloud cover. Sam motioned Jo to descend next. Taking the hemp in her hands, she moved smoothly through the curling white before she came to a canopy of grey silk. Sam touched down right beside her, having followed so closely it was a wonder he didn't kick her in the head.

Mick clipped onto an eyebolt and loosed his repelling line, fat knots were spaced every few feet along it. He signed to them not to follow until he signaled. They waited. Jo clenched and unclenched her toes inside of her boots, wanting to wander, to fidget, but knowing she had to remain silent and still.

A sound like a gull's cry and a tug on the rope told her it was safe to follow. Again, Sam was right on top of her.

Mick waited for them on a catwalk that stretched along the side of the envelope. It stretched far in either direction, hardly seeming even to bend with the shape of the airship's contour.

"How're we going to find him? This thing is enormous," Jo whispered.

Sam touched his finger to his lips and bade them to follow. They shimmied along the narrow planking towards the rear of the craft. A small ladder extended down towards the cabin three quarters of the way back and Sam took the lead this time.

The main cabin attached to the air bladder directly, unlike the Saint Dismus which had a gap between them used to lash cargo. Sam eased down onto another catwalk, narrower than the first. From his belt pouch he pulled out a suction cup and a wrench. The bolts that held the window locks in place were mounted on the outside of the glass.

They were of a peculiar size used only by Army vehicles. Lucky for them, the Saint Dismus had come with a tool kit. The nuts came away easily and Sam pocketed them before using the suction cup to create a handle and hoist the window open. They waited for an alarm, but none came.

Sam leaned inside, glancing towards the aft then the bow before motioning Jo and Mick down off the ladder and onto the narrow catwalk. He eased in first, his long, narrow limbs easily snaking through the small opening. Jo slipped in next leaving the stocky captain to negotiate the heavy window and the sill.

"Maybe Mick should have come in first," Jo breathed in Sam's ear. "We'll be here all night at this rate."

"Patience, dear. We've got time. This is a service corridor to the rear cargo bay, not on the routine patrol. Pity that though, they're missing a lovely view." He nodded towards the bank of tall windows that, although grimy, offered a panoramic view of the tips of Milwaukee's buildings peeking through the fog far below.

Mick tumbled to the floor with a distressing ruckus, letting the window slam behind him. But the sound went unnoticed in the huge ship.

"This way," Sam beckoned and led them back. The corridor ended in a locked door a few yards beyond. "And this is where you come in, little lady."

Jo crouched before it, running her finger along the large keyhole. Peering into it, she could see the shiny tumblers inside. This was a door not often used, which might become a problem. She tried the skeleton key first, levering it this way and that, gauging the pressure needed to move the locking mechanism inside. It felt heavy, but not resistant; well-oiled at least. Quickly unrolling her lock-pick pack she selected a thick shank fitted with the heavy-duty bow. At the narrow collar near the other end of the shank, she fastened on a heavy bit cut with standard Army-issue wards. Just owning those federal key blanks was enough to land a body in prison for ten years. Jo kept her stash safe and secret, only pulling out the big guns like these in emergencies.

Lastly, she spat onto the key and rubbed her saliva across it in as much of a superstitious habit as it was a lubricant. "Saint of Thieves, don't fail me now. I mean to rescue one of our own."

The key slid haltingly into the hole and Jo turned carefully. Too much pressure and she'd snap the bit inside, rendering the lock entirely unpickable and in need of replacement. She breathed through her nerves as she twisted the bow, feeling the wards cut into the bit meet and match up with the tumblers inside the lock. They resisted and Jo steadied her hands. They had plenty of time, Sam said. No one came back like he's told her. No problem.

"I hear footsteps," Mick said.

"Hurry, Jo. I think someone's coming."

"Gimme a minute. This can't be rushed." The key's components protested against the lock and for a terrified instant, Jo felt certain they'd break apart, but the lock gave way with a deep click and the door slid open on silent hinges. She removed the key with as much attention as she'd inserted it, taking care not to bump the bit as she pulled it free. She pocketed it and rolled up her kit.

Mick was already scouting inside, humming a soft all clear for them. Sam darted through the door as Jo closed it behind them. She looked through the keyhole into the corridor. A young woman in a green-gray uniform strolled into view. She scanned the halls and paused to gaze out the windows. Jo signed patrol and stepped away from the keyhole. Behind her, Sam and Mick made themselves scarce as Jo ducked down into the space that would hide her when the door was opened. They heard the officer's footfalls come right to the door before echoing softly away, back the way she'd come.

Jo counted to thirty before creeping back to the keyhole for a look. The corridor stretched empty for as far as she could see. "All clear."

"No guards back here then, eh, Sam?" Mick raised an eyebrow at him.

"I said it wasn't on routine patrol. Maybe they heard a walrus hitting the decks and came to investigate."

Mick's shoulders tensed and he took a menacing step towards Sam.

"Boys!" Jo stepped in between them. "Harry. We are here for Harry. When we get to Beaver Island you two can measure dicks, okay?"

For moment, neither men moved nor spoke. Jo turned Mick away from Sam by the shoulders. "You look that side. Sam, you search that wall. I'll take this center aisle. Now, go!"

Tall stacks of crates and tarpaulin-draped machinery dominated the frigid room. Jo could see why the Eagle crew had stashed Harry back here. She shivered and clapped her hands together, rubbing her fingers to warm them. She had made it nearly to the rear wall when she heard Sam's whistle. Clambering over the boxes in her way, she made a beeline for his position.

The simple pine box had been stenciled with the federal logo above that of the army's. Someone had painted over the crest that signified that the remains belonged to one of the crew of the Eagle and over the paint was written in pencil: unknown federal scout, army?

Impulsively, Jo took out a small jar of powdered chalk she used on locks clogged with grease. Dipping her finger into it, she scrawled *Harry* over the other words.

"Shove over, let me at it." Mick hefted one end easily, leaving Sam and Jo to scramble for the other. Between the three of them, they managed to maneuver the casket into the open area near the door. "Betcha yer glad of the walrus, now, eh?"

"Are we sure it's him?"

Sam glanced around. "This is the only coffin I can see in here. Freshly assembled, too. I can only assume."

"Can we check?"

Mick tugged on his sideburns. "Seems a waste, but at the same time, I'd hate to hoist some stranger's carcass onto my float."

"I didn't bring a pry bar. I think we're going to have to assume it is Harry. Who else could it be? The ship's log accompanying the message didn't mention any other deaths. Now help us with the door, it's going to be tricky getting him out of here." Sam waved Jo back to the door. The corridor was still deserted.

"Looks clear. I am going to scout down the way and check, though." She slinked down the corridor until she met with another door, this one set with a single round window. There was, however, a lock. Glancing into it, Jo could see it was not engaged. "Easy enough to fix and should buy us some time, should it come down to it. Locked doors opened, and unlocked doors shut."

The wards in the bit were different for this lock, simpler. Just a single notch on the bottom was all it took. When she returned to the cargo hold, she found that Sam and Mick had gotten the coffin situated under the window. Jo scrambled up into the narrow ledge outside, then onto the window's frame itself so she could hold the glass open. Sam stepped out behind her and guided the coffin out as Mick pushed.

The pine box teetered precariously on the sill, balanced between the ship and a long drop to a watery grave.

"Careful," Sam panted. "Easy there, I've got to turn it."

That was the worst of it, rocking the coffin back and forth, bringing it out by inches. Jo could only keep the window open and softly offer words of encouragement.

"Didn't really think this all the way through." Mick stopped to mop his forehead. His face was flushed deep red and his hands had already grown raw from handling the coffin's unsanded edges.

"We can't quit, now!" Jo's own strength flagged as she struggled to hold the window open. "Come on, boys, for Harry!" She said it as much for herself as for them.

By inches, the wriggled the coffin out the window and Sam eased it down on its side. He began to lash the ropes to it at once as Mick hauled himself out of the corridor, his hands leaving bloody prints on the window frame.

"It's gonna get rough, buddy, but bear with us, okay? We're taking you home." Mick patted the coffin's side, leaving his mark there as well. He took the cords and wove them through the parachute harness.

"But Mick," Jo protested, easing the window shut with rubbery arms. "You can't do that, if the coffin falls…."

"If Harry goes, I go. We made that pact a long time ago. I should never have let him leave to start with. Ready, Sam?"

Sam scrambled over the coffin to get behind it and push. Mick took up the slack on the cords until the coffin rested at his heels. "Ready."

"All right then. Jo, you've got the gun?"

She stashed the suction cup and patted her hip. "Right here."

"Good. Let's get on with it."

Mick led, his shoulders straining from the very first step. He bore the full weight of the coffin until Sam could get beneath it. Jo waited, watching the corridor with her gun cocked and ready. The ladder groaned loudly and she feared it would not hold them all. But, after what seemed like hours, Mick and Sam began to crest the fullest part of the envelope.

The coffin shifted as gravity tugged it away from the airship's side. Mick's knuckles grew white as he clutched at the ladder.

"Help," he grunted.

Sam pushed with all his might, but the coffin swayed dangerously and threatened to take them all to the bottom of the lake.

"Hold on!" Jo holstered the gun and scrambled up the ladder after them. She swung around to the side of it, wrapping her legs around each side and shimmying up it like a drainpipe. She got around Sam and reached for the cording. With every muscle tensing, she pulled the coffin toward the ladder.

It was slow going. They inched up the fullest part of the great ship's side, each of them tugging against gravity's insistent pull. A hundred times, Jo thought her muscles would betray her and she'd let go of the rope, but she steadfastly clung to the ladder, moving in tandem with the two men hauling Harry's body, offering a small measure of stability to their climb.

The sun dipped below the cloudbank, warming them for a few minutes before vanishing again. There was no sunset, only the gloaming twilight and a very long climb ahead in the dark.

As they neared the larger catwalk above, the ships running lights kicked on, throwing everything into eerie shadows. Mick rolled into the planks, lying there gasping for a long moment while Sam and Jo bore up the coffin's weight. When he could breathe again, Mick rose to his knees and began to pull. Sam bowed his head and let the coffin rest on his shoulders, then began to climb once more. Jo could only continue to take up what weight she could as she clung to the ladder's edge.

The walkway was much wider there and the coffin was easy to bring up onto it. The three of them sank against the icy dew that cloaked the silk envelope of the airship. The ropes had bitten deep into Jo's left hand and the ladder had left bruises on her right.

"We only have to get it below the Saint Dismus, then we can winch it up the rest of the way." Sam looked at Jo. "You up for one more climb?"

She nodded. She wasn't. Not by any stretch of the imagination. But she wasn't going to let them down. Not Mick and Sam who had risked their lives on this venture a dozen times already. And not Harry. No, never Harry.

The single lead from the Eagle's top hung wet with dew in the dark. She gripped it and put the pain away. She hauled herself up, catching the knot below between her knees to rest her throbbing arms a moment. Foot by painful foot, Jo climbed, her heart battering against her ribs. Night had fully settled by the time she reached the rope ladder. She wished she could call for Cora and have her send down the winch, but there would be no one to hold the helm. They were one crewmember short.

She glanced down to the catwalk and sighed. They never could replace Harry.

The rope ladder was not as daunting and she quickly made it to the cabin, then up to the cabin loft beneath the air bladder of the Saint Dismus. Jo's fingers felt so numb she didn't know she'd nicked herself on the winch rigging until she felt the warmth of blood on her hands. Slowly, she cranked down the iron hook, hating the loud grate of the chain as it descended.

Someone rang the bell attached to the hook. It was an old bicycle bell. Three rings: they had contact. Four rings: they were secure. Two more rings: bring it up.

Jo pressed her weight against the handle and the blood welled up across her knuckles. Around and around, she cranked until she could hear her heart thundering and feel the muscles in her arms want to tear themselves apart. The loud bump of the coffin against the strutting came as a shock. Mick and Sam wearily climbed up after.

Together they lashed Harry's coffin to the roof of the cabin.

*****

If the Eagle gave chase, Jo never knew. She collapsed on the floor of the galley after Cora bandaged her hands. Mick and Sam were still beside her when she opened her eyes in the thin, gray dawn. She could smell stale coffee. Cora still stood at the helm, knees trembling and shoulders bunched. Jo could tell she'd been there all night, navigating them to safety.

"Take a break, Cora. I'll grab the helm."

"Make some fresh coffee. The gents should be up and around soon."

"Cora, it's been hours and hours."

"Seven and a half, to be precise. Coming onto the landing field."

"Well, let's get Sam or Mick up so we can land."

"I'll do it."

"Um, have you handed the float before?"

"Yes. Once."

"But…."

"I have to do this, Jo. I have to do this for Harry. Now go and make me some damned coffee, will you?"

"Okay. I can do that. Okay." Jo backed off, leaving Cora at the helm.

In the tiny galley, she stepped around Mick and Sam while she made a fresh pot of coffee. The scent woke them and they sat up stiffly.

"We got any patent medicine left in the first aid kit?" Sam stretched, twisting his back one direction then the other.

"I'll check and see."

"I just want a gun. And someone to shoot me in the head," Mick moaned and slumped against the wall.

"Cora says we're here. Should be landing in a minute or two."

Mick's eyes widened. "Cora's gonna land us?"

Jo handed him a mug of coffee. "She insists. For Harry." Her eyes darted up to the ceiling.

"Coming in," Cora called from the helm. "Hold on, just in case."

Mick sipped his coffee. "What the hell, if she kills us all, I'll die happy, or at least accomplished."

The Saint Dismus slowed and hovered, tilting back and forth a few times before bumping up against something solid that sent a shuddering wave through the whole cabin. Mick hauled himself to his feet and limped towards the main hatch, throwing it wide.

"Halloo!" He shouted down to the few people on the grounds at this early hour. They seemed less than interested in them.

"Submit yer paperwork to the chief." One of the ground crew jerked his head towards a small shack on the edge of the runway before meandering off.

"I'll handle it." Mick dragged out the ship's clipboard and ambled down the gangplank.

Cora leaned against the dashboard, staring up at the ceiling. Jo leaned out of the cabin.

"Hey, can I get a little help?"

One of the ground crew glanced up at her. "With what?"

"Bringing one of your boys home." Jo pointed to the pine coffin still tied securely down to the Saint Dismus' cabin roof. "It's been a helluva night and we could use a little extra muscle."

The fellow scuffed at the ground with a booted toe. "Well, we're Union…."

Jo rustled a dollar coin out of her pocket and flicked it towards the man. "We just need him down off the roof and maybe a vehicle to take him somewhere…suitable."

"Who is he?"

"Harry Argyle."

The man gripped the coin. "Argyle, you say?"

"Harry."

"Yeah, Mathias' son. I know him."

"We'd like to bring him home, if that's okay."

"Yeah. Lemme get the guys."

When Mick returned, Jo had already supervised the loading of Harry's coffin into a flatbed farm truck.

"Nice work," he told her. "Sure saved my hands another helluva workout."

"Where do you want him," the man, Dwight, asked.

Mick set his jaw and glanced out towards the lake. "Is there still a cemetery on the hill overlooking the beach?"

"You know this island well," Jo said.

"Harry and I were born here. I left before him, but he wasn't long to follow. Oh, Harry." Mick pressed his palm atop of Jo's scrawled writing. "Let's lay you to rest."

"We never did check," Cora said, haltingly.

"Does it matter at this point," Sam laughed, darkly. "If it ain't him, I can tell you that I ain't going back to that fed ship to pinch anther coffin."

"Please," Cora whispered.

"I thought you didn't want to see him like that." Jo crossed her arms, stepping between Cora and the coffin.

"Ladies, please, are you crew or cats?" Mick waved over one of the other runway crew. "Can I get a crowbar and a little help, here?"

Dwight obliged, putting his substantial weight behind the push. The pine lid creaked open with a gagging stench. Dwight dropped the crowbar and staggered back, but the Saint Dismus crew leaned in.

The body within had caved in on itself. Dirt and leaves still clung to the tattered remains of a heavy, army-issue wool coat. The flesh, once thawed, had purified and dissolved, staining the dark olive wool with a black and oily mess. There was no locket.

"Can we turn him?" Cora didn't look like she wanted to touch him. "To look for the tattoo?"

Mick reached in and took the body by the shoulder, but the bones came loose in his hands. "He's too far gone."

Jo craned her neck to look at the body to look at another angle. "Does it look right? Harry was taller, don't you think?"

"He's missing his legs from mid-shin down. And a big part of his head. He's going to look a little short."

"You folks gonna bury this poor sap? The foreman's going to be here soon."

They all looked towards Mick, even Cora.

"What do you want from me?" Mick ran his finger along the sleeve of the dead man's coat. "Harry, that you, brother?"

"Let's go." Jo shoved the coffin's lib back in place. "Harry was one of us. Let's do right by him."

*****

Jo thought she would never finish digging. But as the sun broke free of the steel grey clouds, they patted the last of the dirt on top of the fresh grave. Cora knelt back at the edge of the turned earth, tears streaming down her face. She hobbled away and returned with a handful of tiny white and purple wildflowers. They trickled from her shaking fingertips.

"Bless you, Harry. We loved you."

"And we still do." Jo bowed her head and murmured what small snatches of prayer she could recall from the convent school too many years ago.

Sam brought over a rough wooden cross fashioned from scraps of the coffin and a few other bits from the Saint Dismus. He had written HARRY across it with a fine, steady hand; much better than Mick or Cora could have done, or even Jo herself. Together, they crammed the marker into the head of the grave.

Lastly, Jo brought out the pair of iron manacles, the set that used to hang over the helm; the ship's lucky charm. She draped them around the cross.

"Rest in peace, Harry."

They shared a moment of silence before turning back towards the waiting ship. Mick slipped Dwight and his fellows a few more coins and bade them to watch over Harry until their return.

"Dwight says he has a brother running bother on fed ships up on Lake Erie, waterside. Says he might could use some sky support. He's going to send word about us, tell him we're coming."

Sam nodded. "Sounds promising."

Jo agreed. "But he better not send that word by pigeon."

"Why not? At least that way we'll eat!" Cora cracked a smile.

As Saint Dismus lifted off once more, turning east into the sun, the morning light shone down on the plot, casting a shadow of a cross and shackles upon the grave.

Engine 316

Nick Valentino

Horse hooves clomped against the dry Earth, the din so loud that it rattled the riders as if their heads were tin cans filled with rocks. The repetitive squeak of metal joints accompanied the roar as shiny metal leg braces latched to the horses flashed in the March sunlight.

Three men died to acquire the braces, but Rube Thornton was sure the sacrifice was worth the hardware. For short distances the braces enabled a fit horse to keep up with a train at full speed. Like Rube, the two men riding behind him were masked with bandanas, their tinted goggles pulled over their eyes and each man fitted with leather harnesses fashioned from ammunition bandoleers. The trio approached the caboose of the mighty L&N steam locomotive with a brass number 316 affixed over the back door. Rube pulled a long rifle with a clawed spear attached to the top and an oversized canister on the side. Holding the barrel in the air he signaled his band to pick up speed to match the train. The plume of dust behind the horses grew into a twenty-foot cloud.

Rube leaned into his horse and steadied the rifle. With a click of the trigger, the rifle popped and exhaled a whine of steam that fired the rope latched hook forward. The projectile slammed into the back of the caboose and penetrated the back door. Once the line was taut, Rube latched the rifle against his bandoleer. He glanced back at his men and pumped his fist in the air. On the third gesture all three men leaped off their horses. In a stomach jarring motion the men were pulled through the air and to caboose by their tethers slamming them against the back window, but landing them on the back platform without injury.

"I told you it would work," Rube barked over the clank of the train.

The other men got to their feet and withdrew their weapons including some oddly shaped handguns.

"This better be as good as you say, Rube. Those horses alone could have fetched us a pretty good price," the tallest and thinnest man in the group said.

Rube glared at the man. "It'll be good, Leonard. This is secret government property and if we can get it nothing, but an airship will stop us."

Another man removed his bandana revealing a scared and unshaven face. "Let's get it over with then. The Pinkertons were right on our heels at the train depot."

Rube nodded. "Okay then. Jim you take the front, then me, then Leonard."

Jim's lips tightened as he reared back and kicked the door to the caboose with a heavy boot. The lock cracked and the door flew inward.

Leonard lifted his tinted goggles. "Well, if there are soldiers guarding this thing, they know we're here now."

With his double-barreled pistol aimed forward, Jim rushed into the caboose nervously pointing his gun in every direction. Rube followed behind pulling his goggles around his neck.

"There should be someone here," Jim said.

Rube checked the front door that was locked. "Maybe the hook scared them off. The other door is locked."

The men inspected the small caboose room that was little more than a wooden car with a chair nailed to the floor and a small desk with an affixed oil lamp. A series of pipes extended across the ceiling and the words 'Always Be Prepared For Slack Action' was hand painted on the wall.

Rube pressed his revolver against the front door lock and fired. "On to the next car, gentlemen."

Leonard and Jim flinched at the unexpected shot. The gang had been robbing trains for two years and Rube's behavior became increasingly bold after each hold-up. The only reason he and his brother Jim started a life of crime was due to a massive crop failure on their farm in Texas. While Jim often teetered on quitting the gang while he still had his life, Rube's insistence that they move on to the next town and target sometimes seemed threatening. Each heist was slightly bigger than the last, but they never before had attempted something federal. If caught, the three remaining gang members were shoe-ins for the gallows.

With his pistol forward, Rube stepped out of the door to the caboose and back into the Alabama sunlight. He glanced down at the speeding tracks below and with a sudden move he leaped over the gap and onto the next train car. With his greasy brown hair flapping in the wind he turned and waved his gun at the two men in the caboose.

"Was that a threat?" Leonard asked.

"Don't know."

Jim stepped forward hopping over the gap and onto the small ledge of the silver cargo car with Rube. Leonard followed. Rube wiggled the door handle.

"It has multiple locks. I can feel it. Leonard, give me the safe opener."

Leonard reached into his hip bag and produced a wheeled device with a row of teeth in the middle like a giant spur and handed it to Rube. Rube inspected the saw blade teeth and gently inserted it in the jam or the door. Grabbing the lever, he wound it like a giant watch. The blades slowly turned making the safe opener roll along the side of the door like an oversized can opener. Jim grabbed the handle and helped his brother twist the lever making the opener split the door faster. After ten laborious minutes the last lock snapped. Rube handed the safe opener back to Leonard, drew his gun and put his shoulder into the door.

He stumbled into the dark train car and tripped over a cargo box on floor sending him to the ground. Leonard and Jim dashed in behind him with guns drawn.

Jim picked is brother up by the arm. "You alright?"

Rube winced as he stood. "Yeah."

The only light came from the door they just broke through illuminating the oversized train car. In the back was a huge object covered with a burlap tarp that fit in the car with only a few inches to spare. Lined up in front of the object were four human shaped metal sculptures.

Leonard cocked his head. "What the…"

Rube took a step forward. "Looks like suits of armor. But why-"

Before Rube could finish his sentence, the eyeholes in the suits of armor flashed with magnesium white light causing the gang to shield their faces. The grind of metal on metal creaked through the train car as the suits of armor rose to their feet.

"Shoot!" Rube yelled.

Still covering their faces, Rube's gang fired their handguns, bullets ricocheting off the thick iron walls. Complete blind chaos ensued. Rube tried to open his eyes, but the light from the figures burned as he tried to aim his weapon. He heard one of the suits fall hard against the floor, but he had no idea who shot it. The armored people machines stepped forward in unison.

"Get outside!" Rube ordered.

The men fumbled over themselves, but managed to find the door to the small ledge. Jim and Rube pressed their backs against the outer wall.

"What are those things?" Jim asked.

Before anyone could answer the metal grinding inside came to a halt and immediately followed with a barrage of gunshots. Bullets flew out of the door like a swarm of lead bees. Dozens of them slammed into Leonard lifting him off his feet and throwing him over the small security rail. Jim instinctively reached for him earning him a bullet through the top of his forearm, but Leonard's limp body flopped between the train cars and slipped under the caboose with a horrifying series of crunches.

More bullets zipped out of the open door, but after a few seconds the gun play stopped. Jim and Rube looked at each other with wide eyes.

Rube leaned into his brother's ear. "You okay?"

With tight lips, Jim nodded.

"Can you shoot?"

Jim glanced at his arm that was bleeding profusely and nodded again.

"On three then. One, two… three."

Rube crouched low around the door while Jim stuck his pistol over his brother's head. The eyes of the machines had faded into what looked like dying flash bulbs. The brothers quickly aimed and fired at the remaining lights. Only three were left standing and they hit two before emptying their guns. Jim holstered his gun and grabbed Rube by the shirt to pull him out of harms way. Another series of bullets flew through the door with a fraction of a second to spare.

Rube reached for a coil of rope looped on his belt. "Reload."

Jim dutifully snapped the fat cylinder of his revolver open and jammed bullets in as quickly as possible. With expert speed, Rube tied a slipknot in his rope.

"I'm up high, you shoot low. Ready? Go!"

Rube exposed himself in the door, raised his lasso and flung it at the last automaton. Just as the rope settled around the machine's head, Jim landed two shots; one in the shoulder and one in the chest, making it stagger backward. Rube yanked the lasso toward him and before it could get another shot off, it slammed into the floor.

Jim rushed in, jumped on the machine and shot it two more times in the head at point blank range. Sparks erupted like a miniature firework show illuminating the train car. Rube drew his gun and sauntered in inspecting the damage. A cloud of gunpowder filled the air barely leaving enough oxygen to breathe. Rube attempted to wave it out of the speeding train with his bandana, but it did little good.

"Are they all destroyed?" Rube coughed.

"Looks like it. I've never seen anything like this. What are they?"

Rube straddled one of the bullet-ridden guards turning its head with his boot. It looked up at him with two broken glass eyes. "I've heard about these things. Rich people have them as servants and maids. I didn't believe it really and I never would have thought they would be used as guards."

Jim wrapped his bleeding arm in his bandana and made another pass inspecting the automatons. "They're ugly bastards. That's for sure."

"That's the idea. They're made to look frightening."

"It's not so satisfying to kill something that ain't alive, especially when they shot up Leonard. Someone owes us a life."

Rube's lip curled. "Agreed."

"How much you think these things cost each?"

Rube grunted letting the automaton's head slump sideways. "It doesn't matter. That's not why we're here. We'll be able to get ample revenge with this."

Rube stepped over the broken machine and grabbed the enormous tarp in the back of the train car and pulled it aside revealing a tooth-grooved wheel as tall as his shoulders.

Jim's mouth fell open. "What is it?"

"Remember that army sergeant in Bellevue Texas?"

"Yeah. What about him?"

"He squealed about this so I wouldn't shoot him. He said it was a land ship. Like a Navy boat on wheels. He said nothing could stop it except a bomb. Bullets can't even penetrate it."

Rube pulled the tarp back further showing two massive gun barrels protruding from the iron plated land ship.

"It does look like a Navy ship," Jim exclaimed. "How does it run?"

"Coal and steam. The sergeant said the army got it from Lemuria and that's what they're going to be using on the front lines of their war. Little brother, we are going to have ourselves a pay day of a lifetime."

"I'll never understand why the Germans would change their name."

"I guess its part of their plan; it makes them a new country in their eyes."

"Well, what do you want to do with this thing? Sell it back to the government?"

Rube glared at Jim. "We're going to do much more than that. I've got information that the government has been hiding bars of gold at Fort Duffield in Kentucky. We're going to ride this train all the way to the Louisville stop and drive this thing right into the fort. If it has as much firepower as I was told it should an easy job."

"Why didn't you tell me or any of us about all of this?"

"No one needed to know. One squealer and the whole plan would be thrown to the dogs."

"And how do you plan on moving the gold once we've broken in? The whole army will be after us."

Rube smiled and stroked his thin mustache. "I have an airship coming that can hold millions of greenbacks worth of gold. We're flying it to Mexico and we are done. Now that Leonard is gone, we split it three ways, you, me and the airship pilot."

Jim's heart raced. What he thought was a routine train robbery with new horse speed braces turned into a complete government heist and retirement plan to Mexico. Rube was always the planner of the two, but Jim never would have thought a simple farmer could turn into such a criminal mastermind.

"I'm impressed. So this is it? This is our last heist."

Rube bit his lip. "Afraid so. Everyone in the gang has been killed or caught. I figure we better quit before we end up the same way. If we can do this we'll be the most famous outlaws in the world... and the richest."

Jim smiled and embraced his brother. "Let's do it, Rube."

The men tied the door to the train car shut with Rube's lasso and after prying an oil lamp from the wall they set about inspecting the land ship. The innards of the beast were cramped and could hold about four men. There was a driver's seat, a station for a lookout, a gunner's post and a spot in the rear to feed the boiler. The machine was stocked with coal and compression tanks were filled and connected to the massive guns around the sides. The machine even had wooden boxes of ammunition labeled with the Lemurian seal of the dragon.

"Rube, what does Sprenggranate mean?"

Rube sat in the driver's seat attempting to figure out what the levers and pressure gauges would do. It seemed much more complex than he imagined. "No idea, Jim. What's it on?"

"A box of cannon balls."

"Well, don't worry about it until you have to shoot one. Do you know how to shoot one of those things?"

Jim paused. "Not really. I assume it's like any other pressure machine."

Rube wanted to chastise his brother, but thought it unwise to say anything discouraging. "Well, keep studying it. We'll be in Louisville by the evening for sure and you'll need to know how to fire those cannons."

*****

As the warm air of the day gave way to the chill of dusk, the L&N train began to slow. Houses and buildings became more frequent as the train made a large turn into a dirty city with a large hill at its center.

A high-pitched squeal emanated through the train car. Rube's head snapped up from the steering controls of the land ship. "We're slowing down. That sound is the breaks."

"Are we in Louisville?"

"No. It's too early. We're at least a few hours away." Rube pulled his timepiece from his pocket. "Maybe three hours."

The train rattled and vibrated harder as it continued to slow.

"What are we going to do? Where are we?" Jim asked.

Rube looked around the small confines of the land ship. "I don't know, Nashville maybe? They will surely inspect this car if we completely stop."

Jim paced back and forth with his hands on his head.

"Get ready Jim. We're going to have to drive this thing sooner than we thought."

"Rube, we can't just take this all the way to Fort Duffield. We should run now."

Rube slammed his fists against the steering controls. He bit his lip and thought about their situation. As much as he didn't want to give up his marvel of machinery he knew Jim was right. If they took the land ship out now the odds of survival were slim to none.

"Damnit. Okay come on, grab your gun and let's get out of here Jim."

The two scrambled out of the top hatch of the land ship and into the dark train car. The engine significantly slowed and Rube unwound the rope on the door and peered out into the night. Dim lights glowed from clusters of inner city buildings that consisted of a strange mix of shanties uncomfortably placed between multi-storied brick structures.

As the train squeaked to a stop Rube and Jim stepped out on the small walkway on the rear of the train car. They were in a train yard that located in a gulch in the city. Surrounded by motionless trains the two hopped off and weaved their way through the maze of locomotives. Clouds of low hanging steam from inert steam engines hung in the air making the gas and oil lights blur around the train station.

"Where are we going?" Jim asked.

Rube paused and quickly surveyed the scene. "Anywhere is good. Maybe we can make it deeper into downtown. This is definitely Nashville."

Rube led his brother down the tracks in hopes to find an outlet to escape into the city. Dozens of trains surrounded them and Rube heard near by voices. He grabbed Jim by the shirt and pressed him against the nearest train car. "Shh."

The voices faded for a moment and Rube took a minute to glance around their hiding place. He nodded his head to keep moving. The brothers circled the steam engine when the saw two men loading a crate on a platform.

"Hey! Wait! Stop! I know you," a voice called from above.

Rube and Jim's head snapped up simultaneously to see a conductor staring at them through the open window of the engine.

Jim pulled out his gun, but Rube grabbed his brother's hand. "Don't shoot!"

His voice rang across the train yard. It might as well have been a gunshot. The two men dropped the crate, looked at Rube and Jim and dashed up a series of iron steps out of harm's way. Immediately, people began to emerge from the train station and silhouettes of curious lookers appeared in the train station windows.

Jim got his hand free and fired a shot toward the conductor that rang off the iron steam pipe.

Rube panicked. "Back to the car!"

Jim wanted to shoot at the onlookers indiscriminately so they would look away, but his brother already put several yards between them. He turned and sprinted to catch up to his brother.

Rube was lost in the mass of train cars. Most of them looked the same and he wasn't sure where they came from. "What was the number? What was the train number he saw in that Alabama field?" He thought to himself.

The voices grew into shouts as people from above directed yard workers and possibly policemen to Rube and Jim's whereabouts. The brothers rounded a few trains, Rube looking at each number he passed hoping to recognize the digits. Loud footsteps banged against the metal stairs of the train station and the shouting grew from a few men to what sounded like dozens.

Rube drew his gun, but just before he spun around to find a firing position, he noticed a great red and black steam engine with the number 316 over the window staring him right in the face. "Jim! This is it!"

Jim's eyes were wide. Rube wasn't sure Jim comprehended what he was saying, but his little brother followed him regardless. They ran down the train cars until they saw the caboose and Rube with gun held forward hopped back on the car with the broken door and into the black car. Tripping over the smashed automatons the brothers scurried over the debris and climbed up the land ship. An orange glow emanated from the top hatch as Jim had left the oil lamp burning inside the vehicle. Rube would normally chastise his brother for such an action, but this time the light was a welcome mistake.

"Start it up and load those guns!" Rube ordered.

Jim opened the coal box that was already full and fumbled with a tin box of matches. Rube jumped in the driver's seat and clutched what he thought were the forward and reverse controls. Jim lit three matches and threw them into the coal that caught fire instantly due to some sort of liquid accelerator.

"The fire's started, but it will take a few minutes before we get any power," Jim sputtered.

Rube looked back at his panic stricken brother. "Close the door and work the lever next it to pump the heat in the water. It's just like those new tractors back at the farm."

Jim did as he was told and latched the iron door then pushed and pulled the lever that pumped compressed air into the heat source. After a few minutes of hard work the water began to boil inside the armored cylinder. The voices increased in volume. They were surrounded and the only way out was if Rube could get the vehicle moving. He pulled the long lever next to him that made a row of glass spheres illuminate inside the cabin. He grabbed the two sticks in front of him and pushed them forward. The land ship blasted out a deafening screech of steam and lurched forward inside the train car scraping the side of the train car wall. Rube pulled the sticks back to the middle position and thrust them forward again. Again, the land ship's engine screamed and with full force, the spiked wheels dug in the floor and rolled forward. It was slow at first, but in the few seconds it took to reach the back of the train car, the machine was rolling quickly. A head splitting sound of metal ripping metal made Rube's eyes vibrate causing him instant nausea.

Before he knew what he'd done the land ship crashed through the back of the train car tearing it open like a tin can. It continued to roll smashing into the caboose that lifted the front end of the machine into the air. Rube was sure the thing would flip over, but it continued to move forward. The wheels gripped the caboose walls and climbed upward until the weight collapsed the last train car completely. Dozens of voices screamed and shouted from outside. Rube tried to ignore them staring into the darkness from the tiny slit cut in the machine to guide the land ship.

Jim had fallen down, but was huddled over a box of ammunition that he somehow managed to pry open. The land ship bucked as it rolled over the rest of the train and Rube jerked the controls to the left. He aimed for an embankment of the gulch right next to the station building. He had no idea where he was going, but it was the only spot he could see that didn't have a train blocking his path. The sounds of bullets pinged off the side of the machine. Unsure what the land ship could actually withstand, he pushed the controls forward as far as they could go making the pressure gauges around him spike in unison.

Flashes from gunfire briefly lit the surroundings like smoky flashbulbs from a camera. Rube's mind swirled trying to concentrate on reaching the embankment that in a few seconds he hit and rolled up quickly. It didn't matter what he did; if caught the Thornton brothers would surely be hanged. Even though the chances were slim this was the only way out. If he couldn't plow his way to safety maybe he could strike a deal for the return of the land ship for him and his brother's lives.

Once the mechanical beast leveled off, Rube glanced back at Jim who was trying to get to his feet with a round shot the size of a grapefruit cupped in his hands. "Get that loaded!"

Jim stood as quickly as he could, tripping over his own feet. Pressing his shoulder into the wall he steadied himself and slid the iron ball into the cannon breach. He closed the door and twisted the pressure nozzle attached to the back.

"I think it's ready!" Jim yelled.

Rube plowed up a cobblestone street next to the train station and toward a large thoroughfare he glimpsed. There wasn't much to see through the driving slit, but Rube knew there were people all around him, many of them still firing their weapons.

"There are people all around us. Just fire the cannon!"

Jim gripped the handles on the cannon and tried to look down the barrel to aim. With only a confusing mix of blackness and distant building lights, Jim pulled the finger trigger. The cannon rocked violently with a quick whooshing suction sound and quickly blasted a single shot that deafened the men inside the land ship. The shot rushed through the air and slammed through the train station doors. A second later, the shell exploded sending a shock wave through the first floor followed by a ball of fire that spilled through the windows.

The sound alone made Rube let go of the controls to cover his ears. He stood up from the driver's seat while the land ship still rolled forward and looked at Jim who had fallen on the floor again. "Get up! Get up!"

Jim didn't hear him. The ringing in the brother's ears overpowered any other sound. Rube came to his senses realizing he left the machine running. Falling back in the seat, he peered through the slit and pulled the controls to the side to correct their path. As the ringing in his ears began to subside, a new barrage of bullets tickled the land ship's armor.

"Jim if you can hear me, load the cannon and fire it again!"

Jim said something back, but Rube couldn't understand him. The land ship turned the corner and onto a wide street lined with businesses and packed with people and horses. Utter chaos had ensued on the streets people were running in every direction to avoid the mechanical monster. Even through his stinging ears, Rube could hear the cries from the people around him. It was as if the entire town was yelling. The controls were crude so it took a lot of strength just to get the thing to turn so Rube went straight down the road into the heart of downtown.

Out of nowhere the whooshing sound came again and another shot rang from the land ship. This time the shell hurtled down the street and ultimately hitting a feed store that erupted into a large cloud of debris and without warning collapsed in on itself. Fiery beams and chunks of stone rolled onto the street enveloping everything on the street. Rube turned the controls again and snapped through an electric guide wire for a trolley car sending sparks flying into the night sky that rained down like a fire breathing dragon. Rube couldn't help wondering of the residents that were trampling each other to get out of the way thought that the devil himself had emerged from the train yard. Rube's attitude changed. It didn't look like there was anywhere to drive this machine to safety. In a maddening moment, he embraced the power he now possessed, even if it was only for a short time.

In a last ditch effort to keep moving, Rube turned the land ship down a smaller street and up toward a series of fancier buildings. "Jim, can you give me another shot?"

Jim had already gotten another shell out of the wooden crate, but his spirit looked broken. Even in the dim light of the cabin, Rube could see he was covered in sweat and possible blood. Jim acted on his brother's orders alone for survival. The new street was devoid of people which gave Rube some room to maneuver without rolling over anyone. He just had to make sure he didn't run into a building.

Just as Rube took a heavy breath of hope for escape, soft thuds followed by boot steps rumbled around the land ship. Strange cracked voices echoed from outside.

"Target acquired."

"Roger. Initiating sequence."

"…Neutralization in progress."

"What's that Rube? What's going on?" Jim yelled.

Rube looked through the slit, but was only confused by the motion outside the machine. "Someone's on the land ship! Get your gun!"

Before Rube could pull the pistol from his holster, a chrome object the size of a small candlestick struck him in the shoulder and clunked on the floor.

"What the…"

A flash of blinding white light filled the innards of the land ship. Pressure engulfed Rube's body making him squeeze his head to stop the pain. Unknowingly, he kicked the controls and the machine careened into a building. The pain from the light explosion made the impact a minor inconvenience. Rube rolled out of the seat and onto the floor where he pressed his head even tighter hoping the pain would subside. The land ship came to a halt as the sound of bricks thundered against the armor. Only a few lights remained lit inside, but Rube could see his motionless brother next to the cannon. As he squirmed on the floor two men jumped inside the land ship from the top hatch. Rube was sure he was dead and seeing the grim reaper himself. The men dressed in tight black clothes with smooth black helmets that covered their faces held huge indescribable rifles, the likes of which he'd never seen.

"One neutralized, one conscious," the reaper closest to Rube said.

Rube coughed blood as the reaper pulled a black box off his belt and held it toward him. A high-pitched whine sounded from the box and Rube felt a sting in his shoulder. Next a wave of pain shot though his body burning every muscle, shaking him uncontrollably. The seconds felt like minutes of the most intense pain Rube could comprehend. His mind went white as his last thought was that death was much more painful than he imagined.

*****

Rube coughed again waking him up, his spittle pink with blood. White light from the ceiling burned his swollen eyes. He blinked repeatedly trying to get his bearings. He tried to wipe his face, but his hands were strapped to the arms of a chair with a soft, but firm material. He sucked in a panicked breath realizing that his head and legs were also strapped to the chair. Although he couldn't turn his head he could see his brother still motionless strapped to a chair next to him. The room was most peculiar. The walls were covered in stark white tile and the light from the ceiling came from strange long tubes affixed to metal rectangles. There wasn't a window at all just tile-covered walls and a single door with a tiny barred hole in the top.

Clicking sounds came from the door and it slowly opened. A rotund man with a bushy mustache walked in. He wore a suit jacket, a formal knotted tie and thin oval spectacles. Rube thought he appeared to come from a fancy supper.

"Rube and James Thornton," the man said. "You boys have caused quite a fuss. You know you're quite famous for your train robberies. Lucky for us you stuck your nose in the wrong place."

Rube said the first thing that came to his mind. "I'm in Hell aren't I?"

The man belly laughed. "Not yet."

"What's this all about then? Is my brother alive?"

"Yes your brother is alive. Life is going to change for you both Mister Thornton. Somehow your simple robbery has gotten the attention of some very important people. Let me introduce myself; my name is James McKenna. I'm associated with The Pinkerton National Detective Agency."

"What about those grim reapers? Who were they? What happened to me and my brother?"

McKenna chuckled again. "Grim reapers, eh? Some would call them that. See, Mister Thornton, you saw something that you were never supposed to see. Actually, you operated something you should have never touched."

"The land ship?"

"I have no idea how you ever heard about that thing. I imagine that you stumbled upon it with sheer dumb luck, but to actually get in it and try to drive it? My boy, what were you thinking?"

Rube felt the need to spill any information he possessed in hopes of getting some favorable treatment. "I thought my boys and I could rob the bars of gold at Fort Duffield in Kentucky with it. This was our last heist. Honest. We were going to retire in Mexico after that."

McKenna's eyebrow raised forming a sharp point on his head. "Good lord! You know about Fort Duffield as well? The fellows are going to have a ball asking you questions."

"What does that mean? I'll tell you whatever you want," Rube pleaded.

McKenna cleared his throat. "Don't grovel Mister Thornton. I'll level with you. The Pinkerton National Detective Agency is a group of people that have protected the United States throughout its history. We look out for the best interests of this country and we have no bounds. The men that collected you, the reapers as you call them, are not of this time. They're from a distant time that I'm guessing you can't understand."

"I don't understand," Rube agreed.

"They are from a future time, my dull headed boy. See, the United States needs to constantly progress and sometimes the Pinkertons are called upon to make sure that our newly reunited country does so at an accelerated rate. What you just drove through the city was an advanced Lemurian tank being shipped to a new facility to be copied for our military use."

"A...tank?"

"That's what they call it in later days," McKenna said.

"You're telling me those reapers are from the future? As in twenty years from now? How is that possible?"

"Much further than twenty years from now."

"Why are you telling me this? Are you going to kill us?"

"Not literally, Mister Thornton. Your death will be reported in the papers and on official record as occurring on October 9th 1890 by being gunned down in the streets of Linden, Alabama. Your brother's obituary will read that he will die next year on October 5th 1888 of consumption in jail."

"How do you know this? What are you going to do with us?"

"They've decided to take you with them, Mister Thornton. You and your brother will disappear from this time and never be heard from again. We have a story already written for the rest of your lives here in 1887."

Rube shuddered. "What are they going to do with us?"

"That I don't know, Mister Thornton. Let's hope it's more pleasant than the gallows which is all you would get if you remained here."

A knock came from the door.

McKenna's face lit up. "Ah, they're here. I'm sorry you got into this mess, Mister Thornton. Consider yourself lucky. You get to see something that few men get to witness. The future."

McKenna turned and opened the door. A thin man with a white coat and a white cone shaped mask over his nose and mouth walked in holding a glass syringe. McKenna left the room shutting the door behind him and the man in white kneeled next to Rube who was literally shaking in his bonds.

"Wha... What are you going to do to me?"

The man in white didn't speak. He calmly rolled up Rube's sleeve rubbed his arm with alcohol and slid the needle into a vein in his arm. Rube tried to fight against his restraints, but nothing budged.

Rube instantly felt sleepy. His eyes began to close involuntarily. "You... have to tell... me..."

The man in the white coat stood and locked eyes with Rube. "You killed a lot of people today Mister Thornton. When you wake, Hell will take on a whole new meaning. You will wish the gallows were your fate for the rest of your days."

Rube tried to speak, but the drug prevented him from opening his mouth. He struggled fruitlessly against his bonds, but his limbs felt like a hundred pounds each. Rube's eyes flickered, his last vision as he fell unconscious were of the horrors that awaited him in another time. In one day, a once great train robber, Rube Thornton was now thrust into the dark unknown of a time not yet happened. Man's ultimate Hell.

An Odd Demise

Allan Gilbreath

Last night lied to me. The night sky had a lovely rosy hue to it as the sun sank behind the rooftops. I believe the rhyme goes "A red sky at night and tomorrow a delight. Red sky in the morning, please take warning." The look on the sergeant's face told me it should have been a red morning.

"Begging your pardon, Sir." The sergeant stopped speaking until I fully met his gaze. I knew of this man. He always carried himself with the dignity of his station. "The Chief Inspector has asked for you personally."

I rose and gestured slightly towards the door. "Do you know why he is asking for me?"

"I suspect it has to do with that bit of unpleasant business in Covent Gardens this morning. The whole affair sounds a bit unnatural, if you take my meaning, Sir."

I followed him down the hallway to the Chief Inspector's office. Covent Gardens has had an unsavory reputation for decades. The whole area is infested with a wide variety of mankind's basest of indulgences and sins. We are gradually reforming the area, but old traditions die hard. As we reached the door, the sergeant opened it for me and stood aside for me to pass.

"Thank you, Sergeant." I nodded to him. Being an inspector meant that you had spent a number of years in uniform. Some inspectors seem to forget that fact. I don't. I entered to find the Chief Inspector sitting behind his very organized desk with a pensive look on his face. "Good morning, Sir. You asked for me?"

"Yes, James, I did. You are doing well I assume?"

"Yes, Sir. Doing quite well. I believe we are making excellent progress in the community."

"Ah, yes. The community." He stopped and stroked his gray moustache in a thoughtful manner. He seemed to be choosing his words very carefully. "That is why I asked for you this morning."

"Yes, Sir." My curiosity had been peaked back with the sergeant. Now, this case obviously had ramifications if it was garnering attention at this level. The Chief Inspector motioned for me to sit down while he thought.

"I have a driver waiting for you. We've been called to a case that I need solved in a reasonable manner. From what I have been told, there is already speculation of unnatural forces at work. That is the last thing we need in this day and age." He clasped his hands and pressed them to his lips for a moment before continuing. "Such talk undermines rules and authority. So, I can't have the Commissioner having to explain that Welch witches, black magic, crazed gypsies, or evil Masonic plots are responsible. Am I making myself clear?"

"I believe so, Sir. May I ask the nature of this issue?"

"Actually, I don't want to influence you before you begin your investigation. Use whatever resources you find prudent and keep me informed of your progress." The Chief Inspector stood and walked me to the door. "I do mean any and prudent. I will be checking."

"Thank you for your confidence, Sir. I will do my best." I stood. Opportunities like this make or break careers for most inspectors. I clearly saw that in the Chief Inspector's eyes.

"I know you will. Thank you, James."

The sergeant pulled the door closed after I stepped into the hall. Just what was the Chief Inspector getting me into? I know I have a funny reputation for taking lots of notes and performing a wide range of interviews. I have always found that if you ask enough people enough questions, you will find a way through the lies and misdirection. I also caught the veiled reference to my association with a known intellectual and inventor. We were children together and have kept each other's company all these years. Yes, he would be prudent.

"Sir, the driver is at the front."

"Sergeant, I just need to grab my pad and then we will go and see this mystery."

The sergeant looked at me. "We, Sir?"

I smiled at the man. "We, Sergeant Heston. The Chief Inspector said for me to use any resource that I find prudent. As you seem to already have some knowledge and opinion of what I am about to see, you will be coming with me."

The sergeant looked halfway between shocked and making a run for it. He took a deep breath and resigned himself to his fate. "Yes, Sir."

*****

Sergeant Heston stepped out of the carriage first and stood aside for me. The dilapidated boarding house loomed ominously in front of us. A quick glance up and down the block revealed more of the same. In better neighborhoods, people have a tendency to gather and watch anytime that a number of officers are present. In neighborhoods like this one, people will stop and watch for a moment. However, as soon as they come to the attention of an officer, they lower their eyes and move on as quickly as they can without arousing suspicion.

"This way, Sir." An officer prompted me to enter the squalled building. I flipped open my notepad and began recording my thoughts on the environment. While the interior was slightly better than the exterior, I had no intention of touching anything I didn't have to. We walked up a flight of stairs and arrived at an open door with a few officers standing just inside the room. The senior officer saw me in the doorway.

"We were told to expect you, Inspector Peele." The officer motioned to the contents of the room. "We've made sure to keep the contents unmolested."

"Thank you, officer. That was very good of you to do so." I honestly expected to see a body by now. Instead, I looked around at a dingy, yellowed, threadbare flat. "What do we have here?"

All of the officers looked uncomfortable at my question. The senior officer took the lead. "This is the domicile of Mr. Cedric Clarke. We responded to a complaint by the landlady. She feared that something had happened to her tenant."

I noticed that the other officers kept looking away from us so I followed their eyes deeper into the flat to where a chair should have been sitting at a small table. I walked closer. "Is this what was found?"

The senior officer swallowed hard and answered, "I'm afraid so, Sir."

I stepped up the edge of an area of tile floor covered in scorch and ash. In the center of the area lay the end of a chair leg and a workman's boot. I turned the chair leg over and about with the back side of my pen. The top showed the char of a bit of wood fallen from the fireplace, otherwise, I couldn't see anything spectacular about it. The leather at the top of the boot also showed a similar exposure to heat. I pushed it about from one side to another. It felt oddly heavy. As I pulled it towards me, a faint curl of smoke wisped from the inside. Still with my pen, I pulled the boot around to the point where I could look inside. I sank slowly to one knee as I tried to make sense of what I saw. The boot was still occupied. Looking down the leather tunnel, I could clearly make out the top of the shinbone and the surrounding flesh. Not surprisingly, the contents looked as charred as the chair leg. The words of the Chief Inspector now made perfect sense. The local press was going to make a complete spectacle of this. I rubbed my chin thoughtfully. Yes, I was going to have to find a reasonable solution to this, quickly.

"Sergeant, would you mind asking the landlady for a few bags, a whisk, and a dustpan. We need to gather all this up. Put everything in separate bags as possible."

"Yes, Sir."

Sergeant Heston gave the other officers in the room a bit of a shrug as he headed downstairs. While I waited on his return, I examined the rest of the flat. All the walls had a sooty yellowed look to them. All the windows, mirrors, and glassware possessed an oily coating of some type. The doors were all intact. As an odd note, the entryway door even had a padded draft catcher at the bottom. Nothing else in the flat looked burned. Even the table sitting close to the scorched areas was intact. The surface possessed an interesting array of scratches, gouges, and other damage, but nothing singed. I didn't know what it would take to burn away a human body, but I was fairly certain that there had not been an immense bonfire in the center of this room. I could see no evidence of a wife or children, so our dearly departed was a bachelor. Judging by the wardrobe, he was a common man, a laborer at best, but, more likely, a man of darker character. The fact that there was half a bottle of strong spirits and four glasses on the table spoke to his less than temperate nature.

The mantelpiece took my attention. The heavy candles appeared softened, wilted if you will, as if they had been left on a sunny window ledge too long. I carefully jotted down each fact that I felt I might wish to look over later. I had just finished my last entry when Sergeant Heston walked into the flat carrying the items I requested. I noticed he had an uncertain look on his face.

"Thank you, Sergeant. If you don't mind, please give me a hand." I decided to give all the gathered officers a lesson and let the poor sergeant off the hook, so to speak. I pulled down my sleeve over my fingers to avoid touching the items. They may be coated with something, not to mention the uneasy feeling of picking up a disembodied foot. We put the chair leg and the boot in separate bags. Then, I swept up the char and ash and we placed it in a third bag. "Sergeant Heston, please take these down to the carriage. I will be along shortly."

I turned to the senior officer. "If would you be so kind as to escort me to the landlady, I have a few questions for her."

The senior office stood to an informal attention. "Please, come this way, Sir."

I followed him out of the flat and down the stairs to an equally distressed flat on the lower floor. The senior officer nodded to his junior at the door as he passed. The younger man stepped back a bit to let me pass. The senior officer did the introductions. "Inspector James Peele, this is Mrs. Margot Emms, the landlady. Mrs. Emms, the inspector has a few questions for you."

The poor woman looked like a rabbit in a snare. I decided to try to put her at ease. "Mrs. Emms, I know it has been a very trying day so far. I will try to keep my inquiries brief. May we sit?"

She looked at me oddly, as if expecting rough treatment, then looked relieved. "Oh, where are my manners. Please sit, sit."

I didn't embarrass her by dusting off the chair. I just made a mental note to send the pants out for a cleaning and pressing at the end of this day. Once we had both been seated, I turned to a clean page. "I am sure, by now, that you know we have a bit of unfortunate business."

"Yes, Sir. My boy's the one that found all this."

"How did he find all this?"

"Well, every morning, he makes the rounds prompt like at 7:00 and knocks on all the doors so everyone knows the work day is here. When he got to Mr. Clark's room, he noticed that the door knob was warm. Not burning hot, mind you, but warm enough to come tell me. I tell you, it's unnatural it is."

"What is? Please go on." The truth is more likely that the boy makes his rounds just before dawn so that those who need to be up and out can be gone before they are noticed.

"Well, I went up and that knob was warm in the hand. I used me pass key and opened it up. That's when I saw that boot just sitting there with a bit of smoke coming out of it. It's like the Devil himself come in here to claim that man."

"How was the condition of the room when you opened the door?"

"It wasn't flaming or anything like that. My late husband had put the tile in the rooms when we took this place. Said it made it easier to wash out after the tenant left."

I had to agree, the tile floor made it much easier to conceal a wide variety of activities. I kept taking notes; some had to do with her answers others had to do with what I could see. She had a peephole in her front door and from her vantage point she could see everyone who came and went from the main door. "Do you happen to know what time Mr. Clarke arrived last night?"

Mrs. Emms leaned in towards me and gave me a bit of a half wink. She had seen me notice the hole in her door. "They don't know I can see the comings and goings around here. Mr. Clarke wasn't exactly most timid of tenants. He's bit fond of his darts, cards, and his drink. However, I heard him come in early for him, around midnight."

"Did he come home alone or have any callers?"

"Oh, he came in with his three mates, but they didn't stay too long. I try to run a respectable house."

"I am sure you do." I agreed with her and kept her talking. "Do you happen to know what Mr. Clarke did for his living?"

She shifted around in her chair. I could tell we had reached the point in the questions where she would have to start editing the truth to cover her own indiscretions. I have made it a habit to respectfully watch people's faces as they talk. Card players say that everyone gives away their cards in the eyes. I find that something in the face will always betray you.

"I believe Mr. Clarke found work down at the market or at the Royal. He always paid his rent on time." Mrs. Emms looked happy with her answer. I find it interesting that people that are used to being a bit dodgy will provide you with some type of personal testimonial that actually has nothing to do with the question, but sounds like it may have something to do it. The truth was that he was most likely a laborer, card player, and a hustler. The Royal was a pub known for its dubious activities.

"Just a few more questions if you don't mind." She nodded so I continued. "Would you happen to know the names of the gentlemen that visited last night and the name of your clergyman? I would like to personally ask him to stop by and make sure that we have made your facility truly safe. I would also like him to see the other gentlemen, just in case." I knew she wouldn't give me the names if I asked a straight question. By adding the clergyman and the thought of something unnatural, she should be more than happy to give me the information I needed, eventually.

"Oh, I see Pastor Hayes. Do you know him?"

I smiled. "Yes, I am sure that we do. I will send word for him to stop by. Who else does he need to see about this unfortunate event?"

After several more minutes of verbal dodging, she finally gave into her fears of the supernatural and gave me the names. All the while, I kept making notes. Periodically, I would glance up at the officers at the door. The looks on their faces indicated to me that they might have taken a bit more direct approach to the interrogation. I will trust my information above the other methods. At length, I concluded that Mrs. Emms had no further useful information for me. I wasn't concerned with whatever petty plots may be going on here. I had a cremated mystery to solve.

"Mrs. Emms, thank you so much for your time. I will endeavor to resolve this matter as soon as possible." I rose to my feet and extended my hand. Mrs. Emms took it with slight apprehension. I could tell she was trying to discern what she might have told me or not. "You have been a great help."

"Thank you, Inspector." She cast me a quick glance under the pleasant face. She would be very happy to have our presence out of her house.

I walked directly towards the front of the boarding house and out to the carriage. Once clear of Mrs. Emms' earshot, I pulled a page out of my notebook and handed it to the senior officer. "Please take a few of your lads over to the Royal and see if you can find these men. I will need to interview each of them. I should be along in about an hour or two."

He looked over the list. "We're acquainted with these gentlemen. It shouldn't take us too long. We'll bring them down to the station for you."

I thought about that for a moment. "Actually, I would prefer to speak with them at the Royal if I could."

The bemused look on the senior officer's face told me that he had been warned that I was an odd one. No matter, I had been instructed to bring this case to a reasonable end and that was what I intended to do.

"As you say, Sir." The senior officer took my nod as permission to carry on. I then joined Sergeant Heston at the carriage. I wrote an address on a piece of paper and handed it to the driver.

As I entered, I could see Sergeant Heston watching the bags as if he expected serpents to slither forth at any moment.

"Sir, are we taking the remains to the undertaker?" Sergeant Heston asked hopefully.

I smiled at the question. "No, Sergeant, we are not. We're off to see a friend of mine who may be able to shed a little light on this event. I would like to hear your opinion while we travel."

The poor sergeant looked uncomfortable at expressing his opinion, but like any good man in the field, he soldiered up. "My opinion, Sir." He took a deep breath and looked hard at the bags. "Sir, I am afraid that this all looks very unnatural. I've family out in the countryside and it takes a serious fire to burn away the chicken bones left over from dinner. I'm not sure what I think."

"Sergeant, I happen to agree with you completely." I have to admit that I enjoyed the shocked look on the man's face. "It does look unnatural. This means that there is some component to this affair we haven't seen yet. When we find the missing piece, it won't look so mysterious."

"So you are suspecting foul play as opposed to devilish intervention?"

"Sergeant, I think when we interview these mates of his we will find that at least one of them will guide us to a reasonable solution."

He nodded affirmatively to my assertion and we finished the last few minutes of the ride in a professional silence.

As the carriage came to a stop, once again, Sergeant Heston got out first and held the door for me. We stood in front of the Essex Machine Shop. A man wearing goggles and a kerchief over his mouth leaned into the open doorway at our approach. We could hear him call out into the building that they had visitors. By the time we reached the open doorway, a lean man with tousled hair, rolled up sleeves, and a sweaty brow approached excitedly.

"James, come in. Come in. So good to see you." Duncan Essex, proprietor, extended to me his slightly oil stained hand. We shook warmly.

"Duncan Essex, I would like to introduce Sergeant Heston. He is assisting me with an inquiry today."

Sergeant Heston shook his hand. "A pleasure, Sir."

"This must be a very interesting inquiry or have I been up to something I shouldn't have been?" Duncan motioned us to follow him deeper into the building as he spoke.

We walked by the gentleman we saw at the door. He was loosening bolts on some kind of device that looked like the Lord of the Underworld himself had designed it. I couldn't even begin to guess what purpose such a diabolical device could serve. Sergeant Heston stared unabashed.

Duncan stopped at a mostly clear workbench. "I assume that you have something for me in the bags."

"I must warn you, you are about to see something both horrible and fascinating." I took the bags from the sergeant and placed them on the table. "We have a bit of unpleasant business this morning." I picked up a rag from the table and opened the first bag. I laid the chair leg out on the table.

"A house fire is enough to be a situation of interest to the CID?" Duncan looked at the chair leg without impression.

"No, we are talking about something far more bizarre." I opened the second bag and, using the rag, set the boot on the table. I waited in silence for Duncan to make the same discovery I did.

"Is that what I think it is?" Duncan looked from me to the sergeant then back to the boot.

"I am afraid so."

Duncan grabbed on his leather gloves and searched about for a pair of tongs. "May I?"

I nodded affirmatively. Duncan gripped the heel as he slipped the tongs into the boot. After a series of tugs, twists, and long pulls, the socked foot emerged to the light of day. Involuntarily, both the sergeant and I took a step back. Duncan, on the other hand, seemed completely enthralled by the gruesome artifact. He turned it this way and that. The sock had been worn to the end of its usefulness and one could clearly see that Cedric had been in need of a pedicure.

"I think you see why I came to you. I need to know how something like this can happen without burning down the building. I have plenty of notes about the scene and …"

A great noise rose up like some mechanical beast roaring to be fed and overwhelmed us from the front of the shop. The hideous machine we passed on the way in had been activated. The Johnny bar swung back and forth like the one on a train engine while the savage metallic jaws began to leap forward and attempt to eat the poor technician. He watched it perform for a moment or two, then threw the hand switch to the off position. The great metal beast ground to a halt.

Sergeant Heston couldn't contain himself. "What in the name of All Saints Day is that contraption?"

Duncan looked up as us as if he had heard nothing out of the normal. "Oh that. That's a deflesher from the leather shop. We are giving it a service. They have some big orders coming and need everything in good working order."

"A deflesher? What kind of mind designs such a thing?" The sergeant stammered.

"The kind that has something that needs to get done." Duncan answered flatly as he continued to ponder the disembodied foot. "I assume the CID will reimburse me for any expenses incurred?"

"Yes, I am authorized to use whatever resource I find prudent." I flipped through my notes. "This has to work without added fuel and it can't burn down the house around it. The chair and the body were both destroyed, but a table nearby was untouched. The room was stained, but the tile flooring kept the burn from spreading."

"Good." Duncan looked absolutely elated at the challenge. "Come see me tomorrow morning and I will show you whatever we find. By the way, did you recover any ash or char from your scene?"

Sergeant Heston pointed to the remaining bag on the desk. "We were quite careful with it."

"Ahh, very good. Gentlemen, we will try to not let you down. James, you should really come by for dinner sometime when work is not so pressing."

"We'll have dinner soon, Duncan. In the morning then." We all shook hands, then the sergeant and I led ourselves past the beast of a machine and back out to the carriage. We instructed the driver to take us directly to the Royal.

*****

The afternoon sun found nothing to flatter in the pub. This place had seen a lot of hard wear. The officers had done their job efficiently. Since we were looking for locals, I hadn't expected it to be difficult to locate the men. I was pleased to see that none of them appeared any worse for the experience of being escorted here.

"Sergeant, if you would, give me a hand here." I began pulling a couple of tables together. The sergeant lent a hand. Quickly, we had enough room for all of my guests. The officers had each man sitting alone at distant tables, one might guess in an informal interrogation formation. I motioned to the three men I had requested. "Gentlemen, please join me over here."

The officers eyed both the men and me suspiciously. The men looked uncertain as they slowly approached my makeshift dining table. "Have a seat gentlemen, please, sit."

I believe that Sergeant Heston had begun to catch on to my methods. He assumed the role of host and guided each of them into their seats. The other officers began to drift together over by the bar. They looked like they now expected a show.

"Sergeant, I believe it is lunch time. See if there is anything available to eat." I looked at each of the men. "Some sandwiches would be nice."

"I will see what we can do." Sergeant Heston headed to the bar.

"As I am sure each of you already know, my name is Inspector James Peele. I am conducting an inquiry into a bit of unpleasant business involving Mr. Cedric Clarke. I understand that each of you were at his flat last night." I could see in their eyes that they had already heard the news of his bizarre fate.

Sergeant Heston arrived at the table with a basket of hard boiled eggs and a wedge of cheese. "Nigel has put a kettle on and says he'll pull together some sandwiches."

"Thank you, Sergeant." I picked up an egg and knocked it on the scarred table just hard enough to crack the shell. I nodded at the basket while I peeled my egg with my fingernail. The gathered men, suspiciously, each picked up an egg and followed suit.

"Since, I have introduced myself, please…"

They each looked at each other then back at me. Then from my left to right, they spoke.

"Basil Young."

"Newell Gauden."

"Ellery Bates, Sir."

"Well Basil, tell me about Cedric last night. What was he doing here at the Royal?"

Basil swallowed a bite of egg quickly. "Cedric was doing the rendering. He was planning on doing suet pies tonight. They're really quite good."

Newell added, "Old Cedric put the strips of fried meat and the crunchy bits in a basket on the bar."

I could see Nigel approaching with a tray. "Ah, the tea is here."

Our conversation paused while Nigel did his best to serve the tea. I am sure he was much better at pulling a pint, but he tried hard. His hands shook so, it was a wonder anything made it to the inside of the cup. I thanked him as he scurried back to the bar. As he walked away, I noticed the edges of his heavily stained leather apron had frayed from age and use. Nigel wore the clothes one would expect of a man of his station, however, he wore the same kind of boots as Cedric. I picked up my cup and blew at the steam.

"Ellery, how was your evening last night?"

"Me, Sir?" Ellery looked stricken.

"Yes. Did you play darts? Cards?" I prompted.

"I finished up at the livery and came down for a pint. I beat Newell here two out of three sets at the darts."

Newell loosened up a bit. "Oh, only just. You was just lucky that's all."

"I'm known to toss a few myself. How did the game go?" Like all devoted dart enthusiast they could recall nearly every toss and the tactics. I let them tell me about the whole set. All three of them joined the conversation and continued eating the eggs and cheese while sipping tea. Soon, we were just four blokes having a bite. Periodically, I could see one officer or another rolling their eyes at my apparent free lunch on the CID. I smiled to myself. Just as the story of the game wrapped up, Nigel and Sergeant Heston came to the table with a small platter of beef sandwiches. They set them in the middle of the table while we continued to chat. I gave the Sergeant a bit of a nod and a quick look at Nigel. The sergeant understood perfectly. I returned to my inquiries.

"So when did Cedric decide go back to his flat?" I hoped the good nature would continue.

Ellery stepped up. "Old Cedric has a bit of the dropsy now and again. After he had taken up the suet and set the fat to the side, he said he was feeling a bit light in the head. Lenny, the overnight man was already here, so he told Cedric to get off his feet. We all sat out here and had a pint with him."

Basil added, "He started looking a bit pale, so we walked him back home. Normally, a good stiff shot of the whiskey will set him right. He said he had a bottle."

"We went by that crazy old busybody of a landlady. You can see her eye at the hole in the door. Daft old bat, don't think anyone knows she's there." Newell commented between bites.

"I poured everyone a shot and left Cedric with my last cigar. We left and come back down here." Ellery concluded.

The men ate their sandwiches while we talked. They relaxed and told me in great detail about the mostly legal activities of last night. There was a bit of gossip and drinking; no one could remember anything out of the ordinary. The detail at which these men spoke told me volumes.

We had finished our luncheon and they sensed I was done with them. Basil looked hard at me and spoke in a lowered voice. "Can you tell us something? We heard that Cedric got took by the Devil himself. Burnt him up to just about nothing!"

"You have aided my inquiry more than you can know. I assure you that by this time tomorrow I will be able to tell you what actually happened to your friend." I rose to my feet. "Thank you for your time. If needed, I can send word to your employers that you were in my charge." A quick look at their faces told me that that was the last thing they wanted. "No? Then, good day, gentlemen. Thank you for your time."

Newell returned, "Thank you for the lunch. That was very kind of you, Inspector."

The three left as I walked to the bar to settle the tab with Nigel. The man looked absolutely shocked at payment. The gathered officers all looked at the doorway like the entire morning had been a complete waste of time. Their collective dark mood changed when I paid Nigel to feed them as well. They might think I am as mad as a hatter, but they will remember they got a lunch out of the deal. I put the receipt in my pocket and motioned for the sergeant to come with me. Once in the carriage and on the way back to station, we could talk.

"Thank you for your assistance, Sergeant. What did Nigel have to tell you?"

"I assumed you wanted me to warm him up while you buttered those three." Sergeant Heston looked proud of himself. "Turns out that Cedric has been under the weather a bit lately. Nothing serious, just gets tired easily. He confirmed that bunch was eating up all the fried strips and playing darts most of the time he was there. They're regulars. Most folks in a place like that are there most every evening. They take their business elsewhere, if you take my meaning, Sir."

I flipped through my notes and reconfirmed facts with the sergeant. Page after page, we covered everything. Since Nigel had on a leather apron, I asked if there had been others hanging in the back. Sergeant Heston could only remember seeing one. Overall, I was pleased with how that went. Soon, the carriage stopped in front of the station. I could see the Chief Inspector glancing out his window at our arrival.

"Sergeant, meet me at the Essex Machine Shop at 8:00 in the morning. I have a feeling that the Chief Inspector is waiting to have a word or two with me."

Sergeant Heston looked a touch worried to leave me to my fate, but took me at my word. "Good luck, Sir. I'll be there."

At that, I walked in as if nothing out of the ordinary had happened all day long. I didn't get past the front desk before a junior officer inconspicuously intercepted me and escorted me to the front of the building. He stopped at the door and stood at attention. I took a deep breath and entered without knocking. I was certain that I was expected.

"Good afternoon, James."

"Good afternoon, Chief Inspector."

"How has your investigation proceeded?"

"I believe I have made substantial progress."

"You believe." At those words the Chief Inspector stopped speaking and took an exaggerated breath. "I believe we are discussing two very different days."

"How so, Sir?"

"Well, the day I have reports on involve you removing human remains from the crime scene with a dust pan and a bag. Then you suggested to the landlady that it might not be a bad idea to have the clergy stop by to make sure the house was cleared of influences. I assume that you have also been out to see that grease monkey friend of yours. Next, you had three men rounded up and detained at a pub, where you bought them lunch and chatted about darts. After which, you let them go on their own recognizance. After that, you purchased lunch for everyone else. I assume you are going to turn that receipt in and expect reimbursement. You also had Sergeant Heston opening doors and waiting tables. Since I don't see any bags with you, I assume you have left the remains with someone other than the undertaker. Have I missed anything?"

"No, Sir. The Chief Inspector is very well informed." I waited.

"Did you understand my request this morning for a reasonable resolution?"

"Yes, Sir. I am confident that tomorrow I will be able to bring this affair to a mundane conclusion."

He stared at me with a mix of fury and awe. I certainly had my druthers as to which way his mind was going to go. He pursed and unpursed his lips. This action created the effect of a grey fuzzy caterpillar undulating under his nose. "In the meantime, the press is running with the story that my lead inspector asked for the clergy at the scene of an unnatural event, then went to lunch with locals at a nearby pub."

"Sir, the press was going to run with the unnatural angle no matter what we did. I simply gave them the angle I wanted them to pursue."

"James, for your sake, you had better package this whole affair up nicely with a bow on top, or the Commissioner is going to have both of us in a box."

"I understand completely, Sir. I will have my conclusion tomorrow."

The Chief Inspector looked at me then slowly smiled. "Tomorrow will be interesting, to say the least."

*****

Sergeant Heston met me promptly at 8:00 at the Essex Machine Shop. Our approach went unnoticed due to the metallic mayhem emanating from the building. As we entered the door, we got to see the great diabolical machine in full operation. The workman at the end of the jaws was expertly positioning a sheet of cured, but unfinished leather as the bits of excess flesh mechanically were stripped away. I noticed a faint burning smell as the machine went about its work. I looked from a distance until I saw that small strips of shaved off leather would get caught in the moving parts. If the parts moved fast enough, they could make the leather shavings smolder. A shout over the din took our attention and directed it to the back of the building. Duncan waved his arms, motioning us to come to him.

We followed him to a back room where a slaughtered pig lay in various parts on a metal work table. A number of attempts at cremation lay there in mute evidence to Duncan's activities.

"James, we have tried about everything. I'm afraid I can't duplicate your event." Duncan waved his arm over the mostly raw evidence. "Now, I can confirm one fact for you."

"What is that?"

"Part of the contents of the bag of char were these flakes of something that looked like bone. We found that if you burn the pig bones long enough they will flake off like that. So I am afraid that your poor man did indeed burn."

"Why a pig?" Sergeant Heston had to ask.

"Well, mostly, it is big enough. I assumed if I could get this to work, we would know what happened. As it is right now, I may have to agree with the morning rags." Duncan scratched his head as if he were still trying to figure out another angle. "I even went so far as to just stick a candle in and let it go. It went out as soon as it got to the flesh."

"Sir, the tabloids are saying we went to a nice luncheon while the Devil himself walked Covent Gardens. It wasn't very flattering." Sergeant Heston look distressed. "But they had a few nice comments about the Pastor."

I chose to ignore the Sergeant's comment for now. I honestly expected Duncan to be showing me how to make a pile of ash at this point. I looked at all the failed experiments. I needed more information. "Duncan, let's take it from the top. There is something here that we are missing."

Duncan leapt to the task. "First, we tried a bit of an accelerant. A spot of spirits?" He slid one piece to the end of the table and poured a measure of clear liquid on it, then touched a match to it. Blue flames engulfed the meat and a pleasant aroma began to rise. A few moments later, the flames had spent their fuel and extinguished. "We would have to keep adding fuel to keep it burning. So this wasn't it."

Duncan moved down the table to the next piece. "For this one we tried an ignition source." Duncan picked up a small knife and stabbed a slit through the skin. Into the slit, he pushed a small tapered candle and lit it. We watched in silence as the flame swayed back and forth in the slight breeze of the shop. As the flame reached the level of the skin, it began to pop and sear. As the candle melted away a bit more, the edges of the slit began to crisp and burn. It began to smell like meat grilling.

My hopes rose with each sputter and pop. I could actually see the oils cooking out of the skin and adding to the flame. However, once the wax was exhausted, the small flame withered and died.

Duncan continued his demonstrations, moving down the table. Even assuming the chair burned first failed. He simulated that with a small pile of kindling. As with the earlier failures, once the fuel was gone the flame went out. "Now, we were able to partially replicate your results over here at the furnace. If we leave it in long enough, we can cremate it. But, that doesn't answer not burning down the house."

The on again off again racket at the front kept trying to tell me something. While Duncan and Sergeant Heston stood at the furnace examining the evidence, I walked back out front and up to the source of the noise. I tapped the young man on the shoulder and motioned for him to turn off the fearful device.

After the noise died, he pulled his earplugs out. "Yes, Sir. What can I do for you?"

"I noticed that the shavings get caught up in the works there." I pointed to a couple of spots for emphasis. "And the working parts can get very hot."

"Oh, yes, Sir." He pulled a metal tool out of his pocket with a bent tip on it. "That's why it's in for service. They didn't keep it clean enough, so we had to break it down and give it a good service." He used the tool to pull the waste leather out of the cracks and crevices.

"I've noticed this if that stuff gets hot enough, it smolders. How long will that burn?"

"Oh that fluff will smoke that like for hours."

I excitedly shook the man's hand. "Thank you! Thank you very much indeed. You have been a tremendous help."

As I turned, I nearly bumped into Duncan and Sergeant Heston. They could see the elation in my eyes.

"Sir, what have you learned?"

"Yes, James. Out with it."

"Sergeant, I need you to take word to the Chief Inspector that I have found a reasonable solution to the final disposition of Mr. Cedric Clarke. If he would like a demonstration of what happened, he can join us here at the shop. That is, if you don't mind Duncan."

"I certainly wish to see this solution of yours." Duncan agreed.

"I will be back as soon as possible, Sir." Sergeant Heston turned for the door, but Duncan caught his arm.

"Take my coach."

*****

I had a few minor details to attend to before my demonstration. Fortunately, Duncan's shop had everything I needed. Within the hour, Duncan's coach, accompanied by the Chief Inspector's, pulled up out front. I waited by the back table for everyone to gather. It was show time.

The Chief Inspector strode directly up to me. "James, I understand from the Sergeant that you can provide me with the reasonable explanation I requested."

I looked him directly in the eyes. "Yes, Sir. I believe I can. If you will indulge me for a moment."

I turned back to the table and uncovered all of my ingredients. "We have to start with Mr. Cedric Clarke's activities on the evening he died. He tended bar at the Royal, where he also did a fair amount of cooking. As a matter of fact, he was planning on suet pies for the next evening. So, he spent the evening rending down the fatty meats. His mates sat the bar with him. We will let this hog's leg represent the late Mr. Clarke. We noticed that the barkeeps at the Royal wear leather aprons like butchers do. Since they do a fair bit of that at the pub, it is not surprising that Mr. Clarke's apron had become soaked in the rendered fat. Since his apron was not at the pub the next morning during our inspection, we can assume he wore it home. His friends mentioned that Mr. Clarke suffered from dropsy, a heart condition. He did not feel well, so they escorted him home. They had a shot of whiskey with him and left. The landlady independently verifies their account of the events."

The Chief Inspector nodded, but waited expectantly. Sergeant Heston posed the actual question.

"So how did Mr. Clarke come to his ultimate fate if he was alone and alive?"

"The answer to that eluded me until about an hour ago. Let's stage the final event. Chief Inspector, if I could ask you to light a cigar for me."

The Chief Inspector did as requested. After a few satisfied puffs, he turned it over to me.

"After his friends had left, Mr. Clark lit the cigar left with him. Sadly, the shot of whiskey that had revived him from the dropsy in the past failed this time. After a few puffs, Mr. Clark either passed out or died."

I sat the hog leg up and draped a fat soaked sheet of leather over it with the bottom curled up slightly. I had rendered a bit of the hog at the furnace while waiting. "Mr. Clarke's lit cigar fell into his lap and came into contact with the leather apron." I dropped the cigar into the curl. "The tile floor would not give any flame a chance to advance and the draft stopper at the front door would have kept any smoke or odors from escaping into the common hallway. The reason the doorknob was only warm was that there was never a large flame, just the slow burning of an oil-soaked wick, just like any oil lamp."

As I spoke, the heat of the cigar set to work on the rendered fat. Just like I had seen during Duncan's candle demonstration, the oil began to form up. The difference was that now it had something larger to act upon. Within a few minutes the cigar began to absorb the fat.

It is amazing how long grown men will stand there and watch a cigar slowly burn. Just as the Chief Inspector stepped forward for a closer examination, a small flame appeared on the leather. Over the course of the next hour, the leg continued to slowly consume itself.

"There was neither foul play nor the Devil involved. Just a poor man tragically reduced back to the ashes and dust from which we all came."

Artificial Love

Dwayne DeBardelaben

Riley toyed with the lift valve absent-mindedly as the ferry hovered silently over the loading dock. Thick cables stretched eight hundred feet downward to the transport platform where the third train of the day edged forward, allowing cars to be disconnected and stored as needed for the trip across Bottomless Gorge. At this height, he couldn't hear the sounds below, but his mind filled in the grinding screech of steel on steel, the hard thunk of switching levers being pulled to direct each boxcar to its travel position, and the ever present hiss of pressurized hot water escaping the confines of its pipes.

"There's no way we'll finish before shift end," said Riley as he gauged the slow progress below. Billows of white smoke poured from the train's stack, like tiny cotton tufts floating along the edge of the canyon.

"Probably not," replied Larry, "and Momma Wutherton don't pay no overtime either."

Riley chuckled at the maternal image of Wutherton Transit. It fit, in many ways, since the company controlled so much of their lives. Ever since the Harvesters picked him up from his father's farm, Wutherton had housed him, fed him, trained him, and even provided a wife, Penny, so he could start a family. He had always wanted a family, but the thought of having children with *her*, of even trying to have children with her, made the prospect of working late seem attractive. His chuckle faded to a sigh as he envisioned the stony silence, the cold chill in the house, and the inevitable, disapproving look that said, "Riley Owens, you are an absolute failure of a man!"

"Dang, Riley! You still down about that woman?"

Riley spun away from the mesh platform and walked back into the control room. "She makes me feel like a cow turd someone just stepped in - not only am I a piece of crap, but I've gone and ruined someone else's day as well."

Larry followed close behind. "Then give her to me, 'cause she's one fine looking female."

"Yeah, she looks good alright, but there's more to life than a pretty face and full body."

"You sure you're a guy?" Larry never saw the glove that smacked him in the face.

Two hours later, after the train had been safely conveyed across, the two friends coptered down to the ground. The blades rhythmically chopped the air, providing a steady, soporific, background as they floated slowly downward, like dandelion seeds hanging lazily in the air. As he surveyed the Wutherton compound below, the tension in Riley's chest eased momentarily. *Momma* had made quite an investment in the eastern edge of Bottomless Gorge. Not only did Wutherton provide ferry services across for people and trains, they also had a very nice sanitarium that stayed busy year round. Several scenic overviews jutted out from the wide walkway running the length of the property. Tourists, whether seeking the thrill of an adventure on the river so far below, or the rejuvenating effects of the famous spa, always left singing the company's praises.

Riley and Larry guided the one-man copters to the designated landing area behind the stables. A lift balloon would return them to the airship tomorrow morning.

"How 'bout some grub?" suggested Riley as they walked toward the horses, anything to delay the inevitable awaiting for him at home. He could hear his horse, Mellow, stirring at the sound of his voice. The horse, at least, was glad to see him.

Larry shook his head, "Nah, Marie would get her feelings hurt. She always has something tasty fixed when I get in."

Riley gave a half-smile. "That's a good wife you've got there, Larry."

"She feeds me good," agreed Larry as he opened the stall for his horse, "and she's always willing, if you know what I mean. But she's not much of a looker."

"There's more to life than--."

"A pretty face, blah, blah. I know, I know, but you don't know how good you got it buddy." Larry spun up onto his horse's back and grinned at his friend, "Look, Riley, you just gotta figure out how to make her act like you want. In the meantime, just think about how she looks. That should get you by for awhile."

*****

The tinny sound of the piano did nothing to brighten Riley's mood as he settled in at the table for dinner. Bug Eye's was fairly typical, as far as saloons go, not much of a family environment, but they did have decent food at a decent price.

Salomé brushed by his table on her way back to the kitchen. "Want the usual, Riley?"

"Sure," he sighed, "might as well."

"Be just a minute, Hon," she said, flashing him a gap-toothed grin.

Despite his sour disposition, Riley laughed at the older woman. He suspected Salomé was not her real name, but she insisted her mother named her after the biblical character. He asked her, on occasion, whether or not she had cut off anyone's head. "Four", she replied every time. Most nights, including tonight, he didn't believe her, but on the rare occasion when she displayed a foul temper, he wondered if there might just be a few headless corpses buried in the dry desert ground somewhere.

As he waited for the food, Riley surveyed the room. A constant influx of visitors, some definitely out of place in a saloon, usually provided enough entertainment for the evening. A portly, boisterous man sat at the bar, informing everyone of the dangers of giving in to the advances of beautiful women. Riley chuckled to himself, guessing the man's warnings to be more theoretical than experiential. He gazed further and saw a younger couple sitting near the door, holding hands and whispering. Newlyweds, no doubt, enjoying the varied attractions of the Wutherton compound. An older gentleman sat next to them, reading a book and nursing a glass of brandy. A meaty hand on his shoulder interrupted his reverie.

"Quite an interesting set of folks in here tonight," said a husky voice behind him.

Riley shook off a brief surge of adrenaline and replied, "Sure is." He twisted away so he could get a clear look at the man. The stranger stood a couple of inches taller than Riley, and sported a pencil-thin mustache that drooped a little at the corners of his mouth. Everything from the feather stuck in his bowler to the intricate gold watch chain hanging from his vest pocket, gave an image of self-importance, or at the least, arrogant self-confidence.

199

Riley decided he didn't like the man. "Sorry, didn't get your name."

"Fritz," said the stranger as he sat down beside Riley. "Mr. Owens, you're an intelligent man, I can see that. Much more intelligent than your average sky-jockey."

Riley briefly wondered how the same statement could serve as an insult and a compliment at the same time. "What in the world would make you think I'm smart, Fritz?" He said the man's name as if spitting out a bite of apple with half a worm missing.

The man smiled and stood back up and said, "Because you watch people, Mr. Owens. You absorb the situation and take mental notes."

Riley started to ask how Fritz knew his name, but the man interrupted again. "I've got a solution for your wife problem, if you're interested, but it will take some hard work on your part. Think it over, and if you want my help, talk to me tomorrow. In the meantime, enjoy your dinner. This one's on me." Fritz flipped a golden eagle into the air and then walked out the front. Riley caught the coin and stared at the still swinging half-doors leading to the street, wondering just what the man meant. Was he offering to kill Penny? Did he have some way to brainwash her? What kind of work would he have to do?

"Here ya go," said Salomé, setting a plate down on the table. She punched him in the shoulder and said, "I recognize that look, Riley Owens. Not sure what you're thinkin' Hon, but you'd better eat before it gets cold."

Riley shook his head quickly, clearing the cobwebs, and said, "Thanks Salomé, what would I do without you?"

"Starve."

He laughed, "Nah, I'd just have to eat with *her* every night. Could be worse, I suppose. Anyway, here's a tip for you." He handed her the coin from Fritz.

Salomé's eyes grew wide at the treasure in the palm of her hand. "Riley, you can't do this! That's three months salary!"

"Then do your job, woman, and get me another drink," he said with a wink.

The older woman's smile made him forget, temporarily, about going home.

*****

Riley leaned back in the saloon chair, exhausted from the day's work, and more than a little hungry. He had slept poorly the night before, plagued by disturbing images of his wife being kidnapped by living, mustachioed derbies. Each hat had arms, legs, and several sets of fangs. The dreams were easy enough to trace, but what truly bothered him was the joy that coursed through his heart as he saw the demon-derbies carry her away.

He expected the meaty hand on his shoulder. "Hello, Fritz," he said without looking.

"So, have you decided you want my help?" The big man sat next to Riley, putting his bowler on the table in front of him.

Riley sighed and looked at the semi-stranger. He couldn't make himself look in the man's eyes, especially if it meant killing Penny, so he focused on the tips of his mustache. The hair tapered to sharp points that just touched the corners of his mouth.

"I want to hear what you have to say."

Both men glanced up as Salomé approached the table. "Who's your friend, Riley?"

Riley coughed and said, "Salomé meet Fritz. Fritz, Salomé."

The man stood up from his chair, took the waitress' hand in his own, kissed one knuckle, and said, "Fritz Nielson at your service, my lady."

Salomé blushed, not something Riley ever expected to see, and he was surprised at how much younger it made her look. She took a moment to recover and then asked, "Is there something I can get you gentlemen? Riley, I expect you want the usual, but what about you, Mr. Nielson?"

"Fritz, please, and thank you, but no thank you on the food."

She smiled at him for a moment, and then turned toward the kitchen, calling out over her shoulder, "Be just a minute, Riley."

The two men sat in silence until Riley asked, "So, what do you have to say, Mr. Fritz Nielson?"

The taller man put a hand to his face and absent-mindedly traced a line from his brow to the tip of his nose, repeatedly, as he spoke. Somehow, in Riley's mind, the act humanized the strange man, made him less ... impersonal.

"Artificial love," said Fritz.

"What?" Riley drew his head back sharply, not understanding.

"Your wife is attractive, is she not?"

Riley reluctantly agreed, "Yeah, she's a looker alright. But that's only skin deep."

Fritz nodded slightly and asked, "What if there was a way to have her beauty on the outside, but something more loving, more appreciative on the inside?"

Riley felt a surge of relief; perhaps the answer wouldn't involve killing her, just changing her somehow. "That sounds nice, but I'm not sure exactly what that means."

"Mr. Owens, you have seen the incredible technology afforded us in this day and age--trains, airships, the telegraph. With the power of coal and steam to drive our inventions, there is no limit to human imagination."

The man's words intrigued Riley. He wanted to understand how things worked. He spent more time studying the engine of his airship than piloting it. Still, he maintained a steady composure, determined not to get his hopes up for anything real. "So, how does that help me?"

The kitchen door opened, and Salomé walked in with a hot plate and cold beer. Riley's mouth watered as she set the food down. "Eat while it's hot, Hon." She turned to the other man and asked, "Are you sure you don't want anything, Mr. ... uh, Fritz?"

The man smiled, but shook his head.

"Okay, just let me know if you change your mind," she said as she headed to another table.

Fritz waited until she was out of earshot, then continued, "It helps *you* when *you* realize we can build an artificial version of your wife."

"I don't understand. What do you mean?" He took a bite of stew and waited for a reply.

Fritz laughed softly and then said, "By using the right materials, we can build a frame that is identical to your wife. The skin will be just as lovely, just as supple, and just as pliable as hers. On the inside, we will place a device I've been perfecting for years."

Riley's skepticism flared. "Fritz, I don't want some strange doll or puppet for a wife. I want someone to talk with, to laugh with, to do ... uh, other things with. Are you telling me your device will make this thing, this doppelganger, act like the wife I want?"

"Yes," said Fritz, simply, as if he had just commented on the weather.

Riley swallowed another bite and reached for his beer. "Assuming I believe you, which I don't, I remember something my father told me. Before he let me find my own way with the Harvesters, he used to say there's always a reason someone does something. It may not look like it sometimes, but that just means you're not looking in the right place."

Fritz smiled, condescendingly it seemed to Riley, and said nothing. Since Riley could be stubborn as well, especially with a hot meal in front of him, he said nothing either. He took a bite, then took a drink, then took another bite followed by another drink.

Eventually, the condescending smile faded from Fritz's face. He looked toward the ceiling and said, "Your wife's beauty is unsurpassed, Mr. Owens, and I have a wealthy patron, a very wealthy patron, who desires her as his own."

"Why not just take the real one?" suggested Riley. "After all, it's not like I'll fight very hard to keep her."

Fritz seemed, for the first time since he appeared the day before, a bit uncomfortable. He took a deep breath, then sighed most of it away and said, "I tried, but she said she wouldn't leave you."

"Really?" The thought of Penny meeting another man during the day seemed surreal. Come to think of it, the thought of Penny doing anything during the day, other than planning his misery, seemed surreal. Riley had plenty of time for daydreams as his airship traversed the gorge, and those idle moments usually involved going home and finding a note from Penny, explaining how she had reached her limit and decided to leave.

"Don't get the wrong impression, Mr. Owens. Her devotion is not born of love, rather pride." Fritz traced the same line on his nose again. "Leaving you under the current circumstances would stigmatize her in ways that are far worse, to her, than the hell you share together every day."

Riley chuckled, knowing that Fritz Nielson's guess as to her motivation was wrong. She didn't worry about being stigmatized, she simply realized that her greatest joy in life lay in making his life as bad as it could possibly be, and leaving him would rob her of that.

"On the other hand, a fully functional replica of her left here will not only make life better for you, but also, potentially, free her to leave."

"Why not create a copy for your patron?" asked Riley.

It was Fritz's turn to chuckle. "Mr. Owens, my patron desires the real thing, and did I mention that he is very wealthy?"

"I believe you did."

"Not only will you be left with a fully functional replica of your wife, but you will also be amply compensated."

The money meant little to Riley, but the prospect of a life where he looked forward to coming home after work was intoxicating. He drained his beer, and, in a moment of impetuous certainty, or perhaps desperation born of dying dreams, said, "What do you need from me?"

The taller man sighed, in apparent relief, and said, "I need pieces of your wife."

"Like a finger or toe?" he said, half-joking, half-wondering if one of her fingers could be evil all by itself.

Fritz brushed aside the humor and said, "While those would do wonderfully, my device can do with much less. I'll need nail clippings and a lock of hair."

Riley rolled his eyes. "Might as well ask me to strap on a set of wings and fly trains across the gorge myself, if you think she'll ever let me cut her hair."

Fritz pressed on. "We'll also need material that helps define her personality - a journal perhaps."

"Will a diseased cactus stump do?"

Fritz ignored him again, but the taller man's eyes widened slightly, highlighting the importance of his next demand. "And I will need your help during the evening to construct the device. We will start tomorrow, Mr. Owens. I'll see you when your shift ends." Fritz Nielson donned his bowler and headed for the door, stopping briefly to say goodnight to Salomé. Riley could see her flush from across the room, and he smiled, in spite of himself.

She eased her way to Riley's table and cleared the dishes. "What a nice man, Riley. Where'd you find him?"

"He found me," said Riley. He reached for his pocket, intent on digging out enough coin to pay for dinner.

Salomé touched his arm. "No need for that. You gave me enough last night to cover it."

*****

Riley eased the door shut behind him and took off his boots. The house was dark, no lamps or candles left burning for him, but moonlight filtered through the windows illuminating his path. The dry air had cooled considerably in the three weeks since he began work with Fritz Nielson. In spite of the mild evening breeze, he still felt a bead of sweat on his brow as he faced another night with her.

Maybe I can ease into bed and she'll stay asleep, he thought as he finished getting undressed. He folded his clothes into a neat pile, which he then took with his boots and entered the bedroom.

"What's her name?" The voice, so sultry, so damning, startled him, and he dropped everything to floor. She laughed, "Typical. I said 'What's her name?'"

"Who's name?" asked Riley in return, gathering the clothes and depositing them in a chair. His eyes adjusted, and he saw her sitting up in bed, her face buried in soft shadows.

"The harlot you're seeing every night."

Her words cut. Even though he despised his life at home, he would not cheat on her. "Like I told you before, I'm working extra these days."

"Are they paying you extra too?" she asked.

"No. You know how Wutherton is about money."

Penny turned her head slightly away from him, a subtle movement that conveyed more disgust than a thousand words.

This shouldn't still hurt, thought Riley as he climbed into bed. "It won't be for much longer," he said. He lay on his side, with his back to her, and pulled the cover up tight against his chin.

"Why do you let them treat you like that?" she asked. "Why don't you stand up for yourself?"

Riley sighed and rolled over. As much as he disliked her, and her constant berating, he always stopped breathing, for just a moment, when he saw her face. He remembered the day he met her. The on-hands, ferry training class had just ended, and he headed for the showers, thinking about how much he loved the work, when his boss introduced him to Penny. She smiled, and his heart stopped, or at least that's what he thought at the time. In retrospect, his boss singing his praises and talking about how far he would go in the company probably explained her interest, but all he could see was her smile.

Whirlwind, or whirlpool, it all depends on your perspective, and before either of them realized it, they were married. The first few weeks had been exciting, but then something changed. She asked about his ambitions in the company, and he shrugged his shoulders, saying it didn't matter what he did as long as they were happy. But the questions continued, and he found himself angling for a promotion, which he soon got. But that wasn't enough, it seemed, as she asked about the next possible advancement within the company. He continued to work hard, but the joy of piloting, the joy of studying and understanding the machinery, disappeared. He soon found himself not talking to Penny when he got home. It was easier than dealing with her criticism.

To make matters worse, Larry, his best friend, came in daily with stories of how his wife, Marie, treated him - special dinner, special attention, special words spoken during special time. Marie wasn't beautiful, by any stretch, but Riley would have traded for her in a second. And so things went from bad to worse, until one day, only bile and venom remained.

"I used to love my job," he said, staring at the black emptiness of the ceiling.

Penny snorted in disgust and rolled away from him, but Riley still heard her mutter, "You used to be a man."

"Can I have a lock of your hair?," he said, throwing the words out in the open, bracing himself for the onslaught.

"Why," she asked without moving, "so you can make a voodoo doll and burn it?"

For a solid week, Riley had avoided the question, even though Fritz said he had to have the hair to finish the next step. Riley had peered into the heart of the device, watching gears spin and white-blue lightning arc across small gaps, and wondered, for the hundredth time if he should just stop. Then he would hear her voice in the back of his head, reviling him for not "finishing the job," and his resolve would strengthen. The first question was easy, knowing she would give a sarcastic response. The real key would be his follow up. And, after much consideration, he decided to throw her off guard with a thoughtful sentiment.

"I thought it might be nice to have something to remind me of you during the day."

He expected more sarcasm or a fresh attack, instead silence filled the room for several seconds, and then Penny left the bed and returned moments later. She held a pair of scissors in her hand and said, "How much do you want?"

Of all the responses he imagined, this never crossed his mind. "Uh ... a couple of inches would be good."

She pulled a long tress from over her shoulder, and cut a thick lock, leaving a noticeable gap in her otherwise perfect appearance. "Here," she said as she handed it to him, "but I want some of yours to remember you as well."

He nodded, still stunned by her compliance. Maybe, he thought, this won't be so hard.

*****

"We need her journal," said Fritz. He fastened an access panel to the back of a humanoid shape lying prone on his workbench. A cheaply rented hotel room had served as a laboratory for the two men over the course of four long weeks.

Riley had watched, and participated, in amazement as Fritz guided their efforts in fashioning the outer shells, and then assembling the intricate inner device. He asked questions, which Fritz usually ignored, and tried his best to understand the principles behind the machine. He thought he understood some of it, but most of the time he simply followed orders. And when they managed to get skin, or something very similar, to grow on the surface of the outer shells, he knew it could work.

"I still don't understand why the journal is so important," said Riley.

Fritz sealed the panel with a strip of material that dissolved, leaving a seamless, smooth patch of skin. "Personality, Mr. Owens. Just like the device needed a physical piece of your wife to emulate her beauty, it needs a piece of her mind to emulate her personality."

"But her personality is the problem."

"Personality is a template, not an absolute. We want her to be her as much as possible, with a few minor adjustments."

"I told you before, I'm not even sure if she has a journal. I've never seen her write in one before."

Fritz responded with clenched teeth, "She has a journal, Mr. Owens! Can you please find it tonight, or must I come over and do it myself?"

Riley recoiled slightly. He had never seen Fritz angry before. The air of confidence he portrayed, bordering on arrogance, left the impression of perfect self-control. "I'll take care of it, Fritz. If a journal exists, I'll find it."

Fritz regained his composure quickly. "Good," he said. "Now, before you leave tonight, let's take a look at the fruit of our labors." He tapped a rhythmic sequence on the back of the humanoid, and it sat up. It appeared to take a breath, opened its eyes, and smiled.

Riley momentarily forgot to breathe.

Later that evening, he found the journal, and took it to work the next day. Penny would surely discover it missing, but by that time, it should be too late to matter. The day passed slowly, and when their shift ended, Larry, as usual, declined dinner and went home. Riley scarfed dinner quickly causing Salomé to raise an eyebrow, even though she said nothing, and he soon found himself in the hotel room facing Fritz and a perfect copy of Penny. She wore a light brown dress, billowing at the hips, with white lace embroidering around the neckline.

"I still can't get over how much it looks like her," he remarked, handing the journal to Fritz.

"Did you read it?"

"The journal? Not really. I opened it to make sure what it was, and then put it in my satchel." He walked up to his artificial wife, and inspected her face in detail. "Amazing," he muttered several times to himself.

"Then I suggest you read it aloud to our guest, Mr. Owens. After all, she needs some personality now, doesn't she? And I would also suggest you start referring to it as she. She will consider herself to be the real thing." Fritz executed a series of taps on the back of each Penny and said, "She is ready. What you say to her now will factor into her own self-perception."

Riley nodded and opened the journal. He recognized the date on the first page -- the day they first met.

I know Mr. Trammel introduced me to Mr. Owens today in hopes I would be attracted to him. Mr. Owens is a handsome man, but there is more to attraction than mere visage, and on that account, I can say most faithfully that there is indeed hope. The first mannerism I noticed, with some degree of concern, was his eyes. They did not dart to and fro as if directed by the random firing of juvenile or partially coherent thoughts. No. He studied Mr. Trammel as the older man spoke, nodding ever so slightly at key points of interjection, and when I found myself with occasion to utter a response, he studied me. The effect was, to say the least, somewhat disturbing, yet, at the same time, oddly exhilarating. I felt both analyzed and appreciated. Perhaps there is more to Mr. Owens than simple lackey of the Wutherton empire; perhaps he is a man capable of charting his own course.

Riley flipped to the next page and continued reading.

Mr. Owens paid me a visit this evening. His knowledge of appropriate courting is atrocious. He sat on the divan next to me, uninvited! I tolerated his behavior, much to my own hesitation, because he intrigues me so. And, I'm ashamed to admit, because he smelled so ... masculine. It took considerable self-control to remain focused on proper decorum.

Riley grinned, despite himself, remembering how Penny had blushed whenever she was near him in those early days.

I was blessed with a rather unexpected visit from Mr. Owens this afternoon. His shift as ferryman ended early due to inclement wind conditions, or so he proffered, although the sky appeared rather calm to my untrained eye. He assured me the dangerous winds were at elevations to high for the natural eye to discern. And the truth is I cared not whether the wind blew hard or soft, only that my heart fluttered as he touched my arm. As he explained, in laborious detail, the principles behind the ferry, and how piloting could be improved with training and innovation, I was once again reminded of his clear intellect and insight. Surely this man will make a name for himself one day.

She never said any of this to me, thought Riley as he read. Many of the entries dealt with the mundane: work, dining, friends, and even family back home. But an increasing number focused on their growing relationship.

Riley brought me a rose today! How beautiful, how magnificent, how incredible that this delicate flower could survive in this desert air. When I noted that Wutherton does not stock roses, he replied that he gathered seeds from a friend...

Larry, thought Riley. *Larry had seeds, brought from the east when he last visited his mother.*

... and cultivated the plant within the confines of his own room. Not only am I growing fond of, very fond of, an extremely intelligent and insightful man who understands the cogs and gears of machinery, he is also an accomplished botanist. Is there no end of surprise from my Riley? He is so unlike my father, who squandered away his abilities and fortune and left his poor wife, my mother, destitute and unable to provide for her own children. The mere semblance of a woman that remained as her life lay wracked by turmoil after turmoil is one that I will not become. I am thankful with an unbounded gratitude for the affections of my Riley. In him I find myself able to relax and let worry flow from my mind like a gentle stream trickling down a mountainside.

Riley kept reading, allowing part of his brain to translate the written words into meaningful sound, but the other part of his mind detached from the process, and he contemplated his wife and her motivations. A side of her emerged that he had not seen before, and as he reinterpreted his marriage, he grew uncomfortable.

I am distraught. Concern weighs on my mind as if great blocks of granite have been secured to my own, weak shoulders. Earlier, as I contemplated the challenges and adventures of an uncertain future - uncertain, true, but one also pregnant with potential - I dared broach the subject with the one I hoped to share my innermost burdens and dreams. With genuine excitement, with ideas bursting forth from my mind, I asked my dear Riley of that future. His reply left me weakened and stunned. He professed his love, which delighted me as always, but then he professed no concern nor care for provision for the future. He shrugged his shoulders - a coarse gesture that left me adrift in a sea of confusion and sorrow. Could he truthfully care so little for our future that he shrugs away responsibility and forethought? Does he shrug away our lives because he cares so little for me? Am I worth so little to him? NO! I choose to believe that the burdens of the day left my dearest Riley in a mental state such that he knew not what he did, or said. Tomorrow he will confess that his plan assuages all concerns and I will once again feel safe and loved. Today ... this day ... is but aberration.

Riley stopped reading and handed the journal to Fritz, who sat in motionless silence the whole time. "I think that's enough," he said.

Fritz took the book and replied, "Indeed it is Mr. Owens. The time has come to change the rest of your life."

Riley looked at the replica of his wife, breathtakingly beautiful, and said, "I don't want her hurt, Fritz. She may be an insufferable pain, but I don't want her to hurt, or die."

"Not to worry, Mr. Owens," he said. "You have my word as a gentleman that I will take care of her. If I do not convince her to come with me, then I shall leave her where she most desires. After all, she does have certain ... motivations of her own."

"What do you mean?"

"You'll see soon enough," said the taller man. He directed the Penny replica to the door, and beckoned for Riley to follow. "To your house, Mr. Owens. The climax is upon us. "

*****

Riley's heartbeat pulsed in his ears, like some hidden drum signaling his arrival. His hand hesitated on the doorknob; his next step would cross a threshold of no return. He took a deep breath, and walked in. He expected Penny to be in bed, since it was later than usual, so his reaction bordered on comical when he saw her, fully dressed, in a light brown dress with white lace, waiting for him inside the doorway.

She laughed, "Why, Riley, you look as if you've just seen a ghost."

"Why aren't you in bed?"

"Why aren't you in bed?" she echoed.

He swallowed the lump in his throat and said, "I've been busy."

She smiled, and Riley's heart stopped for a moment before she continued, "That answer works for me as well." He shook his head, puzzled, and then his confusion grew even more when she raised her voice and motioned toward the door, "Mr. Nielson, you may come in now."

Riley spun to face the man with whom he had been working, every night, for the past month. "She's expecting you?"

"Indeed she is, Mr. Owens." He stepped aside, and allowed the replica of Penny to enter the room.

Penny chuckled softly and said, "Mr. Nielson, she is remarkable."

Riley spun back to his wife and said, "You know about this too?"

She walked over to him, and ran her fingers through his hair. "Riley, Mr. Nielson has confided the truth to me as well. I am aware of your desire for a more docile version of me."

Riley looked from Fritz Nielson, to the replica, and then to his wife before finally asking, "And you have no problem with that?"

"Of course not, Riley dear," she said, her voice smooth and inviting. "After all, this wonderful device of Mr. Nielson offers a world of possibility." She turned to the bedroom and said, "You may come out now." The bedroom door opened, and a perfect replica of Riley emerged, wearing his clothes. "You're not the only one dissatisfied with this marriage, Riley. You destroyed us as you withdrew from me, leaving me no choice but to follow the dreams of another," she said as she glanced at Fritz.

Riley studied his twin across the room. It was almost like looking in a mirror. "So where do we go from here?"

Fritz took a step forward and said, "We go to my vessel."

Riley watched in utter amazement as Penny followed Fritz, and their identical twins, out the front door. He had no choice but to follow as they walked down the lane and out toward the empty desert. Half an hour later found them well distanced from the Wutherton compound, standing before a strange, pyramidal machine. An enormous cog spun slowly inside the base of the machine, driving a complex set of gears, spurred onward by small, crackling bolts of the same white-blue energy he saw inside the replica device.

"You are more than capable of understanding this," he said, looking directly at Riley, "but it is best if you don't, so please don't ask."

Riley ignored the request, studying the machine. "What does it do?" he asked.

Fritz sighed. "It transports me, Mr. Owens, much as your airship does for the trains it ferries across the gorge. This carries me across a different type of gorge."

"Are you sure you won't explain it to me?" asked Riley. "I learned some of the principles of your replica device in a relatively short time."

"Quite certain," he said. "Undoubtedly you will discover much on your own in the days ahead."

Penny watched her husband's eyes as he scrutinized the machine, taking in every detail. She could almost see his mind working at his brow wrinkled and eyes scanned. She felt herself becoming mesmerized all over again.

"Mr. Nielson," she asked, wanting to break the spell, "is there anything more you need from me?"

"Only Mrs. Owens ... Penny ... that you remember all we have discussed. Without that careful attention, the results may be less than optimal."

"I shall pour my heart into it," she said as she squeezed replica-Riley's arm affectionately.

"In a moment," he continued, "I will need your cooperation, but first I must speak with your husband."

Fritz walked away from the vessel and motioned for Riley to follow. Riley reluctantly followed, not wanting to take his eyes off the machine. When they were sufficiently out of hearing range, Fritz spoke.

"Mr. Owens," he said, "I know the revelations of this evening have come as a surprise, but please know I have been working in good faith with you."

"Makes me wonder what else you haven't told me, Fritz."

"I deserve that comment," said the taller man. "But you have to believe that my goal has been not only to improve your life, but also the life of Mrs. Owens. She may not desire the life my patron has in mind for her, preferring instead some idealized version of you, but regardless of her choice, she deserves her own measure of happiness."

Riley thought of the journal entries and nodded, "I suppose our marriage had its share of disappointments for her as well."

"So it seems," said Fritz. "But let's not concern ourselves with that. What is critical is how you interact with your version of Penny."

"What do you mean?"

"Right now, the device inside your replica is very much in a learning mode, and it will be for some time. It is very important that you treat her, the device, with very special attention and care. If you do so, the reward will be exactly what you've been longing for."

Riley nodded, Fritz's admonition mirroring his own thoughts. He had already decided he was going to give special attention to *his* Penny. He glanced back at Fritz's vessel. "I didn't ask before, Fritz, but will ... uh, relations be normal with the replica."

It was one of the few times Riley saw Fritz Nielson smile and laugh. "Yes, Mr. Owens, she will be quite normal. In fact, the day will soon come where you forget altogether that she is a copy."

"Children?" asked Riley, not knowing the full capabilities of the device.

Fritz continued smiling and said, "It is unlikely, Mr. Owens. However, the device is adaptive and may surprise us both."

Riley sighed and said, "Shall we finish this?"

"Indeed, let us return." And the two men headed back. When they reached the company of the others, Fritz said, "I'm going to need help. There are two levers, on opposite sides of my vessel that must be pulled simultaneously in order to activate the machine."

"Are we in any danger?" asked Riley.

"Not at all," said Fritz. He walked to the far side of the device and said, "Penny, if you will please come over here."

Penny and her replica both walked after Fritz. "How quaint," said the real Penny. "She thinks she's me."

Riley shook his head in disgust at his wife's ability to complain in any situation. The two versions of Penny, one real, one artificial, disappeared around the ship, and he stood alone with his own replica. Everything looked the same-- the hair, the features, even the clothes. He shuddered involuntarily, ready for the *thing* to be gone.

Fritz walked back around the vessel, holding Penny's arm. "And now, my dear, we must be off. I hope you will consider my patron's offer."

Penny smiled and said, "I will consider anything, Mr. Nielson."

"Please go inside and wait. I will only be a moment."

Riley watched Penny enter the strange vessel, and his heart skipped. Once again he questioned his resolve, but his memories of misery remained fresh. Riley put his hands on the lever and asked, "Is she going to be safe? I mean the real Penny?"

Fritz smiled again. "Yes, Mr. Owens. In fact, she will be better than safe. She will be happy." He ushered the replica Riley into the vessel and said, "Hang on tightly, Mr. Owens. It will be a unique experience, I assure you. Wait for my signal to pull the lever." And Fritz disappeared inside.

A couple of minutes passed before he heard Fritz's voice echo from beneath the machine platform. "Please pull the levers on the count of three."

Riley tensed. "One ... two ... three." And he pulled.

The air instantly crackled as the white-blue energy leapt from the base of the machine and raced around its surface. It swirled clockwise and then counter-clockwise, ebbing and flowing faster and faster until a vortex above the vessel started pulling. Riley held tight to the lever, but he noticed the pull wasn't one of a vacuum or gravity, rather it seemed to be coming from inside his body - inside every part of his body. His fingers held firm, but he felt as if his bones were slipping out through the pores of his skin. Then, just as suddenly, it was over, and the machine vanished.

On the other side of the clearing stood *his* Penny, holding tightly to her lever. *It's done*, he thought as walked over and took her hand. "Are you alright?"

Something nagged at the back of his mind, but then she smiled and Riley momentarily forgot to breathe.

*****

That night was like a second honeymoon for Riley and *his* Penny. He couldn't believe how incredibly lifelike she acted. Every detail, every mannerism, had been duplicated, save anger and animosity. She looked on him with eyes of desire and love.

He skipped dinner at Bug Eye's the next day in order to get home as quickly as possible. And he was rewarded with a hot dinner and wonderful conversation.

"Penny," he said softly as they lay in bed that evening, "I'm thinking of applying for flight supervisor tomorrow. I've studied the engines carefully for some time now, and I have several ideas about improvement. But I need to move higher into management in order to implement them. What do you think?"

She sighed softly, the sound of contentment, not resignation, and said, "Riley, I want you to be happy, and I will support any decision you make."

Life got better and better every day. He found himself eagerly anticipating the end of his shift, so he could return home to his wife. They talked about everything, except Fritz. He decided that subject was one to be buried in the past. In fact, he rarely thought of Penny as a replica anymore. She was simply his wife.

It took Riley three years, but he eventually got the promotion. At dinner that evening, he excitedly explained his new position, and how much opportunity it provided, when she interrupted him.

"Do you know how much I love you?" she asked.

"Almost as much, Penny, as I love you." She smiled, and Riley thought, *This may be artificial love, but my happiness is real.*

The greatest surprise though, came with Penny's pregnancy later that same year. The replica simulated morning-sickness so convincingly he looked for baby clothes and a crib, and he made tentative plans for having the birth in private so no one would discover the truth about her. However, when Penny's slim figure began to fill out, Riley remembered what had nagged at the back of his mind the night Fritz had departed.

His Penny, the one that remained with him after the strange vessel disappeared, the one he had come to love with all his heart, the one who treated him like a king, the one he would move heaven and earth to please .... *his* Penny had a small, two inch gap in her hair.

He smiled, realizing the truth didn't matter anymore. He genuinely loved Penny, but the question of why remained one that puzzled him the rest of his life.

*****

Fritz watched the swirls of space-time resolve into the walls of his laboratory and sighed with relief. He reached over, tapped a sequence on the backs of the two replicas, and smiled as they slumped into inactivity.

"You've served your purpose, my friends," he said as he exited the vessel. "Hopefully you won't be needed again."

An attractive brunette sat on a stool, watching his movements with alert, analytical eyes. "So it worked?" she asked.

Fritz grinned, grabbed the brunette by the hand, and spun her into a tight hug. "It sure did!" He took his thumb and forefinger and lightly pinched her on the arm. "And the proof is in the pudding, wouldn't you say?"

She laughed and kissed him for several long seconds. "Do you think they ever figured it out?"

"Well," said Fritz, as he looked at an ancient photograph of Riley holding Penny and a smiling baby boy, "we know your grandfather did. After all, it was his journal that helped us understand the truth, but we may never know about your grandmother."

The brunette motioned for Fritz to follow her out of the lab. "It really doesn't matter, does it? She may have thought he was a replica, but when you act, in every way, as if you love something, then eventually that becomes the truth, doesn't it?"

He laughed and said, "I guess the only difference between artificial love and real love is just a matter of time."

Phoenix
H. David Blalock

The great man died on August 15, 1872 at the age of 81. George Dillon had lived the majority of his life in the quiet halls of universities, spending his time studying the latest scientific advances and dreaming about flight. It was his fondest dream that man might one day wing through the sky, borne on the winds like the birds that populated the aviary he maintained in his estate outside Atlanta until Sherman's troops burned it down. He never quite recovered from that loss; the destruction of a lifetime's work in a few moments of wartime flame. His age had saved him from the Union soldiers' bullets, but they left him with rubble and ash as punishment for living south of the Mason-Dixon Line.

He spent his remaining years rebuilding, innovating, and inventing. Once, he had told James that perhaps the fire outside Atlanta back in '64 had been the best thing to happen. It made him look at things again, re-examine things, re-evaluate things. He had become blinded to new ideas, snug in the familiar surroundings of his family estate. From the comfort of his rocking chair on the spacious porch overlooking the garden tended by half a dozen slaves, he had indulged in Kentucky whiskey and long discussions on the emerging physical sciences with students and other men of similar interest. After being released by the Union, he had stood and bleakly watched the rag-pickers sort through the rubble of his life until, blinded by tears, he had wandered into a hostel in Athens.

Looking back, James Mayberry never knew if it had been fate or chance that put him in the same hostel as the old man on that day. Beating the dust of five days hard travel from Rome off his chaps, he coughed the rest out of his throat before downing nearly a gallon of water. The barkeep laughed at him when he asked for whiskey.

"Whiskey?" The man, filthy from the top of his balding head to the ample belt James could see behind the bar, snorted. "Damn Yankees drank it all. We got green beer, water, and some milk. That's it."

Mayberry swung his saddlebags back over his shoulder, blinking at the dust that stirred up. "Never mind. Still got a room, or did the Yanks take them, too?"

The barkeep scowled at him and looked him up and down. "Where you from, boy?"

James reached into his jacket and produced a gold eagle. He tossed it at the startled barkeep. "Carolina. Room."

The barkeep squinted at the coin, bit it experimentally, and then grinned. "Comin' right up." He reached under the bar and produced a key ring. He thumbed through them briefly, then pulled one off the ring and handed it to James. "Down the hall, third room on the left. Best room in the house. Even got a view of the..." He stopped, and then frowned again, reflecting on something. "No. Not anymore." He shook himself. "Anyhow, third on the left."

"Any grub left?" Mayberry asked before the barkeep could stash the eagle.

"I'll get Mandy to bring you some cheese and sausages," he said as the eagle disappeared into his apron. "Have a seat in the parlor."

James looked around, noticed what the barkeep probably considered the "parlor": a sitting area next to the front door. An elderly man sat staring at nothing in one of the three chairs that made up all the furniture. He plunked his saddlebags down by the chair across from the old man and sank down into the worn cushions with a grateful sigh. The noise didn't even make the old man raise his head. Mayberry leaned down and pulled off his left boot, shaking the sand out of it before setting on beside the chair and reaching for the other. As he finished emptying that boot, someone cleared her throat. He looked up at the teenage girl dressed in faded gingham, wearing a stained apron, holding a plate.

"Ah, lunch!" he said. He nodded at the girl as he took the plate. "Thanks much, dearie."

"You are most welcome, sir," she replied, with a little curtsy.

James lifted an eyebrow at her as he snapped a sausage in half. "Them's right fancy manners, girl," he said. He pointed at her. "Mandy?"

She nodded. "Learned 'em in Miss Bridges' Home for Girls," she said proudly, with a tiny toss of her head. "Best place around, 'til the Yankees come."

He grinned at her and chewed on the meat. Breaking off a bit of the cheese, he nodded at the old man. "What's his problem?" he asked the girl.

She glanced at the gentleman and leaned toward James conspiratorially. "That's Mister Dillon. Used to own a big house outside Atlanta. Ain't got no family. Sons died in the war. Wife died years ago."

James grimaced. He'd seen plenty of people ruined by the war, but never anybody that old. Most of the folk were young enough to start over, or had family to tide them over until they could find their way again. Poor old soul, he thought. James held out the plate to the man.

"Share a meal, Mister Dillon?" he asked.

He'd been at Bull Run and seen dead men in the field that had eyes more alive than the pair that turned on him then. The old man stared at him, through him, as if he wasn't there, and then looked away again without a word.

"It ain't much, I give ya that," James went on. "Still, man's gotta eat." Dillon remained unresponsive. James looked at Mandy. "How long's he been like this?"

She shrugged. "Two, three weeks. He eats a little oncest in a while. Pa tried to get him to eat oncest or twicest, then give up."

He sat back down and set to the rest of the meal, glancing at the old man periodically to see if the sausage's aroma wakened anything there. After a few minutes, Mandy wandered off, leaving them alone. James finished the plate and put it on the floor by the chair, wiping the grease from his lips on his sleeve.

"Man, that was good," he said out loud, patting his belly. "Been livin' on beans 'n' hardtack for the last week." He looked closely at Dillon. The man appeared to be looking at something, but Mayberry couldn't figure out what it might be. "Dillon?" he asked. "Dillon!"

The man blinked back into the room from wherever he had been and looked at James as if seeing him for the first time. James stuck his hand out.

"James Michael Mayberry," he offered, "but people just call me James."

The man took his hand absently. "George Dillon," he said vacantly.

"Pleased to meet ya, George Dillon," James said brightly. "I'm just on my way through to Charleston," he went on when Dillon smiled weakly in response. "Got me a job at a livery waitin' there for me."

"That's nice," Dillon mumbled.

"What's your line, George Dillon?"

The old man blinked several times. "Excuse me?"

"Your line. What do you do?"

For a moment Mayberry was afraid the man was going to lapse back into his comatose state, then Dillon sighed heavily. "I was a professor of physical sciences."

"A professor, huh?" Mayberry repeated. "Now, that's interesting. I met a professor in Nashville, at that University there, a few months back. Maybe you know him."

Dillon smirked. "I doubt it."

James ignored the remark. He scratched his chin as he thought. "Let's see. What was that name?"

"Really, I don't know anyone in Nashville," the old man said.

Mayberry shrugged. "Well, never mind then. So, where do you do yer professorin'?"

"I'm retired."

"Retired? I didn't think professors retired. I thought they went on teaching till the end," James laughed.

"I retired several years ago."

"Yeah? So, what do you do now?"

Dillon's face paled and James immediately regretted asking the question. Obviously, that was exactly what the man had been asking himself for the last several weeks. James kicked himself mentally. Luckily, Mandy appeared at just that moment with another plate of cheese and sausages. She offered it to Dillon, who thanked her quietly and took it, only to stare absently at it as it sat in his lap. James pressed forward, unwilling to let the man slip back into his funk.

"You were saying?" he prompted.

The old man started. "I...I, uh, I used to research... that is, I used to study new ideas." He picked up a sausage and looked at it the way one would look at something extraordinarily odd.

"New ideas? Like what?" James said.

"Well," Dillon said, reluctantly, "ideas that other people thought were strange."

Mayberry stared at Dillon expectantly. The old man took a tentative bite out of the sausage and dropped the rest back on the plate as he chewed.

"Go on," James said.

Dillon swallowed and stared for a long time at him. Mayberry got the impression the man was gauging exactly what to say, sizing up how much of what he had to share would be acceptable and how much would be either too technical or too odd. At last, Dillon carefully put the plate on the floor and brushed at imaginary crumbs on his pants legs. He took a breath.

"I was studying ways to fly," he said, almost defiantly.

It was Mayberry's turn to blink. He looked from the man to the bar to see if anyone else had heard that. Turning back, he stroked his chin. "Fly, you say?"

"Yes. Fly."

Mayberry sat back in his chair and thought. The man might be off. He'd been through a lot, that was obvious. And he was quite old, could be senile. Still, Mandy hadn't said anything about the man being anything other than depressed, and that little minx certainly couldn't have passed on such a sweet tidbit as senility if it was there to be revealed. She had all the earmarks of a first-rate gossip brewing in that little brain of hers. James imagined a few hours with her and he would know the secrets of everybody in Athens, Georgia, and maybe most of the county thereabouts.

But, if the man wasn't senile...

"Fly, you say," was all Mayberry could manage.

"Yes, and I was just on the verge of finishing my research when the war broke out," Dillon said, a bitter edge to his voice.

"You mean, like in a balloon," Mayberry ventured, remembering the observation balloons he'd seen a couple of times near battlefields. "Well, that's not so strange."

"No, not like a balloon. Like a bird," Dillon said firmly. "Powered flight with directional control, not subject to the vagaries of the wind or even the weather."

James nodded silently, trying to keep the disbelief out of his manner. "Like a bird?"

"You see, Leonardo da Vinci drew up plans for several flying machines," Dillon said, his demeanor changing as he spoke. His eyes brightened, and his face actually glowed with a warmth Mayberry hadn't previously seen on the man. "Most of them were gliders, and one of them was a strange screw-winged contraption. I haven't been able to figure out what that was supposed to be. But the gliders, now that was different. Gliders are easy; they just fall in a controlled manner. There's no real trick to that. Air resistance, gravity, the same thing that a sycamore seed uses, or some spiders. Anyway, I took one of the glider designs and improved on it." He smiled to himself. "I built a small compressed air device that drove the wings. Now, it didn't fly far, mind you, but it did fly across the grounds and into the lake..."

"Wait!" Mayberry barked. "It flew?"

"Yes," Dillon said, irritated. "Haven't you been listening? It flew about two hundred yards. Now, if I can work it where I can put a small plant aboard the craft itself, one that will continually compress the air I need for the hydraulic lines to run the wings, I could make it fly, oh, I don't know, several miles, perhaps."

James shook his head. How did he get into this? The old geezer was obviously off his rocker. Flew?

"It would take a little time and some skill with the..." Dillon broke off suddenly. He made a small choking sound. "With the..." He looked at James with tear-filled eyes. "It's gone. It's all gone." He dropped his face into his hands and sobbed.

James reached over to pat the man on the shoulder.

"There, there, old fella," he said.

Dillon shook him off. "You don't understand," he snapped, looking up at Mayberry. "My laboratory was unique. It wasn't just another place to repeat experiments done hundreds of times before for the entertainment of bored students. It was a place of invention, a place of vision. I was on the verge of things greater even than simple flight. I was ready to make the next step. I..." He stopped abruptly and turned his face away.

"Look, Mister Dillon," James said, "I don't know much about science. I'm just a simple fella from a small town tryin' to get by, but it sounds to me like you need to get back on yer horse."

"It's not that simple," Dillon argued.

"Sure it is," James insisted. "You pick up where you left off 'fore Sherman."

"No, no, no, no!" The old man thumped his knee with his fist. "The equipment is gone, the work is burnt, don't you understand? The war has set me back years. I simply don't have that much time left in me."

"Do you have to start over completely? I mean, I don't pretend to be no scientist, but it seems to me a bunch of the work should be behind ya already. Stuff ya don't need to do again, mistakes and such."

Professor Dillon stared at him, but Mayberry thought something changed in the man's face as the seconds ticked by.

"You're right," Dillon said, finally. "By God, man, you're absolutely right!" He bolted to his feet, startling James. "I never realized it, but the majority of my preliminary work amounted to finding out what didn't work. When I hit on the answer, it came quickly thereafter." He began to pace more animatedly than James would have guessed a man of his age might. "The boilers, the hydraulics, the guts of the equipment would have survived the fires relatively intact. If the rag-pickers couldn't carry it on their backs, they would have ignored it. That means most of it will still be there!" He startled Mayberry again with a high-pitched laugh. "It could be done!"

"That's the spirit!" Mayberry smiled, recovering himself.

"But I'm going to need help," the man went on, almost to himself. "Without the staff, I won't be able to do the heavy work needed." He looked at James. "You. Are you in a hurry to get to Carolina?"

"Well, I..."

"What would the livery pay you?"

Mayberry scratched his jaw in thought. "I suppose about a dollar a week. Maybe a dollar, two bits."

Dillon reached out and grabbed his forearm. "I'll pay you three dollars a week." He fumbled in his waistcoat and produced a leather billfold. "Here's two weeks' pay in advance, Union blankets."

James stared at the money. The oversized paper looked tempting, but he preferred the security of gold. Still, they were Union currency, and the CSA notes that circulated would likely be worth next to nothing soon. He could trade the paper for gold when the hostilities died down, and it wasn't like he savored the idea of another couple of months on the road.

He reached out for the money, and a new partnership was born.

Over the next two weeks, they worked to rebuild the professor's laboratory. Dillon bought a small building at the edge of town and rented a wagon from the local livery to cart the remains of his old workshop. James couldn't make hide nor hair of anything they crated up and carried, but the old man was as energetic now as he had been lethargic there in the hostel. Mayberry came to realize the man had a mind sharper than anyone he had ever met before. It was as if the man had spent his whole life learning, and it showed. He knew about chemicals, and physics, and scientific theories, and things called atoms, and molecules, and stuff about weather like air currents, and cumulus clouds, and turbulence, and hundreds of other things.

And he talked incessantly, as if he had so much inside, he couldn't contain it all. It spilled out in a constant stream of words and ideas.

Mayberry learned by osmosis. The things the old man said began to make a kind of odd sense to him. He realized one day that Dillon's talk was as much to fill him in on the work as fill in the silences that surrounded their efforts. James realized the old man was teaching him, and was flattered at the attention. Nobody had ever thought he was good enough for something like that. Even his father, God rest his soul, hadn't expected much more of him than that he help out in the fields and feed the animals. His commanding officers had expected nothing from him, but obedience and not to get shot without their permission. It was nice to know that somebody thought he could be more than just a tool. His respect and affection for the old man grew daily.

Finally, all the equipment that could be salvaged from the ruins of Dillon's estate had been moved and stacked neatly in the new laboratory building. Mayberry was checking the tack on the livery wagon, getting it ready to return, when Dillon appeared beside him, watching quietly as he ran his fingers along the lines. He peered at the rings and the buckles, walked back to the wagon and looked for broken slats or missing spokes in the wheels. It wouldn't do to give the livery any excuse to gouge them for any more than they had already paid. The war had jacked up prices on nearly everything, and they had paid three times what they should have had to for the rental. Dillon quieted James' argument by telling him that there were things more important than money, something James was never quite convinced was true.

"Headed back to town?" Dillon asked as he climbed up on the bench.

"Yup."

"Well," the old man said, forming his words slowly, "I want to thank you for your help. I couldn't have done it without you."

Mayberry wrapped the rein around his hand and looked down at Dillon. "What do you mean? I'll be back in a coupla hours."

The professor cleared his throat nervously. "I can't pay you anymore," he admitted. "I've spent everything to put things back together."

Smiling, James leaned over toward Dillon. "Well, then, I guess I need to get another job."

The old man's face fell and he nodded at his shoes.

"You need a laboratory assistant?" James asked.

Dillon looked up in surprise. "What? But I can't pay you..."

Mayberry leaned back and laughed. "You can't get rid of me that easy, professor. Besides, after all this work, I want to see this thing fly." He snapped the reins and smiled to himself as he headed away.

They settled into rebuilding the following day. For weeks, Dillon and Mayberry worked from sunrise to sunset until one day the old man stood in the middle of the workshop, hands on his hips, and looked around, satisfied. He grinned at James and announced that the real work could finally begin.

Mayberry didn't have the heart to let Dillon know that the money to buy the groceries and the odd new piece of equipment came from his own late night forays into the war-torn city. Atlanta was still a smoking ruin in many places, full of the rag-pickers who swept in behind the ravaging enemy forces. They stripped the conquered populace of what little was left, themselves living on not much more. They were human vultures, picking clean the skeletons of the killed cities, just as their avian counterparts picked clean the bones of the fallen soldiers. Eventually, they would move on, following the armies south and eastward toward fresher prey, but for now they provided cover for James' own work. Rain came at times and finally put out the fires, but the damage would not disappear for months. He told himself it was necessary, what he did, even as he waded through the mud and debris, but some nights it was hard to watch as property owners fought with the scavengers. Especially the nights they lost their battles. He was glad Dillon never asked where the money came from.

It may have been that Sherman's army destroyed Dillon's work, but in a kind of ironic twist, it was what Sherman left behind that had rebuilt it.

Dillon settled into his work with gusto, his garrulous nature in full bloom. Mayberry learned of the history of steam engines, from the toys of ancient Greece, to the great iron horses that crisscrossed the country. Dillon's enthusiasm was contagious, and, in spite of himself, James became fascinated with the da Vinci ideas and drawings. The longer he worked, the more he was amazed at the brilliance of the professor. The man was definitely years ahead of his time, perhaps decades. He seemed to work magic with the steam plants, to manipulate the hydraulic systems with an alacrity that spoke of years of familiarity. In a startlingly short period, less than three weeks, a prototype appeared in the three acre plot behind the little workshop building.

It looked somewhat like a da Vinci glider, but a small steam-plant clung to the fuselage in front of the cockpit. The water tank balanced the weight of the plant by stretching throughout the rear of the glider, ending just before the rear stabilizers. Once the lines were primed, suction from the plant pistons would pull water from the tank through lines that ran on either side of the cockpit toward a holding tank near the boiler to prevent loss of pressure. Dillon had designed something he called the "spinner" and mounted it on the front of the vehicle. It was based on the design of a sycamore seed, which whirled as it dropped from its parent tree, traveling away on the wind and falling softly at distance. Dillon's reasoning was that, if the sycamore seed could in essence fly, its derivative should be able to do so as well. Powered by the engine to which a straight axle connected it, the vehicle, dubbed an "aerocraft", should be able to fly for as much as a mile before needing to refuel. On the ground, it would roll on four modified wagon wheels whose axles spanned the width of the fuselage and attached to the body of the craft by a steel grid that would be released at lifting off to reduce the overall weight. Landing would be a little bumpy, James supposed, but there didn't seem to be any other way.

The war ended as Mayberry watched the development of this device with an increasing faith in the professor's ideas. The more he knew, the more he was convinced that the aerocraft would indeed fly. In fact, the itch began to develop within himself to be the one to test that aerocraft. He actually began to hope that Dillon would let him be the first person to fly like a bird, to get into that cockpit and lift off from the earth and feel the ground fall away and rush underneath. His sleep, what he got after his nocturnal efforts, became filled with imaginings about just that. And Dillon's speculations about the experience only fueled his anticipation.

At last, the day came. Dillon flit around the workshop like a schoolboy, alternately elated and panicked as last minute preparations went smoothly or hiccupped. James brought the rental wagon to pull the aerocraft around to the front of the workshop and onto the road. As the old man fretted over the aerocraft, minutely examining every part, James unhitched it and moved the wagon back toward the building. As he fixed the craft's restraining ropes to the hitching post in front of the laboratory building, he saw Dillon stand back from the aerocraft and nod his head.

"It is ready," the professor announced. "After all this time, it is finally ready."

James hopped down from the wagon and walked to stand beside him. "Congratulations, professor. Sure is a beaut."

"Yes, she is," Dillon agreed, proudly.

They stood admiring their work for a moment, then James asked the question.

"Now what?"

It took a moment before the old man turned to look at him. "What?"

James indicated the craft. "Now what? You gonna make it fly?"

Dillon looked back at the aerocraft, his face betraying the fact that he might have meticulously planned and built it, but he had never thought past that. In spite of everything, he was nothing more than a technician, a person who was a magician with theory, but had no idea how to actually put theory into practice. His mouth opened and shut several times as the impact of that realization set in.

"It needs a pilot," Dillon said to the craft.

James laughed. "It would seem so."

The professor put a hand to his forehead and closed his eyes. "What a fool. Did I think it would fly on its own? It needs a pilot."

"I'll do it," James said, his heart thumping hard. "I know how it works and I can handle the controls."

Dillon shook his head firmly. "No, I will do it. I designed it; the risks are part of the picture. My picture."

"Professor, how old are you?"

The old man frowned at him. "What does that have to do with it?"

"Seventy? Seventy-five?"

"I'm seventy-four. Again, what does that have to do with it?"

"Let's say this thing does fly," James said. "Are you sure it's safe?"

"As safe as I could make it," Dillon replied tersely.

"What if something goes wrong?"

The professor paused, considering his response. James pressed ahead.

"Could you survive a crash?" he asked.

Dillon started. His mouth opened and shut again, without a word uttered.

"Let me do this, professor," James said softly. "I ain't done much in my life to make much difference to nobody. You, you had your time at the university, your studies and your letters. Me, I'm just a hired hand. I'm expendable." He dry swallowed at that admission, but went ahead with the argument he had been rehearsing for weeks in his head. "If I get my head broke open, you can get another pilot. You need to keep yer brains in yer skull, if the aerocraft needs fixin'."

The old man eyed him critically for several seconds, then slowly nodded. "You're right, of course. I probably wouldn't survive a crash. Still, you've come to mean more to me than just a hired hand, son." He smiled and put a hand on James' shoulder. "You're not expendable."

James stood speechless in shock. In all the time they had worked together, the old man had never so much as addressed him as anything but 'Mayberry'. It had never occurred to James that the man felt anything like affection toward him, although James had come to think of Dillon as the closest thing to a father since his own had died. Part of the reason he was willing to sit in that cockpit had to do with making sure Dillon didn't take that risk. He pulled himself together with an effort.

"Well, that's as may be," he said. "I should still be the one to fly it."

The professor shook his head again. "No, we'll get somebody else to do it."

"Professor, look around you. Take a good look."

The old man's forehead creased in puzzlement. He cast about, taking in the burned out buildings, the wagons bringing supplies for those families that remained. From where they stood in the road, they could see people making their way southward, refugees from Sherman's march returning to their destroyed homes. Most were grim-faced, filthy with the mud and despair of the long road they traveled. Even the children were subdued, the atmosphere of dread and anxiety dampening their natural exuberance. They were the aftermath, the survivors of the end. Most were coming back to start over. Some were coming back to bury their dead, say their goodbyes, and move on. Ahead of them would be disease and hunger, without much hope for relief from the new Federal government that was already mourning its own tragic losses. Both sides bore deep scars, scars that would take more than just a few days to heal, scars that would blind those who could help to the needs of those who needed that help most desperately.

James watched Dillon's face as he took in the scene. Slowly, it dawned on the man what James meant. There was no one here that would care anything about his work. They had more immediate concerns. Survival was foremost, an overriding need that dwarfed his own. Somewhere down the line, in a few years maybe, his work would get more attention, would generate more interest. For now, Mayberry was his only option.

He turned back to James and nodded silently. "Very well. I understand."

James stripped off his leather gloves. "I'll stoke the plant," he said.

It only took a few minutes to build up enough pressure to start the spinner moving. James cranked the heat up until the gauges stood a microscopic bit below red line and the aerocraft strained at the ropes that anchored it. Donning the laboratory goggles Dillon insisted he wear, Mayberry climbed into the webbing stretched across the fuselage between the water tank and the little boiler, tucking his legs under him to avoid the hot metal. He made one last check of the gauges, then turned the valve that connected to the wing hydraulics. Slowly at first, then faster and faster, the wings moved, jointed in the middle to mimic the motion of their avian pedigree. The aerocraft pulled hard at the restraining ropes.

"Let go, professor!" James shouted over the noise of the wings and boiler.

Dillon pulled the knots loose and the aerocraft leapt forward.

The great man died August 15, 1872 at the age of 81. George Dillon had lived the majority of his life in the quiet halls of universities, spending his time studying the latest scientific advances and dreaming about flight. And then, one day in 1865, he had watched as his dreams came true. His protégé, James Mayberry, would go on to be the first man to fly across the Atlantic, making the trip from New York to London in three days, arriving September 3, 1872.

Ultimate Weapon

Jeff Harris

Glancing at his wrist chronometer, James reached forward and pushed a lever forward, lining it up with two other shiny brass knobs on the array of instruments before him. Looking around the cabin of his airship, he checked the various dials and switches with an efficient glance before settling back in the high backed leather seat. Shiny brass, copper, and polished wood surrounded him along with a dizzying array of valves, switches and knobs.

This was a nice ship, he thought to himself. Far better than the last one he had stolen. A small single man airship, the best that modern science could provide, had been left all alone. This was an opportunity too good for a resourceful entrepreneur like himself to let pass by, so he took it. In this modern day of steam and electricity, it took a certain skill and a bit of knowledge to fly one of these things, and a different set of skills to steal one.

Looking out through the front view port, James considered his options. As the youngest son of minor noble from a cadet branch far from the seats of power, he had to make his own way in the world. As a near penniless youth when he left home, he had nonetheless left a tidy sum on deposit with the Bank of England due to his various "adventures". Still, being born noble gave him certain advantages, both in gaining access to various places, and with the law.

Within moments of seeing this particular ship, James already knew of a buyer who would take it off his hands. With the ship sailing towards the mountains, it was time to search the various compartments and cubbyholes to see what he had acquired.

He began rummaging through the various polished wood cabinets. Within moments he savored a delightful cabernet with his feet propped up against the control panel. In his other hand was a strange object of brass and glass with a single switch. Carefully examining the thing, he found a tiny inscription etched into the filigreed plate on the bottom.

It read "*Accerso nex ut totus humanus*", basic Latin. Perhaps the creator of this thing was one of those that believed that Latin was only for scholars, he thought. He was wrong. In English, it read "to bring death to all humanity".

It was only a partial message... or a warning. Nowadays, every crackpot who even had a basic understanding of bending the aether was building a doomsday device. Of course, none of them ever worked... yet.

Either way, even a small device could be lethal, so best not to take a chance.

"Not a bad idea" he said to himself, "I could get some shiny junk parts and build fake doomsday devices to sell to paranoid rich people... Not a bad idea at all."

The rich and the aristocracy were always paranoid. They had no reason. Society had not really changed in hundreds of years. Sure there was an occasional war... more like a skirmish. Constitutional monarchy was the way of the world. It made things work. Other than a few small tribes in New Guinea and maybe somewhere in the unexplored depths of the Congo or Brazil, the aristocracy and the landowners controlled everything. It was a good system.

There was no starvation, no hunger; everybody had what he needed. The ruling classes provided a basic stipend for all persons, and all had the opportunity to better themselves to a degree. They could even become aristocrats themselves, although it was pretty rare.

Still, theft and assassination still occurred, so the nobility often had a fail-safe to ensure their continued existence.

His thoughts were interrupted by a loud explosion off his port bow, followed by the tic tic tic sound of shrapnel hitting his airship. James looked up to see a much larger airship bristling with weapons closing rapidly.

Dropping the device to the deck James vented gas and turned his small ship into a steep dive. The larger ship followed smoothly, coming down directly over the top of his ship and forcing him down.

James knew he was beat. The big ship was faster, better weaponed, and he was being out flown. Gently, he set the small ship down and vented the bag, settling into a small clearing below. The larger ship stayed just above him and stopped in mid air, barely a foot above the top of the smaller ship.

James pocketed the strange little device, secured the ship, and disembarked. Two rope ladders dropped from the larger ship and it disengaged a dozen rough looking armed men.

The men approached James, who stood very still watching them carefully. The leader, wearing a dark blue long coat and beat up captain's hat said, "Stand and deliver!"

Pirates. This might work to his advantage. If they had been bounty hunters or militia his chances would have been less… much less.

James took his most aristocratic pose. "How can I help you….gentlemen?"

The pirate leader looked back at his crew and laughed, "Well it looks as if we have come upon a bit of a whoopsie little aristo, all alone and unprotected." He looked back at James and raised his pistol. "I hate to trouble your lordship," he sneered, "But we require your ship and gold."

James stood his ground. "And you gentlemen will leave me unmolested and in peace if I comply?"

"Maybe a bit of molesting and maybe a few pieces…" He laughed again as the pirates began to close in.

James pulled the strange little device from his pocket and raised it above his head. "Stop!," he ordered, "or we are all dead."

The pirates froze in their tracks looking to their leader for direction.

The pirate leader eyed James uncertainly. "And what be that thing you hold so proudly?"

"This 'thing' as you call it, is a weapon designed to cause destruction on a massive scale. All I have to do is press this little button and …"

The pirate laughed. "I have heard some tall tales…"

James pressed the button.

The world seemed to twist momentarily and bright light filled the air. A horrendous sound that seemed to come from everywhere at once filled James ears. He dropped the artifact and half ran and half stumbled away, vomiting and reeling.

He didn't stop until night was falling.

He didn't know what it was. He didn't really want to know. Whoever had created that infernal device had somehow reached through time, space, and dimension to bring forth a sonic weapon with so much destructive ability… It was inhuman. It was sickening. There were things that man was not meant to endure.

The last he had seen of the pirates, they were fleeing in terror. Even so, he wouldn't go back to his ship. It wasn't worth it. He remembered the visual images put out by that horrid device: A young woman twitching as if she was having a seizure, obviously in pain... and the strange words projected in the air: MTV Brittany Spears.

Some things man was not meant to see.

Gathering himself, James began the long trek back to civilization.

Long Shots
Kirk Hardesty

The last thing the mechanic chose to do before leaving the garage was to polish the roadster's hood ornament. Three vertically interlocking Cs made up the brass marker, which somewhat resembled three chain links. The C's stood for the Covington Carriage Company.

The roadster was a six year old model and it had seen much better days, but it had never before been driven so fast as it had earlier that day during the speed trials at the Washington Road Course outside of Chicago, Illinois. The steamer was far from the prettiest entry and she finished last in the field of twelve qualifying automobiles. But the mechanic knew the old girl had a couple of secret weapons under her shiny black hood. One secret was an engine of unique design that used spent steam from the first two cylinders to power the next two and then the next two. Very little steam was expelled from the auto's exhaust, so very little energy was unused by the efficient power plant.

The black roadster with bright red fenders, red running boards and red doors was far different from the polished cars she would have to run against the next day. The 200 mile Fourth of July Road Challenge was different from any other race in the U.S. and the leading steamer manufacturers had taken to using the derby to show off their newest roadsters to the 20,000 or more fans who would pack the grandstand and fill in all around the hay bale lined dirt road course.

The mechanic stuffed his rag in the left back pocket of his coveralls and stepped a little to the right to admire the fancy script number 17 painted in glossy black upon the red door. Then he heard the sound of a step from behind him. He turned expecting to see the Derby Sheriff there to tell him it was time to leave the impound garage until morning when all the drivers and mechanics would be allowed back inside to prepare for the start of the race.

Instead, he was surprised to see the impeccably dressed owner of one of the auto companies that had an entry in the race. It was the owner of the company that had originally built the roadster that the mechanic and his brother would race in the next day.

Howard Covington stepped up to him, extended his hand and asked, "Gary Wilson?" The two men shared a firm handshake. "I'm-"

"Howard Covington," Gary finished for him. He didn't even try to keep the surprise out of his voice. "I'm sorry sir. I didn't mean- It's just that-"

"That's quite alright, Mr. Wilson." The voice was pleasant, friendly. "No harm done."

"No, sir. Thank you. What can I do for you Mr. Covington?" Gary was uncomfortably realizing that his face and hands were dirty and he pulled the rag from his back pocket and began rubbing at his hands with it. He was acutely aware of his grimy coveralls as he looked over the finely tailored pinstripe suit, highly polished black shoes and felt derby hat adorning the other man.

Covington removed his hat. "You can relax Mr. Wilson. May I call you Gary?" At the mechanic's nod he continued, "Gary, I wanted to personally commend you on your engine's performance today. I saw the time trials and I was impressed with how fast that little roadster of mine came through the straightaways on the course."

"You were here? Of course you were. You have the '09 in the race... thank you." Gary peered at the man's open smile, deep blue eyes, and tussled curly blonde hair. He seemed genuine.

"Yes, I watched all the drivers to see how they handle their steamers. I will be driving the Covington entry tomorrow."

"You?" Gary remembered the firmness of the other man's grip, noticed the confidence in his wide stance and the almost imperceptibly raised chin.

Covington walked around the number 17 car looking at the modifications Gary had made to the suspension, noticing the way the running boards were not quite straight and the small dents in the doors and fenders that at a distance were hidden under the bright paint. "I don't need to run the trials," he said, glancing at Gary, "but I don't trust anyone else to drive my cars in races against other drivers. I must and I will win tomorrow."

The Covington entry had won the July 4th Challenge for the last three years.

Having completed a circuit around the old roadster, he stopped in front of Gary. "I built only two hundred of the Ought Fours. Where did you get this car?" Gary explained how he had acquired the wrecked car from one of his customers at the Wilson brother's Garage in Morris, 35 miles southwest of Chicago. "Bickles, right? So he gave the car to his teenage son after all. Pity that. But then, I might not have met you otherwise, now would I?"

"Well, I-" began Gary.

"I want to offer you a job." Covington cut in with a tone that expected agreement. "My nephew is an apprentice in Detroit at the shop where you had your engine block cast. It seems your design caused quite a stir there. My nephew couldn't get his hands on the drawings, but his description of the motor caught my attention. I was pleased to see you here again this year and even more pleased that you made the field this time."

He stepped around Gary and began walking briskly towards the garage door where the Derby Sheriff stood with his hands on his hips. "You should be riding along beside me," he said as he strode away.

"I'm riding with my brother!" As the words came out, Gary worried that they must have sounded rude.

"Of course you are," came the response drifting across the garage. "I'm talking about the next race, Mr. Wilson."

*****

Ritchie was wide awake as soon as his eyes opened. Dreams of steam and dust faded from his memory. All he could think was - it's race day! He popped out of bed and into the washroom where fresh water and towels awaited him. He lost no time taking care of his business. He dressed in pitch black trousers and red silk shirt, grabbed his black leather racing jacket and bounced down the stairs to find his brother similarly dressed and busy in their spotless garage sweeping at a very clean concrete floor.

All the tools were safely stowed in the large wooden toolboxes. Ritchie knew that if he rolled any of the boxes away from the walls, the floor under each of them would be clean. The steam powered, chain driven wench was at the end of its overhead rail at the back of the garage. Betsy, the engine that powered the wench and anything else Gary wished to put steam power to, purred along contentedly behind the same back wall. The three work bays were empty. Gary and Ritchie had cleared out all the scheduled work in anticipation of this day.

"Good morning, Rich."

"Good morning, Gare."

"There's bread and butter on the table." Ritchie walked behind the stairs and into the living area where on the table sat a basket of thickly sliced bread, a plate of fresh butter and a bottle of ice cold milk. He made quick work of the food while Gary secured the garage and shut off the flame to Betsy's boiler.

*****

At the race course the cars were lined up side by side facing out onto the track. The Covington number 1 car was closest to the start/finish line. The Wilson brother's number 17 was at the other end of the line farthest away from that line.

The pre-race inspections were over. Some extra time had been taken with the 17 car after Gary told the Derby Sheriff about the second secret weapon waiting under the hood. The cars had been driven around the track to warm up the boilers and then shut off for the inspection and race start. The driver and mechanic teams looked on with interest from the other side of the roadway as the inspection of the 17 car took a few minutes longer than one would think was necessary to verify that the boiler fire was completely out. Three race officials each took turns under the black hood. Then the all-clear was signaled and the racing teams braced, pulling on goggles and gloves.

At the crack of the starter pistol the teams foot-raced across the track, each driver jumping into his car and each mechanic darting under the hood or trunk or lifting the passenger seat to spark the natural gas or kerosene to heat the boiler; except for the crew of the 17 car.

Both Wilson brothers jumped into their seats. Gary turned a small dial in front of him on the dash, and then pushed a button beside it. He peered into a glass in the dash to see a glow of fire and said "Fire!" turning his grinning face to Ritchie. The younger brother smiled largely back at him as he pulled back on the drive lever protruding from the floor and pushed forward on the throttle lever mounted to the steering column.

As the other eleven mechanics had just gotten to the point where each was starting their respective boilers, the number 17 slid out of line and onto the road course. The packed grandstand roared. A few of the drivers gesticulated and shouted at race officials. Surely, this must be cheating. One driver got out of his car to run over to the 17, but Ritchie left him in the dust. He scrambled back to his car as his mechanic railed at him.

The number 17's second secret weapon had been a battery operated spark for the pilot light, verified by mirrors through the glass in the dash board.

Gary concentrated on the pressure gauges monitoring the boiler and the natural gas as well as the water. He tweaked several dials on the dash in front of him giving Ritchie all the steam he could coax out of the old Covey Roadster.

The race was on.

*****

Ritchie glanced quickly at the several gauges mounted on the dashboard as he wrestled the roadster through the last set of s-curves. Satisfied with the boiler pressure, he put the heel of his right hand on the throttle lever mounted on the steering column and shoved it all the way forward. The car leaped ahead in response and the rear end squirmed a bit as the tires vied for traction on the dirt road.

"Ritchie, mind the tires!" warned Gary, belted in as the driver was, over on the passenger side of the machine.

The driver spared a glance at his older brother whose red and black checkered cap was long since gone, his dark brown hair, goggles and clothing covered in road dust, gripping the bar protruding out of the dash board with both hands.

"I've got this, Gary!" Ritchie shouted back as his eyes darted to the small rearview mirror mounted to the top center of the dash. All the other cars were eating his dust and bathing in the little steam the roadster gave up. They were on the straightaway now, about to roar past the start/finish line in front of the stands. There the roadster would hit its top speed. Ritchie wanted to go faster than anyone else ever had.

The crowd leapt to its feet as the old roadster, painted fire engine red with shiny black hood and fenders, shot past. It was far ahead of the rest of the pack. The red wheel spokes looked like translucent disks and the spectators could barely make out the black number 17 painted on the red door through all the dust kicked up, but they all knew the Wilson brothers' steamer as it flashed past the start/finish line and into the final lap.

Waves of cheering washed over the two and Ritchie laughed. He roared with glee. Gary looked over and once again saw the boy he'd taught to ride a bicycle after their father had died. And he began to laugh too as the roadster flashed past the crowded grandstands. Using a dial on the dash in front of him, he turned up the kerosene to make sure the boiler stayed hot enough to maintain pressure while the steam flow was wide open. The car flew past the stands toward the track's first wide curve to the right.

Ritchie charged into the curve as if the rest of the racers were right on his tail, waiting until the last instant to cut the throttle and press the brakes. He knew he wasn't driving the most nimble machine in the race, so he made up for the car's shortcomings both with his driving skills, and with the powerful new steam engine which itself was a reflection of his brother's mechanical skills. The car rocked on its suspension and its wheels skidded a bit. Ritchie worked the steering wheel back and forth to keep the car under control and shot into the next wide curve going to the left. In this way, he stayed on the edge of control through the opening curves and into the short straightway which ended in a near hairpin curve to the right.

He worked that short straight stretch of road for every bit of speed he could get and as he popped the throttle back and started to press the brakes he glanced at the mirror to see the closest competitors had gained on them in the curves. He threw the car into the tight turn and the rear tires lost the road causing the car to try to spin around.

"Ritchie, the tires, damnit!" Gary raged, but Ritchie was lost in the moment, turning the car into the skid, quickly working the front wheels back and forth with his left hand and bumping the throttle forward and back with his right until the rear wheels caught and they were off into a series of alternating tight and wide turns leading to the last decent straightaway and the set of s-curves to finish the track.

Ritchie barked back, "Watch the pressure, Gare! I've got this!" and Gary busied himself making sure the machine was working at peak performance. He backed the boiler pressure down with one dial and adjusted the fuel flow to compensate with another. Then he glanced back to see why his brother seemed so concerned. The racers closest to them were already blasting through the dust cloud that Ritchie's skid had produced. The chasers were coming on strong, the Covington car leading them in the chase.

Gary knew that only one thing scared Ritchie and it wasn't high speed or the thought of crashing. Ritchie loved driving as fast as he could and he never thought of crashing even though in the past they'd had some minor crunches into the bales of hay lining race courses.

Ritchie was afraid of losing a race that he ought to have won. Fear was showing in the tension on Ritchie's face as he struggled through the turns. He was not quite keeping the old roadster under his control, and was losing ground to those behind as he fought to ride the skids he was causing by going faster than he should have. And as they approached the third straightway, that fear was turning into anger, shown by his clenching jaw.

The last right hand turn before the setup to the s-curves was the one that got them. Ritchie was already skidding, but must have gauged that he could control it as they came out of the turn. Midway through, he rammed the throttle all the way forward.

"Ritchie-!" was all Gary could get out as the sliding car drifted to the outside of the turn and the left side wheels got into the loose dirt beside the course. It was over then, but Ritchie would not give up. He fought the coming spin and the car slid sideways into the hay bales, causing a plume of dirt and dust to burst into the air. Losing almost none of its velocity, the car flipped over the hay bales.

To Ritchie and Gary it seemed as if, after a great lurch accompanied by a loud pop, the ground rapidly turned sideways and then soared over them. For a disorienting instant everything was silent and then the earth slammed into the passenger side of the car and the world was dust and long terrible crashing sounds. Steam hissed, and from somewhere there were urgent shouts.

The car landed on its side after a spectacular mid-air roll and continued to roll along the ground, over and over. Tires and body parts flew off. Track-side spectators fled in all directions away from the disaster. The smashed roadster finally came to rest, right side up. Dust began settling. Steam was rising from under the car. Back on the track, all the other cars flashed past on their way to the finish line.

The brothers had both instinctively ducked down as the car had been aloft. Ritchie slowly sat up, pulling off his goggles and looking around as the air cleared of dust and steam. Gary was slumped over, left hand on the dashboard bar, right arm hanging out of the car at an odd angle. He was moaning and tried to sit up, but his right arm seemed to hinder him. He winced and gingerly tried to slide his body left to pull the arm back into the ruined car.

"Hold on, Gare, don't move!" Ritchie worked at the straps across his lap to free himself.

Men were running up to the car now, one asking "Are you alright?" He seemed amazed that they were even alive. "Get them out!" someone said. "Don't move them!" exclaimed another. A multitude of men's voices fell around them as Ritchie freed himself and began to work on his brother's straps. The sound of a siren wailed as it approached.

In the distance, the crowd roared for the photo-finish among three cars at the end of the race. Everything was a million miles away except the dirt covering them and his brother slumped to the left almost onto Ritchie.

He got the straps loose and stood, holding onto the hood where the windscreen should have been. He leaned over Gary to try to gently grasp the oddly dangling arm by the wrist and get it into the car. He wanted to make Gary more comfortable. A grey suited bystander saw this and grabbed the arm as if to hand it to Ritchie. "Ah, shit!" yelled Gary and jolted back, his arm flopping onto the seat beside him. He grabbed his left shoulder with his right hand.

"Hey!" Ritchie shouted at the man. He plopped back down on the seat and with both hands lifted Gary's dirt encrusted goggles to look at his eyes. Gary's blue eyes seemed to roll in their sockets for a few seconds and then they looked around, his head not moving against the backrest.

"Are you alright?" Ritchie's own blue eyes were wide, seeming all the wider for the clean circles around them where his goggles had been on his dirt covered face. Steam and sweat made mud tracks down his dirty, worry furrowed face.

Gary straightened, pulling his limp left arm onto his lap and surveyed the heap of a car, steam rising from the hoodless engine and from under the seat where they sat. The siren wailed louder and seemed insistent. He brushed at some of the dirt on the left knee of his trousers. "How'm I gonna fix this?" he whispered and let his head fall back onto the top of the seat. His eyes closed against the harsh sun.

Relief washed over Ritchie's face, "You'll be fine. You'll be alright," he said. He looked intently at Gary's arm, wanting to and not wanting to touch it.

The people near the car on Ritchie's side parted, and white coated men carrying black medical bags dashed up. "Are you injured?" The first one leaned over and yelled into Ritchie's ear. Another sprinted around the front of the car to where Gary sat with his head still tilted back and his eyes closed.

"I'm not hurt," Ritchie answered the man almost as loudly, although he was beginning to notice a burning in the back of his neck and at the base of his skull, "but his arm...," he raised his own left arm across his body to indicate Gary.

Unable to yank the car doors open, the ambulance team began to carefully lift the pair out of the wreckage as newspaper photographers flashed them. Breathless reporters finally bolted onto the scene to shout questions at Ritchie, Gary, the crowd, and the men extracting the Wilson brothers.

*****

Two days later, in the mid afternoon, Ritchie sat alone, halfway up the steps in the garage while Gary walked around the dusty wreckage of the number 17. Gary had his right arm in a sling to keep from doing more injury to his dislocated shoulder. Both men were bruised and sore. Ritchie's head was in his hands and he stared at the bottom of the stairs.

"Axle's broken, steering's bent, all the brake drums are cracked or split, the boiler's torn open, the gas tank is punctured--we were really lucky there Rich," his brother groaned in response, "the frame's bent if not cracked. Pretty much the only thing that might not be destroyed is the engine."

Gary walked around the scrap heap for a few minutes ticking off in his mind the things that were fixable and the things that weren't. Not much was. The car was left with only one splinter spoked rear wheel still on so it sat at an angle. The two left side fenders were no longer attached. They sat in a corner looking like large pieces of dusty red crumpled paper. The hood was crumpled but still on the car. The right side fenders and side board were bent up at almost a ninety degree angle. Gary peered under the hood and tried to move it with his good hand. The car groaned in response. It sat in a puddle of water and lubricants. The hood ornament was nowhere to be found.

A sedan pulled up outside, purring. Gary looked as the driver got out and opened one of the rear doors. Even before he got out, Gary knew who it was buy the golden inlaid triple C ornament above the door handle.

Covington strode in like the garage was one of his own. Gary slowly walked over to meet him not quite half way.

"So, as soon as you are able I would like to have you at my Engineering Division in Detroit." There was no question in his voice. He looked around the garage with a keen eye.

"Well, sir…"

"Come now. You have a fine garage here, but when I look around this establishment I don't see the work of a mechanic. I see the work of an engineer." His eyes were following the workings of the overhead wench, the chain, the gear and shaft protruding from Betsy on the other side of the wall. He looked at the other shafts and gears that Gary could affix to Betsy in a moment for any number of tasks such as horizontal pulling.

Gary looked at him in his flawlessly fine suit. Ritchie raised his head just enough for his confused eyes to take in the man and the auto behind him.

"All those mechanics riding with the drivers at the race were engineers. We don't need mechanics anymore. If a steamer suffers a breakdown requiring a mechanic's attention, that car is out of the race. The mechanics seat is a place of honor held by the chief engineers who design those cars. You belong in one of those cars."

Gary looked around the garage thoughtfully. Betsy had been the engine from their father's tractor. Clyde, the truck they used for hauling and towing, was the farm truck their father had bought just before the accident. Gary had modified everything as he needed to.

After their father had died, Gary took over the farm. They lost their mother during Ritchie's birth. They were alone and for years they had continued their father's work. But the big farms were increasingly relying on better and bigger machines. Steam was supreme and Gary could not keep up, especially as farming efficiency drove down the prices of produce. One by one the family farms had sold out and moved on.

Gary had always enjoyed working on the farm's machinery more than working the farm itself. Ritchie would do anything that involved driving, but it took supervision to make sure fields were cut, plowed, harvested. If Ritchie took Clyde to town you were lucky if he brought back anything he had been sent for. He loved to drive.

One day, Gary sold the farm and the two of them bought the garage and made a business doing what Gary loved. Ritchie learned and even enjoyed working on steamers. By careful management of their money and excellent mechanical workmanship, they had managed to save enough money to get a car and race the smaller oval tracks. Eventually, they had enough to build the racer.

The number 17 was gone now and Gary didn't know how they would replace it without dipping farther into their savings than Gary was willing to go. And he knew Ritchie would argue with him to do just that.

"I can have all of this moved and set up just as it is in Detroit." Covington interrupted Gary's thoughts and brought his attention back to the owner of one of the finest steamer manufacturing companies in the country. Covington was pulling his black gloves on as if preparing to go. As if all had been decided.

Ritchie's voice came from the stairs, "What the..."

"I've got this, Ritchie," Gary said firmly. "No, thank you, Mister Covington. I prefer to work on my own time and schedule, and with my brother."

The man finished setting his gloves just right then glanced at Ritchie, the busted up number 17 and finally his blues eyes rested on Gary. "Then sell me the engine. That car won't ever roll again. I'll give you one thousand dollars for it." He saw the look on Gary's face, "I'll give you two thousand and the car I won the race with."

Covington straightened as if this were his final offer. Gary considered. He had bought the wreck that he'd turned into the number 17 for $150. His engine cast had cost a thousand including all the parts he'd made himself to make the unique design function. The derby had paid ten thousand dollars to Covington who didn't need the money.

Gary glanced at Ritchie. The poor young man was shaking his head. That fear of losing was stealing over his face. He still thought the 17 could be salvaged. Then Gary almost laughed.

"I will sell you the designs for the engine for ten thousand dollars." Gary enjoyed the flicker of surprise that passed over Covington's face.

The auto tycoon's eyes lost focus as he calculated. "You will build no more of that design?" He asked.

"I will not."

"Done." He tugged on his gloves once more. "I will have my attorney come by first thing in the morning with some papers for you to sign and a check. He will receive the designs from you." Covington turned on his heel and strode out of the garage to the car where his driver held open the door.

"Gary?" Ritchie sounded tentative.

"I've got a better design in mind, Rich." He walked over to the bank of levers on the back wall and pulled one. The wench began tracking out toward the crumpled number 17.

"Let's see what's left of this engine. Maybe we can use it in a car for the oval tracks." Ten thousand dollars would build a very nice car for the ovals and a real shocker for next year's Fourth of July Challenge Derby.

About the Authors

Rachel Pixie

Rachel Pixie is a student at Indiana University of Bloomington. She is a Memphis native with prior publications under the name of Chronicles Bailey. She is the winner of the Darrell Award for Best Short Story for her story *Tamer* featured in *Dragons Composed* (Kerlak Publishing). She has been writing stories since she was six years old and is working on her first novel between school and everything else.

Jared Millet

Jared Millet is a librarian in Birmingham, AL and is the moderator of the Hoover Library Write Club. His short fiction has previously appeared in *Shelter of Daylight Vol. 3* and *WTF Mysteries*. Follow him online at http://jaredmillet.blogspot.com.

Stephanie Osborn

Stephanie Osborn is a former payload flight controller, a veteran of over twenty years of working in the civilian space program, as well as various military space defense programs. She has worked on numerous Space Shuttle flights and the International Space Station, and counts the training of astronauts on her resume. Of those astronauts she trained, one was Kalpana Chawla, a member of the crew lost in the Columbia disaster.

Stephanie holds graduate and undergraduate degrees in four sciences: Astronomy, Physics, Chemistry, and Mathematics, and she is "fluent" in several more, including Geology and Anatomy. She obtained her various degrees from Austin Peay State University in Clarksville, TN and Vanderbilt University in Nashville, TN.

Stephanie is currently retired from space work. She now happily "passes it forward," tutoring math and science to students in the Huntsville, AL area, elementary through college, while writing science fiction mysteries based on her knowledge, experience, and travels.

M. Keaton

M. Keaton has been writing professionally for over two decades, fiction and non-fiction, across four genres and three age groups (sci-fi, fantasy, horror, mystery and child, young adult, adult respectively). His short work has appeared most recently in Ray Gun Revival and Abyss & Apex. He has two novels currently in print, *Speakers and Kings* (epic fantasy) and *Calamity's Child* (space opera). He has served as Bard in Residence for both the Northwest Arkansas and Missouri Renaissance Festivals. More information is available on his website http://archangelpress.net.

Angelia Sparrow

Angelia Sparrow is a middle-aged trucker living quietly in the MidSouth with her husband, four kids, and two cats. She has been writing professionally since 2004, when her story, *Prey*, was published. Her novel, *Nikolai*, a dark future Pygmalion story, was released in 2008. In between, she has produced 35 short stories, and 6 more novels, both alone and with Naomi Brooks, her writing partner. She can be reached through her website: http://www.angelsparrow.com.

Sidney M. Reese

Professor Sidney Reese is the Creator of Gnawed Faces (http://www.gnawedfaces.com), an art/photography/modeling company devoted to bringing the art of the macabre to the world. Originally from Memphis, TN, he currently resides in Huntsville, AL and is hard at work on the next chapter of the Chronicles of Atlantis. He would like to thank his family and friends for their continued support and dedicates his story to his grandmother, Ruby Moss.

Kimberly Richardson

After being found as an infant crawling among old books in an abandoned library, Kimberly Richardson grew up to be an eccentric woman with a taste for listening to dark cabaret or jazz music while drinking tea, reading books in every genre, and writing stories that cause people to make the strangest faces. Her first book, *Tales From a Goth Librarian*, was published through Kerlak Publishing in March 2009 and was named a Finalist in the USA Book News Awards for Fiction: Short Story for 2009. *Tales From a Goth Librarian* was also named a Finalist in the 2010 International Book Awards for Fiction: Short Story. Kimberly is also the Editor of the Steampunk anthology *Dreams of Steam*. Her family, albeit normal, loves her as much as she loves them. She currently resides in Memphis, Tennessee.

Dale Carothers

Dale Carothers lives in South Dakota with his wife, Sara. He helped to found a local science fiction and fantasy writing group and is hard at work on a new batch of short stories. His work has appeared in *Electric Spec, Kaleidotrope, Aoife's Kiss, Afterburn SF,* and *Silver Moon, Bloody Bullets: An Anthology of Werewolf Tails.* Visit him at http://dalecarothers.wordpress.com.

Missa Dixon
Missa Dixon wears many hats: scientist, mathematician, Reiki master, metaphysical practitioner, animal communicator, teacher, podcast host, and now, she has added professional writer to her list of accomplishments. Having suffered with a learning disability all her life, Missa never thought she could write; however, through the encouragement of her friends she finished her first short story and to her surprise it was accepted into the *WTF Mysteries* anthology. Encouraged by her success, she is currently working on two full-length books dealing with the metaphysical world; one interviewing animals, the other dealing with a broad range of metaphysical topics. Missa currently lives in a rural community outside of Memphis, TN on a half acre with her two dogs. Please visit her website http://www.missadixon.com and her podcast Missa's Urban Home on Blog Talk Radio.

Stephen Zimmer
Originally born in Denver, Colorado, Stephen Zimmer is an author and filmmaker based out of Lexington, Kentucky. He is the author of the epic urban fantasy series The Rising Dawn Saga, which currently includes *The Exodus Gate* and *The Storm Guardians,* and the epic medieval fantasy Fires in Eden Series, which launched with *Crown of Vengeance* in the fall of 2009.

As a writer/director in independent film, his credits include the indie feature "Shadows Light", and the horror short film "The Sirens". Stephen maintains a year-round appearance schedule at conventions and other events. Updates and information about Stephen can always be found at http://www.stephenzimmer.com

Sara M. Harvey
Sara M. Harvey is an author, costumer, and Steampunk enthusiast. Her paranormal Steampunk series from Apex Publishing (*The Convent of the Pure, The Labyrinth of the Dead,* and the forthcoming *The Tower of the Forgotten*) have garnered rave reviews from the Steampunk community. Sara lives in Nashville, TN with her husband and too many dogs.

Nick Valentino

Nick Valentino's Steampunk adventure novel, *Thomas Riley* (Echelon Press), is the first in a series of alternative history books about two Victorian-era weapons designers that are forced into enemy lands to undo an alchemic mishap. His YA Steampunk short story series, *The Young Alchemists* (Echelon Shorts), was released January 2010 with a second entry coming in May. He currently lives in Nashville, Tennessee.

Allan Gilbreath

Allan Gilbreath denies that he was raised by wolves, but still enjoys quiet moonlit evenings. He is an accomplished skeptic, cook, gardener, computer geek, martial artist, and avid student of arcane knowledge. Allan is also a nationally recognized and award-winning author, publisher, speaker, and instructor. He has appeared on television, stage, radio, web/podcast, and tours the country in live appearances. He enjoys serving on convention panels and can cover a wide range of topics from the serious to the outrageous. In his adult vampire novels, *Galen* and *Dark Chances*, he links sensual fantasy with danger and predation to excellent effect. His exceptional use of plot tension between the various characters sets a wonderful stage for the little details that bring it all to life. Allan's Jack Lago supernatural mysteries are known for their attention to detail and suspense. His short stories have appeared in numerous anthologies. For more information please see: http://www.kerlakpublishing.com.

Dwayne Debardelaben

Dwayne, his wife Dana, stepdaughter Ashley, cat-that-thinks-it-is-a-dog Zorro, and a dog-that-thinks-it-is-a-cat Sandy, all live in Huntsville, AL near Monte Sano.

His story was inspired by the certainty that his wife would surely replace him with a perfect replica if he failed to keep her supplied with chocolate, flowers, and snippets of romantic stories. In between pleasing a HIGH maintenance wife, working a "real" job, and sleeping occasionally, he manages to work on several writing projects.

Artificial Love is Dwayne's first foray into the realms of Steampunk. You can comment on the story and follow his overall writing progress at http://dwayne.debardelaben.org.

H. David Blalock
H. David Blalock has been writing for print and the Internet for more than 35 years. His work has appeared in print and web magazines such as *Alternate Species [UK]*, *Gateway SF, Alternate Realities, Raven ElecTrick, The Harrow, Writer's Hood, Intrigue, The Three-Lobed Burning Eye*, and anthologies like *Monsters From Memphis* (Zapizdat Press), *Tales of Fantasy* (Kerlak Publishing), *Heaven and Hell* (Speculation Press), *Fundamentally Challenged* (Turner Fiction), and *Dragons Composed* (Kerlak Publishing). His novel *Ascendant* (Sam's Dot Publishing) will be shortly followed by a second in the series, *Emperor*. David currently lives in west Tennessee area with his wife Maria.

Jeff Harris
A long, long time ago in a state far away (California) a scream was heard in the maternity ward of the Brookside Hospital: "It's alive!!!" Jeff "Ugly Shoes" Harris was born on a sultry midnight in August in the days of legend. Those were the days that mighty creatures and strange monsters walked the earth (of course, referring to his first wife). Jeff appeared on stage at the tender age of 5 years, sitting in with his father's surf band "The Untouchables" in San Francisco, California. He was fired the next day.

Since then, he has been fired from many venues and bands, some even firing him before he ever played. In 1969, he received a personal letter from music producer and legend Dick Clark telling Jeff that, although they had never met, and he had not heard him play, Jeff was fired. Jeff is currently appearing at most Sci-Fi cons with his band "The Cemetery Surfers", and can be heard on his weekly comedy podcast "KURU Radio" (Parental advisory- not for kids). On the way, he has written a book (The Ghost hunters Field Guide), appeared at the rockabilly hall of fame, been seen occasionally on MTV, recorded 9 albums, appeared on over 40 more, won the 1989 North Bay Comedy Competition in California, been married 3 times, and drank a lot of beer.

Jeff is an avid science fiction fan and has several short stories sitting on publisher's desks and in their trashcans. He once received a fortune cookie that read "A psychic will lead police to your body."

Kirk Hardesty

Kirk has been reading and writing science fiction and fantasy since the 5th grade. He also writes poetry and has been published in the *Aurorean* and *Penny Dreadful* as well as anthologies published by the Alabama State Poetry Society. This is Kirk's first published short story. He lives in the woods of central Alabama with a few dogs, a cat, and the love of his life, Jerri.

Discover other fine Kerlak publications at:

http://www.kerlakpublishing.com

LaVergne, TN USA
17 August 2010
193640LV00004B/1/P